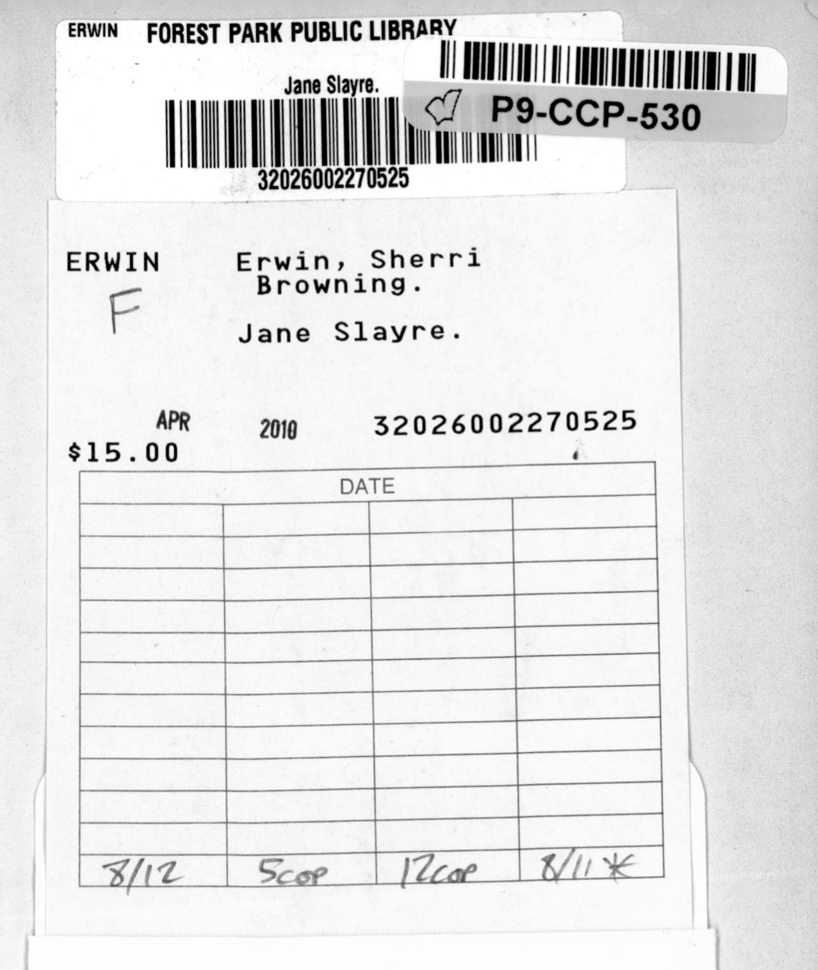

DATE			
8/12	5cop	12cop	8/11 *

JANE SLAYRE

CHARLOTTE BRONTË
AND SHERRI BROWNING ERWIN

GALLERY BOOKS
NEW YORK LONDON TORONTO SYDNEY

In memory of Kathleen Givens—
a generous, witty, and most wonderful friend,
gone far too soon. I love you, man.
Always.

Gallery Books
A Division of Simon & Schuster, Inc.
1230 Avenue of the Americas
New York, NY 10020

First Gallery Books trade paperback edition April 2010

GALLERY BOOKS and colophon are trademarks of Simon & Schuster, Inc.

For information about special discounts for bulk purchases, please contact Simon & Schuster Special Sales at 1-866-506-1949 or business@simonandschuster.com.

The Simon & Schuster Speakers Bureau can bring authors to your live event. For more information or to book an event contact the Simon & Schuster Speakers Bureau at1-866-248-3049 or visit our website at www.simonspeakers.com.

Designed by Jaime Putorti

Manufactured in the United States of America

10 9 8 7 6 5 4 3 2

Library of Congress Cataloging-in-Publication Data

Erwin, Sherri Browning.
Jane Slayre / Charlotte Brontë and Sherri Browning Erwin.
p. cm.
1. Brontë, Charlotte, 1816–1855. Jane Eyre—Parodies, imitations, etc.
2. Governesses—Fiction. 3. Vampires—Fiction. 4. Fathers and daughters—Fiction. 5. Mentally ill women—Fiction. 6. Charity-schools—Fiction. 7. Married people—Fiction. 8. Country homes—Fiction. 9. Young women—Fiction. 10. Orphans—Fiction. 11. England—Fiction. I. Title.
PS3555.R95J34 2010
813'6—dc22 2010000176

ISBN 978-1-4391-9118-7
ISBN 978-1-4391-9129-3 (ebook)

CHAPTER 1

THERE WAS NO POSSIBILITY of continuing my walk that night. We had been wandering, indeed, in the leafless shrubbery an hour after dark, but since Mrs. Reed had picked up a scent (Mrs. Reed, when there was no company, hunted early), I was sent home so the others could stalk their prey.

I was glad of it. I never liked long walks, especially on chilly evenings. Dreadful to me was the coming home in the raw midnight, with nipped fingers and toes, and a heart saddened by the death of the poor thing they'd dined on, raw, right in the middle of the wood. Not that I frequently watched as they took their meal. I avoided accompanying them on the hunt as often as I could.

In fact, I interfered with their efforts by inadvertently making noises to scare off whatever beast they'd settled on draining for their dinner. Unlike my cousins, my senses didn't sharpen at night. My inability to see in the dark, combined with my natural lack of physical grace, led me to trip over tree roots, branches, fence posts, or even my own two feet. Most often, once Mrs. Reed's nostrils flared to indicate a scent on the air, I ran home alone to face the chidings of Bessie, the nurse, both humbled by my consciousness of my physical inferiority to Eliza, John, and Georgiana Reed, and delighted I didn't share their condition.

The said Eliza, John, Georgiana, and their mama had returned and were now clustered in the drawing room. Mrs. Reed lay on a sofa by the fireside and, with her darlings about her (for the time sated), looked perfectly happy. Me, she had dispensed from joining the group, saying, "I regret to be under the necessity of keeping you at a distance; but until I hear from Bessie and can discover by my own observation that you are endeavouring in good earnest to acquire a more fierce and bold disposition, a more athletic and controlled manner—something quieter, stealthier, more unnatural as it were—I really must exclude you from privileges intended only for ruthless, bloodthirsty little children."

"I don't like blood," I responded matter-of-factly. "And I wouldn't be as clumsy if we could go out during the day."

I'd returned home without disturbing their hunt. I'd eaten my steak as rare as I could stand for my dinner, which was admittedly not very rare indeed. Though Mrs. Reed longed for me to develop some tolerance to blood, I preferred my potatoes and spinach to anything that had actually lived. Bessie was often required to recount what I'd left on my plate or if I'd woken before dusk to steal a glance of sunlight out the window.

A breakfast room adjoined the windowless drawing room. I slipped in there and lit a lamp. The Reeds preferred to keep the house dark, even during their waking hours in the night. I found the bookcase and soon possessed myself of a volume, taking care that it should be one filled with pictures. I mounted into the window seat and sat cross-legged. Having drawn the red velvet curtain nearly to a close, I did my best to confine the lamp's light to my hiding spot. Folds of scarlet drapery shut in my view to the right hand; to the left were the clear panes of glass, protecting, but not separating, me from the drear November eve. At intervals, while turning over the leaves of my book, I studied the aspect of that moonless winter night. I couldn't see far for the rain, and thank goodness. Who knew what dead thing they'd left out on the lawn for the servants to remove in light of day?

I returned to my book—*Bewick's History of British Birds*. Sometimes, during the daylight hours through which I was demanded to sleep, I could hear the birds outside caroling and carrying on. I longed to see them in the daylight, to watch them twitter and flit. Once, in a late afternoon, I'd chanced to move the heavy curtains and catch a glimpse, but John Reed had also been awake and sneaking up on me right in time to be singed on the hand by a ray of sunshine streaming in through the folds. His screams roused the entire household and I had quite the thrashing for it. Was I trying to kill my cousin? He who was so kind to let me live and not drink my blood at tea?

Mere pictures of the birds, mixed in amongst sunlit images of foreign lands, were to content me. Each picture told a story of life lived during the daytime hours, mysterious often to my undeveloped understanding and imperfect feelings, yet ever profoundly interesting. As interesting as the tales Bessie sometimes narrated on winter evenings, when she brought her ironing table to the nursery hearth. She allowed us to sit about it and, while she got up Mrs. Reed's hunting habit, fed our eager attention with passages of murder and mayhem passed down by her own Romanian grandmother. Sometimes, if I woke in the afternoon and she chanced to be awake and in good humour, she would tell lighter stories for my ears alone, tales of love and adventure taken from old fairy tales or folk songs.

With Bessie busy elsewhere, I contented myself with the *Bewick's* on my knee. I feared nothing but interruption, and that came too soon. The breakfast-room door opened.

"Boh! Madam Mortal!" cried John Reed. He paused. He found the room apparently empty. "Where the devil is she! Lizzy! Georgy! Jane is not here. Tell mama she is run out into the rain—bad human!"

It was well I drew the curtain, and I wished fervently he would not discover my hiding place. John Reed would not have found it out himself. He was not quick of any sensation that normally served his kind at the hunt; but Eliza just put her head in at the door and said at once—

"I smell her from here. She is in the window seat, to be sure, Jack."

And I came out immediately, for I trembled at the idea of risking close contact with the said Jack at a time when he'd barely finished his dinner and probably thirsted for more.

"What do you want?" I asked with feigned boldness.

"Say, 'What do you want, Master Reed?' I want you to come here." Seating himself in an armchair, he intimated by a gesture that I was to approach and stand before him.

John Reed retained the form of a schoolboy of fourteen years old, four years older than I, for I was but ten. Large and stout for his age, with a greyish pallor, wide features, heavy limbs, and large extremities, he gorged himself habitually of prey, which gave him consistently red eyes and a leonine awareness, as if he were always on edge, ready to pounce on his next snack. He ought now to have been at school, but a fiendish child was used to waking at night and sleeping during the day. Besides, he would have frightened the others in class, and it would have been a tad suspicious had he risen through the ranks but remained all of fourteen in appearance.

John had not much affection for his mother and sisters, and an antipathy for me that I suspected derived from hunger. He pulled me close and sniffed me, not two or three times in the week, or once or twice in the day, but continually. Every nerve I had feared him, and every drop of blood in my veins coursed faster when he came near.

Some moments I was bewildered by the terror he inspired. I had no appeal whatever against either his menaces or his inflictions. The servants feared offending their young master lest he devour one of them, and Mrs. Reed was blind and deaf on the subject. She never saw him lick or bite at me, though he did both now and then in her very presence, more frequently, however, behind her back.

Though it was my habit to obey him, I did not approach. Something in his glowing eyes hinted at a craving not yet sated. It was possible that he didn't get his fill of the stag or bear or whatever creature they'd feasted on. One day, I feared he would not be quenched with just a taste of my blood but would drink me dry or, worse, make a monster of me as he had one of the footmen, James, a poor lad who had once thwarted him and now had to forage in the night for bats or barn rats to eat his fill, being too small of stature to hunt effectively on his own.

"Hold out your hand," he ordered. I stood my ground, hands behind my back. "Approach," he repeated, louder, sounding slightly annoyed, "and hold out your hand."

The room was small and no one would answer my screams. Whether I went to him voluntarily or waited for him to get me made little difference if my fate was to be John Reed's dessert. Disobeying him might only fire his blood and force him to stop toying with me at last and do the deed.

I approached and, as ordered, held out my hand. He smiled the leering half smile he used when we were alone.

"Very good, my dear canapé." He took my arm and roughly forced my sleeve up. His bulbous nose met my skin and traced a slow, damp trail up my forearm to the tender inner elbow, as far up my arm as my sleeve would expose.

Sighing, he paused a moment as if to take in my essence or to gather his wits. As he had no wits to gather, it must have been my essence giving him pause. Abruptly, he jerked me down into the chair, onto his lap, pulling my head to the side to better access my neck. With the pad of a finger, he stroked my throat.

"Your blood. I feel it thrumming through your veins." His breathing slowed. I couldn't see his face, but I imagined his pupils narrowing, a predator going in for the kill. I knew he would soon strike, and while dreading the bite, I mused on what it might be like to be one of them, to live forever in the dark with no hope of ever returning to the light. While Mrs. Reed did not give me leave to go out of doors in the daytime, in the back of my mind I kept the notion that I *could*. One day, given the right conditions, I would walk out and turn my face to the sun. John Reed was not going to take that dream from me.

I jerked free of his hold and sprang across the room.

With his superior build and skills as a hunter, he was on me immediately, shoving me to the floor and rolling with all his weight atop me. No doubt he read fear in my face, for he fed on it, twisting my arms up over my head and pinning me motionless beneath him. He licked my cheek, his tongue burning a path from chin to brow. I closed my eyes, squeezing tight, as if not seeing him would make him go away, but his breath was hot on my face and redolent with the smell of blood and entrails, his earlier repast. My stomach lurched.

"You taste sweet for such a vile, bitter little thing," said he, "sweet enough to be my reward for catching you sneaking around before you could hatch another scheme. Perhaps I should make you one of us and force you out into the sun. Then you'll understand the pain you cause when you lift the curtains during the day."

"I was only reading," I said in my own defence. I was not in habit of answering John Reed's accusations. My care was in how to endure whatever punishment he sought to inflict upon me. But now, his tone held new seriousness. I had always known he was on the edge of carrying through with his most severe possible threat, and at last he seemed ready to do his worst.

"Show the book." He let me up to fetch it, both of us well aware that he would pin me down again, mouse to his cat, at his convenience.

I retreated to the window seat and returned to offer him the volume.

He flipped the pages, pausing at a scene of a gull soaring over a turbulent sea, clouds just beginning to cover a high midday sun. His eyes widened with an unmistakable look of envy. He slammed the book shut and threw it to the hearth, nearly pitching it into the fire.

"You have no business to take our books. You are a dependent, Mama says. You have no money. Your father left you none. You ought to beg, and not to live here with gentlemen's children like us."

"Soulless fiend children," I corrected boldly, drawing a gasp from Georgiana and Eliza, who stood watching just inside the door.

He nodded, unfazed. "You're disgustingly mortal. We'll live forever while you age and rot."

I would not be so certain, I thought, and did not know from whence such a strong supposition took root. I suddenly had an image of myself standing over John Reed, a wooden stake in hand. I had no idea where I would acquire a stake, let alone find the strength to plunge one through John Reed's heart, but the idea brought a queer little smile to my lips.

"Was that a laugh, Jane Slayre? At me?"

I shook my head, the smile departing.

"Georgiana and Eliza, did you not hear it as well? The wretched little mortal thinks she has a reason to laugh! I'll teach you to respect our power. Go and stand by the door, out of the way of the mirror and the windows."

The Reeds could not stand to be near reflective surfaces, to find no self-image staring back. Most of the mirrors in the house had been removed, but the servants kept one in the breakfast room, a room seldom used by the Reeds since nature had forced them into the habit of hunting their meals out of doors.

I did as told, looking around futilely for a weapon as I crossed the room. I looked up just as he sprang to action, landing on me with enough force that we rolled several times to the side until I struck my head on the corner of the door. It made me dizzy, but I maintained consciousness enough to know the blow had left a cut, and the blood enticed John Reed to quiet contemplation of my head. My anger flared along with his nostrils at my scent.

"Wicked and cruel boy!" I said. "You are like the monsters from Bessie's tales, like Vlad the Impaler!"

Bessie often told of Vlad, of his cruelty and thirst for blood. I suspected she told the tale as a subtle warning to me not to thwart the Reeds, especially John; but suddenly, I was not afraid. He could do his worst, kill me even, but he could not force me to become one of his kind. I would not sacrifice my soul, as no doubt all of the Reeds had given theirs.

"What! What!" he cried. "Did she say that to me? Did you hear her, Eliza and Georgiana? Won't I tell Mama? But first—"

I felt him grasp my hair and my shoulder and lick at the drop or two of blood that had trickled down my neck.

"So sweet," he said. His fangs pierced my neck, a quick, sharp burn, and I was sensible of somewhat pungent suffering. These sensations for the time predominated over fear, and I received him in frantic sort. He drank until I began to weaken, and I had the vision again of my standing over him, victorious at last. I had no weapon, barely any consciousness, and yet I knew that I could fight. Fight! Something in me screamed. Fight! Live!

I rammed my knee up and connected with tender flesh.

"Rat! Rat!" he bellowed.

Aid was near him. Eliza and Georgiana had run for Mrs. Reed, who had gone upstairs. She now came upon the scene, followed by Bessie and Mrs. Reed's maid, Abbot.

I lived in dread of Abbot. She frightened me far more than the vampyres, for I wasn't certain what she was. I only knew that her limbs frequently detached and she had a devil of a time putting them back on. Sometimes, when Abbot nodded off for a nap and the Reed children were feeling especially naughty, they took delight in rearranging her as if she were a puzzle. Unfortunately, Abbot nodded off frequently, as she was not very vigorous, and the Reeds were always naughty. But what Abbot lacked in enthusiasm she made up for in strength. She held me by the collar with toes where her fingers should have been and pulled me away from John.

I heard, "He's going to eat her, Mama! May we all join in?"

"No, no, dears! Her common blood will bring on fevers, maybe apoplexy! We only eat what we kill out of doors, or nobility!" Mrs. Reed's insistence on purity of blood kept the servants feeling safe in her presence, but John Reed had occasionally shown that his appetite could overcome even this prejudice.

"But she smells tolerable," Eliza said. I imagined her inching closer, fangs extended.

"She laughed," Georgiana pointed out, as if to add to her mother's argument about my disgusting common nature. "She nearly drove us all out of mind with her unmitigated mirth."

"What a wanton to tempt Master John with laughing and bleeding." This from Abbot, monotone as ever but dutifully indignant on her mistress's behalf. "As if she *wanted* to be eaten."

Then Mrs. Reed subjoined, "Take her away to the red room and lock her in there, away from my children." Four hands were immediately laid upon me, and I was borne upstairs.

CHAPTER 2

I DRIPPED BLOOD ALONG THE carpet all the way, a circumstance that greatly strengthened the bad opinion Bessie and Miss Abbot were disposed to entertain of me. I believed John Reed's fang had pierced an artery, for the flow came fast and would not stop though I tried to press the wound and dab at it with my sleeve. Abbot took my attempts to stanch the bleeding as fighting her off and held me tighter, confining my arms, until she fell asleep midwalk and nearly dropped me. Bessie caught me and nudged Abbot.

"Help me lift her, Miss Abbot. She's dazed."

"For shame." The lady's maid woke and took me entirely out of Bessie's hands, holding me, again, by the dress. "What shocking conduct, Miss Slayre, to entice your benefactress's son, your young master."

I hardly had the strength to speak, yet I found my voice. "Master? Am I a servant? Am I to let him feed at will?"

"No, you are less than a servant, for you do nothing for your keep. And to laugh at Master Reed? There, sit down, and think over your fit of levity."

They had got me by this time into the apartment indicated by Mrs. Reed and had thrust me upon a stool, but I had such trouble sitting upright that I immediately lost my balance. Levity? I grew lighter by the minute.

"If you don't stop bleeding, we'll have to bandage you up," said Bessie. "Miss Abbot, lend me your kerchief."

The cadaver-thin Miss Abbot reached inside her sleeve, and I recoiled. I dreaded to think of something so close to Miss Abbot's pasty skin touching my own. If her hand came with it, I might lose my potatoes and spinach on the red room's carpet.

"Don't take it off," I cried. "I'm nearly done bleeding."

Bessie clucked her tongue, reached in a pocket for her own handkerchief, and began dabbing at my neck. I shifted a little on my seat, seeing two Bessies for a brief moment, and tried not to swoon.

"She's never done anything like this before," Bessie said to Abbot, as if I were no longer present.

"It was always in her" was the reply. "I've heard Missus often enough and I agree with her opinion about the child. She's an underhanded little thing. She wants to be like them."

Like them? My heart revolted, but I did not care to correct the notion for fear of losing my breath. My head swam.

Bessie didn't answer, but addressed me. "You ought to be aware, miss, that you are under obligations to Mrs. Reed. She keeps you. If she were to turn you off, you would have to go to the poorhouse."

Miss Abbot joined in. "And you ought not to think yourself on an equality with the Misses Reed and Master Reed, because Missus kindly allows you to be brought up with them. They have a great deal of money, and you have none. It is your place to be placid, and if Master Reed wants a taste now and then, so be it."

A taste? No doubt the bloodless Abbot thought it nothing to simply offer a sample.

"What we tell you is for your own good," added Bessie. "You should try to stay out of the way and be quiet. Then, perhaps, you would have a home here."

"Come, Bessie, we will leave her; I wouldn't have her heart for anything." Indeed, even an animal's blood took preference over my common sort. "Miss Slayre, when you are by yourself, something bad might be permitted to come down the chimney and fetch you away."

I could not imagine much worse than with whom I currently resided. They went, shutting the door behind them. The red room was a square chamber, seldom slept in, I might say never, indeed, unless a particular noble the Reeds fancied came to visit. It was one of the largest and stateliest chambers in the mansion. I could not see well in the dark, but I remembered the layout from coming in once on an afternoon before Bessie came to fetch me and said it was too early to be up and I had best return to my own chamber.

A bed supported on massive pillars of mahogany, hung with curtains of deep red damask, stood out like a tabernacle in the centre. An ample cushioned easy chair sat near the head of the bed, white, with a footstool before it, looking like a pale throne. The two large windows, with their blinds always drawn, were half shrouded in falls of similar drapery. The carpet was red. The table at the foot of the bed was covered with a crimson cloth. The walls were a soft fawn colour with a blush of pink in it. The wardrobe, the toilet table, and the chairs were of darkly polished old mahogany.

The room was chill because it seldom had a fire; silent, due to the remote location far from the nursery and kitchen; solemn, because it was known to be so seldom entered. The housemaid came here on Saturdays to wipe from the furniture a week's worth of dust. Mrs. Reed herself, at far intervals, visited it to review the contents of a secret drawer in the wardrobe, where were stored divers parchments, her jewel casket, and a miniature of her deceased husband; and in those last words lies the secret of the red room—the spell that kept it so lonely in spite of its grandeur.

Mrs. Reed had been a vampyre nine years. In this chamber she breathed her last mortal breath at her husband's side. Here, Mr. Reed had bitten her and transformed her, as he had been attacked and transformed on the road home from his sister's—my mother's—funeral. Bessie said that Mrs. Reed didn't want her husband to suffer through the curse of immortality alone, but I suspected that Mrs. Reed cherished the idea of eternal life more than she even cared for her husband.

It seemed Mr. Reed alone suffered agonies over his new soulless state. He had never been much for the hunt, and being required to kill to feed his cravings left him feeling forlorn and most unsettled, according to Bessie's assessment, though she was fairly new to the Reeds' service at the time. Mrs. Reed suffered no such pangs of conscience. She adjusted to her new situation as easily as learning a new mode of dance for a society ball, but her husband remained morose.

Mr. Reed, trusting in Mrs. Reed's ability to maintain the household and provide proper care for his children and infant niece, enlisted a mercenary to drive a stake through his heart, turning him instantly to a pile of fine dust, thus ending his earthly tortures in the very room where he'd turned his wife into a vampyre. A sense of dreary consecration had since guarded the red room from frequent intrusion.

Unable to contemplate eternal life without her darlings, it was not five years before Mrs. Reed gave in to John Reed's pleading to make him a vampyre, too. Georgiana and Eliza followed. Aside from turning her children, Mrs. Reed stayed true to the last promise she made Mr. Reed, to never turn another living being to her own altered state—most especially not me, for I did not deserve, nor want, the honour.

My seat, to which Bessie and the bitter Miss Abbot had left me half-conscious, was a low ottoman near the marble chimneypiece. The bed rose before me. To my right was the high, dark wardrobe, with subdued, broken reflections varying the gloss of its panels. To my left were the muffled windows and the empty frame of what I guessed had once had been a great looking glass. I was not quite sure whether they had locked the door, and when I tried to move to check, I fell to the floor.

All looked colder and darker from my low vantage point. I struggled to my knees, crawled to the window, clutched the curtains, and tore them open before I fell back again to the carpet. I slept, perhaps an hour or more, but woke again to darkness. How I wished it could be the sun!

Somehow, I found strength to return to my stool. I shook with fear, or perhaps rage. John Reed's vicious attacks, his tyranny, occupied my mind. What if he struck again? How could he be stopped? I felt my head, my hair sticky with dried blood, and my neck, still sore at the wound, the handkerchief Bessie bound me with damp but not soaked. I thought of Eliza, headstrong and selfish but still respected, asking for a taste of me, her mother's admonishment delivered to protect Eliza from my common taint rather than to save me from harm. I was glad Georgiana hadn't asked. She, with her spoiled temper, was universally indulged and might have been allowed a sample, just small enough to satisfy without putting her in danger of contamination.

Georgiana's beauty, her pink cheeks and golden curls, seemed to give delight to all who looked at her, and to purchase indemnity for every fault. John no one thwarted, much less punished; though he tortured servants, snacked between meals on the little peachicks and barn cats, stripped the hothouse vines of their fruit, and broke the buds off the choicest plants in the conservatory. He liked to call his mother "old girl," too. He bluntly disregarded her wishes, often tore and spoiled her silk attire, ridiculed her appearance for the dark shadows under her eyes that were similar to his own; and he was still "her own darling." I dared commit no fault. I strove to fulfill every duty. And I was termed naughty and tiresome, too cheerful, and sneaking, from dusk to midnight, and from midnight to dawn.

"Unjust!" said my reason. Why should I suffer their accusations and live with John Reed's bullying and without the sun? Could I run away? Where would I go? How would I find food? Might it be worth it to take the chance even if death was my reward? I would die free of the Reeds, at least, and with a bright sun shining to warm my limbs as I passed.

How cold I was without a fire. I began to shake with chills, or was it weakness? I couldn't run away when it was a struggle to remain sitting upright, let alone attempt to stand or walk. Yet my mind reeled.

Gateshead Hall sheltered a family of vampyres, an undead maid, some two dozen mortal servants who were paid well for their silence and their service, and me. Where did I fit in? I was like nobody there.

Eventually darkness began to make way for day. The clouded night grew lighter with the dawn. I heard the rain begin to stop, and the howling wind give way to tranquil breezes. I grew colder still, but my heart warmed. My courage rose. The Reeds would soon be off to bed, and I might be forgotten and get a glimpse of sunlight. I might see the day break, bright and beautiful, over the valley beyond the fields surrounding the house. My cheer returned.

What delirium had led me to think such thoughts as I had? I was aware that I never wished to be like the Reeds, and nothing could have induced me to drink another being's blood, most especially John Reed's. If he came to me now and gave me the choice that my uncle's attackers had reportedly given him, to drink or die, I would indeed choose death and not be sorry for it. But to give up without a fight? To admit defeat at John Reed's hands? Never. I did not have it in me to concede. Running away and dying of want would as much be giving John Reed his triumph as if I drank of his blood after he began to drain me of mine.

I would live to see the sun. There, it came up over the field, just peeking out from a cloud. I drew closer to the window and squinted through the pane only to fall from the ottoman again. On the floor, I let the light wash over me, warming me and growing brighter as it rose. Or was it all a dream? I closed my eyes, I thought for just a second, but when I opened them again, the light was gone. As I sat squinting through the darkness towards the dimly gleaming windowpanes, I began to recall Bessie's nighttime tales of dead men coming back to earth as ghosts to right past wrongs or simply to visit those once known to them. Again, I might have slept. What happened next was more likely the result of losing so much blood, making my head swoon, my imagination wax fantastic, instead of any real occurrence.

A light shone brighter through the window, a small dot of light not large enough to be the sun, yet growing brighter and larger as it neared until it almost filled the room. I heard a voice, a deep male voice—my uncle Reed?

"Jane," he addressed me. "Dear Jane."

"Uncle?" I responded, a little frightened to contemplate that he was speaking to me. I could not see him, only light, bright yet soothing light that blinded me to all else in the room.

"Jane, you are a Slayre. You must fulfill your destiny."

"My destiny?"

"To slay. It's in your Slayre blood. Your aunt and your cousins need you to end their earthly tortures. They're abominations. Monsters. Only in death can they be reunited with their mortal souls. Save them, Jane, as only you can."

"I don't believe they want saving. And how—" What did he ask of me? To slay? I was but a child, too easily injured myself. Yet my mind flashed to my earlier vision, standing over John Reed with a wooden stake in my hand. "How would I begin to know what to do?"

"When the time is right, you will know. Seek out your kindred spirits, your family. There are Slayres living still. You must find them, study with them."

"I know no other family." My heart raced. Family? Someone else, besides the Reeds, who might care for me, take me in, dare I hope—might love me? "My parents are dead."

"Your parents died attacking a band of vampyres. Your father's brother, a master slayer, sent for me. His life's vocation, hunting vampyres, was too dangerous to allow for the safety of an infant in his care. Though estranged from my sister due to her marriage to your father, who was inferior to her in birth and station, I was a magistrate with a wife and children of my own, a suitable situation for raising a baby. Quite honestly, I missed your mother. I loved her. I wanted to make amends."

"And so you agreed to take me in?"

"But on the way home, a terrible thing happened."

"The vampyres."

"The county was rife with them at the time, before your uncle brought the region under control. They surrounded me. Fortunately, tucked away as you were in a basket under the carriage seat, they never found you."

"Oh, Uncle!" My heart ached. If not for me, my uncle Reed might never have been transformed. No wonder my aunt Reed hated me so! I could hardly blame her.

"You were an infant, an innocent. I'm only glad that I could keep them from finding you."

"By becoming one of them!"

"Not my wisest choice. And now you must undo my crime of bringing such a curse home to my family. Save them. Save them all!"

"But how?" I cried.

"If they are repentant of their choices and eager to reclaim their souls, you need only drive a stake through the heart and end the torture."

I barely contained my laugh. Repentant? Even if I could manage to drive a stake into John Reed's heart, I could not imagine he would ever be repentant. My uncle charged me with a heavy task, nay, an impossible one.

"All things are possible, Jane. You have the tools, the natural ability. You merely need the training and the discipline."

"I can be disciplined," I offered, eager for him to believe me. I couldn't say as much for the tools or ability. Had he seen me run? "But where to seek the training? You speak of family. How can I find them?"

The light grew dim. The room, silent.

"Uncle?" I called to him. "Please!"

I must have shouted in my sleep, for surely it had been a dream. Upon opening my eyes, I saw Bessie and Abbot leaning over me, their faces bathed in candlelight. Bessie checked my wound and pressed a hand to my forehead.

"Miss Slayre, are you ill?" said Bessie.

"You were making a fuss," Abbot intoned.

"I want to go to my chamber," I said. "Please, let me go."

"Have you seen something?" Bessie demanded. "I saw a light from under the door and I thought a ghost had come."

The servants all believed in ghosts, and why shouldn't they? They lived with vampyres, and Abbot. And of all rooms to be considered haunted, the red room was at the top of the list. Yet, they had left me in here. Alone. And bleeding. In the cold darkness without fire or even a candle. I took hold of Bessie's hand, and she did not snatch it from me.

"No ghosts. She has screamed out for attention," declared Abbot in her usual monotone. "And what a scream. If she had been in great pain, one would have excused it, but she only wanted to bring us all here. I know her naughty tricks."

"She has been bleeding," Bessie observed, as if it had escaped Abbot's attention. "The flow seems to have stopped, but she might have lost too much."

"What is all this?" another voice demanded, Mrs. Reed's. She came along the corridor in her nightcap and gown, ready to settle in for a good day's sleep. She cut it perilously close to sunrise all for the sake of furthering my punishment. Perhaps I should have been flattered. "Abbot and Bessie, I believe I gave orders that Jane Slayre should be left in the red room until I came to her myself."

"Miss Jane screamed so loud, ma'am," Bessie pleaded. "You would let her wait until evening?"

"Let go of Bessie's hand, Jane" was her answer. "You'll win no sympathy from me. Your problems are brought on by yourself and well deserved. It is my duty to show you that tricks will not be tolerated. You will stay the day here, and it is only on condition of perfect submission and stillness that I shall liberate you at nightfall."

I said nothing. I formed great plans to watch the sun rise and arch over the azure afternoon sky for as long as I could manage to keep my eyes open. Punishment indeed.

If only I hadn't been so weak as to faint at her feet before realising my fantastic dream.

CHAPTER 3

AT DUSK, I WOKE with the feeling I'd had a wonderful dream, and seeing before me a beautiful white glow. I heard voices, too, speaking softly as if desiring me not to hear. I became aware that someone was handling me, lifting me up and supporting me in a sitting posture. I rested my head against a pillow or an arm and felt easy. In five minutes more the cloud of bewilderment dissolved. I knew that I was in my own bed, and that the soft glow was the nursery fire. Day gave way to night. A candle already burned on the table. Bessie stood at the bedside with a basin in her hand, and a gentleman sat in a chair near my pillow, leaning over me.

I felt an inexpressible relief, a soothing conviction of protection and security, when I knew that a stranger was in the room, an individual not belonging to Gateshead, and not related to Mrs. Reed.

Turning from Bessie, I scrutinised the face of the gentleman. I knew him. It was Mr. Lloyd, an apothecary sometimes called in by Mrs. Reed when the servants were ailing. For herself and the children, she avoided medical attention at risk of exposing them all for what they were. Vampyres weren't often in need of physicians, besides.

"Well, who am I?" he asked.

"Mr. Lloyd."

"Yes. You're doing well." He smiled, took my hand from where it gently gripped the lace edge of the coverlet, and held it. "You're colour is returning, though I dare observe there's not much colour to return. How long has it been since you've been in the sun?"

"Mrs. Reed's not one for sunlight," Bessie interjected too quickly. "She believes it bad for the complexion, sir, if I may."

Mr. Lloyd pursed his lips, as if he knew more than Bessie suspected. "Hm. That might be the way of it for her, but this child"—he smiled again, turning to me—"this little one needs sunshine, fresh air. A few afternoons out of doors would work wonders. Don't you like the outdoors, Jane?"

I nodded. If only I could roam the hills with the sun shining overhead! My heart soared. It seemed too much to hope.

"I'll see to it she gets out more," Bessie answered dutifully.

"Very well." Mr. Lloyd had no reason to disbelieve her.

I had no idea if she meant to keep her word. Still, my nerves tingled with excitement—to be given time to play outdoors in the sun! True, there were not many fine days in mid-November, but I could make the most of what I had.

Mr. Lloyd issued further instructions that I was to sleep through the night, not to be disturbed, and he should call again the next day. To sleep at night! I didn't think sleeping would be a problem. As delighted as I was at the prospect of sleeping at night and going out during the day, I still felt weak and light-headed from my injury. He took his leave, and Bessie claimed the chair at my bedside.

"Do you feel as if you should sleep, miss?" asked Bessie rather softly.

"Oh, yes. Without a doubt." I feared that she would try to keep me up, to stay in step with the Reeds and their regular schedule.

"Would you like to drink, or could you eat anything?"

"No, thank you, Bessie."

"Then I think I shall go wake the others, for it is past six o'clock. But you may call me if you want anything in the night."

Wonderful civility this! It emboldened me to ask a question. "Bessie, I will be able to play in the sun, won't I? I won't turn into a vampyre just because John Reed took more than a taste of my blood?"

Bessie smiled. "No, dear. He would have to take even more than that, and then you would have to have a fair taste of his as well. You won't turn into a vampyre. And I will speak with Mrs. Reed. I believe Mr. Lloyd has offered a solution to benefit all of you. It's sheer folly to expect you to keep up with them, different as you are. If you sleep at night when they're awake, and they sleep during the day when you're up, you won't have to tolerate much of John Reed."

Or Mrs. Reed's prejudice. But Bessie's main objective, I supposed, was to make sure Mrs. Reed no longer had to tolerate seeing much of me.

"It's a wonder Mrs. Reed had not thought of it before now. I suppose she felt it somehow disloyal to her promise to Mr. Reed to raise you as one of her own."

"But I'm not one of her own," I said defiantly.

"No indeed. Get some sleep, then. You'll be better soon, no doubt."

Bessie went into the housemaid's apartment, which was near. I heard her say, "Martha, come and wake them with me. I daren't for my life be alone with John Reed if he's still hungry for blood. He took enough from that poor child last night. She might die. We should have called for the apothecary sooner if Mrs. Reed hadn't been in such a state that he should guess at her condition."

Martha Abbot clucked and made some disagreement on the risk

of exposure to the Reeds and how much I might have cost them with my antics. They both went to the other part of the house, where the Reeds kept to closed caskets in windowless rooms during the day.

I tried to sleep, but my head ached and I kept thinking about strolling the orchard in the afternoon. At last, the fire and candle went out, and sometime after that I must have fallen asleep.

Next day, by noon, I was up and dressed and sat wrapped in a shawl by the nursery hearth. My spirits soared, but I felt physically weak and broken-down, too weak to go out of doors. I had the curtains open, and I could watch birds flitting, from windowsill to rooftop, from rooftop to sky. It was almost as good as being out. I felt cheered to know the Reeds were all shut up for the day while I was able to sit up and glory in it. I tried not to seem overjoyed lest Abbot and Bessie report me to Mrs. Reed as unabashedly pleased with my situation.

Abbot was sewing in another room. I had no idea when she slept if she stayed awake during the day and still managed to serve the Reeds all night. Perhaps it explained her narcolepsy. Bessie had been down to the kitchen, and she brought up a tart on a certain brightly painted china plate, whose bird of paradise, nestling in a wreath of rosebuds, had been wont to stir in me a most enthusiastic sense of admiration; and which plate I had often petitioned to be allowed to take in my hand to examine more closely, but had always hitherto been deemed unworthy of such a privilege.

This precious vessel was now placed on my knee, and I was cordially invited to eat the circlet of delicate pastry upon it. I smiled at it. It smelled sweet, of berries, and the crust glistened with a sprinkling of sugar. No chunk of meat was left bleeding on my plate, no sign of juice or entrails. I took a bite. "Thank you, Bessie."

Bessie asked if I would have a book. Sun outside my window, sweets, and a book! I felt thoroughly spoiled and not about to question my good fortune, even if it might fade as soon as the apothecary returned to declare me nearly recovered.

"*Gulliver's Travels?*" I suggested. She went to fetch it and returned, reclaiming the seat beside me.

Yet when this cherished volume was now placed in my hand, I put down the book and begged Bessie to indulge me with one of her fairy stories instead. She spun a tale of forest-dwelling elves while I finished my tart.

After eating, I began to feel tired again, but a pleasant sort of tired, not weary. Bessie opened a little drawer, full of splendid shreds of silk and satin, and began making a new bonnet for Georgiana's doll. Meantime she sang:

"In the days when we went gypsying, a long time ago."

I listened always with lively delight; for Bessie had a sweet voice—at least, I thought so. Usually, I found an indescribable sadness in the Gypsy melody, but now, I heard a new sweetness in Bessie's lovely tones. Her voice seemed higher, clearer, the tone more upbeat and merry.

"Come, Miss Jane, don't cry," said Bessie as she finished.

I felt my cheeks. "Was I crying? But I feel so content. Is it possible to cry when one is happy?"

Bessie smiled. "Yes, Jane. I believe it is."

She spoke as if she'd had experience with it. I trusted her opinion, for what I felt was far from sadness.

In the afternoon, Mr. Lloyd came again.

"What, already up!" said he as he entered the nursery. "Well, nurse, how is she?"

Bessie answered that I was doing well.

"She's still very pale. Come here, Miss Jane. Your name is Jane, is it not?"

"Yes, sir, Jane Slayre."

"Well, Miss Jane Slayre, have you any pain?"

"No, sir."

The good apothecary looked me over, head to toe. I stood before him in my heavy cotton gown, a shawl draped over my shoulders. My strength seemed to increase with his appraisal. I managed to stay on my feet as he fixed his small, grey gaze on me steadily. He had a good-natured face.

"How did you hurt your head yesterday? And what made those peculiar marks on your neck?" He gestured to where the shawl covered my bite marks.

"She had a fall," said Bessie, again putting in her word.

"A fall! That might explain her head, but her neck?" He tugged the shawl and it slipped down my shoulder, revealing the tiny scrapes where the bites had been.

"John Reed bit me" was my blunt explanation. Let Bessie scold me for making an accusation. "He knocked me down, and then he bit me. Mrs. Reed accused me of provoking him and ignored my bleeding to shut me up in a room."

Bessie gasped. "Child's play, sir. It did get a bit out of hand. But I tended the girl. She was carefully monitored."

A loud bell rang for the servants' dinner. He must have known what it was when he turned to Bessie. "That's for you, nurse, you can go down. I'll give Miss Jane a lecture till you come back."

No doubt Bessie would rather have stayed, but she was obliged to go because punctuality at meals was rigidly enforced at Gateshead Hall.

"You were bleeding and left alone?" Mr. Lloyd asked once Bessie was gone.

"Bessie checked my wounds, and then I was left alone. In the dark. I saw a ghost."

I saw Mr. Lloyd smile and frown at the same time. "A ghost! Is that all? Ghosts shouldn't frighten you. You're at least nine years old. I'm wondering what else you might have seen. Something worse than ghosts perhaps?"

I pondered. Should I reveal Gateshead's secrets? I didn't know if Mr. Lloyd would believe me or accuse me of fits of fancy. "I wasn't afraid of the ghost, not once I recognised his voice as Mr. Reed's. He died protecting me. I think he meant to do so again."

"Protecting you from what? Your cousin's bullying?"

Unwilling to say more, I simply nodded.

"Are you afraid he will attack you again?"

"Not while the sun shines." I glanced at the window, sad to see the sun setting, nearly gone. "I wish I had somewhere else to go."

"Away from your aunt and cousins, truly? You have no other family?"

"I have no father or mother, brothers or sisters."

Mr. Lloyd produced a snuffbox from his waistcoat pocket, took some, and put it back. "Don't you think Gateshead Hall a very beautiful house? Are you not very thankful to have such a fine place to live at?"

"It is not my house, sir; and Abbot says I have less right to be here than a servant."

"Bah, but you can't be silly enough to wish to leave such a splendid place?"

"If I had anywhere else to go, I should be glad to leave it; but I can never get away from Gateshead until I am a woman."

"Perhaps you may—who knows? Have you any relations besides Mrs. Reed?"

"I think not, sir."

"None belonging to your father?"

"I don't know. I asked Aunt Reed once, and she said possibly I might have some poor, low relations called Slayre, but she knew nothing about them."

"If you had such, would you like to go to them?"

I reflected. I had seen poverty, and it looked even less appealing than living with vampyres, Abbot, and a potential ghost. "No. I should not like to belong to poor people."

"Not even if they were kind to you?"

I shook my head. I could not see how poor people had the means of being kind. I had not yet learned enough of poverty to see anything noble in it.

"But are your relatives so very poor? Are they working people?"

"I cannot tell. Aunt Reed says if I have any, they must be a beggarly set." I did not repeat that Uncle Reed said I had another uncle, a master slayer. How to explain? Besides, his job was too dangerous to care for a child, and I was not ready to face more danger than John Reed provided regularly.

"Would you like to go to school?"

I scarcely knew what school was, but if Bessie's occasional accounts of school discipline, gathered from the young ladies of a family where she had lived before coming to Gateshead, were somewhat appalling, her details of certain accomplishments by these same young ladies were, I thought, equally attractive. Besides, school would be a complete change. It implied a long journey, an entire separation from Gateshead, an entrance into a new life.

"I should indeed like to go to school. Very much."

"Well, well! Who knows what may happen?" said Mr. Lloyd as he got up. "The child ought to have change of air and scene," he added, speaking to himself. "Nerves not in a good state."

Bessie now returned; at the same moment the sound of Mrs. Reed calling out for Abbot could be heard from the hall.

"Is that your mistress, nurse?" asked Mr. Lloyd. "I should like to speak to her before I go."

As he was a lowly apothecary, I didn't think Mr. Lloyd in any danger from Mrs. Reed right around her usual feeding time. I thanked him and bid him good-night.

Bessie invited him to walk into the breakfast room and led the way out. In the interview that followed between him and Mrs. Reed, I presume, from later occurrences, that the apothecary ventured to recommend my being sent to school, and the recommendation was readily enough adopted. I overheard Abbot discussing the subject with Bessie when both sat sewing in the nursery after I was in bed.

"Missus was, she dared say, glad enough to get rid of such a scheming, vengeful child, who always looked as if she were watching everybody, and ready to find a way to do us all in." Abbot, I think, gave me credit for being a sort of infantine Guy Fawkes.

On that same occasion I heard more to expand upon what my uncle Reed's ghost, real or imagined, had told me. Miss Abbot spoke of my father, a wicked demon slayer who passed himself off as a poor clergyman; that my mother had married him against the wishes of her friends, who considered the match beneath her; that my grandfather Reed was so irritated at her disobedience, he cut her off without a shilling. That after my mother and father had been married a year, my mother's training was complete and she went out slaying with my father, conduct most unbefitting a lady! My parents were on a mission to rid a large manufacturing town from a ravenous band of vampyres when they were outnumbered and surrounded. They died fighting together.

Abbot seemed to think it was right that they should die, as if they attacked poor helpless vampyres out of some sort of misguided prejudice. I suppose she must have forgot what it was like for the Reeds before they were turned and considered all their acts since to be somehow right and good because they were, after all, gentility. Abbot's thoughts reflected her mistress's so well I suspected she was grown in a laboratory from a bit of Mrs. Reed's brain, had Mrs. Reed any little bit to spare.

Bessie, when she heard this narrative, sighed and said, "Poor Miss Jane is to be pitied, too, Abbot."

"Yes," responded Abbot. "But I suspect she's got too much of the Slayre blood in her." A long pause ensued in which she must have fallen asleep and then woken herself with a loud snore to continue as if she hadn't missed a beat. "Like her parents, that one. Watch and see."

"I don't think her capable of real violence, Abbot, such a weak little thing," Bessie defended. "At any rate, if she were lovely and athletic like Miss Georgiana, you would no doubt have more faith in her potential."

"Yes, I dote on Miss Georgiana," said Abbot somewhat listlessly, as if reading from a script. "Bessie, you had better get some rest. The

Reeds are out late hunting and won't be in need of you, but you'll be up early with your charge."

"Indeed. I will have to wake Jane early so she gets used to her new schedule. I'm glad Mrs. Reed can spare me to take care of her properly."

"No one else would be up for the task. Besides, the Reeds are grown as much as they will be. They haven't much need of a nurse."

"True enough," Bessie said, though her tone seemed to offer some disagreement with her words. "Well, Abbot, good night."

CHAPTER 4

TWO DAYS AFTER Mr. Lloyd's visit, I'd finally recovered my strength enough to venture out of doors. At midday! I nearly stripped off my cloak and danced under the sun, it felt so glorious shining down on me. Unfortunately, a chill wind blew, despite the sun's brightness, and I was forced to wrap my cloak tighter around me to keep out the breeze. Cold as it was, nothing could stop me. I ran across fields, jumped over rocks and twigs, and relished the pricking in my expanding lungs. My heart raced. My spirits lightened. I shouted out with glee, not even caring if they could hear me in the house. Let them shake in their coffins. I was free to roam.

A little later in the day, I was gathering small twigs to build a house for my doll when I had a sudden inspiration, a memory of my vision. I was standing over John Reed with a stake in my hand. Oh, the power it inspired! The house was forgotten. I found a fine-edged stone and started rubbing it against the twigs, sharpening them to a point.

After a while, I decided the rock wasn't doing the trick and I stole into the kitchen and pocketed a tiny dagger when cook wasn't looking. Though only a small one, just large enough to pare potatoes, it allowed me to whittle fat twigs to a fine point. I spent half the afternoon experimenting with branches of different shapes and sizes. When I found what I felt was just the right size twig and worked it to the sharpness for a stake, I practised stabbing it into the ground, imagining John Reed's body in the dirt. Satisfied, I found more twigs, gathered them up in my tucker, and went to a soft, little hill at the side of the house where I could whittle to my heart's content, or until my fingers froze. From then on, I made it my habit to work on a few branches a day until I'd built up a stockpile and I was able to return the dagger as easily as I'd taken it.

Days and weeks passed from Mr. Lloyd's visit and there was no word of my going to school. I never bothered to ask about it, as I was quite content since Mrs. Reed had put me out of her company and allowed me to keep separate hours from the family's. Occasionally, I met up with her in the hall as she was making preparations for the hunt, but she merely narrowed her eyes and stepped around me as if I were a mess on the rug. If she noticed the improved colour in my cheeks from spending hours in the sun, my more robust frame since I'd been permitted proper food, my improved energy from spending hours out of doors running through fields, she didn't comment on it.

My cousins seemed to notice, however. Eliza and Georgina, evidently acting according to orders, spoke to me as little as possible. I noticed their gazes narrowing on me, much like their mother's, only theirs seemed to linger in shrewder assessment. Did I perhaps look a little prettier to them now that I lived a healthier mortal lifestyle? And why should it bother them?

John thrust his tongue in his cheek whenever he saw me and once attempted chastisement. More determined than ever to stand my ground, I snarled at him, as if warning him away in a language he might understand, that of wild beasts. Once I dared show him a wooden stake I'd taken to keeping with me at all times, hidden in my pocket or up a sleeve. He ran immediately to his mama.

"Don't talk to me about her, John. I told you not to go near her. She is not worthy of notice. I do not choose that either you or your sisters should associate with her."

Here, leaning over the banister, I cried out suddenly, and without at all deliberating on my words, "They are not fit to associate with me."

Mrs. Reed was a rather large woman, a fierce hunter who alone could devour more than half of what she killed, and she flew at me like a whirlwind, taking the stairs three or four at a time. She crushed me against the wall and dared me to move much less speak to her children again. Her sharp canines, bared, glowed in the lamplight. If she had ever been tempted to attack me, she had hid it well until now.

I checked my fear to address her as calmly as I could manage. "What would Uncle Reed say to you, if he were alive?"

"What?" Mrs. Reed backed away, her black eyes returning to their usual cold, composed, and lifeless state.

"My uncle Reed is in heaven now, reunited with his conscience and his soul. Don't think he doesn't watch over you and wish you to find your way to eternal peace and comfort as well. He sees all."

Mrs. Reed soon rallied her spirits. She jumped at me again, gripped my shoulders and shook me most soundly, then slapped me across the face and left me without a word. Once she walked away, I realised that I'd had a firm hand inside my tucker, gripping the sharpened stake, the entire time I'd been under attack. How close I might have come to using it.

Bessie had words for me that night before bed about minding my station and keeping to my place. For once I did not feel humbled by the words. No, indeed. I felt empowered, not wicked, courageous, not ungrateful. I'd found the power to stand up for myself, and it felt better than I ever imagined it would.

November, December, and half of January passed away. Christmas and the New Year had been celebrated at Gateshead with the usual festive cheer. Presents had been exchanged, dinners and evening parties given, old friends invited and unexpectedly consumed later in their beds. From every enjoyment I was, of course, excluded. My share of the gaiety consisted in witnessing the nightly attiring of Eliza and Georgiana, for Bessie was needed in the duty, and seeing them descend to the drawing room dressed out in thin muslin frocks and scarlet sashes, with hair elaborately ringleted. And afterwards in listening to the sound of the piano or the harp played below, to the passing to and fro of the butler and the footman, to the jingling of glass and china as refreshments were handed out, to the broken hum of conversation as the drawing-room door opened and closed. When tired of this occupation, I would retire from the stairhead to the silent nursery. There, though somewhat sad, I was not miserable.

To speak truth, I had not the least wish to go into company, for in company I was rarely noticed. I could run down the stairs screaming that the Reeds were vampyres and that blood would be spilled, and no one would pay me any more mind than a mouse stealing a crumb.

Instead I sat with my doll on my knee until the fire got low, glancing round occasionally to make sure that nothing worse than myself haunted the shadowy room. I would show my doll the stakes I had cut that morning and how I planned to use them if my cousin vampyres dared to come near. She approved wholeheartedly, love that she was.

When the embers sank to a dull red, I undressed hastily, tugging at knots and strings as I best might, and sought shelter from cold and darkness in my bed. To this bed I always took my doll. I could not sleep unless it was folded in my nightgown, a stake tucked into its dress as I had a stake tucked into the sleeve of mine. When it lay there safe and warm, I was comparatively happy, believing it to be happy likewise.

Long did the hours seem while I waited for the shrieks of dying company and listened for the sound of Bessie's step on the stairs hours after she was done helping to clean up while the footmen buried corpses with some ceremony on the grounds in unmarked graves. Sometimes Bessie would come up in the interval to seek her thimble or her scissors, or perhaps to bring me something by way of supper—a bun or a cheesecake—then she would sit on the bed while I ate it, and when I had finished, she would tuck the clothes round me, and twice she kissed me and said, "Good night, Miss Jane."

It was the fifteenth of January, about nine o'clock in the morning. Bessie had gone down to breakfast. My cousins were sleeping off their repast, a lighter meal than they'd become accustomed to during the holidays as they had gone back to hunting wildlife with the end of the season's celebrations. I was making my bed, having received strict orders from Bessie to get it arranged before she returned. Having spread the quilt, checked my store of stakes in the pillowcase, and folded my nightdress, I went to the window seat to put in order some picture books and dollhouse furniture scattered there, then stopped and tried to see out the window through the frost. For days, it had been too cold to go out, overcast and grey. I breathed on the window to clear a space, just in case some of the sun's rays poked through the clouds.

From this window, I could usually see the porter's lodge and the carriage road, and just as I had dissolved enough frost from the panes to look out, I saw the gates thrown open and a carriage roll through. Carriages did not often come to Gateshead, so I watched with growing interest. It stopped in front of the house. The doorbell rang loudly.

Bessie came running upstairs into the nursery. "Miss Jane, take off your pinafore. What are you doing there? Have you washed your hands and face this morning?"

I was spared the trouble of answering, for Bessie seemed in too great a hurry to listen to explanations. She hauled me to the washstand, inflicted a merciless but happily brief scrub on my face and hands with soap, water, and a coarse towel, disciplined my head with a bristly brush, took off my pinafore, and then, hurrying me to the top of the stairs, bid me go down directly, as I was wanted in the drawing room.

I would have asked who wanted me—not Mrs. Reed surely, as she was still abed—but Bessie was already gone and had closed the nursery door upon me. I slowly descended. I stood in the empty hall. Before me was the drawing-room door, and I stopped, curious and a little intimidated.

"Who could want me?" I asked inwardly, as with both hands I turned the stiff door handle, which, for a second or two, resisted my efforts. "Who could it be?"

The handle turned, the door opened, and passing through and curtsying low, I looked up at—a black pillar! Such, at least, appeared to me, at first sight, the straight, narrow, sable-clad shape standing erect on the rug. The grim face at the top was like a carved mask. Surely not a vampyre, as he was out so early in the day, but I then startled at the sight of Aunt Reed, seated at the fireside behind him. Mrs. Reed interrupting her sleep to venture out about the house in daylight hours? This was an important meeting to be sure.

"This is the little girl respecting whom I applied to you," Mrs. Reed said, gesturing for me to come forward.

I swallowed hard. He turned his head slowly towards where I stood and, having examined me with the two inquisitive-looking black eyes, which twinkled under a pair of bushy brows, said solemnly, and in the deepest bass voice that bounced like thunder off the walls, "Her size is small. What is her age?"

"Ten years," I said, willing to speak for myself instead of waiting for Aunt Reed to speak for me.

"So much?" was the doubtful answer that seemed to echo in the room, and he prolonged his scrutiny for some minutes. Presently he addressed me. "Your name, little girl?"

"Jane Slayre, sir." In uttering these words I looked up. My courage waned a little. He seemed to me a giant, but then I was very little.

"Well, Jane Slayre, and are you a good child?"

"I am." I narrowed my eyes at Mrs. Reed to judge her reaction.

She cleared her throat. "Perhaps the less said on that subject the better, Mr. Bokorhurst."

"Sorry indeed to hear it! She and I must have some talk." He settled in the armchair opposite Mrs. Reed's. It groaned under his weight, which was not significant except for his height. He was not stout. "Come here."

I stepped across the rug. He placed me square and straight before him. What a face he had, now that it was almost on a level with mine! What a great nose! And what a mouth! And what large, prominent teeth! Perhaps he was a vampyre who had found a way to tolerate the daylight? Or something worse? One of the demons from Bessie's fairy tales?

"No sight so sad as that of a naughty child," he began, "especially a naughty little girl. Do you know where the wicked go after death?"

"They go to hell" was my ready answer. "With the unrepentant slain vampyres."

He laughed as if he found this fantastical. It reassured me a bit. I didn't dare glance at Mrs. Reed. "And what is hell? Can you tell me that?"

"A pit full of fire."

"And should you like to fall into that pit, and to be burning there forever?"

"No, sir. Especially not with the vampyres." Mrs. Reed would catch my meaning, that my life hadn't been so far removed from hell as it was.

"What must you do to avoid it?"

I deliberated a moment. "I must keep in good health, not die. And most especially avoid sacrificing my soul for the false promise of eternal life."

"Children younger than you die daily. I buried a little child of five years old only a day or two since—a good little child, whose soul is now in heaven. It is to be feared the same could not be said of you were you to be called hence."

Not being in a condition to remove his doubt with Mrs. Reed standing by ready to discredit me, I only cast my eyes down on the two large feet planted on the rug and sighed, wishing myself far enough away.

"I hope that sigh is from the heart, and that you repent of ever having been the occasion of discomfort to your excellent benefactress. Do you say your prayers night and morning?"

"Yes, sir."

"Do you read your Bible?"

"Sometimes."

"With pleasure? Are you fond of it?"

"I like Revelation, and the book of Daniel, and Genesis and Samuel, and a little bit of Exodus, and some parts of Kings and Chronicles, and Job and Jonah."

"And the Psalms? I hope you like them?"

"No, sir."

"No? Oh, shocking! I have a little boy, younger than you, who knows six psalms by heart, and when you ask him which he would rather have, a gingerbread nut to eat or a verse of a psalm to learn, he says, 'Oh! The verse of a psalm! Angels sing psalms,' says he. 'I wish to be a little angel here below.' He then gets two nuts in recompense for his infant piety."

"Psalms are not interesting," I said. Most especially not for a meager two nuts.

"That proves you have a wicked heart and you must pray to God to change it, to give you a new and clean one, to take away your heart of stone and give you a heart of flesh."

I was about to ask how that change of heart was to be performed. Did he act as God's intermediary? Did *he* mean to perform an operation to change my heart? I was, after all, a girl of ten and prone to flights of imagination. I could picture him reaching in and pulling my heart out, still beating. But Mrs. Reed interposed, telling me to sit down. Perhaps I had said enough.

"Mr. Bokorhurst, I believe I intimated in the letter which I wrote to you three weeks ago that this little girl has not quite the character and disposition I could wish. Should you admit her into Lowood school, I should be glad if the superintendent and teachers were requested to keep a strict eye on her, and, above all, to guard against her worst fault, a tendency towards deceit. I mention this in your hearing, Jane, that you may not attempt to impose on Mr. Bokorhurst."

Her words were perhaps intended as a warning to keep me quiet, but she did not scare me. The problem was that Mr. Bokorhurst would take her word over mine, and she was right that I should not attempt to expose her, for now. She had already made me out to be a bad child and a liar, and I would have a struggle to overcome the reputation she painted for me even as I started fresh in a school.

"Deceit is, indeed, a sad fault in a child," said Mr. Bokorhurst. "It is akin to falsehood, and all liars will have their portion in the lake burning with fire and brimstone. She shall be watched, Mrs. Reed. I will speak to Miss Temple and the teachers."

"I should wish her to be brought up in a manner suiting her prospects," continued my benefactress. "To be made useful, to be kept humble. As for the vacations, she will, with your permission, spend them always at Lowood."

"Your decisions are perfectly judicious, madam," returned Mr. Bokorhurst. "Humility is a Christian grace, and one peculiarly appropriate to the pupils of Lowood. Only the other day I had a pleasing proof of my success. My second daughter, Augusta, went with her mama to visit the school, and on her return she exclaimed, 'Oh, dear papa, how quiet and plain all the girls at Lowood look, with their hair combed behind their ears, and their long pinafores, and those little pockets outside their frocks—they are almost like poor people's children! And,' said she, 'they looked at my dress and Mama's as if they had never seen a silk gown before.' "

"This is the state of things I quite approve," returned Mrs. Reed. "Had I sought all England over, I could scarcely have found a system more exactly fitting a child like Jane Slayre. Consistency, my dear Mr. Bokorhurst. I advocate consistency in all things."

"Consistency, madam, is the first of Christian duties, and it has been observed in every arrangement connected with the establishment of Lowood."

"I will send her, then, as soon as possible, Mr. Bokorhurst. I assure you, I feel anxious to be relieved of a responsibility that was becoming too irksome."

"No doubt, no doubt, madam; and now I wish you good morning. I shall return to Bokorhurst Hall in the course of a week or two. I shall send Miss Temple notice that she is to expect a new girl so that there will be no difficulty about receiving her. And how is Miss Abbot getting on?"

"Abbot continues to serve me well. No cross words, never any trouble, and she has saved me much in the cost of food."

"You're careful, then, that she never gets a taste of meat?"

"Oh, no. Never. She does fall asleep rather too frequently, and there's the problem with her fingers occasionally breaking off in my hair arrangements, but otherwise I am most pleased with her. Thank you for recommending her."

"Very pleased to do so. We're preparing new girls for entering service should you ever want for more. Some of our past errors have been corrected with improved technique. We've learnt to harvest them sooner. It cuts down on the difficulties you mention. If you should like to trade Abbot for—"

"Trade Abbot? No, sir, I wouldn't hear of it. We're all quite comfortable with Abbot now. I thank you again. Good-bye, Mr. Bokorhurst. Remember me to Mrs. and Miss Bokorhurst, and to Augusta and Theodore, and Master Broughton Bokorhurst."

So Mr. Bokorhurst was to credit, or blame, for Abbot's presence? It made me a tad nervous about what sort of school he ran. What was he harvesting? Still, it was a school and a chance to get away from the Reeds and learn something of the world.

"I will, madam. Little girl, here is a book entitled the *Child's Guide*. Read it with prayer, especially that part containing 'An account of the awfully sudden death of Mary, a naughty child addicted to falsehood and deceit.'"

With these words Mr. Bokorhurst put into my hand a thin pamphlet sewn in a cover, and having rung for his carriage, he departed.

Mrs. Reed and I were left alone. I thought she might be in a hurry to return to her bed, but the heavy drapes were drawn and I suppose she was not ready to go back to sleep with the excitement of arranging my permanent departure from Gateshead Hall. She picked up her sewing. I watched her. Some minutes passed in silence.

Mrs. Reed was a woman of robust frame, square-shouldered and strong-limbed, not tall, and, though stout, not obese. She had a somewhat large face, the under jaw being much developed and solid. Her brow was low, her chin large and prominent, mouth and nose sufficiently regular. Her skin was pale, if a little grey, and her hair nearly flaxen. Under her light eyebrows glimmered ink-black eyes, as hard in expression as they were inhumanly opaque. Her menacing expression no doubt helped her to remain an exact, clever manager. Almost no one would dare thwart her. Her household and tenantry were thoroughly under her control. Her children only at times defied her authority and laughed it to scorn. She dressed well and had a presence and port calculated to set off handsome attire.

I turned my attention from her to the tract I still held in my hand outlining the sudden death of the liar, to which narrative my attention had been pointed as to an appropriate warning. What Mrs. Reed had said concerning me to Mr. Bokorhurst, the whole tenor of their conversation, was recent, raw, and stinging in my mind. I had felt every word as acutely as I had heard it plainly, and a passion of resentment fomented now within me.

As if she could read my thoughts, Mrs. Reed looked up from her work. Her eye settled on mine, her fingers at the same time suspended their nimble movements.

"Go out of the room. Return to the nursery." My look or something else must have struck her as offensive, for she spoke with extreme though suppressed irritation. I went to the door and came back again. I walked to the window, across the room, fingered the drapes, and returned to stand in front of Mrs. Reed.

"I am not deceitful. If I were, I should say I loved you; but I declare I do not love you. I dislike you the worst of anybody in the world except John Reed, and this book about the liar, you may give to your girl Georgiana, for it is she who tells lies, and not I."

Mrs. Reed's hands still lay on her work inactive. Her eye of ice continued to dwell on mine. "What more have you to say?"

"I am glad you are no true relation of mine. I will never call you aunt again as long as I live. I will never come to see you when I am grown-up, and if anyone asks me how I liked you, and how you treated me, I will say the very thought of you makes me sick, and that you treated me with miserable cruelty."

"How dare you affirm that, Jane Slayre?"

"How dare I, Mrs. Reed? How dare I? Because it is the truth. You have no soul, no feelings, so how can you guess what I endure because of you? I have done long enough without one bit of love or kindness. To my dying day, I shall remember how you thrust me into the red room and locked me up there, bleeding and in agony over a punishment you made me suffer because your wicked boy struck me and bit my neck to drink my blood. My common blood! I will tell anybody who asks me questions this exact tale. People think you a good woman, but you are bad, monstrous, a murderess! Above all, *you* are deceitful!" And now, my climactic revelation, I pulled the stake out of my skirts. I didn't go anywhere without one anymore. "And if you should let your child near to attack me again, I'll run him through! Right through the heart. Phut!"

I stabbed the air in front of Mrs. Reed's face, making her eyes widen with shock, or perhaps fright?

Ere I had finished this demonstration, my soul began to expand, to exult, with the strangest sense of freedom, of triumph, I ever felt. It seemed as if an invisible bond had burst, and that I had struggled out into unhoped-for liberty. Mrs. Reed trembled. Her work had slipped from her knee; she was lifting up her hands, rocking herself to and fro, even twisting her face as if she would cry.

"Jane, put that away! What is the matter with you? You are suffering under a mistaken notion, surely. We do not act as monsters, but for our own survival. You're having delusions, perhaps? Would you like to drink some water?"

"No, Mrs. Reed."

"Is there anything else you wish for, Jane? I assure you, I desire to be your friend."

"Friend? When you told Mr. Bokorhurst I had a bad character, a deceitful disposition? I'll let everybody at Lowood know what you are, and what you have done."

"You mean with your punishments, surely? Jane, you don't understand these things. Children must be corrected for their faults."

"Deceit is not *my* fault!" I cried out in a savage, high voice.

"But you are passionate, Jane, that you must allow. Now return to the nursery—there's a dear—and lie down a little."

"I am not your dear. I cannot lie down. Send me to school soon, Mrs. Reed, for I hate to live here."

"I will indeed send her to school soon," murmured Mrs. Reed; and gathering up her work, she abruptly quitted the apartment.

I was left there alone, winner of the field. It was the hardest battle I had fought, and the first victory I had gained. I stood awhile on the rug, where Mr. Bokorhurst had stood, and I enjoyed my conqueror's solitude. First, I smiled to myself and felt elated, but this fierce pleasure subsided in me as fast as did the accelerated throb of my pulse. I had actually stood my ground. I had threatened her beloved boy's precious existence should he cross my path again, and I felt full ready to act on my own behalf as necessary.

Something of vengeance, of violence, I had for the first time tasted. As aromatic wine it seemed, on swallowing, warm and racy, burning in my veins, intoxicating. I could not sit still. I went to the breakfast room and opened the drapes and the glass door. The frost reigned unbroken by sun or breeze through the grounds, a fairyland painted in white. It looked so pure, so cleansing, as if nothing bad had ever touched it or crawled under soil to roots. I wanted to be a part of that fresh, white scene.

I stepped out. I breathed deep and let the frigid air fill my lungs, needles piercing, pricking me back to life. I walked along, delighting in the silent trees, the falling fir cones, the congealed relics of autumn, russet leaves, swept by past winds into heaps and now stiffened together. I leaned against a gate and looked into an empty field where no sheep were feeding, where the short grass was nipped and blanched. Snowflakes fell in intervals to settle on the hard path.

"Miss Jane! Where are you? Come to lunch! You naughty little thing!" she said, catching up to me. "Why don't you come when you are called?"

I knew well enough it was Bessie, but I could not force my feet to move, as if I had become part of the frozen scene. Her presence did not break the enchanted mood. When she drew near, I threw my arms around her. "Come, Bessie, don't scold."

"You are a strange child, Miss Jane," she said as she looked down at me, "a little roving, solitary thing. And you are going to school, I suppose? And won't you be sorry to leave poor Bessie?"

"What does Bessie care for me? She is always scolding me."

"Because you're such a queer, shy little thing. You should be bolder."

"Ha!" I laughed. She clearly had not heard from Mrs. Reed. "I don't think that should be a problem now."

"Nonsense! I will worry when you are at school, no Bessie to look after you. But you are rather put-upon here, that's certain. My mother said, when she came to see me last week, that she would not like a little one of her own to be in your place. Now, come in, and I've some good news for you."

"What could be better than the beauty of this day, Bessie?"

"Child! I believe you've been out too long. Perhaps your brain is freezing. We shall go in. Missus and the young ladies and Master John will be in bed all afternoon, and you shall have tea with me. I'll ask cook to bake you a little cake, and then you shall help me to look over your drawers, for I am soon to pack your trunk. Missus intends you to leave Gateshead in a day or two, and I will let you choose what toys you like to take with you."

That afternoon lapsed in peace and harmony. In the evening, Bessie stayed with me quite late instead of running off to her duties with the Reeds. She told me some of her most enchanting stories and sang me some of her sweetest songs. My life had improved tremendously at Gateshead just as I was about to leave it for the great unknown.

CHAPTER 5

FIVE O'CLOCK HAD HARDLY struck on the morning of the nineteenth of January when Bessie brought a candle into my closet and found me already up and nearly dressed. I was to leave Gateshead that day by the 6:00 a.m. coach. Bessie was the only person yet risen. She had lit a fire in the nursery, where she now made my breakfast. I was not hungry, but Bessie pressed me in vain to take a few spoonfuls of the boiled milk and bread. In the end, she wrapped some biscuits in a paper and put them into my bag, then helped me on with my pelisse and bonnet and we left the nursery.

As we passed Mrs. Reed's bedroom, Bessie said, "Will you go in and bid Missus good-bye? She hasn't been settled long. She may still be awake."

"I won't take that chance. She came to my room last night when you were gone down to supper and said I need not disturb her or my cousins in the morning. She told me to remember that she had always been my best friend, and to speak well of her and be grateful to her accordingly."

"What did you say, miss?"

"Nothing. I covered my face with the bedclothes and turned from her to the wall."

"That was wrong, Miss Jane."

"It was quite right, Bessie. Your Missus has not been my friend."

"Miss Jane, don't say so! They live differently from us, to be sure, but that's in their very nature. What seems odd or cruel to others makes sense to those who come to understand."

"I'll never understand. Their very existence is in conflict with nature. Good-bye to Gateshead!" cried I, as we passed through the hall and went out the front door.

The moon was set, and it was dark. Bessie carried a lantern. Raw and chill was the winter morning. My teeth chattered as I hastened down the drive. There was a light in the porter's lodge. When we reached it, we found the porter's wife just kindling her fire. My trunk, which had been carried down the evening before, stood corded at the door. It wanted but a few minutes of six, and shortly after that hour had struck, the distant roll of wheels announced the coming coach. I went to the door and watched its lamps approach rapidly through the gloom.

"Is she going by herself?" asked the porter's wife.

"Yes."

"And how far is it?"

"Fifty miles."

"What a long way! I wonder Mrs. Reed is not afraid to trust her so far alone."

Trust? I did not say that she had little reason to trust me, nor did she. Her need to be rid of me exceeded her interest in her protection from what I might say out in the world. She certainly had no concern for my fate. Once I left her gates, she would most likely breathe a sigh of relief. I had no doubt she would risk standing in a window at dawn just to see, with her own eyes, that I would get on that coach and go.

The coach drew up to the gates with its four horses and its top laden with passengers. The guard and coachman loudly urged haste. My trunk was hoisted up. I was taken from Bessie's neck, to which I clung with kisses.

"Be sure and take good care of her," cried she to the guard as he lifted me into the inside.

"Take care, Bessie Lee!" I shouted back, though we were already pulling away, for I did not doubt that she was the one more in need of protection in continuing to live with the Reeds.

Thus was I severed from Bessie and Gateshead, thus whirled away to unknown and, as I then deemed, remote and mysterious regions.

I remember but little of the journey. We passed through several towns, and in a large one the coach stopped. The horses were taken out, and the passengers alighted to dine. I was carried into an inn, where the guard wanted me to have some dinner; but, as I had no appetite, he left me in an immense room with a fireplace at each end, a chandelier pendent from the ceiling, and a little red gallery high up against the wall filled with musical instruments. I walked about for a long time, feeling strange and mortally apprehensive of someone's coming in and kidnapping me; for I believed in kidnappers, their exploits having frequently figured in Bessie's fireside chronicles.

I wouldn't have been surprised had Mrs. Reed hired someone to do the vile deed of capturing me and killing me before I could get to the school and spread stories of life at Gateshead. To what lengths would she go to protect her secret from exposure? But if she'd meant to do me in, it would have been easier to do it at home, if not for fear of being tainted by my common blood. For the first time that morning, I felt my lips curl up in a smile. I should be happy, after all. I had finally made my escape.

Instead, my stomach felt more twisted than the French horn that was left abandoned against the gallery wall. Something wasn't right. If not kidnappers, who—or what—might be lurking about? I heard someone approaching and I moved quickly to stand in the dark corner behind the door. I saw a fellow passenger, the woman who had boarded the coach some miles past Gateshead, being led by the hand. Her guide was an older man with a ridiculous mustache.

"This way, my beauty," he said. "I can show you such things as you never imagined."

"As I never imagined? I only wanted to see the crystal you mentioned for sale. I could probably resell it for double the price in town."

He took her in his arms. "You won't be getting to town."

That's when I saw his bared fangs. I started to cry out in warning, but the guard returned and the vampyre hid with his prey behind the gallery.

I stepped out of the shadows.

"There you are," the guard said. "Come along. We'll be getting back on the road."

"But my fellow passenger." I wish I had known her name. "She's there!"

I pointed to the gallery and reached in my pockets, prepared to pull out a stake in case the vampyre took the guard unawares. But the guard looked and came back, apparently seeing nothing. Perhaps they'd slipped away out a back entrance?

"There's no one there, child. Come."

"But, the woman—"

"Eh, she didn't pay full fare. If she misses her ride, she'll find another."

Afraid for what sort of ride she might find, I stared into the dark room as the guard lifted me to carry me away. I was only a child. What more could I say?

Once more I was stowed away in the coach. My protector mounted his own seat, sounded his hollow horn, and away we rattled over the stony streets. As the misty afternoon waned into dusk, I began to feel that we were getting very far indeed from Gateshead, and very cheerful for it. The country changed. Great grey hills heaved up round the horizon. As twilight deepened, we descended a valley, dark with wood, and long after night had overclouded the prospect, I heard a wild wind rushing amongst trees.

It was as if a knot of tension finally uncoiled in my stomach, allowing me to find a sort of relaxed inner peace. I fell asleep. I had not long slumbered when the sudden cessation of motion awoke me. The coach door opened, and a person like a servant stood at it. I saw her face and dress by the light of the lamps.

"Is there a little girl called Jane Slayre here?" she asked.

"Yes," I said, and was then lifted out. My trunk was handed down, and the coach instantly drove away.

I was stiff with long sitting, and bewildered with the noise and motion of the coach. Gathering my faculties, I looked about me. Rain, wind, and darkness filled the air; nevertheless, I dimly discerned a wall before me, and a door open in it. Through this door I passed with my new guide. She shut and locked it behind her. There was now visible a house or houses—for the building spread far—with many windows, and lights burning in some. We went up a broad, pebbly path, splashing wet, and were admitted at a door; then the servant led me through a passage into a room with a fire, where she left me alone.

I stood and warmed my numbed fingers over the blaze. There was no candle, but the uncertain light from the hearth showed, by intervals, papered walls, carpet, curtains, shining mahogany furniture. It was a parlour, not so spacious or splendid as the drawing room at Gateshead, but comfortable enough. I puzzled to make out the weapons hanging in a row down the wall as if treasured works of art—swords, with long blades that gleamed in the firelight. I supposed someone was a collector, perhaps one of the teachers. The door opened and a woman entered. Another woman followed close behind.

The first was a tall lady with dark hair, dark eyes, and a pale and large forehead. Her figure was partly enveloped in a shawl. Her countenance was grave but gentle, her bearing erect. I guessed she might be around twenty-nine years of age, her companion some years younger.

"The child is very young to be sent alone," said the tall lady, putting her candle down on the table. She considered me attentively for a minute or two. "She had better be put to bed soon. She looks tired. Are you tired?" she asked, placing her hand on my shoulder.

"A little, ma'am."

"And hungry, too, no doubt. Let her have some supper before she goes to bed, Miss Miller."

"But, perhaps we should wait and see first? In case—"

"Nonsense. She is clearly full of life, and there's no meat to be had. Is this the first time you have left your parents to come to school, my little girl?"

I explained to her that I had no parents. She inquired how long they had been dead, how old I was, what my name was, and whether I could read, write, and sew a little. She touched my cheek gently with her forefinger. "I hope you should be a good child."

Mr. Bokorhurst's conversation with Mrs. Reed came to mind, but I shut it out. Yes, I recalled his connection to Miss Abbot, but so far, the women who greeted me seemed nothing out of the ordinary. No waxen pallor, extended fangs, or misarranged limbs. I reasoned I was safe enough. I would prove myself a good child with nothing to fear at my new school.

The tall woman now left me to the more ordinary Miss Miller. Miss Miller, red-faced and careworn, was hurried in gait and action like one who had a multiplicity of tasks on hand. She looked, indeed, what I afterwards found she really was, an underteacher.

She led me along, passing from compartment to compartment, from passage to passage, of a large and irregular building. We emerged from the total and somewhat dreary silence pervading that portion of the house and came upon the hum of many voices as we entered a wide, long room, with great tables, two at each end.

A congregation of girls of every age, from nine or ten to twenty, sat on benches around the tables. Seen by the dim light of the candles, two on each table, their number to me appeared countless, though not in reality exceeding eighty. They were uniformly dressed in brown stuff frocks of quaint fashion, and long holland pinafores. They were apparently going over tomorrow's lesson. The hum I had heard was the combined result of their whispered repetitions.

Miss Miller signed to me to sit on a bench near the door. She walked up to the top of the long room. "Monitors, collect the lesson books and put them away!"

Four tall girls arose from different tables and went around gathering the books.

"Monitors, fetch the supper trays!" Miss Miller said, once the books were gathered and put away.

The tall girls went out and returned presently, each bearing a tray with a thin oaten cake divided into portions, and a pitcher of water and a mug in the middle of each tray. The portions were handed around. Those who liked took a draught of the water, the mug being common to all. When it came to my turn, I drank, for I was thirsty, but did not touch the food, excitement and fatigue rendering me incapable of eating.

Once the meal was over, Miss Miller read prayers, and the classes filed off, two and two, upstairs. By the time I reached my room, I was so overcome with weariness that I barely noticed what sort of a place the bedroom was, except that, like the schoolroom, it was long. Tonight I was to be Miss Miller's bedfellow. She helped me undress. Once tucked in, I glanced at the long rows of beds, each filled with two occupants. In as little as ten minutes, the single light was extinguished, and amid silence and complete darkness I fell asleep.

The night passed rapidly. I was too tired even to dream. When I opened my eyes, a loud bell was ringing. The girls got up quickly and started dressing. Day had not yet begun to dawn, and rush-lights burned in the room. I rose reluctantly. It was bitter cold, and I dressed as well as I could for shivering, and washed when there was a basin at liberty, which did not soon occur as there was but one basin to every six girls on the stands down the middle of the room. Some barely shivered, seemingly insensitive to the cold. I couldn't imagine that I would ever get used to such extreme frigidity inside.

Again, the bell rang. All formed in file, two and two, and I joined in as in that order we descended the stairs and entered the cold and dimly lit schoolroom.

"Form classes!" Miss Miller said.

A great tumult succeeded for some minutes, during which Miss Miller repeatedly exclaimed, "Silence!" and "Order!" When it subsided, I saw them all drawn up in four semicircles, before four chairs, placed at the four tables. All held books in their hands, and a great book, like a Bible, lay on each table before the vacant seat.

A distant bell tinkled. Immediately three ladies entered the room; each walked to a table and took her seat. Miss Miller assumed the fourth vacant chair, which was that nearest the door, and around which the smallest of the children were assembled. I was called to this inferior class and placed at the bottom of it.

Business now began. The day's prayer was read, then certain texts of Scripture were said, and to these succeeded a protracted reading of chapters in the Bible, which lasted an hour. By the time that exercise was terminated, day had fully dawned. The indefatigable bell now sounded for the fourth time. The classes were marshaled and marched into another room to breakfast. How glad I was to behold a prospect of getting something to eat! I felt weak and somewhat nauseated from going almost entirely without food the previous day.

The refectory was a great, low-ceiling, gloomy room. On two

long tables smoked basins of something hot, which sent forth a far from inviting odor.

"Disgusting! The porridge is burnt again!" some of the taller girls whispered amongst themselves, but loud enough that I overheard.

"Silence!" One of the upper teachers, a small, smartly dressed woman, claimed the head position at of one of the tables. A more buxom lady, also perhaps an upper teacher, presided at the other.

I looked in vain for the woman who had first greeted me yesterday. Miss Miller occupied the foot of the table where I sat, and a strange, elderly lady, the French teacher as I afterwards found, took the corresponding seat at the other board. A long grace was said and a hymn sung. A servant brought in some tea for the teachers, and the meal began.

Ravenous and now faint, I devoured a spoonful or two of my portion before I discerned the vile flavor, reminiscent of when Abbot had lost a thumb in the soup. I saw girls taste the food and try to swallow it, but in most cases the effort was soon relinquished. Some girls must have been forewarned, for a few didn't take bowls at all. The breakfast period ended, and no one had breakfasted. I saw one teacher take a basin of the porridge and taste it. She looked at the others.

"Abominable stuff! How shameful!" the stout one whispered.

A quarter of an hour passed before lessons again began. Miss Miller went to the middle of the room.

"Silence! To your seats!" she called out.

In five minutes the confused throng was resolved into order. The upper teachers resumed their posts, but still, all seemed to wait. Ranged on benches down the sides of the room, the eighty girls sat motionless and erect.

I looked at them, and also at intervals examined the teachers. To my relief, none of them looked to be vampyres or demons, but I'd learned not to judge from appearances. One teacher was fair and stout. Another, dark with a sharp, pinched face. The French teacher had grizzled white hair, but a friendly face. And Miss Miller, poor thing! She looked purple, weather-beaten, and overworked. As my eye wandered from face to face, the whole assembly suddenly rose simultaneously, as if moved by a common spring.

What was the matter? I had heard no order given. Before I knew what had happened, the classes were again seated. All eyes were now turned to one point. Mine followed in the general direction and encountered the person who had received me last night. She stood at the bottom of the long room, on the hearth. Cold as it was, there was a fire at each end of the room. She surveyed the two rows of girls silently and gravely. Miss Miller approached and seemed to ask her a question, and, having received her answer, went back to her place.

"Monitors of the first class, fetch the globes!" Miss Miller said.

While the monitors were following orders, the lady consulted moved slowly across the room. Seen in broad daylight, she looked tall, fair, and shapely. On each of her temples her dark brown hair was clustered in round curls according to the fashion. Her dress, also in the mode of the day, was of purple cloth, relieved by a sort of Spanish trimming of black velvet. A gold watch shone at her girdle. Here was everything I imagined a truly great lady of fine breeding to be. She was Miss Temple—Maria Temple, as I afterwards saw the name written in a prayer book entrusted to me to carry to church—the superintendent of Lowood.

Miss Temple took her seat before a pair of globes placed on one of the tables, summoned the first class round her, and commenced giving a lesson on geography. The teachers called lower classes. Repetitions in history and grammar went on for an hour. Writing and arithmetic succeeded, and music lessons were given by Miss Temple to some of the elder girls. The duration of each lesson was measured by the clock, which at last struck twelve.

The superintendent rose. "I have a word to address to the pupils. You had an inedible breakfast. You must be hungry. I have ordered that a lunch of bread and cheese shall be served to all."

The teachers looked at her with surprise.

"It is to be done on my responsibility," she added in an explanatory tone to them, and immediately afterwards left the room.

The bread and cheese were brought in and distributed to the delight of most of the school. It surprised me to see that some did not seem to share the excitement and remained bent over their work at tables, even when the order was given to head out to the garden. Curious, that! I was all for heading outdoors. Most girls put on coarse straw bonnets with strings of coloured calico and cloaks of grey frieze. I was similarly equipped, and, following the stream, I made my way into the open air.

The garden was a wide enclosure surrounded with walls. A covered veranda ran down one side, and broad walks bordered a middle space divided into scores of little beds assigned for the pupils to cultivate. When full of flowers they would doubtless look pretty, but now, at the latter end of January, all was wintry blight and brown decay. I shuddered as I stood and looked around. It was an inclement day for outdoor exercise; not positively rainy, but darkened by a drizzling yellow fog. The stronger amongst the girls ran about and engaged in active games. A smaller group of pale and thin ones herded together, I assumed for shelter and warmth, in the veranda.

As yet I had spoken to no one, nor did anybody seem to take notice of me. I stood lonely enough, but I was used to solitude. I leaned against a pillar of the veranda, drew my grey mantle close about me, and tried to forget the cold that nipped me to the core and made me long for a glimpse of the sun I hadn't seen in days.

I looked around the conventlike garden. At the far side, a field seemed to lead to another yard, and what looked like gravestones rising up from the ground. So close to the school? I had to be mistaken. Though I supposed that girls did take ill and die through a long winter as cold as it was in the bedrooms. I put it from my mind and looked back up at the house—a large building, half of which seemed grey and old, the other half quite new. The new part, containing the schoolroom and dormitory, lit by mullioned and latticed windows, had a churchlike aspect. A stone tablet over the door bore this inscription:

LOWOOD INSTITUTION. THIS PORTION WAS REBUILT BY NAOMI BOKORHURST, OF BOKORHURST HALL, IN THIS COUNTY.

I read these words over and over. I felt that an explanation belonged to them. I was still pondering the signification of *Institution* when the sound of a cough close behind me made me turn my head. I saw a girl sitting on a stone bench near me. She was bent over a book, on the perusal of which she seemed intent. From where I stood, I could see the title—it was *Rasselas;* a name that struck me as strange, and consequently attractive. In turning a leaf she happened to look up.

"Is your book interesting?" I asked.

"I like it," she answered after a pause of a second or two, during which she examined me.

I glanced over her shoulder at the book. A brief examination convinced me that the contents were less intriguing than the title. I saw nothing about fairies, nothing about genies, no bright variety seemed spread over the closely printed pages.

"Can you tell me what the writing on that stone over the door means?" I ventured to interrupt her again. "What is Lowood Institution?"

She looked at me as if I'd sprouted another head. "This house where you are come to live. It is partly a charity school. You and I, and all the rest of us, are charity children. I suppose you are an orphan. Is not either your father or your mother dead?"

"Both. They were killed before I can remember." It seemed an important distinction to me that they were killed and did not die by natural causes.

"Well, all the girls here have lost either one or both parents, and this is called an institution for educating orphans."

"Do we pay no money? Do they keep us for nothing?" Mrs. Reed gave the impression she was taking great care and expense to send me away to school. Was it not so?

"We pay, or our friends pay, fifteen pounds a year for each."

"Then why do they call us charity children?" I took some offence at the word. I was not from a poor family. The Reeds could well afford to send me to a proper school.

"Because fifteen pounds is not enough for board and teaching, and the deficiency is supplied by subscription. Different benevolent-minded ladies and gentlemen in this neighborhood and in London give to support us."

Perhaps Mrs. Reed was one who provided more than the fifteen pounds. "Who was Naomi Bokorhurst?"

"The lady who built the new part of this house as that tablet records, and whose son overlooks and directs everything here."

Mr. Bokorhurst indeed. The mere mention of him made me shudder. "Why?"

"Because he is treasurer and manager of the establishment."

"Then this house does not belong to that tall lady who wears a watch, and who said we were to have some bread and cheese?"

"To Miss Temple? Oh, no! I wish it did. She has to answer to Mr. Bokorhurst for all she does. Mr. Bokorhurst buys all our food and all our clothes."

"Does he live here?" I wished to avoid him as much as possible.

"No—two miles off, at a large hall."

"Did you say that tall lady was called Miss Temple?"

"Yes. And the one with red cheeks is called Miss Smith. She attends to the work and cuts out—for we make our own clothes, our frocks and pelisses, and everything. The little one with black hair is Miss Scatcherd. She teaches history and grammar and hears the second class's repetitions. And the older one who wears a shawl is Madame Pierrot. She comes from Lisle, in France, and she teaches French."

"Do you like the teachers? The little black-haired one?"

"Miss Scatcherd is hasty—you must take care not to offend her."

"But Miss Temple is the best—isn't she?"

"Miss Temple is very good and very clever; she is above the rest because she knows far more than they do."

"Have you been here long? Are you an orphan?" I asked.

"Two years. My mother is dead," she said with little emotion, as if it might have happened long ago or she had learned not to express her sorrow.

"Are you happy here?"

"You ask rather too many questions. I have given you answers enough for the present. I want to read."

But at that moment, the dinner summons sounded. All reentered the house. The dinner was served in two huge tin-plated vessels, whence rose a strong steam redolent of John Reed's dirty old socks. I found the mess to consist of indifferent potatoes and something unidentifiable, possibly turnip greens, mixed and cooked together. I ate what I could and wondered whether every day's fare would be as bad. After dinner, we immediately adjourned to the schoolroom. Lessons recommenced and were continued until five o'clock.

Soon after 5:00 p.m. we had another meal, consisting of a small mug of coffee and half a slice of brown bread. I devoured my bread and drank my coffee with relish, but I craved more. The girl seated near me offered hers in a listless, uninterested voice.

"Don't you want it?" I asked. She looked so pale and thin. Her face had an odd, drawn quality that reminded me of Miss Abbot back at Gateshead.

"No." A simple answer. Instead of elaborating on it, she walked away and left her food. I ate hers quickly in case anyone around me staked a claim. I wondered if Mr. Bokorhurst had enlisted her to the school. Did her body parts fall off? I made a mental note to watch her in case she should be prone to falling asleep without notice.

A half hour's recreation succeeded, then study; then the glass of water and the piece of oat cake, prayers, and bed. Such was my first day at Lowood.

CHAPTER 6

THE NEXT DAY COMMENCED as before, getting up and dressing by rushlight. This morning we couldn't even wash, for the water in the pitchers was frozen. The weather had changed the preceding evening, and a keen northeast wind had whistled through the crevices of our bedroom windows all night long.

That day I was enrolled as a member of the fourth class, and regular tasks and occupations were assigned me. At last I was no longer a mere spectator at Lowood, but a participant, an active captain in command of my own destiny. At first, as I was little accustomed to learn by heart, the lessons appeared both long and difficult. The frequent change from task to task, too, bewildered me. I was glad when, about three o'clock in the afternoon, Miss Smith put into my hands a border of muslin two yards long, together with needle, thimble, and thread, and sent me to sit in a quiet corner of the schoolroom with directions to hem the same.

At that hour most of the others were sewing likewise; but one class still stood round Miss Scatcherd's chair reading, and as all was quiet, the subject of their lessons could be heard. It was English history. Amongst the readers I observed my acquaintance of the veranda. At the commencement of the lesson, her place had been at the top of the class, but for some error or inattention to stops, she was suddenly sent to the very bottom. Even in that obscure position, Miss Scatcherd continued to make her an object of constant notice.

"Burns," the teacher said. The girls here were all called by their surnames, as boys are elsewhere. "Burns, you are standing on the side of your shoe. Turn your toes out immediately." Followed soon by "Burns, you poke your chin most unpleasantly. Draw it in." And next: "Burns, I insist on your holding your head up. I will not have you before me in that attitude," and on and on.

A chapter having been read through twice, the books were closed and the girls examined. The lesson had comprised part of the reign of Charles I, and most of the girls appeared unable to answer the sundry questions about tonnage and poundage and ship money. Still, every little difficulty was instantly solved when it reached Burns. Her memory seemed to have retained the substance of the whole lesson, and she was ready with answers on every point.

I kept expecting that Miss Scatcherd would praise her attention; but, instead of that, she suddenly cried out, "You dirty, disagreeable girl! You have never cleaned your nails this morning!"

Burns made no answer. Why did she not explain that she could neither clean her nails nor wash her face, as the water was frozen? As far as I was concerned, Miss Scatcherd was almost as bad as a vampyre. I studied her closely in case I could catch a glimpse of razor-sharp canines. Was it an accident that she sat far away from any windows?

Miss Smith drew my attention by requesting me to hold a skein of thread. While she was winding it, she talked to me from time to time, asking if I had ever been at school before, if I could mark, stitch, and knit. Until she dismissed me, I could not pursue my observations on Miss Scatcherd's movements.

When I returned to my seat, the lady was just delivering an order of which I did not catch the import. Burns immediately left the class, headed into the small inner room where the books were kept, and returned in half a minute, carrying a bundle of twigs tied together at one end. This ominous tool she presented to Miss Scatcherd with a respectful curtsy. The teacher instantly and sharply inflicted on her neck a dozen strokes with the bunch of twigs. The skin broken, a drop of blood rolled down her neck, but not a tear rose to Burns's eye. Two girls near me groaned, seemingly as moved by the sight of the stoic, bleeding Burns as I was, only they stared after her with a queer look, as if hunger, in their eyes. Curious, that.

I forgot them and paused from my sewing because my fingers quivered at the spectacle of Burns's beating with impotent anger, but not a feature of her pensive face altered its ordinary expression.

"Hardened girl!" exclaimed Miss Scatcherd. "Nothing can correct you of your slatternly habits. Carry the rod away!"

Burns obeyed. I observed as she emerged from the book closet. She was just putting her handkerchief back into her pocket, but the trace of a tear glistened on her thin cheek. I couldn't imagine how the injustice escaped the notice of most of the girls. A few in Burns's group, such as the two girls near me, stared after her with seeming fascination. The rest seemed blind to the entire scene, or at least they ignored it. I could not ignore it. I intended to speak to Burns again as soon as I could manage.

The evening play-hour I thought the pleasantest fraction of the day at Lowood: the bit of bread and the draught of coffee swallowed at five o'clock had revived vitality, if it had not satisfied hunger. I looked for Burns as I wandered as usual amongst the forms and tables and laughing groups without a companion, yet not feeling lonely.

I passed the windows, occasionally lifting a blind to look out on the snow. A drift was already forming against the lower panes. Probably, if I had lately left a good home and kind parents, this would have been the hour when I would most keenly have regretted the separation. I'd packed my doll, along with some stakes, but I did not dare pull her out in company, lest anyone see me. I did not notice any of the girls to have childlike possessions from home. The doll would stay in my pack, guarding the stakes, which might yet come in handy. I thought of Miss Scatcherd.

I derived a strange excitement from thinking of the stakes that I tried to attribute to the wildness of the wind instead. Doubtless the weather made me reckless and feverish. I wished the wind to howl more wildly, the gloom to deepen to darkness, and the confusion to rise to a clamour.

Jumping over forms and creeping under tables, I made my way to one of the fireplaces. There, kneeling by the high wire fender, I found Burns absorbed, silent, abstracted from all round her by the companionship of a book, which she read by the dim glare of the embers.

"Is it still *Rasselas*?" I asked, coming behind her.

"Yes, and I have just finished it." She closed the cover.

I sat down by her on the floor. "What is your name besides Burns?"

"Helen."

"I'm Jane. Jane Slayre. Do you come a long way from here?"

"I come from a place farther north, quite on the borders of Scotland."

"You must wish to leave Lowood." I certainly wouldn't wish to stay if I were beaten and abused like Helen Burns and I had anywhere else to go.

"No! Why should I? I was sent to Lowood to get an education, and it would be of no use going away until I have attained that object."

"But that wicked Miss Scatcherd! How do you bear it?"

"Wicked? Not at all! She is severe. She dislikes my faults."

"Severe? She might as well be a vampyre." I paused in case Helen showed any reaction to my statement. No glimmer of recognition. I went on, "And if I were in your place, I should dislike her. I should resist her. If she struck me with that rod, I should get it from her hand and—" Dear reader, I stopped myself before I said I should stab it through her heart. "I should break it under her nose."

"Probably you would do nothing of the sort. But if you did, Mr. Bokorhurst would expel you from the school. That would be a great grief to your relations. Besides, the Bible bids us return good for evil."

I wondered that anyone could be so good as Helen Burns truly seemed. I felt that she considered things by a light invisible to my eyes. If vampyres lived and reveled on earth, why, then, couldn't angels? I wondered if Helen Burns could be one of those heavenly beings.

"You say you have faults, Helen. What are they? To me you seem very good."

"Then learn not to judge by appearances. I am, as Miss Scatcherd said, slatternly, as well as careless, forgetful, and prone to daydreams. When I should be listening to Miss Scatcherd and collecting all she says, often I lose the very sound of her voice and fall into a sort of dream that I am in Northumberland, and the noises I hear round me are the bubbling of a little brook that runs through Deepden, near our house. This is all very provoking to Miss Scatcherd, who is naturally neat, punctual, and particular."

"And cross and cruel," I added aloud, and possibly a demon, I thought to myself.

Helen Burns kept silent at my accusation.

"Is Miss Temple as severe to you as Miss Scatcherd?" I asked, unable to fathom that one who looked so pure and right as the lovely Miss Temple would allow Miss Scatcherd to be so abusive.

At the utterance of Miss Temple's name, a soft smile flitted over Helen Burn's grave face. I breathed a sigh of relief. Miss Temple must be all that I assumed, and more.

"Miss Temple is full of goodness. It pains her to be severe to anyone, even the worst in the school."

"And when Miss Temple teaches, do your thoughts wander then?"

"No, certainly, not often; because Miss Temple has generally something to say which is newer than my own reflections."

"Well, then, with Miss Temple you are good?"

"Yes, in a passive way. I make no effort. I follow as inclination guides me. There is no merit in such goodness."

"I believe there is a great deal. You are good to those who are good to you. If people were always kind and obedient to those who are cruel and unjust, the wicked people would have it all their own way. They would never feel afraid, and so they would never alter, but would grow worse and worse. When we are struck at without a reason, we should strike back again very hard. I am sure we should—so hard as to teach the person who struck us never to do it again."

Helen smiled. "You will change your mind, I hope, when you grow older. As yet you are but a little untaught girl."

A little untaught girl who had stood up to injustice. Helen Burns might be older and more schooled, but she truly had no idea of evil. Once I'd faced John Reed and gave free vent of my feelings to Mrs. Reed, my life had changed. I believed I was very much in the right.

"I don't know if I will change." I thought of my uncle Reed's visitation. Would he have encouraged me to pursuit of defence against evil were it truly wrong?

"It is not violence that best overcomes hate—nor vengeance that most certainly heals injury."

"What then?" I challenged her. There was no walking away from a vampyre should one decide to make you his dinner. Only in fighting back did one stand a chance, and that most effectively when one knew appropriate techniques. Eventually, perhaps, I would find my people. I would train and learn.

"Love your enemies; bless them that curse you; do good to them that hate you and despitefully use you."

"Then I should love Mrs. Reed, which I cannot do; I should bless her son, John, which is impossible."

In her turn, Helen Burns asked me to explain, and I poured out the tale of my sufferings and resentments, without actually mentioning that the Reeds were unnatural in any way. Though I had threatened Mrs. Reed with exposure, it was another thing to actually tell what she was to those who might not understand. I had already been accused of lying and deceit to Mr. Bokorhurst. The last thing I wanted was to encourage such a reputation on myself. Besides, I had no idea how Helen would react to such news, or if she would believe me at all. In the rest, though, I had no restraint. Of their regular treatment of me at Gateshead, I spoke as I felt, bitter and truculent, without reserve or softening.

Helen heard me patiently to the end. I expected she would then comment, but she said nothing.

"Well," I asked impatiently, "is not Mrs. Reed a hard-hearted, bad woman?"

"She has been unkind to you, no doubt, because perhaps she dislikes your cast of character, as Miss Scatcherd does mine; but would you not be happier if you tried to forget her severity, together with the passionate emotions it excited? Life appears to me too short to be spent in nursing animosity or registering wrongs."

Helen's head, always drooping, sank a little lower as she finished this sentence, as if she were suddenly spent. A monitor, a great rough girl, presently came up.

"Helen Burns," she said in a great loud voice. "If you don't go and put your drawer in order and fold up your work this minute, I'll tell Miss Scatcherd to come and look at it!"

For all the monitor's volume, her words had no intonation, as if she were an automaton. Like the girl who had given me her food at my first evening meal, this one also reminded me, oddly, of Miss Abbot at Gateshead. Something about her pallor and the sunken hollows of her cheeks. I wondered if she, too, had been giving up her meals.

Helen sighed as her reverie fled and, getting up, obeyed the monitor without reply or delay.

CHAPTER 7

DURING JANUARY, FEBRUARY, AND part of March, the deep snows, and, after their melting, the almost impassable roads, prevented our stirring beyond the garden walls, except to go to church. Within these limits, we had to pass an hour every day in the open air. Our clothing was insufficient to protect us from the severe cold.

One afternoon (I had then been three weeks at Lowood), as I was sitting with a slate in my hand, puzzling over a sum in long division, I caught sight of a figure just passing. I recognised almost instinctively that gaunt outline. When, two minutes after, all the school, teachers included, rose en masse, I didn't need to look up to ascertain whose entrance they thus greeted. A long stride measured the schoolroom, and presently beside Miss Temple, who herself had risen, stood the same black giant who had frowned on me so ominously from the hearthrug of Gateshead; Mr. Bokorhurst, buttoned up in a black coat, and looking longer, narrower, and more rigid than ever.

Too well I remembered the perfidious hints given by Mrs. Reed about my disposition, the promise pledged by Mr. Bokorhurst to inform Miss Temple and the teachers of my vicious nature. All along I had been dreading the fulfillment of this promise. Would Miss Scatcherd find a new potential whipping girl? Perhaps Helen Burns could step aside as the notorious slattern of Lowood school.

He stood next to Miss Temple and spoke low in her ear. I did not doubt he was making disclosures of my villainy, and I watched her with painful anxiety, expecting every moment to see her bright gaze turn on me in a glance of repugnance and contempt. I listened, too, and as I was seated quite at the top of the room and his deep voice was much louder and more resonant than he seemed aware, I caught most of what he said, relieving me from immediate apprehension.

"I suppose, Miss Temple, the thread I bought at Lowton will do? I wish the wool stockings were better treated. When I was here last, I went into the garden and examined the clothes drying on the line. There was a quantity of black hose in a very bad state of repair. I was sure they had not been well mended from time to time."

"Your directions will be attended to, sir." She nodded in his direction.

"Also, Miss Temple"—he cleared his throat vigorously—"I find, in settling accounts with the housekeeper, that a lunch, consisting of bread and cheese, has twice been served out to the girls during the past fortnight. How is this? I looked over the regulations, and I find no such meal as lunch mentioned. Who introduced this innovation? And by what authority?"

"I must be responsible for the circumstance, sir. The breakfast was so ill prepared that the pupils could not possibly eat it. I dared not allow them to remain fasting until dinnertime."

"Madam, allow me an instant. You are aware that my plan in bringing up these girls is to ensure they do not become accustomed to habits of luxury and indulgence, but to render them hardy, patient, self-denying. Oh, madam, when you put bread and cheese, instead of burnt porridge, into these children's mouths, you may indeed feed their vile bodies, but you little think how you starve their immortal souls!" Mr. Bokorhurst again paused, perhaps overcome by his feelings.

Miss Temple was looking down when he first began to speak to her, but she now gazed straight in front of her. Her face, naturally pale as marble, appeared to be assuming also the coldness and fixity of that material.

Mr. Bokorhurst, standing on the hearth with his hands behind his back, majestically surveyed the whole school. "And how are our special students? Blending in?"

"Quite well, sir."

My ears pricked at mention of special students. I listened more intently.

"Their devotion and strict obedience should be inspiring countless others. You have followed my instructions to the letter? If one morsel of food passes their lips, it would prove disastrous for the others. If they should come in contact with meat—"

"No meals. Of course. If I may speak plainly, sir, there's not much about them to stir inspiration in others. They exist for work, and work alone. They're responsive, but without the spark and fire of real livelihood—of life—to allow for original thought or creative impulses. I'm afraid—"

I stifled a gasp. She might have been describing Abbot had she only added narcolepsy and detachable limbs! And no meals? How could they exist?

"Afraid, Miss Temple?" He seemed more perturbed at her sudden concern over these "special students" than he had over the idea of comforting us with unauthorised bread and cheese. "There is no room for fear when the Lord calls us to do His bidding."

"What troubles me, Mr. Bokorhurst, is that I'm not sure the Lord would look kindly on your new—"

"You speak too plainly now!" he cut her off in an angry tone. "Have a care, Miss Temple. Have a care. I hired you as superintendent here because I felt you were uniquely qualified with the forward-reaching vision I need to bring Lowood to a shining new future. Perhaps I erred in judgment after all? Miss Scatcherd would be more than willing to take over should you find yourself unworthy of the task."

Miss Temple looked shaken. "No, sir. I'm very pleased with my position and feel capable to continue on."

"Very well." He continued to survey us, his humble subjects.

In that moment, I cared not a whit for Mr. Bokorhurst's supposed mortality. Vampyre or no, I wanted to stake him through the heart for giving Miss Temple a fright. I would absolutely never take the life of another human being. It was out of the question. But Mr. Bokorhurst did tempt me. I found myself wishing I could discover some terrible secret about him, something that might require me to save humanity by removing him from existence.

To avoid discovery during Mr. Bokohurst's entire visit, I had sat well back on the form and, while seeming to be busy with my sum, had held my slate in such a manner as to conceal my face. I might have escaped notice had not my treacherous slate somehow slipped from my hand, falling with an obtrusive crash, directly drawing every eye upon me. I knew it was all over now, and as I stooped to pick up the two fragments of slate, I rallied my forces for the worst. It came.

"A careless girl!" said Mr. Bokorhurst. "It is the new pupil, I perceive. I must not forget I have a word to say respecting her. Let the child who broke her slate come forward!"

Of my own accord I could not have stirred. I was paralysed, but the two great girls who were seated on each side of me set me on my legs and pushed me towards the dread judge. Miss Temple gently assisted me to his very feet.

"Don't be afraid, Jane," she said. "I saw it was an accident. You shall not be punished."

The kind whisper went to my heart like a stake.

Another minute and she would despise me for a hypocrite, perhaps. Fury raged in me at the likes of the Reeds, Miss Scatcherd, Mr. Bokorhurst. Human cruelty could be as vile as any demon's actions. I was no Helen Burns.

"Fetch that stool," said Mr. Bokorhurst, pointing to a high one from which a monitor had just risen. It was brought. "Place the child upon it."

I was placed there, by whom I don't know. I was in no condition to note particulars. I was only aware that they had hoisted me up to the height of Mr. Bokorhurst's nose, and pastille-tinged breath, that he was within a yard of me.

"Miss Temple, teachers, and children, you all see this girl? My dear children, it becomes my duty to warn you that this girl, who might be one of God's own lambs, is a little castaway: not a member of the true flock, but evidently an interloper and an alien. You must be on your guard against her. If necessary, avoid her company, exclude her from your sports, and shut her out from your converse. Teachers, you must watch her: keep your eyes on her movements, weigh well her words, scrutinise her actions, punish her body to save her soul, for this girl is—a liar!"

Mr. Bokorhurst paused, as if for dramatic effect, then resumed.

"This I learned from her benefactress; from the pious and charitable lady who adopted her in her orphan state, reared her as her own daughter, and whose kindness, whose generosity, the unhappy girl repaid by an ingratitude so bad, so dreadful, that at last her excellent patroness was obliged to separate her from her own young ones, fearful lest her vicious example should contaminate their purity. We are prepared to deal with her here. Let her stand half an hour longer on that stool, and let no one speak to her during the remainder of the day." With that, he turned for the door and exited.

There was I, then, mounted aloft at the centre of the room. I was filled with fury at the injustice. Mrs. Reed was the liar, yet was I to bear the punishment for her words? Just as my anger was about to get the best of me, Helen Burns walked by and smiled. She asked Miss Smith some slight question about her work, was scolded for the triviality of the inquiry, and smiled at me as she again went by and returned to her place. What a smile! It lit up her thin face, her blue eyes, like the reflection of an angel.

CHAPTER 8

WITHIN THE HALF HOUR, five o'clock struck. School was dismissed, and all were gone into the refectory. I decided it was safe to get down and I ventured through the darkening room to a corner, where I sank down to the floor. I would have wept, but I found myself laughing when I remembered Mr. Bokorhurst's face contorting as he denounced my evil ways. Laughing alone was not as much fun as sharing the sentiment, and I wished that Helen Burns were with me. I had nothing, no one, and precious little chance of recovering from the horrible impression created by Mr. Bokorhurst by way of Mrs. Reed.

I had meant to be so good, and to do so much at Lowood, to make so many friends, to earn respect and win affection. Already I had made visible progress. That very morning I had reached the head of my class. Miss Miller had praised me warmly. Miss Temple had smiled approvingly in my direction. I was well received by my fellow pupils and treated as an equal by those of my own age. One afternoon visit from Mr. Bokorhurst was enough to erase all the positives and level me low. Could I ever rise again?

I heard a sound nearby and startled. Helen Burns had come in quietly and was crossing the room.

She brought my coffee and bread. "Come, eat something. You need to keep your spirits up. It's not as bad as all that."

Of all people, Helen Burns should know. She suffered regular humiliations without shedding so much as a tear.

"I probably should cry, but I was actually having a laugh. I must be wicked. I can't help but smile when I think of the expression on Mr. Bokorhurst's face, as if he'd swallowed our burnt porridge."

I thanked her for the food, took a bite of the bread, and a healthy swallow of coffee.

"That's better," she said, her soft voice soothing.

"Helen, why are you being kind to one whom everybody regards as a liar?"

"Everybody, Jane? Why, there are only eighty people who have heard you called so, and the world contains hundreds of millions."

"But what have I to do with millions? The eighty are sure to think badly after Mr. Bokorhurst's discourse."

"Jane, you are mistaken. Probably not one in the school either despises or dislikes you. Many, I am sure, pity you much."

"How can they pity me after what Mr. Bokorhurst has said?"

"Mr. Bokorhurst is not a great and admired man. He is little liked here. Had he treated you as a favourite, you would have found enemies all around you. As it is, the greater number would offer you sympathy if they dared. Besides, Jane . . ." She paused.

"Well, Helen?" I put my hand into hers.

She chafed my fingers gently to warm them and went on, "If all the world hated you, and believed you wicked, while your own conscience approved you and absolved you from guilt, you would not be without friends."

I adored Helen for saying so. "As long as I believe I've acted in the right, I can't be wrong?"

"Not to those who know and love you, Jane."

Helen had calmed me. I was about to ask if she was truly one of the heavenly beings sent to keep watch over me when she started breathing fast and began to cough. Angels did not struggle with such mortal afflictions.

Resting my head on Helen's shoulder, I put my arms around her waist. Her spasm waned. She drew me to her and we reposed in silence.

I finally said, "Perhaps it's better not to be one of Mr. Bokorhurst's special students, then."

"Special students?" Helen started a little. "Who told you this term?"

"I overheard Mr. Bokorhurst and Miss Temple speaking of them. Do you know of them? What makes them special?"

She paused. "There are a few students who don't seem quite right to me."

"The ones who don't eat?"

She nodded, leaned closer, and whispered, "Eight of them in all. They took sick last year. We had a case of scarlet fever spread amongst us. Most of the afflicted recovered. The few who had prolonged symptoms were taken away in the night. Many of us supposed them to be dead. We were never told one way or another. But they came back days later, and here they are still well and living amongst us. All except for Ginny Canham. Something happened. She attacked Miss Brockway, tore her to shreds."

"Shreds?"

"Bloody shreds. Miss Temple intervened, but it was too late. There was nothing to be done. Miss Smith was hired to replace her."

"Nothing to be done? But what became of Ginny?"

"Oh, no one knows exactly. Miss Temple subdued her with a sharp blow to the head. Then she was escorted away. Back home perhaps, or—"

"Or?"

"Or she was killed, no hope for it. Do you know what a bokor is?"

"As in Bokorhurst?"

"Indeed," she said. "In Deepden, we had a maid, a lovely woman with dark skin and fire-bright eyes. We took her in and gave her a home after she'd been thoroughly abandoned by the sea captain who had brought her here from the West Indies. She knew things of a strange religion called voodoo. A bokor is a voodoo priest, a type of sorcerer."

"A sorcerer! Of course." Helen seemed surprised at how readily I accepted her tale. "And how does he enchant his victims?"

"He makes them into zombies."

"*Zombies?*" This word, like *bokor*, I hadn't heard.

"A reanimated corpse. A bokor brings the dead back to life, but not the sort of life we know, more of an indentured servitude."

I gasped. Like Abbot! But I didn't want to interrupt Helen's further explanation.

"Zombies serve their master in all things. It's an unnatural way to exist, most against God's will. As long as the zombified remains roam the earth, the spirit of the deceased cannot ascend to heaven. They're most calm, nearly lifeless in demeanor unless—

"Unless they're fed. Feeding encourages them to eat more and crave meat. And once they've tasted flesh, oh dear. I believe it's what happened to Ginny. Only teachers are allowed meat at meals, but somehow Ginny must have got hold of some. It sent her to a frenzied quest for human flesh. Oh, the blood! There was so much blood. I believe she ate a fair amount of Miss Brockway before Miss Temple subdued her, judging from the state of the corpse and the entrails dripping down Ginny's chin. I wish I could forget the sight of it. There's only one way to stop them permanently."

"A stake through the heart?" I ventured, more convinced than ever that Helen Burns was an angel sent to point me on my path.

Helen shook her head and looked at me strangely. "A stake? No. One must remove the heart or head to release the zombie from the curse. They return to death and their spirits are free."

"Remove the heart or head?" I wondered at what strength must be required to entirely sever a head or scoop out a heart. "But if one is not sure . . . if I struck one that was not truly a zombie, I could kill her."

"To be certain," Helen agreed, then started coughing.

I patted her back. "Don't speak of it now. We'll talk more later."

Mr. Bokorhurst, a bokor? It made sense. I reflected on his conversation with Mrs. Reed, trying to recall the full extent. He made mention of new harvests, replacing Abbot. Had Miss Abbot been at Lowood? Was he harvesting dead students to be trained as future domestics? Diabolical!

I had so much more to say to Helen, but we sat silently while she caught her breath. I most certainly did not want Helen, my only friend, to go away and come back not quite right. We had not sat long thus when Miss Temple came in.

"I came on purpose to find you, Jane Slayre," said she. "I want you in my room; and as Helen Burns is with you, she may come, too."

We went. Miss Temple might be in Mr. Bokorhurst's employ, or even under a spell, but I trusted her completely. Whatever reason she had to take part in Lowood's secrets, I would soon find out. For now, we followed the superintendent's guidance through some intricate passages and mounted a staircase to reach her private apartment. It contained a good fire and looked cheerful. Miss Temple told Helen Burns to be seated in a low armchair on one side of the hearth, and, herself taking another, she called me to her side.

"Is it all over?" she asked, looking down at my face. "Are you feeling better now?"

"Indeed. Helen has quite brought me to my senses." I debated how much I could press Miss Temple about the special students and opted to wait before bringing it up. "My mood has much improved. Still, I'm reeling inside from having been wrongly accused. You, ma'am, and everybody else, will now think me wicked."

"We shall think you what you prove yourself to be, my child. Continue to act as a good girl, and you will satisfy us."

"Shall I, Miss Temple?" Was it good to want to kill zombies? I felt somehow it must be. I noticed a sword, like the ones in the parlour, hanging over the mantel and wondered if it had a more necessary purpose than decoration. Dared I ask?

"You will," said she, passing her arm around me. "I have every faith in you, Jane Slayre. And now tell me, who is the lady whom Mr. Bokorhurst called your benefactress?"

"Mrs. Reed, my uncle's wife. My uncle is dead, and he left me to her care." I stuck to the simple facts, leaving out that Mrs. Reed was also dead in her way.

"Did she not, then, adopt you of her own accord?"

"No, ma'am. She was sorry to have to do it, but my uncle, as I have often heard the servants say, got her to promise before he died that she would always keep me."

"Well now, Jane, you know, or at least I will tell you, that when a criminal is accused, he is always allowed to speak in his own defence. You have been charged with falsehood. Defend yourself to me as well as you can. Say whatever your memory suggests is true; but add nothing and exaggerate nothing."

I resolved, in the depth of my heart, that I would be most moderate—most correct without revealing the complete truth of the Reeds' conditions. Having reflected a few minutes to arrange coherently what I had to say, I told her nearly all the story of my sad childhood. Exhausted by emotion, I used language more subdued than it generally was in my repeating the tale of my upbringing. Thus restrained and simplified, without any mention of vampyres, it sounded more credible. I felt as I went on that Miss Temple fully believed me.

I mentioned Mr. Lloyd's coming to see me after what I described as an attack by John Reed that resulted in a knock of the head and not the biting of my neck. I did not spare Mrs. Reed the mercy of leaving off that she'd left me to potentially bleed to death in the red room, though I did not mention the ghostly visitation of my uncle and the path he'd tasked me to follow.

"I know something of Mr. Lloyd," Miss Temple said, after regarding me some moments in silence once I'd finished. "I shall write to him; if his reply agrees with your statement, you shall be publicly cleared from every imputation. To me, Jane, you are clear now."

She kissed my cheek and still kept me at her side. I was a child unused to affection, and I liked Miss Temple showing me some care. She then addressed Helen Burns.

"How are you tonight, Helen? Have you coughed much today?"

"Not quite so much, I think, ma'am."

"And the pain in your chest?"

"It is a little better."

Miss Temple got up, took Helen's hand, examined her pulse, then returned to her seat. As she resumed it, I heard her sigh low. She was pensive a few minutes before rousing herself cheerfully.

"But you two are my visitors tonight. I must treat you as such." She rang her bell.

"Barbara," she said to the servant who answered it, "I have not yet had tea. Bring the tray and place cups for these two young ladies."

When the tray arrived, I delighted in the sight. How pretty, to my eyes, did the china cups and bright teapot look, placed on the little round table near the fire! How fragrant was the steam of the beverage, and the scent of the toast! Tonight was for celebration, not accusations.

"Barbara," Miss Temple called her servant back. "Can you not bring a little more bread and butter? There is not enough for three."

Barbara went out, but she returned soon. "Madam, Mrs. Harden says she has sent up the usual quantity."

Mrs. Harden, be it observed, was the housekeeper, a woman after Mr. Bokorhurst's own heart, made up of equal parts of whalebone and iron. Perhaps literally. She might have been held together by such.

"Oh, very well!" returned Miss Temple. "We must make it do, Barbara, I suppose." As the girl withdrew, Miss Temple added, smiling, "Fortunately, I have it in my power to supply deficiencies for this once."

Having invited Helen and me to approach the table, she placed before each of us a cup of tea with one delicious but thin morsel of toast. She got up, unlocked a drawer, and, taking from it a parcel wrapped in paper, disclosed presently to our eyes a good-size seed-cake.

"I meant to give each of you some of this to take with you, but as there is so little toast, you must have it now." She cut slices with a generous hand.

We feasted that evening as on nectar and ambrosia, and not the least delight of the entertainment was our hostess's smile of gratification as we satisfied our famished appetites on the delicate fare she liberally supplied. Miss Temple and Helen conversed on so many things, books I'd never heard of, world events, and languages unknown. Helen recited some Latin as well as any true scholar, I supposed.

"Miss Temple, I must ask why you have a sword in your room?" I said at length as the evening drew to a close.

"It is a fine saber, is it not? My father was a swordsman," Miss Temple said, taking the weapon down. The blade was safely ensconced in a sheath. "A pirate on the Barbary Coast, to tell the truth, before he retired to Cornwall to marry and raise children. He taught me a few tricks."

She posed like a true fighter, feet planted firmly apart, one arm in the air, the other holding out the sword and waving it boldly. I stood transfixed, filled with admiration as she danced a little circle around us, swishing her sword at imaginary foes. At zombies? I felt more secure knowing of Miss Temple's secret talent.

"Oh, Miss Temple!" I said. "I wish you could teach me your few tricks."

"Perhaps I shall." She smiled, gazing at the weapon as if lost in a memory. After a moment, she placed it back on the hooks over the mantel and embraced us both. "But for now, it's time for bed. God bless you, my children!"

Helen she held a little longer than me. Miss Temple let her go more reluctantly. For her, she a second time breathed a sad sigh; for her, she wiped a tear from her cheek.

On reaching the bedroom, we heard the voice of Miss Scatcherd. She was examining drawers. She had just pulled out Helen Burns's, and when we entered, Helen was greeted with a sharp reprimand.

Next morning, Miss Scatcherd wrote in conspicuous characters on a piece of pasteboard the word SLATTERN and bound it crownlike around Helen's forehead. She wore it until evening, patient, unresentful, and regarding it as a deserved punishment. The moment Miss Scatcherd withdrew after school, I ran to Helen, tore it off, and thrust it into the fire. The fury of which she was incapable had been burning in my soul all day, and tears, hot and large, had continually been scalding my cheek. The spectacle of Helen's sad resignation gave me an intolerable pain at the heart.

CHAPTER 9

ABOUT A WEEK LATER, Miss Temple received a reply from Mr. Lloyd regarding her inquiries. He apparently corroborated my account. Miss Temple had enough faith in me, and Mr. Lloyd's verification of events, that she assembled the whole school, announced that inquiry had been made into the charges against Jane Slayre, and that she was "most happy to be able to pronounce her completely cleared from every imputation." The teachers then shook hands with me and kissed me, and a murmur of pleasure ran through the ranks of my companions.

I felt joy in the sisterhood and affection of my fellow Lowood inmates. For the time, I was able to put the special students and Mr. Bokorhurst to the back of my mind and throw myself wholeheartedly into my studies. I toiled hard, and my success was proportionate to my efforts. My memory, not naturally tenacious, improved with practise. Exercise sharpened my wits. In a few weeks I was promoted to a higher class. In less than two months, I was allowed to commence French and drawing. Miss Temple had also taken me aside to show me how to hold a sword with proper posture, and how to lunge and parry. I returned for a second lesson late in the evening after classes.

"Mr. Lloyd wrote that he suspects you were being raised amongst vampyres," Miss Temple revealed as she showed me how to keep the blade steady while sweeping it through the air. "Speak the truth. I will not fault you."

I lowered the weapon. "Indeed. I wasn't sure anyone would believe me. It sounds so fantastical to say aloud."

"Oh, I believe you. I've known worse things than vampyres, dear child."

I was about to ask her about zombies, but she ended the conversation before I could bring it up.

That night on going to bed, I forgot to prepare the imaginary supper of hot roast potatoes and spinach that had got me through many a night of burnt porridge and meager portions of bread. I feasted instead on the spectacle of ideal drawings that I planned in my head, in the dark, all the work of my own hands: freely penciled rocks and ruins overrun with elves, a blue-eyed angel floating over a peaceful ocean, a Grecian goddess draped in voluminous folds. The angel would of course resemble Helen Burns, the goddess Miss Temple. I imagined, too, my lunging and parrying, thrusting, and hacking a bloodthirsty zombie's head clean off. I was sure I could do it. I tingled at the very thought!

For all of Gateshead's luxuries, I would not trade Lowood, where the riches of opportunity and friendship more than made up for the deprivation of physical comforts such as food and warmth. I fell asleep thinking of it.

But the privations, or rather the hardships, of Lowood lessened with the coming of spring. Sometimes, on a sunny day, it began even to be pleasant and genial, and a greenness grew over those brown beds. Flowers peeped out amongst the leaves. On Thursday afternoons (half holidays) we now took walks and found still sweeter flowers opening by the wayside, under the hedges.

One day, in my wandering, I got carried away following a butterfly through fields and flowers and ended up mindlessly stepping over stones in the little graveyard. I came across one marked for Martha Blake Abbot, and my thoughts turned back to the evil at the heart of Lowood, my new happy place. Would it not be easier to forget such ugliness? What business had I, a mere girl, to investigate matters and attempt to right grievous wrongs? Was it not enough that I had progressed in my studies, made friends, and established myself as a serious student and a good sort of girl?

Miss Martha Abbot, indeed. So she had been part of Lowood, more proof against Mr. Bokorhurst. The grave, no doubt, was empty. Mrs. Reed deserved a zombie maid, after all, did she not? Who better to serve a vampyre mistress? I'd been able to avoid the "Odd Eight" as I'd begun to call the special students, and it made no difference that they were at Lowood with me—as long as they didn't eat. Still, I enjoyed my sword training. I worked with Miss Temple at any opportunity, and lately more often on my own, practicing the moves she taught and improvising some of my own. Once, I asked if she'd ever killed anyone, and she seemed genuinely shocked by the question. But she never actually answered. Curious, that.

April advanced to May. A bright, serene May it was, days of blue sky, placid sunshine, and soft western or southern breezes filling up its duration. Vegetation matured with vigour. Lowood shook loose its tresses; it became all green, all flowery. All this I enjoyed often and fully, free, unwatched, and almost alone. I felt I was still catching up for time lost under Mrs. Reed's rigid rule, stuck inside to sleep during the glorious day and forced to hide in darkness during waking hours. I would have full rejoiced in it if not for the dark reason behind my delightful solitude.

Have I not described springtime Lowood as a pleasant site for a dwelling? Assuredly, pleasant enough; but whether healthy is another question. The forest dell where Lowood lay was the cradle of fog and fog-bred pestilence; which, quickening with the quickening spring, crept into the orphan asylum, breathed typhus through its crowded schoolroom and dormitory, and, ere May arrived, transformed the seminary into a hospital.

Semistarvation and neglected colds had predisposed most of the pupils to infection. Forty-five of the eighty girls lay ill at one time. Classes were broken up, rules relaxed. The few, like me, who continued well were allowed almost unlimited license because the medical attendant insisted on frequent exercise to keep us in health. Had it been otherwise, no one had leisure to watch or restrain us anyway.

The patients absorbed Miss Temple's attention. There was no time for swordplay, though she allowed me to take one of the weapons from the parlour and use it to practise. She lived in the sickroom, never quitting it except to snatch a few hours' rest at night. The teachers were fully occupied with packing up and making other necessary preparations for the departure of those girls who were fortunate enough to have friends and relations able and willing to remove them from the seat of contagion. Many, already smitten, went home only to die. Some died at the school and were quietly and quickly buried, the nature of the malady forbidding delay.

For a time, it seemed we would lose half of Lowood, but then girls began to recover and reappear in the dorm. But had they returned quite the same? I noticed the few who seemed close to death but recovered had come back to us in a somewhat cold and distant state, not quite the same as they'd been before they'd taken ill. They acted more like Mr. Bokorhurst's "special students." I never saw them eat. They no longer took pleasure in simple things, such as days off from classes. They didn't enjoy roaming in the wild outdoors as the rest of us did, but rather they stayed in and memorized psalms. The Odd Eight became the Odd Twenty. I began to suspect that my hours of leisure were over. Something was not quite right at Lowood, and it was time I did something about it.

I could not forget my uncle's words, his charge to me to right wrongs, his insistence that I had it in my blood, the power to effect a change. I was Jane Slayre, and the time had come to act accordingly.

❧

I, and the rest who continued well, enjoyed the beauties of the season. They let us ramble in the wood, like Gypsies, from morning to night. We did what we liked, went where we liked. I used the time to form my plans and to gain in strength and agility.

Mr. Bokorhurst rarely came near Lowood now. Household matters were not scrutinised; the cross housekeeper was gone, driven away by the fear of infection. Her successor, who had been matron at the Lowton Dispensary, was unused to the ways of her new abode and provided with comparative liberality. Besides, there were fewer to feed. The sick could eat little. A fair number of "healthy" ate not at all. Our breakfast basins were better filled. When there was no time to prepare a regular dinner, which often happened, the housekeeper would give us a thick slice of bread and cheese, and this we carried away with us to the wood, where each of us chose the spot she liked best and dined sumptuously.

After a day of trekking through the wood and lifting and moving rocks of various sizes, to build my physique so I could better wield my sword when the time came, I sat with my meal on my favourite seat, a smooth stone rising up from the hillside, which provided a view of the gardens and beyond. I could see the graveyard, though I usually looked towards more pleasant prospects while I dined, and I noticed a fair number of recently dug graves. I left my dinner behind on the stone and drew closer to try to count the number. How many classmates were expected to fill them soon and for how long?

It made my heart heavy to think of the loss. But as I neared, I realised that some of the now fresh graves had but a few days earlier been full. I was certain I had left flowers here, near Miss Martha Blake Abbot's resting place; yet a hole was newly dug in the ground where a grave had been. A chill ran right through me, along my spine and scattering to my fingers and toes. There'd been a new harvest! Which of my friends had now been turned to zombies?

I could not stop girls from dying. The sickness would run its course and leave the victims to their fate. But I had to stop Mr. Bokorhurst from practising his vile art in harvesting the poor corpses and reanimating them into his service. I paced, caught up in wild ideas and flights of my imagination. I didn't even notice that Mary Ann Wilson had joined me. She waited, taking her usual seat on the other side of my favoured stone.

"You seem troubled, Jane," she said as I returned to my seat on the stone.

"Have you noticed anything odd about some of the girls returning from sickbed?" I asked cautiously. One who hadn't been raised by vampyres might not easily believe in bizarre, supernatural occurrences or beings.

She nodded, but didn't even look up from her parcel as she extracted a slice of cold pie. "I suppose the sickness leaves them weak. It will take some time for their vigor to return." She took a large bite of her pie and moaned aloud. "Mm. It is so good, Jane. I can't remember the last time I had meat."

"Meat?" I sat up straighter. "What do you mean, meat?"

"The pie," she said, her mouth stuffed full. "It's mutton."

"Mutton!" My heart raced in alarm. "Why on earth would anyone serve—oh dear."

The new housekeeper, I realised. With Mr. Bokorhurst spending so much time away and Miss Temple occupied with the sick girls, it was possible no one had informed the housekeeper that meat was not to be served to students.

"I must go." I ran off towards the house, leaving my companion and the rest of my dinner behind. In the entry parlour, I took a sword off the wall. This one, with a small handle and a curved blade, was more of a scimitar, really, light and sharp. I shifted it easily in my hands. It would serve me if necessary. I prayed it would not be.

I ran through the empty refectory to the kitchen. The housekeeper was there, cutting pies.

"Who has had the pie?" I asked, not even taking a moment to catch my breath.

"Oh!" The housekeeper beamed. "Nearly everyone! It's quite a success. And Mother always said I wasn't much of a baker."

"Nearly everyone?"

She nodded. "One of the girls took a whole pie to herself."

"A whole pie? Who? Where did she—"

"Oh, there she is now. How was your pie, dear?"

I turned to see Celia Evans making her way through the door, arms outstretched before her. Her mouth shone red in sharp contrast to her greyish pallor. She groaned as she walked. Celia, of course, was one of the original Odd Eight. I wondered at the red on her face—and her pinafore. Blood!

"Stop right there!" I raised my scimitar. Celia groaned again and kept walking, pushing me aside with superhuman strength. I believe I actually flew through the air and landed in a heap on the floor after banging into a rack of pots and pans. I might have lost consciousness briefly, for when I looked up again, I saw Celia leaning over the housekeeper, who was sprawled messily across the kitchen counter next to the neat row of pies. With utmost speed, I flew to Celia to stop her before she—disemboweled the housekeeper. Too late. "No!"

Celia looked at me, a section of bloody intestine dangling like a sausage from her mouth. Dear, dear. Poor Mrs.—heavens, I didn't even remember her name. I was about to attempt a quick prayer for the woman's soul when Celia, hands dripping entrails, started for me—not with any great speed, fortunately. Zombies were strong, but they apparently were not quick. I spread my feet for stability, as Miss Temple had instructed, and bent a little at the knees to improve my flexibility. I held the scimitar aloft, then waited for Celia to get closer, close enough that I might lop her head off.

I waited. She inched forward. Slowly. I waited still.

Oh, never mind. I charged, scimitar extended. "Yah!"

I closed my eyes at the last, fatal second. Not a wise move perhaps. I might have missed. But I did not miss. I felt the sharp edge striking home, severing the flesh at Celia's neck and driving straight through her spinal cord. Either zombies were extremely thin-skinned and fragile, or I was much stronger than I had ever imagined. I looked down at Celia's headless body, pea-green goo oozing from the neck, most definitely dead. But where had her head gone? I looked around, right to left. I supposed it flew into the ovens. I did not have time to make sure. There were more pies, potentially more zombies craving flesh, and more live students out there all too unwilling to provide it.

I left the kitchen and headed back through the refectory towards the classrooms. The special students preferred to work through the day of their own accord. Most of them were still there, gathered around tables, reading psalms aloud in droning, slightly raised whispers. I counted quickly. Eighteen. Celia made nineteen. One missing—

A scream sounded from the library. I hastened there. "Stay back! Stay!" came the cry.

The voice drew me. I entered, turned a corner, and found Rebecca Douglas huddled in the corner between stacks, waving a book at Julia Severn, who groaned and slowly, slowly made her way towards Rebecca.

"I don't know what happened!" Rebecca, near breathless, exclaimed. "One minute she was fine, and then I gave her a taste of my pie and she went wild. She—she bit me!" Rebecca showed me her arm, which now exhibited a good-size welt.

"Stay right there," I ordered Rebecca.

Julia turned towards the sound of my voice, a thin stream of yellow spittle trailing from her lips down her chin. She grunted. Fortunately, it took her so long to turn her body after her head and start after me that I was able to raise my weapon and sever her spinal cord from the back, causing her head to loll in Rebecca's direction. Rebecca shrieked. I gave another solid whack, and Julia was no more.

"Jane," Rebecca marvelled, looking from me to Julia's goo-dripping head and back again. "How could you?"

"Rebecca," I said calmly, "she was going to kill you. And eat you. It was the least I could do. Now go to the sickroom. Have the nurse wrap your wound and send Miss Temple to me at once. Not a word to the other students. I'll take care of all this."

Rebecca, rendered dumb no doubt by the sight of a plentiful pea-green muck gurgling from the cavity of Julia's neck, simply nodded and made her way out of the room. By the time she reached the corridor, the sound of her hurried footfalls indicated she had broken into a run.

Miss Temple would have to leave the sick students in care of the nurse to see to the pressing matter of disposing of three gruesomely dead bodies, wouldn't she? I had just begun to fear she wasn't coming when she suddenly appeared. I met her as she hurried down the hall.

"Miss Temple. We have an unfortunate situation."

"Unfortunate?" She raised a brow. "Of course. I've been meaning to tell you."

"To tell me? How could you know?"

"About Helen?"

"About the zombies. The housekeeper has served mutton pies. Only two seem to have eaten, but—the housekeeper's dead. Rebecca Douglas was terrorized. And Julia Severn and Celia Evans are no more."

"No more? Jane!" She hugged me to her. "How very brave you are! But how did you know? I trust you made use of my instruction?"

I nodded. "With the scimitar from the parlour. It was lighter than the saber I've been practicing with, and quite sharp. Helen told me of voodoo bokors and zombies, and of last year's incident with Miss Brockway."

"Bless her soul. And bless you, dear, still so young! It must have required a good deal of strength." She held me at arm's length and looked me over. "You'll need a new pinafore. Perhaps stockings. But you're unharmed?"

I looked down. Blood and green goo was splattered across my frock and legs. "A bruise or two, perhaps. But unharmed. Now what of Helen Burns?"

Helen had been ill for weeks. So ill that she had been removed from my sight to I knew not what room upstairs. She was not in the hospital portion of the house with the fever patients, for her complaint was consumption, not typhus; and by *consumption* I, in my ignorance, understood something mild, which time and care would be sure to alleviate.

I was confirmed in this idea by her once or twice coming downstairs on warm, sunny afternoons and being taken by Miss Temple into the garden; but, on these occasions, I was not allowed to go and speak to her. I only saw her from the schoolroom window, and then not distinctly, for she was much wrapped up and sat at a distance under the veranda.

"Mr. Bates has been here. He says she'll not be here long."

A wave of panic made me weak in the knees. Helen Burns was numbering her last days in this world, and she was going to be taken to the region of spirits, if such regions there were. I experienced a shock of horror, then a strong throb of grief, then a desire—a renewed necessity to see her; and I asked in what room she lay.

"She is in my room," Miss Temple said. "You may go and see her at once. I will take care of the mess in the—"

"Kitchen," I offered. "The housekeeper and Celia Evans are in the kitchen. Julia Severn is in the library. The others seem to be absorbed by their psalms in the refectory. I don't believe they've eaten."

"Thank God for that. Now go. Go to Helen. I fear there isn't much time."

In Miss Temple's chamber, a small bed covered in white curtains was set up beside Miss Temple's bed. I crossed the room, lifted the curtain, and could make out a form under the bedclothes. I heard a light snoring from behind me, turned, and recognised one of the recently hired nurses, a candle at her side burning dimly on the table. She must have fallen asleep in her chair. I hesitated only a moment to draw back the covers from Helen's face to determine if she was sleeping as soundly as her nurse.

"Helen!" I whispered softly. "Are you awake?"

She stirred and I saw her more clearly now, fever-bright eyes shining from her pale face. Despite her weariness, she seemed quite composed and so little changed that my fear was instantly dissipated. How could she be dying? The doctor must have made a mistake.

"Can it be you, Jane?" she asked in a gentle voice.

"It is Jane. How I've missed you."

I sat on the edge of her bed and kissed her forehead. Her skin was cold and felt like parchment, thin and delicate.

"Why are you here, Jane?"

"No one could keep me away. I needed to see you, my friend. I heard you were very ill, and I could not sleep until I had spoken to you."

"You are probably just in time. When I'm gone, will you bring me flowers, Jane?" She broke off in a fit of coughing.

"Helen!" Her talk distressed me. Gone? Helen? Never! But I started to cry, as if part of me knew the truth that my heart struggled to deny.

She quieted and sighed. I was surprised that Helen's coughing did not rouse the nurse. "Jane, your little feet are bare." I had removed my shoes, stockings, and pinafore before entering for fear of alarming Helen. "Lie down and cover yourself with my quilt."

She patted the bed beside her. I scooted under the blankets. She put her arm over me and I nestled close to her.

"Helen, you mustn't leave me now. We need to work together to stop Mr. Bokorhurst. He's evil, Helen. Those poor girls."

"He must be stopped. You know the way. It's up to you."

"I know the way to free the poor souls from their curse, yes." If I could. I'd gained in strength and stamina, but to free them all and to stop Mr. Bokorhurst?

"Jane, my brave Jane. You've always known. I sensed your strength and your spirit from the start. I'm so glad we've been friends."

"We are friends."

"I am very happy, Jane. When you hear that I am dead, you must not grieve. We all must die, eventually, and I am not in pain. My illness has been gentle and gradual. My mind is at rest. I leave no regrets, and no one to regret me."

"I will regret losing you, Helen. I will!"

"You'll remember me, and the memories will give you joy, I hope. I go to a wonderful new home. I have faith. I am going to God."

"You are sure then, Helen, that there is such a place as heaven, and that our souls can get to it when we die?"

"As long as we meet no impediments."

"Like zombie curses?"

She nodded. "I am sure there is a future state. I believe God is good. I can resign my immortal part to Him without any misgiving. God is my father. God is my friend. He loves us all, and I love Him."

"We will meet again, Helen. I am sure of it."

"That's my Jane, my dear Jane."

I clasped my arms closer around Helen. She seemed dearer to me than ever.

"How comfortable I am!" she said in a sweet, low voice. "That last fit of coughing has tired me a little. I feel as if I could sleep, but don't leave me, Jane."

"I'll stay with you, dear Helen. No one shall take me away."

"Are you warm, darling?"

"Yes," I said. "Quite warm."

"Good night, Jane."

"Good night, Helen."

She kissed my cheek, and I hers, and we both soon slumbered.

When I awoke, it was day. An unusual movement roused me. I looked up. I was in the nurse's arms. She was carrying me back to the dormitory. I knew the truth then: Helen had died in my arms in the night, else Miss Temple would never have allowed us to be disturbed and separated. God bless Miss Temple, and may He love and keep Helen Burns.

CHAPTER 10

WHILE OTHER STUDENTS ROSE and prepared for the day ahead, I was allowed to stay in bed. Miss Miller made the excuses. I was feeling unwell, she said, a stomach complaint not at all resembling typhus. Best they leave me alone to recuperate without affecting, or being affected by, others. I slept for part of the day. For the other, I plotted.

I needed to form a plan with Miss Temple. Clearly she knew all about the zombies and Mr. Bokorhurst's horrific enterprise. Working together, we might meet with success in freeing the affected from the curse before any more of them developed a taste for flesh. I despaired of ever stopping Mr. Bokorhurst entirely.

The next morning, once the others left the room, I rose, washed, dressed, and prepared to go to breakfast. I was hungry, I realised, and I needed to keep up my strength. I ate quickly, picked up my ration of bread and cheese, and set off for the woods to practise my training. Once I'd worked up a healthy glow with physical exertion, I decided to retire to my favourite spot to eat my dinner. Mary Ann Wilson was already there, and she gave me a nod of greeting as she consumed her own bread and cheese.

No more mutton pie for Lowood. Miss Temple had burned them all far from the school, so as not to interest any of the special students with the aroma. I was glad to see that Mary Ann seemed too enamoured of her dinner to gossip today. My mood was reflective, not social. To me, it seemed the sun was shining in tribute to Helen Burns, so bright a soul, and that the birds sang her praises and even the bees hummed hymns in her honour. Later, I would gather flowers and try to find her grave, if she'd been buried yet. I squinted off to the mounds, all freshly patted down. What if Mr. Bokorhurst tried to harvest her? Would I be ready to fight him off? Anything to protect Helen.

"There's talk of resuming classes," Mary Ann said, breaking the golden spell of silence. "Next week, perhaps. Miss Scatcherd was in the library this morning drafting letters to the absent pupils to return to school."

"Do you think they will return?"

Mary Ann shrugged. "Most will want to finish what they started. Mr. Bokorhurst can promise employment to the older girls."

"Employment?"

"Catherine Johnstone and Caroline Henley will be leaving us. Caroline's off to Brighton to be a governess, and Catherine a lady's maid in London. Mr. Bokorhurst announced it last night. You hadn't heard? Ah, but you were in bed. Oh, wouldn't I like to go to London!"

I stifled a groan. Mary Ann wouldn't like to go to London the way Catherine Johnstone was to do it, with a reanimated brain in a shell of a body. She and Caroline had become part of the "special" set since taking ill with typhus. I imagined Catherine hulking around like Abbot, parroting her mistress's speeches and losing her limbs in the wardrobe. Of course, the special students never seemed to have a problem with parts becoming unattached since Mr. Bokorhurst had no doubt perfected his technique, as he'd told Mrs. Reed. It troubled me to think of a zombie working closely with children. What if they were fed meat? I had to speak to Miss Temple right away. There was no time to waste.

"Helen Burns did not envy Catherine a bit. She thought that she would prefer to be sent to Scotland if she were to be a maid. Scotland? La, can you imagine? It's so cold and so far away."

I gasped at the name. "Helen Burns?"

Mary Ann nodded. "Oh, yes. She came back from the sickroom today. We all thought she would never recover. She's still weak, of course, poor thing. But she's back with us."

Back with us? There was only one way that could be possible. The revelation rocked me to my very core. I choked a little on my cheese and spent some minutes coughing.

"Oh dear." Mary Ann jumped down from our perch. "Your cough sounds terrible. Perhaps you should check in with Miss Temple. Miss Scatcherd said that the sickness had likely passed, but perhaps not."

I almost corrected Mary Ann and explained about the bit of cheese, but stopped myself in time. "Miss Temple? Yes. I will seek her out at once."

I could not get back inside fast enough. I left all my things and ran straight for the door. Where could Helen be? I had to see her, yet I dreaded seeing her, all at the same time. Mr. Bokorhurst had been at school, and now Helen had returned. I prayed that Miss Temple would have answers, and while I prayed, I pleaded the case for Helen Burns, God's most devoted little subject.

"Please, God, protect Helen. Don't let Mr. Bokorhurst have robbed her of her chance to fly to heaven."

Before I reached the classroom, I knew Mary Ann Wilson spoke the truth. There, at a table surrounded by ten or so of the "special" others, Helen sat perched on the edge of her chair. She leaned over a book and read, her lips moving, her body rocking slightly with every word.

I approached and placed my hand on her shoulder. So cold! "Helen, how are you?"

She looked at me, but she might as well have looked straight through me to the wall. The absence of life in her eyes, dear reader, how it cut me to the bone! Her eyes, formerly alight with such wit and wisdom as to lend her a divine quality, now appeared dull and grey.

"Jane." At least she knew me. "Leave me. I must read my psalms."

Psalms! Mr. Bokorhurst's favoured psalms. She turned back to her book.

I hesitated. What to say? "Miss Temple wants to see you. She has something for you." Helen continued to read. "An assignment from Mr. Bokorhurst."

Now she stopped reading and rose. "Mr. Bokorhurst?"

"You are to come with me." I took her hand, gently for fear of detachment, and led her from the table. "To Miss Temple's room."

I did not need to guide her down the hall. Her feet, indeed all of her, followed. She clearly knew the way. She chanted as we walked. "Mr. Bokorhurst instructs us to find the Lord in all things. Mr. Bokorhurst alone knows the way to God."

"I believe you know the way, Helen. If only I could set you free to follow your true path."

She ignored me. As much as I wanted to save her, I doubted my ability to do what I had to do. When I looked at her quickly, without allowing my eyes to linger, she was still Helen, my bosom friend, beside me. Dear, sweet Helen Burns.

Perhaps Miss Temple could help me find the strength. We reached her door and I knocked quietly. There was no answer. I opened the door and instructed Helen to go in.

"I do not see Miss Temple," Helen said.

I called out but there was no answer, no sign of the lady or the nurse who had taken her station in the corner to look after the sleeping Helen. The little bed I'd shared with Helen had already been removed.

"Let us sit together," I said to Helen, guiding her to a chair. "Miss Temple will be along shortly. Would you like some tea? We can ring for toast." I had no authority to offer such fortification, but I knew Helen would refuse it.

"No, thank you," she said, proving me correct. "I'm not hungry. Is there a Bible? I would like to read my psalms while I wait."

"Yes. I saw one by the bed." She started to get up. I gestured for her to sit back down. "I'll get it for you."

As I went to the other side of the room to fetch Miss Temple's sword, I heard Helen start to chant a psalm before I'd even returned.

"The Lord is my shepherd, I shall not be in want. He makes me lie down in green pastures, He leads me beside quiet waters, He restores my soul."

I froze in my tracks behind Helen, the unsheathed weapon in my hands. At once, my heart broke for her. I couldn't be certain if the words belonged to zombie Helen or the real Helen somewhere inside her, crying out for help. Her words rung in my ears. *He restores my soul.*

"May God help you, Helen," I said on a sob. "May He keep you and guide you and love you, always, as I have done."

She started to turn towards my voice, but before I could see her face, before I had to look in her eyes and see all over again emptiness instead of Helen, I lifted the sword and brought it, with all my strength, down on her neck. Her head rolled. Her body staggered and fell, slumping to the table. For a moment, I thought I'd made a terrible mistake, that Helen had in fact been alive and I'd killed her. I gasped, dropped the sword, and covered my mouth with my hands. Dear Lord! What had I done?

But then, I caught sight of the green goo dribbling from the orifice where her head had been. Her beautiful, brilliant head! And I knew, on sight of green goo in place of blood, that Helen was indeed no more. I had not taken her life. I had restored her to peace. I fancied I could hear her sweet voice saying, "Good-bye, Jane." I closed my eyes to blink back the tears.

A hand touched my shoulder and startled me. I screamed, I think. I couldn't tell if the sound had actually made it to my lips or if it had only happened in my head, like Helen's good-bye.

"Jane!" Miss Temple's voice. I turned. "I'm glad to see you. We need to talk."

"About Helen? I already know."

She looked and saw the body in the chair. Her arms went around me and she pulled me to her. "Jane."

I had that feeling again, the one I'd had after I'd stood up to Mrs. Reed and showed her the stake intended for her son should he attack me again—a feeling of power and triumph, a fierce pleasure racing through my veins. I'd done the right thing. I'd saved Helen. I'd set her free.

After Miss Temple and I held our own small service and burial for Helen Burns, we returned to Miss Temple's rooms to talk.

I learned that Miss Temple had known about Mr. Bokorhurst's activities for some time, and she greatly disapproved. He'd threatened her with turning her out without a recommendation, and she feared that she would be better served to stay at Lowood to help nurse students to health and look after us than to leave us all to the mercy of a man like Mr. Bokorhurst.

"He truly means well," she said. "He seems to believe he's doing a service for the dead, in keeping their bodies useful after their soul's earthly departure. He would not do anything to harm the girls in life."

"Except for starving us and half freezing us to death. Besides, if he thought he was doing well, he would have no need to threaten you."

"Jane." Miss Temple smiled. "You're so small for your age, and yet you seem so much older than your years."

"I'm much stronger than I look, too. I've been practising."

"As I've seen. The time has come, then. We shall free all the girls from their curses and put a stop to Mr. Bokorhurst's actions at last."

CHAPTER 11

THE NEXT MORNING, WE began our day as usual, with Miss Temple checking on the patients in the sickroom while I rose in the dorm, dressing with the other girls, and keeping watch over the "special students" amongst us. Most girls planned to enjoy their rumored last few days of freedom in the woods. After a brief repast, they took their dinners in parcels and separated from the rest of us to run off into the fields and woods. As usual, the special students gathered at the round tables in the classroom to recite psalms.

Miss Temple waited until everyone settled into activity. She'd sent the teachers on errands, respectively, to the apothecary, to post letters, to procure needles and thread. With the nurse and Miss Miller keeping watch over the girls in the sickroom and the other girls out roaming in nature, we had the schoolroom to ourselves with the special students. Miss Temple informed the zombified girls that Mr. Bokorhurst had important plans for each of them, even the youngest, and that she would be sending them each out of the room to receive instructions from him in the privacy of the library.

Miss Temple hated to lie, but she deemed it a necessity to restore the girls' souls to heaven, where they belonged.

I waited in the library, sword in hand, ready to decapitate them as they entered. One at a time they came in, as Miss Temple sent them, starting with Catherine Johnstone. I stood behind a row of books and coughed, so she would follow the sound and be drawn to the right location. Just as she turned a corner, slice! I delivered a solid stroke, a clean cut. I wished we had planned a little better, though. I had barely enough time to fetch the head and drag the corpse out of the way between two other shelves of books before another zombie came in. Plus, the green goo was already making the floor slippery, as if I were stepping in pea soup. Next came Jilly Richards, Amanda Green, and Millie Harvey.

After the fourth, it became mechanical. I was surprised at my own strength. Eight more came in succession, and I made short work of them all. All except Mona Billings, who somehow got the idea to duck just as I swung the saber. Upon sight of me, she became angry. Angry zombies are strong zombies, as I knew from experience with Abbot. I began striking wildly to keep her away from me in the close space, and I sliced through a few books and cut off one of Mona's hands before I found my bearings again and did the deed. I'd feared that we'd made a mistake and Mona was perfectly mortal after all, but the sight of the oozing green goo warmed my heart and convinced me that we had done the right thing.

By my calculation, we had six more to free, all smaller girls, when I heard a voice that boomed like thunder in the other room. Mr. Bokorhurst!

My heart raced with panic. I ran to the door to listen, nearly slipping on Mona's remains. The zombies were expressing surprise at Mr. Bokorhurst's appearance, and Miss Temple struggled to keep order.

"Where are the others, Miss Temple? I expected to find the older girls leading the group in reciting their psalms. Have you given them orders contrary to my wishes?"

"Yes, Mr. Bokorhurst. I have." I gasped, a little surprised by Miss Temple's easy admission. "The time has come to return your special students to nature, to the heavenly home they deserve."

"Miss Temple! I am astonished. What better home can we give them but one where toil and sacrifice is supported and appreciated?"

"If God intended the girls to continue a life of endless toil and sacrifice, Mr. Bokorhurst, he would have let them live in your care instead of calling them home from their earthly confines. As it is, they are a danger to the others. Though the housekeeper, may she rest in peace, was warned, two of them got hold of mutton pies, and we're lucky there were not more. Now follow Him and let them go!"

"Where is Miss Scatcherd?" he bellowed. "Eve Scatcherd, show yourself! Surely Miss Scatcherd would not stand back and allow you to destroy our careful enterprise?"

Reader, I could no longer stay behind the library door. For my own safety, keeping hidden would have been the wisest choice, but something larger than concern for myself seemed to thrum, nay to pound, in my veins. I heard, or imagined, Helen encouraging me, telling me to stand beside Miss Temple in her rebellion.

I concealed the sword under my pinafore and stepped out in time to see Miss Temple crossing her arms, standing her ground in bold defiance. "I sent her away. I've sent them all away on errands so I could complete my mission to save the girls."

"Save them? You're destroying them!"

"Destroying their earthly remains," I said in a tone so clear and loud I barely recognised it as my own. "What are they but empty shells of girls, once full of life, now forced to do your bidding?"

Mr. Bokorhurst gasped. "Jane Slayre! I should have heeded Mrs. Reed's warnings more carefully. She warned that you would not be easy to control."

"I will not be controlled!" I turned to my former classmates. "Do you not see what he has done? Do you not wish to be free to continue on your path to heaven, where you belong? He is not your master! He will sell you, profit from you, as he sold Miss Martha Abbot to Mrs. Reed. God awaits you in heaven. Stand up! Rise up! Stop Mr. Bokorhurst from using you. Follow your true maker to your heavenly home."

I dropped to my knees, out of breath from my imploring. They would not follow me, a mere girl, a classmate, over one so imposing and authoritative as Mr. Bokorhurst. He had them in a trance. But I thought of Helen and I could not give up. I repeated her last words, from the psalm. "The Lord is my shepherd, I shall not be in want. He makes me lie down in green pastures, He leads me beside quiet waters, He restores my soul."

As I knelt, Mona Billings's hand, which I had tucked in my pocket and forgotten in moving the corpse, tumbled to the floor to land at Karen Marist's zombie feet. She blinked in bewilderment, leaned down, picked up the grisly prize, and bit one of the fingers clean off.

"Mmm." She groaned in pleasure and passed the thing to the zombie student to her left. I immediately rose, ready with my sword, but Miss Temple was prepared, too. She withdrew a dagger from her pocket and pointed it straight at Karen, throwing it with deadly precision, straight to the heart, before the zombie could erupt into a flesh-hungry frenzy.

It would not stop Karen, but would subdue her for the time. Unfortunately, the other girls were still passing around the hand, and Miss Temple would have to waste precious moments to run off and fetch another sword.

"He restores my soul," the girls all repeated in unison, then looked at one another and rose.

Imagine my surprise when the girls began slowly circling Mr. Bokorhurst, chanting the psalm as Helen had, over and over: "He restores my soul. He restores my soul."

They began to tear at Mr. Bokorhurst, ripping at his clothing and his hair. I believe the spectacle of the event, and the justice of Mr. Bokorhurst falling to such a fate, kept Miss Temple and me frozen in place, unable to move. Fortunately, the zombies did not move at any accelerated rate. Miss Temple came to her senses first. "Stop them, Jane! We must stop them."

I waved my saber and took Karen's head before she could come to her senses, then rushed towards the throng around Mr. Bokorhurst. Large as he was, he was no match for the superhuman strength of his zombified subjects. Miss Temple returned with her weapon and began slicing at the others with expert precision. One head, then two, rolled. She spun, leveled a kick at another, and sent her flying across the room. I ran after and took care of that one, but my strength from swinging the sword all day had begun to falter. I only managed to hack her neck half through. Nerves and veins spurted the distinctive green goo, but the head was still attached. I gave another whack and finished the deed.

Mr. Bokorhurst's screams, a sound as loud as the very sky splitting in two, made Miss Miller and the nurse come running into the room.

"Oh dear! They've gone mad!" Miss Miller said, heading for the mob.

Miss Temple managed to behead one more before Miss Miller and the nurse, who clearly knew a thing or two about zombies as well, jumped in and tried beating them away to get to Mr. Bokorhurst before he was completely dismembered and consumed, a task made more difficult as we were all covered in the vile zombie ick.

Off to the side, I remained forgotten, but not helpless. I wrenched the dagger free from Karen Marist's chest and hurled it, with quite good aim, into Maria Grayson. That ought to contain her for the time.

Miss Temple made quick work of the remaining zombies, and the nurse and Miss Miller struggled to drag the bodies aside and assess the damage to Mr. Bokorhurst. Surprisingly enough, he lived! Mr. Bokorhurst remained curled up in a ball on the floor, his head tucked into his arms, legs drawn up to provide further protection from the grasping, revolting zombies.

"You see, Mr. Bokorhurst"—Miss Temple wiped her hands—"I tried to warn you there was danger in your unnatural pursuits."

He was in no position to answer. The nurse coaxed him to a sitting position and began examining him. Miss Miller stood still, blinking repeatedly, as if recovering from a shock. Mr. Bokorhurst bled profusely from the socket of a missing arm, which Miss Temple had tried to pick up to restore, but it was badly chewed. The nurse began bandaging him up. He shook with fright and muttered something unintelligible. I wondered if they had ripped out his tongue, but didn't see it anywhere in the mess. His hair was entirely missing, and a nasty gash was in his temple.

While Mr. Bokorhurst was incapacitated, it was settled, at last, that the returning teachers and students would be told of the sudden recurrence of disease at Lowood and kept from the new makeshift sickroom where the infected girls supposedly lingered. Over the next few days, announcements would be made of their deaths, and the "bodies" buried quickly in the night "to keep others from risk of infection."

"Oh, Jane, my darling girl, we've done it. We've freed the girls and Lowood from the tyranny of Mr. Bokorhurst at last!"

Though I had my doubt that the problem of Mr. Bokorhurst would be solved as easily as a zombie attack, I did not want to spoil Miss Temple's good mood by voicing my concerns. I returned her embrace, shared her delight in our victory, and prepared for the unpleasant task of cleaning up after the dead.

CHAPTER 12

READER, I WAS WRONG to doubt. The tyranny of Mr. Bokorhurst had indeed come to an end. He died in the night from his wounds, after much pain, reflection, and prayer. When the typhus fever, on which all of the deaths had been blamed, fulfilled its mission of devastation at Lowood, it gradually disappeared from thence, but not until its virulence and the number of its victims had drawn public attention to the school.

The last course of infection claimed as many as twenty girls in a week, and inquiry was made into the origin of the scourge, and by degrees various facts came out that excited a high degree of public indignation. The unhealthy nature of the site; the quantity and quality of the children's food; the brackish, fetid water used in its preparation; the pupils' wretched clothing and accommodations—all these things were discovered, and the discovery produced benefits to the institution.

Several wealthy and benevolent individuals in the county subscribed largely for the erection of a more convenient building in a better situation. New regulations were made; improvements in diet and clothing introduced. The funds of the school were entrusted to the management of a committee. The office of inspector was given to one who knew how to combine reason with strictness, comfort with economy, and compassion with uprightness. The school, thus improved, became in time a truly useful and noble institution.

I remained an inmate of its walls, after its regeneration, for eight years: six as pupil and two as teacher; and in both capacities I bear my testimony to its value and importance. My life, after the first eventful year, was free of zombie curses and vampyres; uniform, but not unhappy because it was not inactive. I had the means of an excellent education placed within my reach, a fondness for some of my studies, and a desire to excel in all. I availed myself fully of the advantages offered me. I made friends. I cherished my relationships with my fellow students and teachers. In time I rose to be the first girl of the first class; then I was invested with the office of teacher.

For two years, I discharged my duties with zeal. Miss Temple, through all changes, had thus far continued as superintendent of the seminary. To her devotion and instruction, I owed the best part of my acquirements. Her friendship and society had been my continual solace. She had stood me in the stead of mother, governess, training instructor, and, latterly, companion.

But destiny, in the shape of the Reverend Mr. Nasmyth, came between me and Miss Temple. She had fallen in love with the man who had taken over the deceased Mr. Bokorhurst's duties as clergyman at Bokorbridge Church. When Mr. Nasmyth later found a new position in a far-removed county, he revealed that he loved Miss Temple, too, and he requested her hand in marriage. I could not be anything but overjoyed for Miss Temple, of course.

I saw her in her travelling dress step into a post chaise, shortly after the marriage ceremony. I watched the chaise mount the hill and disappear beyond its brow. Once it was beyond my line of vision, I retired to my room and there spent in reflective solitude the greatest part of the half holiday granted in honour of the occasion. My mentor, and my dearest friend, was lost to me.

From the day she left, I was no longer the same. Without Miss Temple, every warm and settled feeling, every association that had made Lowood in some degree a home to me, was gone. I had imbibed from Miss Temple something of her nature and many of her habits. Peaceful, harmonious thoughts had taken over the violent, wild feelings I'd begun to develop in my youth. I was quiet. I believed I was content. To the eyes of others, usually even to my own, I appeared a disciplined and subdued character.

In the weeks after Miss Temple's—Mrs. Nasmyth's—departure,

I walked about my chamber most of the time. I imagined myself only to be regretting my loss and thinking how to repair it. Eventually, once I reflected on it, I came to a different conclusion; that my mind had put off all it had borrowed of Miss Temple—or rather that she had taken with her the secret thrill I had of training at her side and practicing with weapons. She had given me a gift before she left, a pair of Egyptian daggers with lovely engraved handles. They had belonged to her father, but now I had no chance to use them.

I remembered the excitement I had felt at the visitation from my uncle's ghost and the charge that he had made of me, the power that had coursed in my veins when I'd held the stake up to Mrs. Reed's face, the thrill of decapitating zombies to send so many souls to the heaven they deserved. Certainly I was grateful to have lived so many years at Lowood free from threats or violent challenges. My motive had been to escape the Reed household and to get an education, and I had.

My world had for some years been in Lowood. My experience had been of its rules and systems. At last, I remembered that the real world was wide, and that a varied field of hopes and fears, of sensations and excitements, awaited those who had courage to go forth into its expanse, to seek real knowledge of life amidst its perils. What I wanted was a new place, in a new house, amongst new faces, under new circumstances. It occurred to me that those who want situations advertise. I simply had to advertise in the *Herald*. Satisfied at last, I fell asleep.

With earliest day, I was up. I had my advertisement written, enclosed in an envelope, and directed before the bell rang to rouse the school. It ran thus:

"A young lady accustomed to tuition is desirous of meeting with a situation in a private family where the children are under fourteen (I thought that as I was barely eighteen, it would not do to undertake the guidance of pupils nearer my own age). She is qualified to teach the usual branches of a good English education, together with French, Drawing, and Music."

This document remained locked in my drawer all day. After tea, I asked leave of the new superintendent to go to Lowton, to perform some small commissions for myself and one or two of my fellow teachers. Permission was granted. It was a walk of two miles. The evening was wet, but the days were yet long and I still loved the outdoors in the daytime. I visited a shop or two, slipped the letter into the post office, and came back through heavy rain, with streaming garments, but with a relieved heart.

A week later, I repeated the journey in search of answers to my post. My ostensible errand on this occasion was to get measured for a pair of shoes, so I discharged that business first. When it was done, I stepped across the clean and quiet little street from the shoemaker's to the post office.

"Are there any letters for J.S.?" I asked.

The old lady who kept the office peered at me over her horn spectacles. At last, she presented a document across the counter, with an inquisitive and mistrustful glance. It was for J.S.

"Is there only one?" I asked.

"There are no more," she said.

I thanked her, put the letter in my pocket, and turned homeward. The school rules obliged me to be back by eight, and it was already half past seven. I waited to read until I was back at school and had the chance, after dinner. I took out my letter. The seal was an initial *F.* I broke it. The contents were brief.

"If J.S., who advertised in the *Herald* of last Thursday, possesses the acquirements mentioned, and if she is in a position to give satisfactory references as to character and competency, a situation can be offered her where there is but one pupil, a little girl, under ten years of age; and where the salary is thirty pounds per annum. J.S. is requested to send references, name, address, and all particulars to the direction: Mrs. Fairfax, Thornfield, near Millcote, ——shire."

I examined the document for a long time. The writing was old-fashioned and rather uncertain, like that of an elderly lady. I felt that an elderly lady was no bad ingredient in the business I had on hand. If she turned out to be some sort of demon, I could no doubt handle her well enough if she took the form of someone aged.

Mrs. Fairfax! I saw her in a black gown and widow's cap. Thornfield! That, doubtless, was the name of her house, a neat, orderly spot. Millcote, ——shire. I brushed up my recollections of the map of England. Yes, I saw it, both the shire and the town, some seventy miles nearer London than the remote county where I now resided. I longed to go where there was life and movement. Millcote was a large manufacturing town on a river, a busy place enough, doubtless. Not that my fancy was much captivated by the idea of tall chimneys and clouds of smoke, but I decided that Thornfield would probably be a good way from the town.

The next day, steps were to taken to make arrangements. Having sought and obtained an audience of the superintendent, I told her I had a prospect of a new situation where the salary would be double what I now received (for at Lowood I got only fifteen pounds per annum) and requested she break the matter for me to some of the committee and ascertain if they would permit me to mention them as references. She obligingly consented to act as mediatrix.

A day later, she informed me that Mrs. Reed must be written to, as she was my natural guardian. A knot of dread formed in my stomach. Mrs. Reed! How could she still have a hand in my affairs? A note was accordingly addressed to that lady, who returned for answer, that "she might do as she pleases: I have long relinquished all interference in her affairs." And thank goodness! This note went to the committee, and at last, after what appeared to me a most tedious delay, formal leave was granted for me to better my condition if I could; and an assurance was added that as I had always conducted myself well, both as teacher and pupil, at Lowood, a testimonial of character and capacity, signed by the inspectors of that institution, would be sent to Mrs. Fairfax.

In about a month, I got that lady's reply, stating that she was satisfied, and fixing the day, a fortnight hence, as the time for my assuming the post of governess in her house.

The fortnight passed rapidly. I had not a large wardrobe, though it was adequate to my wants, and the last day sufficed to pack my trunk, the same I had brought with me eight years ago from Gateshead.

The box was corded, the card nailed on. In a half hour the carrier was to call for it to take it to Lowton, whither I myself was to repair at an early hour the next morning to meet the coach. I had brushed my black stuff traveling dress and prepared my bonnet, gloves, and muff. I looked through all my drawers to see that no article was left behind. I could not rest; I was too much excited. A phase of my life was closing tonight, a new one opening tomorrow. It was impossible to slumber in the interval. I left my chamber to pace the corridors.

"Miss." A servant met me in the lobby, where I wandered like a troubled spirit. "A person below wishes to see you."

"The carrier, no doubt," I thought, and ran downstairs without inquiry. I passed the teachers' sitting room, the door of which was half-open, to go to the kitchen, when someone ran out.

"It's her, I am sure! I could have told her anywhere!" cried the individual who stopped my progress and took my hand.

She was attired like a well-dressed servant, matronly, yet still young; good-looking, with black hair and eyes, and lively complexion.

"Well, who is it?" she asked in a voice and with a smile I half recognised. "You've not quite forgotten me, I think, Miss Jane?"

In another second I embraced her. "Bessie! Bessie! Bessie!"

She half laughed, half cried, and we both went into the parlour. By the fire stood a little fellow of three years old, in plaid frock and trousers.

"That is my little boy," said Bessie directly.

"Then you are married, Bessie?"

"Yes. Nearly five years since to Robert Leaven, the coachman. I've a little girl besides Bobby there, that I've christened Jane."

I was touched by the honour and told her so. "And you don't live at Gateshead?"

I hoped for her sake, and that of her children, that she did not expose them regularly to the Reeds or Abbot.

"I live at the lodge. The old porter has left."

"Well, and how do they all get on? Tell me everything about them, Bessie. Have a seat. Bobby, come and sit on my knee, will you?" Bobby preferred sidling over to his mother.

"You're not grown so very tall, Miss Jane, nor so very stout," continued Mrs. Leaven. "I daresay they've not kept you too well at school. Still, Miss Reed is even slighter in figure than you, though I daresay she still stands taller. And Miss Georgiana is stouter, perhaps two of you, but still fancies herself a beauty."

"I am sure she should. Her mother always said so."

Bessie smiled. "They had a carriage made without windows and with heavy drapes to cover every crack so that they could go to London last winter. Everybody admired Miss Georgiana, and a young lord fell in love with her. His relations were against the match; and—what do you think?—Miss Georgiana and her mother and sister made a feast of them! They tried to make the lad into one of them, but he couldn't handle the transformation. He died, poor thing. Miss Georgiana blamed her sister for insisting on having a taste of his blood and draining him too dry before he had a chance to return the favour. Now she and her sister lead a cat-and-dog life together; they are always quarrelling."

"Tragic! And what of John Reed?"

"Oh, he is not doing so well as his mama could wish. He declared himself to be of age to handle the household affairs, but his mother did not agree. He insisted on going off to find his own way in the world. We hear from him but rarely, usually when he has gambling debts to discharge or bodies to hide. He's not much of a hunter. He prefers to attack travellers and passersby, easy targets. He doesn't concern himself if their blood is too common for his tastes."

"Troubling. His mother must be constantly concerned lest he pick up a taint."

"Missus has grown stouter, though she looks well enough in the face. She hunts often to take her mind off her troubles. Mr. John's conduct is indeed a constant worry."

"Did she send you here, Bessie?"

"No. I have long wanted to see you, and when I heard that there had been a letter from you, and that you were going to another part of the country, I thought I'd just set off and get a look at you before you were quite out of my reach."

"I am afraid you are disappointed in me, Bessie," I said, laughing.

"No, Miss Jane, not at all. You are genteel enough. You look like a lady, though rather plain, and it is as much as ever I expected of you. I daresay you are clever. What can you do? Can you play on the piano?"

"A little." I still smarted from the sting of having been called plain, though I treasured Bessie's frankness.

Bessie went and opened the piano in the room, then asked me to sit down and give her a tune. I played a waltz or two, and she was charmed.

"The Miss Reeds could not play as well!" said she exultingly.

"They did eat their music master."

"That's right." Bessie smiled. "I'd forgotten. Mrs. Reed kept them quarantined for a week in case they caught something until she remembered that his grandfather was a viscount. And can you draw?"

"That is one of my paintings over the chimneypiece." It was a landscape in watercolours. I had given it to the superintendent in acknowledgment of her obliging mediation with the committee on my behalf. She'd had it framed and glazed.

"Well, that is beautiful, Miss Jane! It is as fine a picture as any Miss Reed's drawing master could paint, and have you learned French?"

"Yes, Bessie, I can both read it and speak it."

"Oh, you are quite a lady, Miss Jane! I knew you would be. You will get on whether your relations notice you or not. There was something I wanted to ask you. Have you ever heard anything from your father's kinsfolk, the Slayres?"

"Never in my life."

"Well, you know Missus always said they were poor and quite despicable, and they may be poor, but I believe they are as much gentry as the Reeds are. One day, nearly seven years ago, a Mr. Slayre came to Gateshead and wanted to see you. Missus would not admit him. How she screamed when she saw him! And when he came in anyway, she begged him not to slay her. Queer, is it not?"

"Most assuredly." I remembered what my uncle Reed had said about my uncle Slayre, that he lived too dangerously to care for an infant. But perhaps he'd decided I was ready to start training. Would he not be proud to know how I'd handled the zombies?

"Missus said you were at school fifty miles off. He seemed so much disappointed, for he was going on a voyage and the ship was to sail from London in a day or two. He looked quite a gentleman, and I believe he was your father's brother."

"A voyage? To where, Bessie?"

"An island thousands of miles off, where they make wine—the butler told me—"

"Madeira?"

"Yes, that is it—that is the very word. He did not stay many minutes in the house, what with Missus screeching at him. She called him afterward a sneaking murderer."

It occurred to me, not for the first time, that perhaps he was the one who had taken mercy on my uncle Reed and staked him. After all, how many vampyre slayers would Uncle Reed have known?

"That's not very nice of her," I returned, "but as to be expected."

Bessie and I conversed about old times an hour longer, then she was obliged to leave me. I saw her again for a few minutes the next morning at Lowton, while I was waiting for the coach. We parted finally at the door of the Bokorhurst Arms there. She set off for the conveyance that was to take her and her little boy back to Gateshead. I mounted the vehicle that was to bear me to new duties, and a new life, in the unknown environs of Millcote.

CHAPTER 13

I LEFT LOWTON AT 4:00 a.m., and the Millcote town clock was just striking eight in the evening as I sat, in my cloak and bonnet, by an excellent fire in a room at the George Inn. My muff and umbrella rested on the table, and I warmed away the numbness and chill of long exposure to a raw October day.

Reader, though I looked comfortably accommodated, I was not tranquil in my mind. I thought when the coach stopped, someone would meet me. I looked anxiously around as I descended the wooden steps, expecting to hear my name pronounced, and to see some description of carriage waiting to convey me to Thornfield. Nothing of the sort was visible. When I asked a waiter if anyone had been to inquire after a Miss Slayre, I was answered in the negative. I had no resource but to request to be shown to a private room, and there I waited, while all sorts of doubts and fears troubled my thoughts. I had a few stakes tucked away on my person out of habit, old habit indeed, but my daggers, on which I was sure I could rely, were tucked away in my luggage for safekeeping.

A half hour elapsed and I was still alone. I thought to ring the bell.

"Is there a place in this neighbourhood called Thornfield?" I asked of the waiter who answered the summons.

"Thornfield? I don't know, ma'am. I'll inquire at the bar." He vanished, but reappeared instantly. "Is your name Slayre, Miss?"

"Yes."

"Person here waiting for you."

I jumped up, took my muff and umbrella and hastened into the inn passage. A man stood by the open door, and in the lamplit street I saw a one-horse conveyance.

"This will be your luggage, I suppose?" the man asked rather abruptly, pointing to my trunk in the passage.

"Yes." He hoisted it onto the vehicle, which was a sort of carriage, and then I got in. Before he shut me up, I asked him how far it was to Thornfield.

"A matter of six miles."

"How long shall we be before we get there?"

"Happen an hour and a half."

He fastened the door, climbed to his own seat outside, and we set off. Our progress was leisurely and gave me ample time to reflect. I supposed, judging from the plainness of the servant and the carriage, Mrs. Fairfax was not a very dashing person. So much the better. I never lived amongst fine people but once, and I was miserable with them. I wondered if she lived alone except for this little girl. If so, and if she was in any degree amiable, I would surely be able to get on with her.

I let down the window and looked out. Millcote was behind us, judging by the number of its lights. It seemed to be of considerable magnitude, much larger than Lowton. I felt we were in a different region to Lowood, more populous, less picturesque, more stirring, less romantic. We passed a church. About ten minutes after, the driver got down and opened a pair of gates. We passed through, and they clashed to a close behind us. We slowly ascended a drive and came upon the long front of a house. Candlelight gleamed from one curtained bow window. All the rest were dark. The carriage stopped at the front door. A maidservant opened it and greeted me. I alighted and went in.

"Will you walk this way, ma'am?" the girl said.

I followed her across a square hall with high doors all round. She ushered me into a room that had a double illumination of fire and candle to dazzle me, contrasting as it did with the darkness to which my eyes had been for two hours inured. When I could see, however, a cosy and agreeable picture presented itself, a snug, small room with a round table by a cheerful fire, a high-backed armchair, wherein sat the neatest imaginable little, elderly lady, in widow's cap, black silk gown, and snowy muslin apron. She was exactly as I'd fancied Mrs. Fairfax to be, only less stately and milder in appearance. A large cat sat demurely at her feet as she knit. A more reassuring introduction for a new governess could scarcely be conceived. As I entered, the old lady got up and kindly came forward to meet me.

"How do you do, my dear? You must be cold, come to the fire."

"Mrs. Fairfax, I suppose?"

"Yes. Do sit down."

She conducted me to her own chair, then began to remove my shawl and untie my bonnet strings. I begged she would not give herself so much trouble.

"Oh, it is no trouble. I daresay your own hands are almost numbed with cold. Leah, make a little hot negus and cut a sandwich."

"Now, then, draw nearer to the fire," she continued. "You've brought your luggage with you, haven't you, my dear?"

"Yes, ma'am."

"I'll see it carried into your room." She bustled out.

I thought she treated me like a visitor. I little expected such a warm reception.

She returned, cleared her knitting apparatus and a book from the table to make room for the tray Leah brought, then handed me the refreshments. I felt rather confused at being the object of more attention than I had ever before received, and that shown by my employer and superior. As she did not seem to consider she was doing anything out of her place, I thought it better to take her civilities quietly.

"Shall I have the pleasure of seeing Miss Fairfax tonight?" I asked when I had partaken of what she offered me.

"Miss Fairfax? Oh, you mean Miss Varens! Varens is the name of your pupil."

"Indeed! Then she is not your daughter?"

"No, I have no family. I am so glad you've come." She sat down opposite me and took the cat on her knee. "It will be quite pleasant living here now with a companion. To be sure it is pleasant at any time, for Thornfield is a fine old hall. Still, in wintertime one feels dreary in even the best quarters. Of course, I do have Leah, and John, your driver, and his wife are very decent people. Since the end of summer, we have little Adele Varens and her nurse. A child makes a house alive all at once. And now that you are here, I shall be quite gay."

My heart really warmed to the worthy lady as I heard her talk, and I drew my chair a little nearer to hers and expressed my sincere wish that she might find my company as agreeable as she anticipated.

"But I'll not keep you sitting up late tonight," she said. "You have been travelling all day. I've had the room next to mine prepared for you. It is only a small apartment, but I thought you would like it better than one of the large front chambers. To be sure they have finer furniture, but they are so dreary and solitary I never sleep in them myself."

I thanked her for her considerate choice and, as I really felt fatigued with my long journey, expressed my readiness to retire. She took her candle, and I followed her from the room as she led the way upstairs.

The steps and banisters were of oak. The staircase window was high and latticed. Both it and the long gallery into which the bedroom doors opened looked as if they belonged to a church rather than a house. A vaultlike air pervaded the stairs and gallery. I suddenly had a queer feeling, an icy chill snaking through me. Mrs. Fairfax and even Leah had seemed decent and quite right. They aroused in me no suspicions. I felt I could trust and get to know them. But something in the hall as we walked gave me pause. I couldn't tell what it was, and when I was finally ushered into my chamber, it faded fast. My room was much more pleasing to me, a calming haven of small dimensions furnished in ordinary, modern style.

When Mrs. Fairfax had bidden me a kind good-night and I had fastened my door, I took time to gaze leisurely around. The lively aspect of my little room chased off the eerie impression made by the wide hall, the dark and spacious staircase, and that long, cold gallery. The impulse of gratitude swelled in my heart, and I knelt down at the bedside and offered up thanks where thanks were due. At once weary and content, I slept soon and soundly. When I awoke, it was broad day.

The chamber looked such a bright place to me as the sun shone in between the gay blue chintz window curtains, showing papered walls and a carpeted floor, so unlike the bare planks and stained plaster of Lowood that my spirits rose at the view. I thought it a sign that a fairer era of life was beginning for me, one that was to have its flowers and pleasures as well as its thorns and toils.

I rose and dressed with care, obliged to be plain for I had no article of attire that was not made with extreme simplicity. Sometimes, I regretted that I was not handsomer. I desired to be tall, stately, and finely developed in figure. I felt it a misfortune that I was so little, so pale, and had features so unremarkable. However, when I had brushed my hair smooth and put on my black frock—which, Quaker-like as it was, at least had the merit of fitting to a nicety—and adjusted my clean white tucker, I thought I should do respectably enough to appear before Mrs. Fairfax, and that my new pupil would not recoil from me with antipathy. Having opened my chamber window and seen that I left all things straight and neat on the toilet table, I ventured forth.

I paused on the oak staircase. No feeling of apprehension or fear came over me as had the previous night. Perhaps it had merely been nerves, uncertainty of the unknown. I looked at some pictures on the walls, at a bronze lamp pendent from the ceiling, at a great clock whose case was curiously carved and black with time and rubbing. Everything appeared stately to me, but then I was little accustomed to grandeur.

The hall door, which was half of glass, stood open. I stepped over the threshold. It was a fine autumn morning. The early sun shone serenely on embrowned groves and still green fields. I walked out to the lawn, looked up, and surveyed the front of the mansion. It was larger than it seemed last night, three stories high, of proportions not vast, though considerable, a gentleman's manor house, not a nobleman's seat. Battlements around the top gave it a picturesque look. Its grey front stood out well from the background of a rookery, whose cawing tenants were now on the wing. They flew over the lawn and grounds to alight in a great meadow, from which these were separated by a sunk fence. An array of mighty old thorn trees—strong, knotty, and broad as oaks—at once explained the source of the mansion's name.

Farther off were hills, not so lofty as those around Lowood, but yet quiet and lonely hills that seemed to embrace Thornfield with a seclusion I had not expected to find so near the stirring locality of Millcote. A hamlet, whose roofs blended with trees, straggled up the side of one of these hills. The church of the district stood nearer Thornfield. Its old tower looked over a knoll between the house and the gates.

I enjoyed the calm prospect and sunshine, the pleasant fresh air, and even the cawing of the rooks. The beauty of a sunny day had never failed to stir my soul, so deprived had I been of them in my earliest years.

"What, out already?" Mrs. Fairfax peeked out the door to greet me. "I see you are an early riser."

"Yes," I answered, still looking over the aspects of the house and thinking how well it suited Mrs. Fairfax. I finished my surveying, went up to her, and was received with an affable kiss and shake of the hand. I was pleased to see that Mrs. Fairfax was unafraid to step out into the sunshine. I could rule out any chance that she was a vampyre, and her cheerful disposition made it seem equally unlikely that she was a zombie.

"How do you like Thornfield?"

"Very much," I answered, completely at ease.

"Yes, it is a pretty place. But I fear it will be getting out of order unless Mr. Rochester should take it into his head to come and reside here permanently, or at least visit it rather oftener. Great houses and fine grounds require the presence of the proprietor."

"Mr. Rochester? Who is he?"

"The owner of Thornfield," she responded quietly. "Did you not know he was called Rochester?"

Of course I did not. I had never heard of him, but the old lady seemed to regard his existence as a universally understood fact, with which everybody must be acquainted by instinct.

"I assumed that Thornfield belonged to you."

"To me? Bless you, child, what an idea! To me! I am only the housekeeper—the manager. To be sure I am distantly related to the Rochesters by the mother's side, or at least my husband was. The present Mr. Rochester's mother was a Fairfax and second cousin to my husband, but I never presume on the connection. In fact, it is nothing to me. I consider myself quite in the light of an ordinary housekeeper. My employer is always civil, and I expect nothing more."

"And the little girl, my pupil?" At last I thought it was best to ask questions and know what I had got into at the risk of being impolite. A civil employer was a good sign, though vampyres could be civil when they wished.

"She is Mr. Rochester's ward. He commissioned me to find a governess for her, and so I have. Ah, and here she comes, with her 'bonne,' as she calls her nurse."

The enigma was then explained: this affable and kind little widow was no great dame, but a dependant like me. I did not like her the worse for that. On the contrary, I felt better pleased than ever. The equality between us was real and not the mere result of condescension on her part.

As I was meditating on this discovery, a little girl, followed by her attendant, came running up the lawn. She was quite a child, perhaps seven or eight years old, slightly built, with a pale, small-featured face and a redundancy of hair falling in curls to her waist.

"Good morning, Miss Adele," said Mrs. Fairfax. "Come and speak to the lady who is to teach you, and to make you a clever woman someday."

The child approached and pointed to me, addressing her nurse. *"C'est la ma gouvernante!"*

"Mais oui, certainement."

"Are they foreigners?" I inquired, amazed at hearing French.

"The nurse is a foreigner, and Adele was born on the Continent. I believe she never left it until some months ago. When she first came here, she could speak no English. Now she can make shift to talk it a little. I don't understand her. She mixes it so with French. But you will make out her meaning very well, I daresay."

Fortunately I had had the advantage of being taught French by a French lady, and I was not likely to be much at a loss with Mademoiselle Adele. She came and shook hands with me.

As I led her in to breakfast, I addressed some phrases to her in her own tongue. She replied briefly at first. After we were seated at the table, and she had examined me some ten minutes with her large hazel eyes, she suddenly commenced chattering fluently.

"Ah!" she said in French. "You speak my language as well as Mr. Rochester does. I can talk to you as I can to him, and so can Sophie, my nurse. She will be glad. Nobody here understands her. Madame Fairfax is all English. Sophie came with me, over the sea in a great ship with a chimney that smoked—how it did smoke!—and I was sick, and so was Sophie, and so was Mr. Rochester. And, Mademoiselle—what is your name?"

"Slayre—Jane Slayre."

"Slaire? Bah! I cannot say it. Well, our ship stopped in the morning, before daylight, at a great city, and Mr. Rochester carried me in his arms over a plank to the land, and Sophie came after, and we all got into a coach!"

"Can you understand her when she runs on so fast?" asked Mrs. Fairfax.

"Oh, indeed." I understood her well.

"I wish," continued the good lady, "you would ask her a question or two about her parents. I wonder if she remembers them?"

"Adele," I inquired, "with whom did you live when you were in that pretty, clean town you spoke of?"

"I lived long ago with Mama, but she is gone to the Holy Virgin. Mama used to teach me to dance and sing, and to say verses. A great many gentlemen and ladies came to see Mama, and I used to dance before them, or to sit on their knees and sing to them. I liked it. Shall I let you hear me sing now?"

She had finished her breakfast, so I permitted her to display her accomplishments. She placed herself on my knee. Folding her little hands demurely before her, shaking back her curls and lifting her eyes to the ceiling, she commenced a song from some opera about a jilted lover. The subject seemed strangely chosen for an infant singer, and in bad taste. I wondered at her mother teaching her such songs. Adele sang well enough, apparently oblivious of the nature of her song, then she jumped down from my knee, curtsied prettily, and declared that next she would read me some poetry.

" '*La Ligue des Rats,' fable de La Fontaine*," she announced. She then declaimed the little piece with an attention to punctuation and emphasis, a flexibility of voice and an appropriateness of gesture, unusual indeed at her age, which proved she had carefully been trained.

"Was it your mama who taught you that piece?" I asked.

"Yes, and she just used to say it in this way: '*Qu'avez vous donc? Lui dit un de ces rats; parlez!*' She made me lift my hand—so—to remind me to raise my voice at the question. Now shall I dance for you?"

"No, that will do." I laughed at her readiness to exhibit. "But after your mama went to the Holy Virgin, as you say, with whom did you live then?"

"With Madame Frederic and her husband. She took care of me, but she is nothing related to me. I think she is poor, for she had not so fine a house as Mama. I was not long there. Mr. Rochester asked me if I would like to go and live with him in England, and I said yes, for I knew Mr. Rochester before I knew Madame Frederic. He was always kind to me and gave me pretty dresses and toys. But you see he has not kept his word, for he has brought me to England, and now he is gone back again himself, and I never see him."

I passed this information on to Mrs. Fairfax, who simply nodded. She offered no illumination into Adele's relationship to Mr. Rochester, and I suspected she was not quite certain of it herself. I became more curious about my absent master.

CHAPTER 14

AFTER BREAKFAST, ADELE AND I withdrew to the library, which room, it appears, Mr. Rochester had directed should be used as the schoolroom. Most of the books were locked up behind glass doors, but one bookcase left open contained everything that could be needed in the way of elementary works, and several volumes of light literature, poetry, biography, travels, and a few romances. I suppose he had considered that these were all the governess would require for her private perusal, and indeed they contented me amply for the present. Compared with the scanty pickings I had now and then been able to glean at Lowood, they seemed to offer an abundance of entertainment and information. This room, too, had a cabinet piano, quite new and of superior tone, an easel for painting and a pair of globes.

I found my pupil sufficiently docile, though disinclined to apply. She had not been used to regular occupation of any kind. I felt it would be injudicious to confine her too much at first. I had talked to her a great deal and got her to learn a little, but when the morning advanced to noon I allowed her to return to her nurse. I then proposed to occupy myself until dinnertime in drawing some little sketches for her use.

"Your morning school hours are over now, I suppose," Mrs. Fairfax said, stopping me on my way to get my pencils and portfolio.

Through two open folding doors, I entered the room she was dusting. The large, stately apartment had purple chairs and curtains, a Turkey carpet, walnut-paneled walls, one vast window rich in slanted glass, and a lofty ceiling, nobly molded.

"What a beautiful room!" I exclaimed. I had never seen anything like it, so exotic and fine.

"Yes, this is the dining room. I have just opened the window to let in a little air and sunshine, for everything gets so damp in apartments that are seldom inhabited. The drawing room yonder feels like a vault."

She pointed to a wide arch corresponding to the window, a connecting room. I crossed over and looked at it. The pretty drawing room had white carpets, a ceiling of snowy moldings of white grapes and vine leaves, beneath which glowed in rich contrast crimson couches and ottomans.

"In what order you keep these rooms, Mrs. Fairfax!" I said, impressed with her housekeeping. "No dust, no canvas coverings. Except that the air feels chilly, one would think they were inhabited daily."

"Why, Miss Slayre, though Mr. Rochester's visits here are rare, they are always sudden and unexpected. It puts him out to find everything swathed up, and to have the house in an uproar on his arrival. Generally, I think it best to keep the rooms in readiness."

"Is Mr. Rochester an exacting, fastidious sort of man?"

"Not particularly so; but he has a gentleman's tastes and habits, and he expects to have things managed in conformity to them."

"Do you like him? Is he generally liked?" I didn't want to run into a new version of Mr. Bokorhurst any more than I wanted to belong to another family of vampyres.

"Oh, yes, the family has always been respected here. Almost all the land in this neighbourhood, as far as you can see, has belonged to the Rochesters time out of mind."

"Well, but, leaving his land out of the question, do you like him? Is he liked for himself?"

"I have no cause to do otherwise than like him. I believe he is considered a just and liberal landlord by his tenants, but he has never lived much amongst them."

"But has he no peculiarities?" Drinking blood? Digging up corpses? Perhaps losing his fingers in the soup? "What, in short, is his character?"

"Unimpeachable, I suppose." She didn't answer readily. Perhaps something was there, something to give her pause? "He is rather peculiar, perhaps. He has travelled a great deal and seen a great deal of the world, I should think. I daresay he is clever, but I've never had much conversation with him."

"In what way is he peculiar?" I hoped *peculiar* had a different meaning to Mrs. Fairfax than it did to me. I had known something of peculiar, indeed, but my experience was limited. There could be all kinds of peculiar I hadn't even yet imagined.

"I don't know. It is not easy to describe—nothing striking, but you feel it when he speaks to you. You cannot be always sure whether he is in jest or earnest, whether he is pleased or the contrary. You don't thoroughly understand him, in short—at least, I don't. But it is of no consequence. He is a very good master."

A very good master with an unreadable disposition. There was nothing unnatural in that, as far as I could tell. This was all the account I got from Mrs. Fairfax of her employer and mine.

When we left the dining room, she proposed to show me over the rest of the house. I followed her upstairs and downstairs, admiring as I went, for all was well arranged and handsome. The large front chambers I thought especially grand, and some of the third-story rooms, though dark and low, were interesting from their air of antiquity. The furniture once appropriated to the lower apartments had from time to time been removed here, as fashions changed, and the imperfect light entering by their narrow casements showed bedsteads of a hundred years old.

Chests with strange carvings of palms and cherubs' heads, rows of venerable chairs, stools still more antiquated, on whose cushioned tops were yet apparent traces of half-effaced embroideries, wrought by fingers that for two generations had been coffin dust. All these relics gave to the third story of Thornfield Hall the aspect of a home of the past, a shrine of memory. I liked the hush, the gloom, the quaintness of these retreats, in the day, but I by no means coveted a night's repose on one of those wide and heavy beds.

"Do the servants sleep in these rooms?" I asked.

"No, they occupy a range of smaller apartments to the back. No one ever sleeps here. One would almost say that, if there were a ghost at Thornfield Hall, this would be its haunt."

"Ah, do you believe in ghosts, then?" I smiled. Perhaps she knew something of the supernatural after all.

"None that I ever heard of," returned Mrs. Fairfax, smiling back.

"Nor any traditions of one? No legends or ghost stories?"

"I believe not. And yet it is said the Rochesters have been rather a violent than a quiet race in their time. Perhaps, though, that is the reason they rest tranquilly in their graves now. On to the leads," she said. "Will you come and see the view from thence?"

I followed up a narrow staircase to the attics, thence by a ladder and through a trapdoor to the roof of the hall. I was now on a level with the crow colony and could see into their nests. Leaning over the battlements and looking far down, I surveyed the grounds laid out like a map: the lawn closely girdling the grey base of the mansion; the field, wide as a park, dotted with its ancient timber; the wood, dark and divided by a path visibly overgrown; the church at the gates, the road, the tranquil hills; the horizon bounded by an azure sky. No feature in the scene was extraordinary, but all was pleasing.

When I turned from it and passed back to the trapdoor, I could scarcely see my way down the ladder. The attic seemed black as a vault compared with that sunlit scene of grove, pasture, and green hill over which I had been gazing with delight.

Mrs. Fairfax stayed behind a moment to fasten the trapdoor. I, by drift of groping, found the outlet from the attic and descended the narrow garret staircase. I lingered in the long passage to which this led, separating the front and back rooms of the third story. It was narrow, low, and dim, with only one little window at the far end, and looking, with its two rows of small black doors all shut, like a corridor in some Bluebeard's castle.

While I paced softly on, the last sound I expected to hear in so still a region, a laugh, struck my ear. It was a curious laugh: distinct, formal, without mirth. I stopped. The sound ceased, only for an instant. It began again, louder, for at first, though distinct, it was low. It erupted in a clamorous peal that seemed to wake an echo in every lonely chamber, though it originated but in one, and I could have pointed out the door whence the accents issued.

"Mrs. Fairfax!" I called, for I now heard her descending the garret stairs. "Did you hear that loud laugh? Who is it?"

"Some of the servants, very likely. You haven't met them all, you know. Perhaps Grace Poole."

"Did you hear it?"

"Yes, plainly. I often hear her. She sews in one of these rooms. Sometimes Leah is with her. They are frequently noisy together."

The laugh was repeated in its low, syllabic tone and terminated in an odd murmur. This Grace Poole must be quite a character indeed. She sounded otherworldly. I was on my guard.

"Grace!" exclaimed Mrs. Fairfax. The door nearest me opened, and a servant came out, a woman of between thirty and forty. She was solid, red-haired, with a hard, plain face. Any apparition less romantic or less ghostly could scarcely be conceived. I was glad to see she existed in tangible form, but what form? Human or something else, I couldn't tell. "Too much noise, Grace. Remember directions."

Grace curtsied silently and went in. She was polite enough, I supposed. And common. If she were a vampyre, she would have had no reason not to eat the whole house in their sleep by now. She didn't have the grey pallor or slight form of a zombie. What else could she be? A question I would rather leave untested for the time.

"She is a person we have to sew and assist Leah in her housemaid's work," continued the widow, "not altogether unobjectionable in some points, but she does well enough. By the by, how have you got on with your new pupil this morning?"

The conversation, thus turned on Adele, continued until we reached the light and cheerful region below. Adele came running to meet us in the hall.

"Mesdames, vous êtes servies!" she said. *"J'ai bien faim, moi!"*

We found dinner ready and waiting for us in Mrs. Fairfax's room.

CHAPTER 15

THE PROMISE OF A smooth career, which my first calm introduction to Thornfield Hall seemed to pledge, held out as I got to know my situation and my housemates better. Mrs. Fairfax was what she appeared, a placid-tempered, kind-natured woman, of competent education and average intelligence. My pupil was a lively child who had been spoiled and indulged, perhaps shown off on some occasions and left to her own devices on others.

Now and then, while Adele played with her nurse, and Mrs. Fairfax made jellies in the storeroom, I walked the grounds and looked out afar over sequestered fields and I longed for a power of vision that might overpass my earthly limits. I thought of busy towns that I had heard of but never seen, and then I desired more practical experience than I possessed, more of intercourse with my kind, of acquaintance with variety of characters, than was here within my reach. I valued what was good in Mrs. Fairfax, and what was good in Adele, but I believed in the existence of other and more vivid kinds of goodness, and what I believed in I wished to behold.

Some might call me discontented. The restlessness was in my nature. At those times, my sole relief was to walk along the corridor of the third story, backwards and forwards, safe in the silence and solitude of the spot, and allow my mind's eye to dwell on whatever bright visions rose before it.

During my times in the attic corridor, alone with my thoughts, I frequently heard Grace Poole's laugh, the same peal, the same low, slow *ha! ha!* that when first heard had thrilled me. I sensed more to Grace Poole than I had learned on first impression. Perhaps that drew me to the dark spaces of the attic, a sense that some unnatural spirit roamed here, too. I'd ruled out vampyre and zombie, but I didn't know what else there could be. Bessie had told tales of demons, trolls, and ogres. Grace might yet be one of those. I only knew that my Slayre instinct warned me something was not right at Thornfield, and I'd learned to trust that instinct in the past.

I listened to Grace while I paced, her eccentric murmurs even more strange than her laugh. Sometimes I saw her. She would come out of her room with a basin or a plate or a tray in her hand, go down to the kitchen, and shortly return, generally (oh, romantic reader, forgive me for telling the plain truth!) bearing a pot of porter. I made some attempts to draw her into conversation, but she seemed a person of few words.

The other members of the household—John and his wife; Leah, the housemaid; and Sophie, the French nurse—were decent people, but in no respect remarkable. Possibly I'd built some imaginary excitement around Grace Poole just to keep me from boredom.

October, November, December, passed away. One afternoon in January, Mrs. Fairfax had begged a holiday for Adele because she had a cold, and I allowed her a rest from her studies. It was a fine, calm day, though very cold. Mrs. Fairfax had just written a letter that needed posting, so I put on my bonnet and cloak and volunteered to carry it to Hay. The distance, two miles, would be a pleasant winter-afternoon walk. Having seen Adele comfortably seated by Mrs. Fairfax's parlour fireside, and given her a wax doll to play with and a storybook for change of amusement, I kissed her and set out.

The ground was hard, the air still, the road lonely. I walked fast until I got warm, then I walked slowly to look for birds and other wildlife that might be out on the cool afternoon. The church bell tolled three as I passed under the belfry. I was a mile from Thornfield, in an empty lane. Far and wide, on each side, there were only fields, where no cattle now browsed.

This lane inclined uphill all the way to Hay; having reached the middle, I sat down on a stile, which led into a field. Gathering my mantle about me, and sheltering my hands in my muff, I did not feel the full force of the cold, though a sheet of ice covering the causeway where a brook had overflowed proved the temperature was below freezing. From my seat, I could look down on Thornfield. The grey and battlemented hall was the principal object in the vale below me. I wondered if Grace Poole even now walked the leads, and if she could turn into a winged dragon or some other fantastical creature and fly around the house at night. Might I catch a glimpse of her, there, in silhouette hovering over the trees? No, it was only a crow.

I lingered longer than I should, until the sun went down amongst the trees and sank crimson and clear behind them. On the hilltop above me sat the rising moon, nearly full, pale yet as a cloud, but brightening momentarily. I looked towards Hay, half lost in trees and yet a mile distant.

A rude noise broke the evening's peace, a positive tramp, tramp, a metallic clatter. The din was on the causeway. A horse was coming. The windings of the lane yet hid it, but it approached. I was about to get up and start on my way, but I sat still to let the rider pass. I was young, but I had already seen much to inspire superstition, and all sorts of fancies bright and dark tenanted my mind. The memories of nursery stories were there amongst other rubbish, and I knew too well that sometimes stories of fantastical monsters turned out to be quite real.

Perhaps because I was thinking of my childhood and monsters, a queer feeling coiled in my belly, a sort of nervousness the likes of which I hadn't known in years, since leaving Gateshead. Apprehensive, I shot to my feet and I looked from left to right. Indeed, a group of travellers were making their way on foot from the very same direction as the horse, but only just coming into my line of vision. They must have been walking some way ahead of the horse, for I heard the clapping of hooves in the near distance yet as the voices of the group came into earshot. Instinct warned me to duck into a row of bushes so as not to be seen.

"He's coming on fast, Jim. What's the plan?" one man said to another. They were right in front of me now. Through the branches I could make out three sets of feet. If they sniffed the air, they might pick up my scent. Fortunately, the chill of the night probably helped dull their senses, for I had no doubt what they were: vampyres. That queer little feeling might have been an appropriate warning after all.

"We could do the poor injured-traveller bit," one, perhaps Jim, suggested. "You could sit on the stile just there and feign an injury. When he stops, the two of us can jump out and accost him. Voy-a-la, dinner for three."

"It's voilà, you louse. From the French, literally to 'see there.' *Vwa-la*. Very easy. Repeat after me."

I supposed it was Jim who broke out in a guffaw. "Well, la-ti-da, Perfesser. Are we here for a grammar lesson, or to get us some grub?"

"Right, you two," the other one said. "He's coming. He's big. And I'm hungry. We could divvy his horse up, too. What the hell. We don't need a plan. Look at that ice patch, there. He hits that ice and he's down. And there we are, on him and eating in no time flat. He'll be so surprised that he won't even stand a chance to fight us off."

My blood burned in my veins. One innocent traveller, prey to three waiting vampyres? It was wrong. I thought of John Reed. It was just his sort of low trick. None of the vampyres were John Reed, but I pictured him in my mind. I imagined what I would, even after all these years, like to do to him. I had two stakes up my sleeves. I wished I had brought my daggers, but stakes were more effective against vampyres in any event.

"Dibs on the dog," the one that was certainly Jim said. "It's been so long since I've had a good dog."

"It was yesterday, idiot. That pug you sucked down at the pub?"

"That was just a wee thing, barely a snack. I dream of a whole-dog meal."

"You can have the dog. I lived off dog through October. I'm so sick of dog I would be happy to never taste another in my life. He's close now. Hide. Behind the bushes there. We'll get him when he slips."

I breathed a sigh of relief when two of them chose the bushes on the opposite side of the road, but one of them was dangerously close to me. Though it was too dark in the brush covering to see me with any clarity, he might scrape against me if he moved so much as an inch.

The horse approached, near but not yet in sight when, in addition to the tramp, tramp, I heard a rush under the hedge, getting closer. I looked and startled when my eyes made out the form of a tremendous beast, the targeted dog, whose black-and-white colour made him a distinct object against the trees. It passed me, and the vampyres, without noticing, thank goodness. The horse followed—a tall steed, and on its back, a rider. An ordinary traveller taking the shortcut to Millcote, he stood not a chance against three vampyres—without warning or assistance.

Before he passed, I scrambled out of the bushes, stakes in hand at the ready, to wave him down before he hit the sheet of ice glazing the causeway. Unfortunately, he took absolutely no notice of me. I closed my eyes as if I could shut out the sliding sound and an exclamation of "What the deuce now?"

Man and horse were down. The dog came bounding back to see his master in a predicament and, hearing the horse groan, began to bark until the evening hills echoed the sound, which was as booming loud as the dog's great size would allow. He snuffed around the prostrate horse and man, then he ran up to me as if he'd known I was there all along.

Jim was first to come out of the bushes straight after me. As evidence of his love of dogs, or lack of sense, he went straight for the dog to slake his thirst instead of accosting me. The rider was still down, as if trying to gather his bearings, when Jim grabbed the dog around the neck and bit into him. The dog gave a yelp, but never tried to fight, and I dodged straight at them, ably staking the feeding Jim straight through the back into the heart—as I'd imagined I could do to John Reed all those years ago when I played with my stakes and a drawing of John in the dirt.

My aim must have been dead-on, for Jim arched his back, looked as if he would turn and come after me, and dissolved into a heap of dust straightaway! Where there had been a vampyre, there were only some dusty old clothes. I drew closer to look. Dust. Curious, that! I surged with an immediate feeling of satisfaction and triumph.

Vampyres were going to be much easier to dispose of than zombies; much less messy anyway. I brushed my hands and retrieved the stake. Perhaps I had a knack for this sort of thing after all. I reached out to pet the poor dog. His injury didn't seem to be bad, just a small puncture between his shoulder blades. He let me pat his head for but an instant before he sniffed at the pile and trotted off dutifully to check on his master.

Where were the other two? Had they gone stiff with fright at the sight of such capable vampyre slaying from such an otherwise unassuming young lady? At no appearance from them, I followed the dog to check on the traveller, by this time struggling himself free of his steed. His efforts were so vigorous, I thought, gratefully, that he could not be very hurt.

"Are you injured, sir?" I asked.

He was swearing under his breath, words I ought perhaps not to have known, but some of my Lowood inmates had been rough girls from working families.

"Can I do anything?" I asked.

"You must stand aside," he answered as he rose, first to his knees, then to his feet. I didn't move very much away, for he yet looked unsteady on his feet. Indeed, his footing was on the ice and he began to slide. I reached out. He was a large man, quite tall and solid for his size. I couldn't support him, but I must have lent him enough of something to grab on to until his feet found purchase, for he righted himself without taking us both to the ground.

Noise distracted us, a heaving, stamping, and clattering, accompanied by barking and baying, as his horse scrambled on the ice, with the dog running and making a to-do all around him. The stranger urged me out of the way. I stood back and watched, but did not remove myself from the scene. Still no sign of the vampyres, but I sensed them lying in wait. The horse managed to rise and the dog was silenced with a "Down, Pilot!"

The traveller stooped and felt his foot and leg, as if trying whether they were sound. Apparently something ailed them, for he halted to the stile whence I had just risen and sat down. Sure enough, the two vampyres bolted from their hiding places, one gripping me by the waist, the other fighting off the dog, who was no willing victim now that he was aware of the danger. Pilot charged full force at his assailant.

"Don't move and you might live," the man holding me tightly against him whispered in my ear. His breath, surely fetid, heated my neck, but happily I could not smell him through the chill night air.

Live? For another few minutes, perhaps, if I gave in as easily as all that. I elbowed him in the gut, sharp and without restraint, and he recoiled. Before he could recover, I spun around and performed a jumping kick move that Miss Temple had demonstrated with such grace. My skirts flew out awkwardly. I lacked her elegance, but the kick was effective just the same, knocking him to the ground, dazed. I wasted no time in raising my stake and driving it home through his chest. He burst into a fine dust that wafted like smoke in the night breeze.

"If you are hurt and want help, sir, I can fetch someone either from Thornfield Hall or from Hay," I said absently to the lone traveller while looking after what might have become of his dog.

"Thank you. I shall recover. I have no broken bones, I think." He now broke off and groaned as he no doubt tried to move his leg. "Only a sprain."

I spied his dog then, tearing flesh in a zombielike frenzy from the vampyre pinned under him. Of course, it didn't kill the vampyre, but it must have occasioned some pain. The creature struggled to protect his face with his hands. It made it most convenient to reach around to the side of the large, furry beast atop him and jab him right through the rib cage. Strangely, I gave him a solid stab, but he didn't burst. With the vampyre thrashing about to avoid the jaws of the attacking dog, I must have missed. I tried again. Poof! Success. The dog shook the bit of cloth left in his teeth, then groaned as if wondering what had become of his opponent. Still, being a dog, he simply shook his head and trotted quite happily away, back to his master's side.

I crossed the road back to the traveller as well. I hazarded to get close to see what was wrong with his leg, which he still examined with such concentration as to be apparently oblivious of all that had gone on around him. He stood up and tried his foot, but the result extorted an involuntary "Ugh!"

The moon was waxing bright, I could see him plainly. His figure was enveloped in a riding cloak, fur-collared and steel-clasped. Its details were not apparent, but I traced the general points of some height and considerable breadth of chest. He had dark, wild hair framing a tanned face with stern features and a heavy brow. His eyes and gathered eyebrows looked ireful and thwarted. He was past youth but had not reached middle age. He might perhaps be thirty. Though I had no fear of vampyres, I had expected to have some uneasiness around men. Yet I felt no fear of him, and but little shyness. Had he been handsome in the more classic sense, a heroic-looking golden god of a young gentleman, I should not have dared to stand thus questioning him against his will, and offering my services unasked. I had hardly ever seen a handsome youth and had never in my life spoken to one.

If even this stranger had smiled and been good-humoured to me when I addressed him, had he thanked me for my heroic actions in saving his life, I should have gone on my way and not felt any vocation to renew inquiries. But the frown, the roughness of the traveller, and his ignorance to the general chaos in his midst intrigued me. He set me strangely at ease while making me want to stay, even to annoy him with my offer to help. I retained my station when he waved to me to go.

"I cannot think of leaving you, sir, at so late an hour, in this solitary lane, until I see you are fit to mount your horse." Besides, more vampyres might be on the way. I hadn't even imagined them out and about in the world and not safely confined at Gateshead, but here they were. I supposed there might be a great many of them waiting to take advantage of a steady diet of poor, working folk in an industrial town such as Millcote, or, for a treat, perhaps the sweet farmers from a village such as Hay.

He looked at me. "A young woman like you ought to be at home yourself. If you have a home in this neighbourhood. Where do you come from?"

"From just below. I am not at all afraid of being out late when it is moonlit. I will run over to Hay for you with pleasure, if you wish it. Indeed, I am going there to post a letter." Better I, a studied young fighter of evil things, took the journey than one so oblivious of the dangers of the world as he.

"You live just below—do you mean at that house with the battlements?" He pointed to Thornfield Hall, on which the moon cast a hoary gleam, bringing it out, distinct and pale, from the woods, which by contrast with the western sky now seemed one mass of shadow.

"Yes, sir."

"Whose house is it?"

"Mr. Rochester's."

"Do you know Mr. Rochester?"

"No." I laughed a little for it sounded odd to live in the man's house and not know him. "I have never seen him."

"He is not resident, then?"

"No. Not for many months."

"Can you tell me where he is?"

"I cannot."

"You are not a servant at the hall, of course. You are—" He stopped, ran his eye over my dress, which, as usual, was quite simple: a black merino cloak, a black beaver bonnet; neither of them half fine enough for a lady's maid. He seemed puzzled to decide what I was. I helped him.

"I am the governess."

"Ah, the governess!" He rubbed his growth of beard, a dark stubble along his square jaw. "Deuce take me if I had not forgotten! The governess!"

My raiment again underwent scrutiny. In two minutes he rose from the stile. His face expressed pain when he tried to move.

"I cannot commission you to fetch help," he said, "but you may help me a little yourself, if you will be so kind."

"Yes, sir."

"Try to get hold of my horse's bridle and lead him to me. You are not afraid?"

"Of you, not at all. But of the horse? I have no experience. Let us see." I went up to the tall steed. I endeavoured to catch the bridle, but the horse was spirited and would not let me come near its head. I jumped when it snorted near me, and I laughed. I couldn't help it. To be afraid of a horse? How silly. I sobered and tried again, though in vain. I, who had killed vampyres, ended zombies, and conquered a bokor, was mortally afraid of a horse's trampling hooves. The traveller waited and watched for some time, and at last he laughed, too.

"I see," he said. "You might bring me to the horse instead. I must beg of you to come here."

I did.

"Excuse me," he continued. "Necessity compels me to make you useful." He laid a heavy hand on my shoulder and, leaning on me with some stress, limped to his horse. Having once caught the bridle, he mastered it directly and sprang to his saddle, grimacing as he made the effort, for it must have wrenched his sprain.

"Now," he said, releasing his underlip from a hard bite, "just hand me my whip. It lies there under the hedge."

I sought and found it, as well as the muff I had abandoned earlier as I hid along with it.

"Thank you. Make haste with the letter to Hay and return as fast as you can."

A touch of a spurred heel made his horse first start and rear, then bound away. The dog rushed in his traces. All three vanished.

"Like heath that, in the wilderness, the wild wind whirls away," I said into the night air. I took up my muff and walked on.

My help had been needed and, eventually, willingly claimed. I had given it. I was pleased to have done something. At least, I told myself, this was the reason for the fire in my veins, the tingle that ran up and down my spine. The new face, too, was like a new picture introduced to the gallery of memory. Rough-hewn and masculine, it stood out from all the others. The dark whiskers, the bold line of his jaw, here was a man who was used to being in command. No doubt it was injury that rendered him oblivious. The pain must have been great. I imagined him capable of slaying scores of vampyres if left to his own devices, and in good health without injury. The idea of it was still before me in mind when I entered Hay and slipped the letter into the post office. I saw it as I walked fast downhill all the way home.

When I came to the stile, I stopped a minute, looked around, and listened, with an idea that a horse's hooves might ring on the causeway, and that a rider in a cloak, and a Newfoundland dog, might again show up. I saw only the hedge and a pollard willow before me, rising up still and straight to meet the moonbeams. I heard only the faintest waft of wind roaming fitful amongst the trees around Thornfield, a mile distant, and when I glanced down in the direction of the murmur, my eye caught a light kindling in a window. It reminded me that I was late, and I hurried on.

I did not like reentering Thornfield. To pass its threshold was to return to stagnation. To cross the silent hall, to ascend the darksome staircase, was to quell the faint excitement wakened by my walk. I lingered at the gates, then on the lawn. I paced on the pavement. The shutters of the glass door were closed. I could not see into the house, and both my eyes and spirit seemed drawn from it to the sky overhead, a black sea absolved from taint of cloud. The moon ascended in solemn march. Little things recall us to earth; the clock struck in the hall. That sufficed. I turned from moon and stars and headed for the door, but something on the third story caught my notice. Was it Grace Poole sitting in the window, also lost in contemplation of the moon? It probably was, strange woman. Who knew what a waxing moon meant to her? I opened a side door and went in.

The high-hung bronze lamp suffused a warm glow on the staircase that shone into the hall. Yet a light seemed to come from another direction. I followed the glow to see the great dining-room doors stood open and a genial fire burned in the grate, glancing on marble hearth and brass fire irons, and revealing purple draperies and polished furniture in the most pleasant radiance. It revealed, too, a group near the mantelpiece. I had scarcely caught it, and scarcely become aware of a cheerful mingling of voices, amongst which I seemed to distinguish the tones of Adele, when the door closed.

I hastened to Mrs. Fairfax's room. There was a fire there, too, but no candle, and no Mrs. Fairfax. Instead, all alone, sitting upright on the rug, and gazing with gravity at the blaze, I beheld a black-and-white, long-haired dog.

"Pilot?" I said, remembering its name. He got up, came over, and started sniffing my skirts. I caressed him, checking the bite marks on his neck, and he wagged his great tail. I rang the bell, for I wanted a candle.

Leah entered.

"What dog is this?"

"He came with master."

"With whom?"

"With master—Mr. Rochester—he is just arrived."

My heart stopped a second, then started racing. "Indeed! And is Mrs. Fairfax with him?"

"Yes, and Miss Adele. They are in the dining room, and John has gone for the surgeon. Master has had an accident. His horse fell and his ankle is sprained."

"In Hay Lane?"

"Yes, coming downhill. It slipped on some ice."

"Ah! Bring me a candle, will you, Leah?"

Leah brought it. She entered, followed by Mrs. Fairfax, who repeated the news, adding that Mr. Carter, the surgeon, had come, and was now with Mr. Rochester. Then she hurried out to give orders about tea, and I went upstairs to take off my things.

"Mr. Rochester." I repeated the name aloud as I changed in my room. All I could see was that rugged, masculine face. Mr. Rochester, indeed.

CHAPTER 16

Mr. Rochester, it seemed, by the surgeon's orders, went to bed early that night and stayed in bed late the next day. When he did come down, it was to attend to business. His agent and some of his tenants had arrived and were waiting to speak with him.

Adele and I had to vacate the library. While Mr. Rochester remained in residence, it would be in daily use as a reception room for callers. A fire was lit in an apartment upstairs, and there I carried our books and arranged our future schoolroom. I discerned over the morning that Thornfield Hall was a changed place. No longer silent as a church, it echoed every hour or two to a knock at the door, or a clang of the bell. Steps, too, often traversed the hall, and new voices spoke in different keys below. A rill from the outer world was flowing through it, and I loved it. Though, for my part, I would have liked it even better had I got to play a more active role. It seemed vampyres seldom came so close to Thornfield.

Adele was not easy to teach that day. She kept running to the door and looking over the banister to see if she could get a glimpse of Mr. Rochester. I looked for him, too, on the pretext of running after her. She wanted to know what presents he had brought her. Apparently, on the night before, he had intimated that when his luggage came from Millcote, amongst it would be a little box in whose contents she had an interest.

Adele prattled on in French about her present and about Mr.

Rochester. She insisted he must have brought me a present as well, and why should we wait? We should go down to the library and insist upon them. I would not indulge her. Probably vexed with me over my refusal to interrupt Mr. Rochester's business, she made up a little story about how he'd asked about me last night. What was my name? Was I a small, pale little one with eyes like the stars? Adele could be quite inventive when she was eager to have her way.

We remained in our new schoolroom, quite out of the way, and then we dined as usual in Mrs. Fairfax's parlour. It was a wild and snowy afternoon, and we returned to spend it in the schoolroom until dark. Only then did I allow Adele to put away her books and work and to go downstairs, for it was finally silent and Mr. Rochester was likely at liberty at such an hour.

Mrs. Fairfax came in. "Mr. Rochester would be glad if you and your pupil would take tea with him in the drawing room this evening."

"When is his tea time?" I inquired.

"Oh, at six o'clock. He keeps early hours in the country. You had better change your frock now. I will go with you and fasten it. Here is a candle."

"Is it necessary to change my frock?" We had never stood on such ceremony.

"Yes, you had better. I always dress for the evening when Mr. Rochester is here."

I repaired to my room and, with Mrs. Fairfax's aid, replaced my black stuff dress with one of black silk, the best and the only additional one I had, except one of light grey, which, in my Lowood notions of the toilette, I thought too fine to be worn, except on first-rate occasions.

"You want a brooch," said Mrs. Fairfax.

I had a single little pearl ornament, which Miss Temple had given me as a parting keepsake along with the Egyptian daggers. I put it on, then we went downstairs. Unused as I was to strangers, it was rather a trial to appear thus formally summoned in Mr. Rochester's presence. I tripped going down the stairs and couldn't keep my hands from fluttering nervously without great effort. How unlike me to dissolve into nerves! He was just a man. I reminded myself of this, but I let Mrs. Fairfax precede me into the dining room and kept in her shade as we crossed the apartment to the drawing room.

Two wax candles stood lit on the table, and two on the mantelpiece, three more candles than we usually kept lit in Mrs. Fairfax's parlour. Basking in the light and the heat of a superb fire lay Pilot. Adele knelt near him. Half-reclined on a couch, Mr. Rochester had his foot out, supported by a cushion. I knew my traveller with his dark eyebrows, square forehead, and black hair. I recognised his decisive nose, his grim mouth, chin, and jaw. His build, now divested of cloak, I perceived was as solid as I supposed.

Mr. Rochester must have been aware of the entrance of Mrs. Fairfax and me, but he appeared not to be in the mood to notice us.

"Here is Miss Slayre, sir," said Mrs. Fairfax in her quiet way.

He bowed, still not taking his eyes from the group of the dog and child.

"Let Miss Slayre be seated," he said with something in the forced stiff bow, in the impatient yet formal tone.

I sat down quite happily. Had he shown polite interest, he would probably have confused me, but harsh caprice laid me under no obligation. On the contrary, he gave me the advantage of returning his indifference, or worse. Besides, I grew all the more interested to see how he would go on.

He went on as a statue would; that is, he neither spoke nor moved. Perhaps he wasn't oblivious, but was steady and silent by nature. Mrs. Fairfax seemed to think it necessary that someone should be amiable, and she began to talk, kindly, as usual. She spoke of the snow and the roads, of the business visitors he'd had to endure all day, and on the likely frustration of being laid up with a sprained ankle.

"Madam, I should like some tea" was the only thing he said in return. When the tray came, she arranged the cups, spoons, and serving dishes with assiduous celerity. Adele and I went to the table, but the master did not leave his couch.

"Will you hand Mr. Rochester's cup?" Mrs. Fairfax asked me.

I did as requested.

As he took the cup from my hand, Adele, thinking the moment propitious for making a request in my favour, cried out. *"N'est-ce pas, monsieur, qu'il y a un cadeau pour Mademoiselle Slayre dans votre petit coffre?"*

"Who talks of *cadeaux*?" he said gruffly. "Did you expect a present, Miss Slayre? Are you fond of presents?" He searched my face with eyes that seemed dark, irate, and piercing.

I did not fluster. If his intent was to frighten me, he might be in for a surprise. "I hardly know, sir. I have little experience of them. They are generally thought pleasant things."

"Generally thought?" His eyes did not change. "But what do *you* think?"

"I should be obliged to take time, sir, before I could give you an answer worthy of your acceptance." Now I delivered a short little bow as disingenuous as his had been earlier. "A present has many faces to it, has it not? One should consider all before pronouncing an opinion as to its nature."

"Miss Slayre, you are not so unsophisticated as Adele. She demands a *cadeau*, clamorously, the moment she sees me. You beat about the bush."

"Because I have less confidence than Adele has. She says you have always been in the habit of giving her playthings. But if I had to make out a case, I should be puzzled, since I am a stranger and have done nothing to entitle me to an acknowledgment."

"Oh, don't fall back on overmodesty! I have examined Adele and find you have taken great pains with her. She is not bright. She has no talents. Yet in a short time she has made much improvement."

"Sir, you have now given me my *cadeau*. I am obliged to you."

I gave him a genuine nod. "It is the mead teachers most covet, praise of their pupils' progress."

"Humph!" said Mr. Rochester, then he took his tea in silence.

"Come to the fire," said the master when the tray was taken away, and Mrs. Fairfax had settled into a corner with her knitting. Adele and I obeyed. She wanted to take a seat on my knee, but she was ordered to amuse herself with Pilot.

"You have been resident in my house three months?"

"Yes, sir."

"And you came from . . . ? "

"From Lowood school."

"Ah! I know it. A charitable concern. How long were you there?"

"Eight years."

"Eight years! You must be tenacious of life. I should think half the time in such a place would kill me. Indeed, it killed many, if I remember the stories." I could feel his gaze on me but I refused to meet it, preferring to look down at the table.

"That was in my first year." I smiled, recalling the part I had played in it and keeping it my own treasured secret. "It was much improved afterwards."

"Still, to have lived there so long! No wonder you have rather the look of another world. I marvelled where you had got that sort of face, so serious yet so bright-eyed all at once. When you came on me in Hay Lane last night, I thought unaccountably of fairy tales and had half a mind to demand whether you had bewitched my horse. I am not sure yet. Who are your parents?"

I could feel him wishing I would look up, and still I refused. "I have none."

"Nor ever had, I suppose? Do you remember them?"

"No."

"I thought not. And so you were waiting for your people when you sat on that stile?"

"For whom, sir?"

"For the fairy folk. It was a proper moonlight evening for them. Did I break through one of your rings that you spread that damned ice on the causeway?"

I shook my head. "The fairies all forsook England a hundred years ago," said I, speaking as seriously as he had done. "And not even in Hay Lane, or the fields about it, could you find a trace of them."

Mrs. Fairfax had dropped her knitting and, with raised eyebrows, seemed wondering what sort of talk this was.

"Well," resumed Mr. Rochester, "if you disown parents, you must have some sort of kinsfolk: uncles and aunts?"

"No; none." None to acknowledge.

"And your home?"

"I have none."

"Where do your brothers and sisters live?"

"I have no brothers or sisters."

"Who recommended you to come here?"

"I advertised, and Mrs. Fairfax answered my advertisement."

"Yes," said the good lady, who now knew what ground we were upon, "and I am daily thankful for the choice Providence led me to make. Miss Slayre has been an invaluable companion to me, and a kind and careful teacher to Adele."

"Don't trouble yourself to give her a character," returned Mr. Rochester. "I shall judge for myself. She began by felling my horse."

"Sir?" said Mrs. Fairfax.

"I have to thank her for this sprain."

The widow looked bewildered.

I sat still, quite untroubled by his accusations. Better he lived with a sprain than the fate that might have befallen him had I not been present.

"Miss Slayre, have you ever lived in a town?"

"No, sir."

"Have you seen much society?"

"None but the pupils and teachers of Lowood, and now the inmates of Thornfield."

"Inmates indeed." He laughed. "Have you read much?"

"Only such books as came in my way, and they have not been numerous or very learned."

"No doubt you've lived the life of a nun. What age were you when you went to school?"

"About ten."

"And you stayed there eight years. You are now, then, eighteen. And what did you learn at Lowood? Can you play?"

"A little."

"Of course. That is the established answer. Go into the library—I mean, if you please. You must excuse my tone of command. I am used to say, 'Do this,' and it is done. I cannot alter my customary habits for one new inmate. Go, then, into the library; take a candle with you, leave the door open. Sit down to the piano and play a tune."

I departed, obeying his directions. I hid my astonishment that he would even ask for me to excuse his commanding tone. And why should I? Was I not in his employ? But it touched me that he would ask for my consideration on it. I did as he asked. I played.

"Enough!" he called out in a few minutes. "You play *a little*, I see, like any other English schoolgirl. Perhaps rather better than some, but not well."

I closed the piano and returned.

"Adele showed me some sketches this morning, which she said were yours," Mr. Rochester said. "I don't know whether they were entirely of your doing. Probably a master aided you?"

"No, indeed!"

"Ah! That pricks pride. Well, fetch me your portfolio, if you can vouch for its contents being original, but don't pass your word unless you are certain."

"Then I will say nothing, and you shall judge for yourself, sir."

I brought the portfolio from the library.

"Approach the table," said he; and I wheeled it to his couch. He deliberately scrutinised each sketch and painting. Three he laid aside. The others, when he had examined them, he swept from him.

"Take them off to the other table, Mrs. Fairfax," said he, "and look at them with Adele. You"—glancing at me—"resume your seat and answer my questions. I perceive those pictures were done by one hand. Was that hand yours?"

"Yes."

"And when did you find time to do them? They have taken time and thought."

"I did them in the last two vacations I spent at Lowood."

"Where did you get your copies?"

"Out of my head."

"That head I see now on your shoulders?"

"The very same." I was not a zombie. I only had one, and it was not detachable.

He spread the pictures before him and again surveyed them alternately.

"Were you happy when you painted these pictures?"

"I was absorbed, sir, yes, and I was happy. To paint them, in short, was to enjoy one of the keenest pleasures I have ever known."

"That is not saying much. Your pleasures, by your own account, have been few. I daresay, though, you did exist in a kind of artist's dreamland while you blended and arranged these strange tints. Did you sit at them long each day?"

"From morning until noon, and from noon until night. It was vacation. I had little else to do."

"And you felt self-satisfied with the result of your ardent labours?"

"Far from it. I was tormented by the contrast between my idea and my handiwork. In each case, I had imagined something which I turned out to be quite powerless to realise."

"Not quite, I'm guessing. You have secured the shadow of your thought, but no more, probably. You had not enough of the artist's skill and science to give it full being: yet the drawings are, for a schoolgirl, peculiar. As to the thoughts, they are elfish. These eyes you must have seen in a dream. How could you make them look so clear, and yet not at all brilliant? And what meaning is that in their solemn depth? And who taught you to paint wind? There is a high gale in that sky, and on this hilltop. And this last one? Such a terrible sense of justice there. How could you know it? Put the drawings away!"

"Yes, sir."

"It is nine o'clock," he said, glancing at his watch before I could even put the drawings away. "What are you about, Miss Slayre, to let Adele sit up so long? Take her to bed."

Adele went to kiss him before quitting the room. He endured the caress, but he seemed to relish it little more than Pilot would have done, nor so much.

"I wish you all good night, now." He made a movement of the hand towards the door, in token that he was tired of our company and wished to dismiss us. Mrs. Fairfax folded up her knitting. I took my portfolio. We curtsied to him, received a frigid bow in return, and so withdrew.

"You said Mr. Rochester was not strikingly peculiar, Mrs. Fairfax," I observed when I rejoined her in her room, after putting Adele to bed.

"Well, is he?"

"I think so. He is very changeful and abrupt."

"True. No doubt he may appear so to a stranger, but I am so accustomed to his manner. And then, if he has peculiarities of temper, allowance should be made."

"Why?"

"Partly because it is his nature—and we can none of us help our nature. And partly because he has painful thoughts, no doubt, to harass him and make his spirits unequal."

"What about?"

"Family troubles, for one thing. He lost his elder brother a few years since."

"His elder brother?"

"Yes. The present Mr. Rochester has not been very long in possession of the property; only about nine years."

"Was he so very fond of his brother as to be still inconsolable for his loss?"

"Why, no—perhaps not. I believe there were some misunderstandings between them. Mr. Rowland Rochester was not quite just to Mr. Edward and perhaps he prejudiced his father against him. The old gentleman was fond of money and anxious to keep the family estate together, and yet he was anxious that Mr. Edward should have wealth, too, to keep up the consequence of the name. Old Mr. Rochester and Mr. Rowland combined to bring Mr. Edward into what he considered a painful position, for the sake of making his fortune. I never knew the precise nature of that position, but his spirit could not brook what he had to suffer in it. He is not very forgiving. He broke with his family, and now for many years he has led an unsettled kind of life. I don't think he has ever been resident at Thornfield for a fortnight together since the death of his brother without a will left him master of the estate. Indeed, no wonder he shuns the old place."

"Why should he shun it?"

"Perhaps he thinks it gloomy."

The answer was evasive. I should have liked something clearer, but Mrs. Fairfax either could not or would not give me more explicit information of the origin and nature of Mr. Rochester's trials. She averred they were a mystery to her, and that what she knew was chiefly from conjecture. It was evident, indeed, that she wished me to drop the subject, which I did accordingly.

I thought of him all night, that pained look in his eyes when he spoke of my paintings and the feelings that might have inspired them. No doubt he had read some of his personal tragedies into my work. Well, I could indentify with family struggles. Yet I did not pity him. I rather liked him. He was, at least, direct with his words if evasive with his emotions.

CHAPTER 17

FOR THE NEXT SEVERAL days, I saw little of Mr. Rochester. In the mornings he seemed much engaged with business. In the afternoon, gentlemen from Millcote or the neighbourhood called. When his sprain was well enough for him to return to exercise, he rode out a good deal. I would usually be awake to hear him just coming in.

During this interval, even Adele was seldom sent for to his presence, and all my acquaintance with him was confined to an occasional passing in the hall, on the stairs, or in the gallery, when he would sometimes look with a haughty stare in my direction and just barely acknowledge my presence with a nod. Other times, when he would make the effort to bow and smile, I didn't know what to make of him. His changes of mood did not offend me because I saw I had nothing to do with it; the ebb and flow depended on causes quite disconnected with me.

One day, he had company to dinner and sent for my portfolio. I had no idea why he would wish to exhibit its contents, but I was agreeable. Soon after his guests were gone, a message came that I was to bring Adele downstairs.

I brushed Adele's hair and made her neat and checked my own appearance before we descended. As usual, Adele prattled on, wondering whether her presents were at last arrived, and how did her hair look, and was her dress quite the right one for the occasion. I told her she should concern herself more with her behavior than her appearance, and she pouted prettily. A little carton greeted her on the table, and she beamed again.

"*Ma boîte! ma boîte!*" she exclaimed, running towards it.

"Yes, there is your *boîte* at last. Take it into a corner, you genuine daughter of Paris, and amuse yourself with disemboweling it," said the deep and rather sarcastic voice of Mr. Rochester, proceeding from the depths of an immense easy chair at the fireside.

"And mind," he continued, "don't bother me with any details. Let your operation be conducted in silence. *Tiens-toi tranquille, enfant; comprends-tu?*"

She was then absorbed in the contents of the box.

"Is Miss Slayre there?" he demanded, half rising from his seat to look around to the door, near which I still stood.

I caught his gaze, and my heart gave the tiniest little skip. What was it? I'd already established that he did not make me nervous. It must have been excitement at considering a chance for some interesting conversation.

"Ah! Well, come forward. Be seated here." He drew a chair near his own. "I am not fond of the prattle of children, I must explain. Old bachelor as I am, I have no pleasant associations connected with their lisping voices."

I suppose he wanted me to simper or protest, as women might over the dismissal of their children's charms. But Adele was only my pupil, not my child, and furthermore, I found his honesty engaging. Still, I pushed my chair a little back from where he'd placed it, so close to his own.

"Don't draw that chair farther off, Miss Slayre. Sit down exactly where I placed it—if you please, that is. Confound these civilities! I continually forget them. I suppose I should call for the old lady, too."

He rang and dispatched an invitation to Mrs. Fairfax, who soon arrived, knitting basket in hand.

"Good evening, madam. I sent to you for a charitable purpose. I have forbidden Adele to talk to me about her presents. Have the goodness to attend to her."

Adele, indeed, no sooner saw Mrs. Fairfax than she summoned her to her sofa and there quickly filled her lap with the porcelain, the ivory, and the waxen contents of her *boîte*, pouring out, meantime, explanations and raptures in her usual broken English.

"Now I have performed the part of a good host," said Mr. Rochester. "I've put my guests into the way of amusing each other, so I ought to be at liberty to attend to my own pleasure. Miss Slayre, draw your chair still a little farther forward. You are yet too far back. I cannot see you without disturbing my position in this comfortable chair, which I have no mind to do."

I did as I was bid, though I would much rather have remained sitting not quite so close to him. Everything was still, save the subdued chat of Adele and, filling up each pause, the beating of winter rain against the panes.

Mr. Rochester, as he sat in his damask-covered chair, looked different to what I had seen him look before, not quite so stern and much less gloomy. A definite smile was on his lips, and his eyes sparkled. Still, an air of the grim remained about him. I doubted he could help it. His rugged, rough-hewn masculinity leant itself to natural intimidation of others.

He had been looking at the fire, and I had been looking at him, when, turning suddenly, he caught my gaze fastened on him.

"You examine me, Miss Slayre. Do you think me handsome?"

I should have said something conventionally vague and polite, but a different, more provoking answer somehow slipped from my tongue. "No, sir."

"Ah! By my word! There is something singular about you. You have the air of a little abbess. You sit with your hands on your lap, with your eyes generally bent on the carpet except when they are directed to my face, as just now, for instance. And when one asks you a question or makes a remark to which you are obliged to reply, you rap out a blunt rejoinder. What do you mean by it?"

"Sir, I beg your pardon. I ought to have replied that it was not easy to give an impromptu answer to a question about appearances, that tastes mostly differ, and that beauty is of little consequence, or something of that sort."

"Beauty of little consequence? And so, under pretence of softening the previous outrage, of stroking and soothing me into placidity, you stick a sly penknife under my ear! Go on. What fault do you find with me, pray? I suppose I have all my limbs and all my features like any other man?"

"Mr. Rochester, allow me to disown my first answer. I intended no pointed repartee."

"You shall be answerable for it. Criticise me. Does my forehead not please you?" He lifted up the sable waves of hair, which lay horizontally over his brow.

"It is like marble, sir. Shall I compose a sonnet?" My insolence knew no bounds!

"There again! Another stick of the penknife when she pretended to pat my head."

Perhaps he had had too much wine. I did not know what else to say.

"You look very much puzzled, Miss Slayre. Though you are not pretty any more than I am handsome, a puzzled air becomes you. Besides, it is convenient, for it keeps those searching eyes of yours busy with the worsted flowers of the rug, so puzzle on. Young lady, I am disposed to be gregarious and communicative tonight."

With this announcement he rose from his chair and stood, leaning his arm on the marble mantelpiece. In that attitude, his shape was plainly seen as well as his face. What is handsome? I could not truly say. I could allow that his breadth of chest, length of limb, and sound and solid build was indeed more impressive than his face. So much unconscious pride was in his port, so much ease in his demeanor, such a look of complete indifference to his external appearance, and so haughty a reliance on the power of other qualities, that it atoned for a lack of mere personal attractiveness, had one truly been lacking.

"I am disposed to be gregarious tonight," he repeated, "and that is why I sent for you. The fire and the chandelier were not sufficient company for me; nor would Pilot have been, for none of these can talk. Adele is a degree better, but still far below the mark. So, too, Mrs. Fairfax. You, I am persuaded, can suit me if you will. You puzzled me the first evening I invited you down here. But tonight I am resolved to be at ease. It would please me now to draw you out, to learn more of you, therefore speak."

"What about, sir?"

"Whatever you like."

Accordingly I sat and said nothing. I had spent weeks longing for the same thing he now asked for, some interesting conversation, yet when ordered to provide it, I refused to satisfy him. Something in me forced me to thwart him. It made little sense to me, but I would not speak.

"Stubborn? And perhaps annoyed? Ah! It is consistent. I put my request in an almost insolent form. Miss Slayre, I beg your pardon. The fact is, once for all, I don't wish to treat you like an inferior. I claim only such superiority as must result from fifteen years' difference in age and a century's advance in experience."

"I am willing to amuse you, if I can, sir. I cannot introduce a topic without knowing what will interest you, though. Ask me questions, and I will do my best to answer them."

He paced a second, hand on his chin, then his gaze again met mine. "Then, in the first place, do you agree with me that I have a right to be a little masterful, and abrupt, sometimes, on the grounds I stated, namely, that I am older, and that I have roamed over half the globe, while you have lived quietly with one set of people in one house?"

"I don't think, sir, that the fact that you are older than I or have seen more of the world gives you a right to command me. Your claim to superiority all depends on the use you have made of your time and experience."

"Hmph! Promptly spoken. But I won't allow that, seeing that it would never suit my case. I have made an indifferent, not to say a bad, use of both advantages. Leaving superiority out of the question, then, you must still agree to receive my orders now and then, without being piqued or hurt by the tone of command. Will you?"

I smiled. I would accept his reasonable commands merely because, as his employee, he paid me to do so, but it was odd he did not add this to his argument.

"The smile is very well," he said. "But speak, too."

"I was thinking, sir, that very few masters would trouble themselves to inquire whether or not their paid subordinates were piqued and hurt by their orders."

"You are my paid subordinate, yes. Well then, on that mercenary ground, will you agree to let me hector a little?"

"No, sir, not on that ground. But, on the ground that you did forget it, and that you care whether or not a dependent is comfortable in his dependency, I agree heartily."

"And will you consent to dispense with a great many conventional forms and phrases, without thinking that the omission arises from insolence?"

How curious that he seemed so eager to secure my good opinion, or at least to avoid my censure. "I am sure, sir, I should never mistake informality for insolence. One I rather like, the other nothing freeborn would submit to, even for a salary."

"Most things freeborn will submit to anything as long as their price is met. However, I mentally shake hands with you for your answer, despite its inaccuracy. You have proven yourself a worthy partner. Your manner is frank and sincere, no affectation or coldness, or coarse-minded misapprehensions. Not three in three thousand raw schoolgirl governesses would have answered me as you have just done. Don't take this as flattery. As far as I know, you have some intolerable faults to balance your few good points."

"And so may you," I thought, but did not dare to speak. But my eye met his as the idea crossed my mind, and he seemed to read the thought as if I had spoken it.

"Yes, yes, you are right. I have plenty of faults of my own. I am a severe judge of character. I became steered off course at age twenty-one and haven't managed to right myself yet. I envy you your peace of mind, your clean conscience, and your unpolluted memory. Little abbess, a memory without blot or contamination must be an exquisite treasure—an inexhaustible source of pure refreshment. Is it not?"

Would that my memory were without blot. I had no intention of speaking of my own circumstances, however. I turned his question back to him. "How was your memory when you were eighteen, sir?"

"All right then. I was your equal at eighteen—quite your equal. Nature intended for me to be, on the whole, a good man, Miss Slayre. One of the better kind, and you see I am not so. Do not disagree. You have no idea. Take my word for it. I am not a villain: you are not to suppose that I am. In fact, I am a trite commonplace sinner, hackneyed in all the poor, petty dissipations with which the rich and worthless try to put on life. Do you wonder that I avow this to you?"

"A little, sir."

"If you knew the whole of it, you would probably say that I should have been superior to circumstances. So I should. When fate wronged me, I had not the wisdom to remain cool. Dread remorse when you are tempted to err, Miss Slayre. Remorse is the poison of life."

"Repentance is said to be its cure, sir."

He waved his hand. "It is not its cure. Reformation may be its cure. I could reform—I have strength yet for that, if I could only see the use for it. Since true happiness is irrevocably denied me, I've decided that I have a right to get any sort of pleasure I can out of life. And I will get it, cost what it may."

"Then you will degenerate still more, sir."

"Possibly. Yet why should I? Why shouldn't I seek and enjoy some pleasure?"

"It will sting, sir."

"How do you know?" He laughed. "You never tried it, my little abbess. How very solemn you look."

I shrugged. "I only remind you of your own words, sir. You said error brought remorse, and you pronounced remorse the poison of existence."

"I scarcely think the notion that I deserve some pleasure was an error."

"To speak truth, sir, I don't understand you at all. The conversation has got out of my depth. I only know that you said you were not as good as you should like to be, and that you regretted your own imperfection. It seems to me that if you tried hard, you would in time find it possible to become what you yourself would approve, and then you could find happiness and freely seek your pleasures."

"Rightly said, Miss Slayre. I will try hard. We'll see what comes of it."

"Very good, then," I said as I rose.

"Where are you going?"

"To put Adele to bed. It is past her bedtime." I wasn't going to stay too long and wait for him to reprimand me.

"Are you afraid of me?" he asked, his dark brow arching. "You think me a monster?"

"I have no idea what you could have done to make me think you a monster," I said frankly. I wished he would be more clear on it. "But rest assured, Mr. Rochester, I have faced my share of monsters and come out quite victorious. You don't frighten me in the least. Now good night."

"No, wait a minute. Don't run off. We've spoken enough of dark things for tonight. I would prefer to hear you laugh, my little abbess. Oh, don't bristle at the name, just an endearment really. I think you are as naturally austere as I am vicious. That is, not at all. In time, you will relax around me, I think. We will share some laughs and good times. I feel it. You are still bent on going?"

"It has struck nine, sir."

"Never mind that. Adele is not ready to go to bed yet. My position, Miss Slayre, with my back to the fire, and my face to the room, favours observation of our little charge. While talking to you, I have also occasionally watched Adele. Sit. We shall talk of Adele. A safe subject."

Hesitant, I sat down again.

"She pulled out of her box, about ten minutes ago, a little pink silk frock," he said, taking the opposite chair and speaking low. "Rapture lit her face as she unfolded it. Coquetry runs in her blood, blends with her brains, and seasons the marrow of her bones. '*Il faut que je l'essaie!*' cried she. '*Et à l'instant même!*' and she rushed out of the room. She is now with Sophie. In a few minutes she will reenter, and I know what I shall see—a miniature of Celine Varens, as she used to appear at the theater. But never mind that. However, my tender feelings are about to receive a shock. Such is my presentiment. Stay now, to see whether it will be realised."

I stayed. Ere long, Adele was heard tripping across the hall. She entered, transformed as her guardian had predicted. A dress of rose-coloured satin, short, and as full in the skirt as it could be gathered, replaced the brown frock she had previously worn. A wreath of rosebuds circled her forehead. Her feet were dressed in silk stockings and small white satin sandals.

"*Est-ce que ma robe va bien?*" she cried, bounding forward. "*Et mes souliers? Et mes bas? Tenez, je crois que je vais danser!*"

Spreading out her dress, she skipped across the room until, having reached Mr. Rochester, she wheeled lightly round before him on tiptoe, then dropped on one knee at his feet. "*Monsieur, je vous remercie mille fois de votre bonté. C'est comme cela que maman faisait, n'est-ce pas, monsieur?*"

"Precisely!" was his answer. "And, *comme cela*, she charmed my English gold out of my British breeches' pocket. I have been green, too, Miss Slayre. Ay, grass green. My springtime is gone, but it has left me that French floweret on my hands, which, in some moods, I would fain be rid of. I have but half a liking to the blossom, especially when it looks so artificial as just now. I keep it and rear it rather on the Roman Catholic principle of expiating numerous sins, great or small, by one good work. I'll explain all this someday. Now you may take her to bed. Good night."

CHAPTER 18

ON A FUTURE OCCASION, Mr. Rochester did finally explain. It was one afternoon when he chanced to meet Adele and me on the grounds. She ran about and played with Pilot on the lawn. As she was safely occupied, he asked me to walk up and down a long beech avenue within sight of her.

He then poured out the story of his relationship with a French opera-dancer, Celine Varens, towards whom he had once cherished what he called a *grande passion*.

"Miss Slayre, so much was I flattered by her compliments that I installed her in a hotel and gave her a complete establishment of servants, a carriage, cashmeres, diamonds, and whatever her heart desired. In short, I began the process of ruining myself in the received style."

"Are you sure you wish to tell me all, sir?" I boldly put my hand on his arm. "It isn't necessary to inform me."

He shook his head. "Let me finish."

"Very well." I continued walking at his side.

"Happening to call one evening when Celine did not expect me, I found her out. It was a warm night, and I was tired with strolling through Paris, so I sat down in her boudoir to await her, when I bethought myself to open the window and step out onto the balcony. I sat down and took out a cigar." He patted down his jacket and withdrew one from his pocket. "I will take one now, if you will excuse me?"

I excused him. He lit it, placed it to his lips, and breathed a trail of Havana incense on the cold and sunless air.

"An elegant carriage drawn by a beautiful pair of English horses pulled up. I knew it as the one I had given Celine. The carriage stopped, as I had expected, at the hotel door. My flame alighted, though muffled in a cloak—an unnecessary encumbrance on so warm a June evening. Bending over the balcony, I was about to murmur *Mon ange*—in a tone, of course, which should be audible to the ear of love alone—when a figure jumped from the carriage after her, cloaked also, with a hat pulled down low on his head.

"You never felt jealousy, did you, Miss Slayre? Of course not. Your soul sleeps. The shock is yet to be given which shall waken it." He ground his teeth and was silent. He paused a moment, and something at the house seemed to catch his attention. He walked towards it, then turned back. "I beg your pardon. I thought I saw something. I did see. It was my destiny daring me to be happy here in this house. But it is of no consequence."

I stared off towards Thornfield. I didn't know about destiny, but something up in the battlements, a dark figure was just departing. I wanted to say that it was probably just Grace Poole, but he seemed ready to get back to his story, and I did not wish to stop him before he had got it all out. I urged him back to it. "Did you leave the balcony, sir," I asked, "when Mademoiselle Varens entered?"

"Oh, I had nearly forgotten Celine! I probably shouldn't be telling you all this. It's not a proper story for a man to tell his young lady governess, is it?"

"Perhaps not, but do go on. I must know the end now that you've started."

He smiled. "I thought so. All right. I remained on the balcony. I drew the curtain over the door, leaving an opening just wide enough through which I could take observations. I watched. Both removed their cloaks, and there was 'the Varens,' shining in satin and jewels, my gifts of course, and there was her companion in an officer's uniform. I knew him for a young roué of a *vicomte*—a brainless and vicious youth whom I had sometimes met in society. On recognising him, the fang of the snake Jealousy was instantly broken, because at the same moment my love for Celine sank under the weight of realisation. A woman who could betray me for such a rival was not worth contending for; she deserved only scorn. Less, however, than I, who had been her dupe."

"Oh, thank goodness," I said aloud, then wished I could withdraw it. "Not that you were betrayed. I mean thank goodness that she didn't leave a permanent wound."

"You concern yourself with my wounds?" His brow arched.

I couldn't answer for it. "Please, continue."

"They began to talk. A card of mine lay on the table. This brought my name under discussion. Neither of them possessed energy or wit to belabour me soundly, but they insulted me as coarsely as they could in their little way, especially Celine, who even waxed rather brilliant on my personal defects. Now it had been her custom to launch out into fervent admiration of what she called my *beauté mâle*, wherein she differed diametrically from you, who told me point-blank, at the second interview, that you did not think me handsome. The contrast struck me at the time and—"

Adele came running up. "Monsieur, John has just been to say that your agent has called and wishes to see you."

"Very well." He dismissed her. "Ah! I must abridge. Opening the window, I walked in upon them. I liberated Celine from my protection, gave her notice to vacate her hotel, offered her a purse for immediate exigencies, and disregarded her protestations and convulsions. I made an appointment with the *vicomte* for a meeting at the Bois de Boulogne. Next morning I had the pleasure of encountering him, left a bullet in one of his arms, and then thought

I had done with the whole crew. But unluckily the Varens, six months before, had given me this *fillette*, Adele, who, she affirmed, was my daughter. Perhaps she may be, though I see no proofs of such grim paternity written in her countenance. Pilot is more like me than she.

"Some years after I had broken with the mother, she abandoned her child and ran away to Italy with a musician or singer. I acknowledged no natural claim on Adele's part to be supported by me, nor do I now acknowledge any, for I am not her father. Still, hearing that she was quite destitute, I took the poor thing out of Paris and transplanted it here, to grow up clean in the wholesome soil of an English country garden. Mrs. Fairfax found you to train it, but now you know that it is the illegitimate offspring of a French opera-girl. You will perhaps think differently of your post and protégée. You will be coming to me someday with notice that you have found another place and I will need to look for a new governess. Eh?"

"Certainly not. Adele is not answerable for either her mother's faults or yours. How could I possibly prefer the spoiled pet of a wealthy family, who would hate her governess as a nuisance, to a lonely little orphan who leans towards her as a friend?"

"Oh, that is the light in which you view it! Well, I must go in now." He started to go in and turned back. "And you, too. It darkens. There's a full moon tonight. Er, the weather will not be fine. I wish you indoors before dark."

Did he think us in danger from the weather? It seemed fine enough to me. At any rate, we were close to the house. In defiance, perhaps, I stayed out a few minutes longer with Adele and Pilot. We ran a race and played a game of battledore and shuttlecock. I sought in her a likeness to Mr. Rochester, but found none. No trait, no turn of expression, announced relationship. It was a pity. If she could but have been proved to resemble him, he would have thought more of her.

As I was about to suggest another game of shuttlecock, that queer feeling came over me.

"Adele, take Pilot and go straight inside. I'm going to tidy up out here."

She looked at me quizzically, but knew not to question my orders. She shrugged, took hold of Pilot's collar, and allowed him to lead her inside.

I reached into my pocket, palming a stake, and walked a circle, looking carefully around the gardens and down the path. The closer I got to the house, the more the feeling faded. Perhaps I could follow Adele and leave well enough alone. But I couldn't ignore the warning instinct that evil lurked too close for comfort. I turned quickly at the sound of movement in the trees behind the path. Certain something was there, I leaned down to pretend to pick up a shuttlecock. It wouldn't do to let it know I was aware of it.

I straightened up, moved down the path closer to the trees, and hummed a little tune. Whatever it was seemed to respond to my show of nonchalance, for it moved again in the bushes, drawing nearer to me. No doubt it planned to spring on me at any second, and I steeled myself for it. Finally, I heard it coming quickly. I was ready.

I turned before it struck, crouching slightly for agility as Miss Temple had taught me. It made a move to leap on me and missed, flying over my head. I gave a little laugh.

"Laugh at me, will you?" It stood and straightened its lawn shirt and torn breeches.

I crossed my arms, as if waiting for him to ready himself for combat. Ginger-haired and ruddy, he looked not a thing like John Reed, but brought that boy to mind by his apparent fear of being ridiculed. By appearance, he was barely twenty years old. By how badly he'd misjudged his pounce on supposed prey, I guessed he hadn't been a vampyre long. A day was too long, as far as I was concerned.

"I'll give you a moment to compose yourself and rethink your foolish attack," I said. "If you mean to repent, tell me now and I'll set you free."

"Set me free?" He looked around as if astounded by my audacity and slowly closed the distance between us. "Me? I think you're the one in a spot."

"Oh, I'm quite certain I have just the thing for you."

He smiled. "Ah. Are you—are you one of us? Good thing then. Could you, ah—could you give me some advice on hunting, then? I seem to be having a little trouble actually catching anything but rabbits, and that only once. I might starve if I go another day. And now I'm—"

"Dust." I brushed my hands clean after driving the stake home. No wonder he feared ridicule. I couldn't stand hearing him go on and on for another minute. "Now you're dust."

I stepped over his dirty shirt and breeches and made my way indoors.

Not until after I had withdrawn to my own chamber for the night did I steadily review Mr. Rochester's tale. Why had he confided in me? I could not tell, but I was glad he did. His confidence seemed a tribute to my discretion. His deportment had now for some weeks been more uniform towards me than at the first. I never seemed in his way. When he met me unexpectedly, the encounter seemed welcome. He had always a word and sometimes a smile for me. When summoned by formal invitation to his presence, I was honoured by a cordiality of reception that made me feel I really possessed the power to amuse him, and that these evening conferences were sought as much for his pleasure as for my benefit.

So happy, so gratified, did I become with this new interest added to life that I ceased to pine after some mysterious and intangible destiny. I liked to take long walks and recall our previous conversations or the expressions on his face, the sparkling of his eyes as he spoke. Sometimes, my walking turned into running and I wasn't even aware until I nearly collapsed, breathless after miles. My bodily health improved. I gathered flesh and strength.

And should Mr. Rochester ask me now if I thought him handsome? Oh, reader, my answer would be changed! His face was the object I best liked to see. His presence in a room was more cheering than the brightest fire. Yet I had not forgotten his faults. Indeed, I could not, for he brought them frequently before me. He was proud, sardonic, and harsh to inferiority of every description. He was moody, too, unaccountably so. But I believed that his faults had their source in some cruel cross of fate, and I was more impressed than troubled by them. I believed he was naturally a man of better tendencies, higher principles, and purer tastes than such as circumstances had developed, education instilled, or destiny encouraged.

Though I had now extinguished my candle and was lying in bed, I could not sleep for thinking of his look when he paused in the avenue and told how his destiny had dared him to be happy at Thornfield.

Why shouldn't he be? Besides the occasional vampyre on the grounds, what could alienate him from the house? I hoped he did not plan to leave it again soon. Mrs. Fairfax said he seldom stayed here longer than a fortnight at a time and he had now been resident eight weeks. If he went, I did not know how I would bear it.

I hardly know if I had slept or not after my musing, but I startled awake on hearing a vague murmur, peculiar and sinister, that seemed to come from directly above me. I wished I had kept my candle burning. The night was dark. A cloud must have passed over the full moon, as one had surely darkened my spirits. I rose and sat up in bed, listening. The sound was hushed.

I tried again to sleep, but my heart beat anxiously. My inward tranquillity was broken. The clock, far down in the hall, struck two. Just then it seemed my chamber door was touched, as if fingers had swept the panels in groping a way along the dark gallery outside.

"Who's there?"

Nothing answered. A chill ran through me.

It must be Pilot, I told myself. Pilot usually slept in the kitchen, but he had been known to get out and make his way up to Mr. Rochester's chamber. The idea did not calm me. I knew better. Something was out there. Something unnatural.

I heard the laugh again, as if to confirm my suspicions. Demonic and deep, it seemed to be uttered right through the keyhole of my chamber door. The head of my bed was near the door, and I could almost fancy something stood, or rather crouched, there at my bedside. Something wicked. Something terrible. I rose, looked around, and saw nothing.

The laugh sounded again, and this time I knew it came from right behind my door. I put my hand up to the wood in time to feel it reverberate in response. I checked my impulse to call out again. I knew stealth was required.

It gurgled and moaned, and I heard it hulk, limp, or drag off to the third-story staircase. A door had recently been made for those stairs, and I heard it open and shut, then silence.

Grace Poole? I wondered. She seemed the logical culprit. Mundane as she appeared, I suspected yet again that something was wrong with her. Possessed with a devil, perhaps? Or what kind of creature was she? More important, was she dangerous? I did not even take a candle. I hurried on my frock and shawl in the dark, rummaged in my drawer for where I had left my weapons, slid a dagger into my sleeve, slipped a stake in my pocket, and left the room. What I would do if I found her, I had no idea. She must be stopped, but I had to be mindful of the rules of the house.

In the hall, a candle burned just outside my door, as if she'd had the courtesy to light my way. The air was dim, but not from the light. It was more—smoke? I smelled the burning, and I looked and saw the smoke coming out from a door left ajar, Mr. Rochester's door. I didn't even think. I ran inside. Tongues of flame darted around the bed. The curtains were on fire. In the midst of blaze and vapour, Mr. Rochester lay stretched motionless in deep sleep.

"Wake! Wake!" I cried. I shook him, but he only murmured and turned. The smoke had stupefied him. I rushed to his basin and ewer. Fortunately, one was wide and the other deep, and both were filled with water. I heaved them up and threw them at the flames. The bed was deluged and its occupant, too. But he slept on. I flew back to my own room, brought my own water jug, and doused the whole bed again, this time extinguishing the rest of the flames.

The splash of the shower I had liberally bestowed roused Mr. Rochester at last. Though it was dark again, I knew he was awake. I heard him cursing, much as he had on our first meeting when he'd been thrown from his horse.

"Is there a flood?" he cried.

"No, sir," I answered. "But there has been a fire. Get up. You are quite soaked. I will fetch you a candle."

"In the name of all the elves in Christendom, is that Jane Slayre?" he demanded. "What have you done with me, witch, sorceress? Who is in the room besides you? Have you plotted to drown me?"

"Be quiet, sir. Get up. I will fetch you a candle. Somebody has plotted something."

"There! I am up now. But at your peril you fetch a candle yet. Wait two minutes until I get into some dry garments, if any dry there be—yes, here is my dressing gown. Now run! Come right back."

I ran. I brought the candle from the hall. He took it from my hand, held it up, and surveyed the bed, all blackened and scorched, the sheets drenched, the carpet swimming in water.

"What is it? Who did it?" he asked.

I briefly related to him what I knew of it, about the strange laugh I had heard in the gallery, the step ascending to the third floor, the smoke, the smell of fire, which had conducted me to his room, in what state I had found matters there, and how I had deluged him with all the water I could lay hands on.

He listened gravely. His face, as I went on, expressed more concern than astonishment. He did not immediately speak when I had concluded.

"Shall I call Mrs. Fairfax?" I asked.

"What can she do? Let her sleep. Be still. Tell me, what possessed you to go in search of this demonic laugh? Did you not worry that you could be attacked?"

"To have disregarded my own safety would have been the height of foolishness. I was prepared to defend myself."

"How?" he scoffed. "You're but a wisp of a girl!"

"I'm braver and stronger than you would suspect."

"Braver, perhaps." He sighed. "You have a shawl on. If you are not warm enough, you may take my cloak. Wrap it about you and sit down in the armchair. There—I will put it on." He must have seen me shivering, for he grabbed his cloak, wrapped it around me, and made me sit down. "Now place your feet on the stool to keep them out of the wet. I am going to leave you a few minutes. I shall take the candle. Remain where you are until I return. Do not move or call anyone. I must pay a visit to the third story. I need to know you are safe and accounted for until I get back."

"All right," I agreed, but reluctantly.

He went. I watched the light withdraw. He passed softly up the gallery, opened the staircase door with as little noise as possible, shut it after him, and the last ray vanished. I was left in total darkness. I listened for some noise, but heard nothing. A long time elapsed. At last, the light once more gleamed dimly on the gallery wall, and I heard his unshod feet tread the matting.

"I have found it all out," said he, setting his candle down on the washstand. "It is as I thought."

"How, sir?"

"I forget whether you said you saw anything when you opened your chamber door."

"No, sir, only the candlestick on the ground."

"But you heard an odd laugh? You have heard that laugh before, I should think, or something like it?"

"Yes, sir. Mrs. Fairfax says it is Grace Poole. I have met her and found her rather unremarkable, but now I wonder."

"There's nothing to wonder," he said quickly. "It is Grace Poole.

She is, as you say, unremarkable, except perhaps for her penchant to drink. Gin, I believe, was her poison of choice tonight."

"That's all? A tendency to drink? She tried to burn you in your bed."

"Not on purpose. I think she was stumbling about, in her cups, when she got confused trying to find her way back to bed. She must have confused my room for hers and dropped the candle in fright when she heard my snoring. I shall reflect on the subject. Say nothing about it. I will account for this state of affairs. And now, to your own room. I shall do very well on the sofa in the library for the rest of the night. It is near four. In two hours, the servants will be up."

"Good night, then, sir," I said, departing.

He seemed surprised—inconsistently so, as he had just told me to go.

"What!" he exclaimed. "Are you quitting me already, and in that way?"

"You told me to go, sir."

"But not in such a fashion, abrupt, without taking leave. You have saved my life! Saved me from a most excruciating death! At least shake hands."

He held out his hand. I offered him mine. He took it first in one, then in both his own.

"You have saved my life," he said again. "I have a pleasure in owing you so immense a debt." He stood back, paused, and gazed at me. Words almost visible trembled on his lips, but his voice was checked. "I knew you would do me good in some way, at some time. I saw it in your eyes when I first beheld you. People talk of natural sympathies. My cherished preserver, good night!"

Strange energy was in his voice, strange fire in his look.

"I am glad I happened to be awake," I said, and started away. Clearly, he was shaken from the events of the night and nearly overcome.

"What! You will go?" Again he called me back to him.

"I am cold, sir." I laughed at him now.

"Cold? Yes, of course, and standing in a pool! Go, then, Jane. Go!" But he still retained my hand, and I could not free it. Perhaps I did not wish to free it.

"I think I hear Mrs. Fairfax move, sir," I said, an excuse to finally be away.

"Well, leave me." He relaxed his fingers, and I was gone.

I went back to bed, but never thought of sleep. Too feverish to rest, I rose as soon as day dawned.

CHAPTER 19

THE NEXT MORNING, I both wished and feared to see Mr. Rochester. Any number of times I thought I had heard him coming down the hall or entering a room, but when I turned to look, he wasn't there.

The morning passed almost as usual, save for a little excitement about the strangeness of the previous night. No one addressed any of their concerns to me, but I heard John, Cook (John's wife), Leah, and Mrs. Fairfax going on about it.

"What a mercy Master was not burnt in his bed!"

"It is always dangerous to keep a candle lit at night."

"How providential that he had presence of mind to think of the water jug!"

"I wonder he waked nobody!"

"It is to be hoped he will not take cold with sleeping on the library sofa."

Ah, so he had explained it away as an accident with candle. The next incident he could not explain away, and I marvelled at it. John told the women about several cows that were attacked and slaughtered by something in the night. Vampyres in the area again? Predators? A wolf, or pack of wolves? Rabid foxes?

"But the strangest thing," John added, and the thing that occasioned the most trouble of the morning—one of the poor, bloodied cows had been dragged right up to the garden at the side of the house, its entrails left scattered in the thorn trees.

"What kind of animal could do such a thing? So far from pasture?" Leah asked.

Mrs. Fairfax imagined it would take something strong, a bear perhaps. John agreed with the assessment but hated to think of the size of the bear. I alone knew better, but I wasn't talking. A vampyre could have done it. I could imagine their faces if I walked into the kitchen and told them as much. Vampyres had just that sort of vigor and recklessness when they were on the hunt and eager to feed. I had seen it. With my own eyes, though it was many years ago. But Grace Poole a vampyre? Was she in league with others in the town?

Leah and Mrs. Fairfax spent the day scrubbing and setting Mr. Rochester's room to rights. I expected him to put in an appearance in the schoolroom at the very least, but he did not appear. I finally went to check on the progress in his chamber to find Grace Poole herself sitting on a stool at the corner of the room sewing the rings on new curtains. Leah was there, too, cleaning smoke off the windows.

I hesitated in the doorway. I wanted to see how Grace Poole managed to sit in the destruction she had created without showing the slightest hint of remorse. There she was, staid and taciturn-looking, as usual, in her brown stuff gown, her check apron, white handkerchief, and cap. She was intent on her work, perhaps her personal penance, in which her whole thoughts seemed absorbed.

As I'd earlier noted, and rechecked now, she did not have the hard eyes and grey pallor of a vampyre, or the sunken features and listless demeanor of a zombie. What, then, could she be? And how could she carry on as if blameless?

I was amazed—confounded. She looked up while I still gazed

at her. No start, no increase or failure of colour betrayed emotion, consciousness of guilt, or fear of detection.

"Good morning, miss," she said in her usual phlegmatic and brief manner. Taking up another ring and more tape, she went on with her sewing.

"Good morning, Grace." I meant to put her to some test. "Has anything happened here? I thought I heard the servants all talking together a while ago."

"Only Master had been reading in his bed last night. He fell asleep with his candle lit, and the curtains got on fire."

"A strange affair!" I said in a low voice, then I looked at her fixedly. "Did Mr. Rochester wake nobody? Did no one hear him move?"

She again raised her eyes to me, and this time something of consciousness was in their expression. She seemed to examine me warily. "The servants sleep so far off, you know, miss, they would not be likely to hear. Mrs. Fairfax's room and yours are the nearest to Master's, but Mrs. Fairfax said she heard nothing. When people get elderly, they often sleep heavy." Grace paused, then added, with a sort of assumed indifference, but still in a marked and significant tone, "But you are young, miss, and I should say a light sleeper. Perhaps you may have heard a noise?"

"I did," I said, dropping my voice, so that Leah, who was still polishing the panes, could not hear me. "And at first I thought it was Pilot, but Pilot cannot laugh. I am certain I heard a laugh, and a strange one."

She took a new bit of thread, waxed it carefully, threaded her needle with a steady hand, then observed, with perfect composure, "It is hardly likely Master would laugh, I should think, miss, when he was in such danger. You must have been dreaming."

"I was not dreaming," I said with some warmth, for her brazen coolness provoked me. Again she looked at me, with the same scrutinising and conscious eye.

"Have you told Master that you heard a laugh?" she inquired.

"I have not had the opportunity of speaking to him this morning."

"You did not think of opening your door and looking out into the gallery?"

She appeared to be cross-questioning me. The idea struck me that if she discovered I knew or suspected her guilt, she might set her sights of being rid of me. No doubt she was dangerous. I thought it advisable to be on my guard.

"On the contrary," I said. "I bolted my door."

"Then you are not in the habit of bolting your door every night?"

The fiend! She wanted to know my habits that she might lay her plans accordingly!

"Hitherto I have often omitted to fasten the bolt. I did not think it necessary. I was not aware any danger or annoyance was to be dreaded at Thornfield Hall. In future, I shall take good care to make all secure before I venture to lie down."

"It will be wise so to do. A door is soon fastened, and it is as well to have a drawn bolt between one and any mischief that may be about."

I still stood absolutely shocked at what appeared to me her miraculous self-possession and most inscrutable hypocrisy, when the cook entered.

"Mrs. Poole, the servants' dinner will soon be ready. Will you come down?" Cook asked.

"No. Just put my pint of porter and bit of pudding on a tray, and I'll carry it upstairs."

"You'll have some meat?"

"Just a morsel, and a taste of cheese, that's all."

Ha! No doubt she had her fill of meat last night.

The cook here turned to me, saying that Mrs. Fairfax was waiting for me. I departed.

I hardly heard Mrs. Fairfax's account of the cow massacre or the curtain conflagration during dinner, so much was I occupied in puzzling my brains over the enigmatical character of Grace Poole, and still more in pondering the problem of her position at Thornfield and questioning why she had not been given into custody that morning, or, at the very least, dismissed last night. What mysterious cause withheld Mr. Rochester from accusing her? Why had he enjoined me, too, to secrecy? It was strange. A bold, vindictive, and haughty gentleman seemed somehow in the power of one of the meanest of his dependents. So much in her power that even when she lifted her hand against his life, he dared not openly charge her with the attempt, much less punish her for it.

Perhaps Grace Poole was some sort of witch or enchantress? Were the cows some sort of sacrifice to a dark master? I was on my guard, even if Mr. Rochester had let down his.

I gave up my conjectures to join Adele in the schoolroom, where she sat calmly drawing, shading figures as I had shown her.

"*Qu' avez-vous, mademoiselle?*" said she. "*Vos doigts tremblant comme la feuille, et vos joues sont rouges; mais, rouges comme des cerises!*"

"I am hot, Adele, with stooping." I didn't think I had gone red in the face all my life more than I had in the past week. She went on sketching. I went on thinking.

"Evening approaches," I said, as I looked towards the window. "I have not heard Mr. Rochester's voice or step in the house today, but surely I shall see him before night. I feared the meeting in the morning; now I desire it because expectation has been so long baffled that it is grown impatient."

When dusk actually closed, and when Adele left me to go to play in the nursery with Sophie, I did most keenly desire it. I listened for the bell to ring below. I listened for Leah coming up with a message. I fancied sometimes I heard Mr. Rochester's own tread, and I turned to the door, expecting it to open and admit him. The door remained shut.

A tread creaked on the stairs at last. Leah made her appearance, but it was only to intimate that tea was ready in Mrs. Fairfax's room. Thither I repaired, glad at least to go downstairs, for that brought me, I imagined, nearer to Mr. Rochester's presence.

"You must want your tea," said the good lady as I joined her. "You ate so little at dinner. You look flushed and feverish."

"I'm quite well. I never felt better."

"Then you must prove it by evincing a good appetite. Will you fill the teapot while I knit off this needle?" Having completed her task, she rose to draw down the blind, forgetting that it had been drawn all day to hide the sight of cow bits scattered throughout the yard.

"It was a fair day," she said. "Or so John informed me. Mr. Rochester had, on the whole, a favourable day for his journey."

"Journey! I did not know he was out."

"He set off the moment he had breakfasted. He has gone to the Leas, Mr. Eshton's place, ten miles on the other side Millcote. I believe there is quite a party assembled there. Lord Ingram, Sir George Lynn, Colonel Dent, and others."

"Do you expect him back tonight?"

"I think he is very likely to stay a week or more. When these fine, fashionable people get together, they are so surrounded by elegance and gaiety, so well provided with all that can please and entertain, they are in no hurry to separate. Gentlemen especially are often in request on such occasions, and Mr. Rochester is so talented and so lively in society that I believe he is a general favourite."

"Are there ladies at the Leas?" My breath came shallow.

Mrs. Fairfax ticked them off. "There are Mrs. Eshton and her three daughters, very elegant young ladies indeed. And there are the Honourable Blanche and Mary Ingram, most beautiful women, I suppose. Indeed I have seen Blanche, six or seven years since, when she was a girl of eighteen. She came here to a Christmas ball and party Mr. Rochester gave. Miss Ingram was considered the queen of the evening."

The queen of the evening. With Mr. Rochester. For at least a week or more. Not to mention the Misses Eshton. All three. "You saw Blanche Ingram, you say, Mrs. Fairfax? What was she like?"

"Yes, I saw her. Tall, fine bust, sloping shoulders. Long, graceful neck. Olive complexion. Noble features. Eyes rather like Mr. Rochester's, a little darker perhaps, large and black, and as brilliant as her jewels." Like vampyre eyes? "And then she had such a fine head of hair, raven black and so becomingly arranged. A crown of thick plaits behind, and in front the longest, the glossiest curls I ever saw."

"She was greatly admired, of course?"

"Yes, indeed, and not only for her beauty, but for her accomplishments. She was one of the ladies who sang. A gentleman accompanied her on the piano. She and Mr. Rochester sang a duet."

"Mr. Rochester? I was not aware he could sing." Here was yet another point in Miss Ingram's favour. I wondered at her conversational skills.

"He has a fine bass voice, and an excellent taste for music."

"And this beautiful and accomplished lady, she is not yet married?"

"It appears not. I fancy neither she nor her sister have very large fortunes. Old Lord Ingram's estates were chiefly entailed, and the eldest son came in for everything almost."

"But I wonder no wealthy nobleman or gentleman has taken a fancy to her. Mr. Rochester, for instance. He is rich, is he not?" I insisted on torturing myself to the greatest degree. What could I offer next to this Miss Ingram?

"There is a considerable difference in age. Mr. Rochester is past thirty. She is but twenty-five."

And I only eighteen. She had every advantage over me. "What of that? More unequal matches are made every day."

"True. But you eat nothing. You have scarcely tasted since you began tea."

"I am too thirsty to eat. Will you let me have another cup?"

If I hadn't been sick earlier, I was indeed feeling so now.

When once more alone, I reviewed the information I had got; looked into my heart, examined its thoughts and feelings, and pronounced judgment to this effect:

That a greater fool than Jane Slayre had never breathed the breath of life; that a more fantastic idiot had never surfeited herself on sweet lies and swallowed poison as if it were nectar.

"*You*," I said. "A favourite with Mr. Rochester? *You* gifted with the power of pleasing him? *You* of importance to him in any way?"

I was a governess, nothing more, and I was best served to keep my place.

CHAPTER 20

A WEEK PASSED, AND NO news arrived of Mr. Rochester. Ten days, and still he did not come. Mrs. Fairfax said she should not be surprised if he went straight from the Leas to London, and thence to the Continent, and not show his face again at Thornfield for a year to come. He had made it a habit to quit Thornfield in a manner quite as abrupt and unexpected.

When I heard this, I was beginning to feel a strange chill and failing at the heart. I was actually permitting myself to experience a sickening sense of disappointment, but I rallied my wits. Grace Poole had tried to kill him. Was it not best he stayed away? I missed him. This was true. Selfish girl! Was it not better that he was safe from a witch's spells? Away from the risk of falling under evil enchantments? Would marriage to Blanche Ingram not be preferable to losing him to evil purposes?

I reminded myself I had nothing to do with the master of Thornfield, further than to receive the salary he gave me for teaching

Adele and to be grateful for such respectful and kind treatment as I'd received at his hands. I went on with my day's business tranquilly, but vague suggestions kept wandering across my brain of reasons why I should quit Thornfield. I kept involuntarily framing advertisements and pondering conjectures about new situations. Mr. Rochester had been absent upwards of a fortnight when the post brought Mrs. Fairfax a letter.

"It is from the master," said she as she looked at the direction. "Now I suppose we shall know whether we are to expect his return or not."

While she broke the seal and perused the document, I went on taking my coffee at breakfast. It was hot and I attributed to that circumstance a fiery glow that suddenly rose to my face.

"Well, I sometimes think we are too quiet, but we run a chance of being busy enough now for a little while at least," Mrs. Fairfax said, still holding the note before her spectacles.

"Mr. Rochester is not likely to return soon, I suppose?"

"In three days! And not alone, either. I don't know how many of the fine people at the Leas are coming with him. He sends directions for all the best bedrooms to be prepared, and the library and drawing rooms to be cleaned out. I am to get more kitchen hands from the George Inn at Millcote, and from wherever else I can. The ladies will bring their maids and the gentlemen their valets, so we shall have a full house of it. How exciting!" Mrs. Fairfax hastened away to commence operations.

As she had foretold, the three days were busy enough. I had thought all the rooms at Thornfield beautifully clean and well arranged, but it appears I was mistaken. Three women were got to help, and such scrubbing, such brushing, such washing of paint and beating of carpets, such taking down and putting up of pictures, such polishing of mirrors and lusters, such lighting of fires in bedrooms, such airing of sheets and feather beds on hearths, I never beheld, either before or since.

Mrs. Fairfax had pressed me into her service, so Adele was on holiday. I thought of the many Christmases I had been left out and left alone at Gateshead, and well for it considering how the Reeds preferred to celebrate: by eating all their friends. Having visitors was no holiday for me. I was all day in the storeroom, helping Mrs. Fairfax and the cook. I learned to make custards and cheesecakes and French pastry, to truss game and garnish dessert dishes.

I didn't even have time to chase demons or suspect Grace Poole. For the most part, she kept to her portion of the house. I imagined she spent the days up there sewing and laughing to herself, perhaps consulting her spell book.

Others had to have noticed her odd habits, but no one seemed to think anything strange of her except me. I once overheard part of a dialogue between Leah and one of the charwomen about Grace. Leah had been saying something I had not caught, and the charwoman remarked, "She gets good wages, I guess?"

"Yes," said Leah. "I wish I had as good. Not that mine are to complain of. There's no stinginess at Thornfield. But they're not one-fifth of the sum Mrs. Poole receives."

"She is a good hand, I daresay."

"Ah! She understands what she has to do like nobody better. And it is not everyone could fill her shoes—not for all the money she gets."

"I wonder whether the master—"

The charwoman was going on, but here Leah turned and perceived me, and she instantly gave her companion a nudge.

"Doesn't she know?" I heard the woman whisper.

Leah shook her head, and the conversation was of course dropped. All I had gathered from it was that Thornfield held a real mystery, and that I had purposely been excluded from the secret. More proof that I was not half to Mr. Rochester what I thought I had been a mere few weeks earlier.

The next morning the charwoman—disemboweled, with entrails strewn across the lawn and twisted amongst the hawthorn branches—was found in the garden. Thornfield's mystery had taken a darker turn.

Thursday afternoon arrived. Mrs. Fairfax assumed her best black satin gown, her gloves, and her gold watch, for it was her part to receive the company, to conduct the ladies to their rooms, and to direct the servants. Adele, too, would be dressed, though I thought she had little chance of being introduced to the party that day at least. For myself, I had no need to make any change. I should not be called upon to quit my sanctum of the schoolroom.

"It gets late." Mrs. Fairfax entered in rustling state, wringing her hands. "I am glad I ordered dinner an hour after the time Mr. Rochester mentioned, for it is past six now. I have sent John down to the gates to see if there is anything on the road."

John returned and approached the window presently. "They're coming, ma'am. They'll be here in ten minutes."

Adele flew to the window. I followed, taking care to stand on one side so that, screened by the curtain, I could see without being seen. At last, wheels were heard. Four equestrians galloped up the drive, and after them came two carriages. My gaze flew straight to Mr. Rochester. He rode his black horse, Mesrour, and Pilot bounded before him, but I would have known him from the shock of black hair visible under his hat and his fine form in the saddle. Once I could manage to turn my gaze from Mr. Rochester, I noticed that the rider beside him was a woman. Her purple riding habit almost swept the ground, her veil streamed long on the breeze.

"Miss Ingram!" exclaimed Mrs. Fairfax, and away she hurried to her post below.

Bah, Miss Ingram. Out in the daylight, no less. I didn't even have the chance to question that she might be a vampyre. I wouldn't rule out other, less desirable conditions in a wife until absolutely necessary.

More fluttering veils and waving plumes filled the vehicles. Two of the cavaliers were young and dashing. The cavalcade, following the sweep of the drive, quickly turned the angle of the house, and I lost sight of it.

Adele petitioned to go meet the party, but I would not allow it. She cried prettily at the news, but forgot her tears as soon as she caught sounds of the party entering the hall, the joyous stir of ladies' fine accents and laughter blending with the gentlemen's deep tones, the voice of Thornfield Hall's master distinguishable above them all. Light steps ascended the stairs, accented by soft, cheerful laughs and the opening and closing of doors, followed by a temporary hush.

"*Elles changent de toilettes*," said Adele, who had followed every movement. She sighed.

"Yes, I imagine they are changing to even finer dresses to prepare for the evening's entertainments." I checked my own sigh. "Don't you feel hungry, Adele? While the ladies are in their rooms, I will venture down and get you something to eat."

The party devoted the next day to an excursion to some site in the neighbourhood. They set out early in the forenoon, some on horseback, the rest in carriages. Miss Ingram, as before, was the only lady equestrian, and as before, Mr. Rochester galloped at her side. The two rode a little apart from the rest, no doubt sharing interesting conversation. I imagined Blanche Ingram would be agreeable to Mr. Rochester's every point, and it made me smile to think it. I knew he preferred a challenge.

"You said it was not likely they should think of being married," I said to Mrs. Fairfax, who stood near me. "But you see Mr. Rochester evidently prefers her to any of the other ladies."

"Yes, I daresay. No doubt he admires her."

"And she him. Look how she leans her head towards him. I wish I could see her face."

"You will see her this evening," answered Mrs. Fairfax. "I happened to remark to Mr. Rochester how much Adele wished to be introduced to the ladies, and he said, 'Oh! Let her come into the drawing room after dinner, and request Miss Slayre to accompany her.' "

"He is all politeness. I need not go, I am sure."

"I don't know." Mrs. Fairfax sighed. "I observed to him that you were unused to company and he said, 'Nonsense! If she objects, tell her it is my particular wish. And if she resists, say I shall come and fetch her.' "

It was like him, but I was still sure nothing was behind it but politeness. "I will not give him that trouble. Shall you be there, Mrs. Fairfax?"

"No. I pleaded off, and he admitted my plea. I'll tell you how to manage so as to avoid the embarrassment of making a formal entrance, which is the most disagreeable part of the business. You must go into the drawing room while it is empty, before the ladies leave the dinner table. Choose your seat in any quiet nook you like. You need not stay long after the gentlemen come in, unless you please. Just let Mr. Rochester see that you're there and then slip away. Nobody will notice you."

"Will these people remain long, do you think?"

"Perhaps two or three weeks, certainly not more. It surprises me that he has already made so protracted a stay at Thornfield."

As the hour approached, I proceeded, as instructed by Mrs. Fairfax, to find a perch in the drawing room. Adele had been ecstatic all day after hearing she was to be presented to the ladies in the evening, and only the gravity of getting dressed for the occasion could calm her down. She was a perfect little lady, and grave as a judge, as Sophie arranged her curls in drooping clusters, tied her pink satin sash, and adjusted her little lace mittens. There was no need to warn her not to mess her appearance. She sat on a little footstool in the drawing room and took utmost care in arranging her skirts so as to avoid creasing the satin.

I retired to the window seat with a book to keep me occupied. I imagined I would largely escape notice. Still, I wore my best dress, the silver-grey one, purchased for Miss Temple's wedding. My hair was smoothed. My sole adornment, as usual, was the pearl brooch. The room looked lovely. A large fire burned and wax candles dotted the marble mantelpiece and shone on tables all around the room, next to exquisitely arranged displays of flowers in which I had hidden stakes in the event of necessity. Since guests had entered the house, I'd suffered a return of my odd nervous feeling that I'd come to realise anticipated the presence of vampyres. I would study the guests carefully and decide which of them could possibly be one.

A soft sound of rising now became audible. The dining-room curtain was swept back from the arch to reveal ladies getting up from the table and preparing to adjourn to the drawing room. I counted quickly. There were eight of them. The gentlemen must have gone out for their port or a smoke. I was sure they would rejoin the party shortly.

In the meantime, I sat back in my seat and assessed the ladies, who moved together like a flock of birds. Once they were all in, I rose and curtsied, as it would be impolite to do otherwise, but I couldn't wait to get back to my looking on from the side. Only one or two of them nodded in my direction. The others only stared at me.

Adele had better luck in making an impression. She rose after me, as if waiting to make the most of the entrance.

"*Bonjour, mesdames,*" she said with gravity, then looked up as if just waiting for compliments to start pouring in.

"Oh, what a little puppet!" The one I knew at once was Miss Ingram looked down at Adele with a mocking air. I disliked her immediately, but I ruled her out for the vampyre in our midst as I had witnessed her riding in full sunshine.

Another lady, who I would learn was Lady Lynn, remarked, "It is Mr. Rochester's ward, I suppose—the little French girl he was speaking of."

Mrs. Dent kindly took her hand and gave her a kiss.

Amy and Louisa Eshton cried out simultaneously, "What a love of a child!" Then they called her to a sofa, where she sat, ensconced between them, chattering alternately in French and broken English, absorbing not only the young ladies' attention, but that of Mrs. Eshton and Lady Lynn. Adele was spoiled to her heart's content, but were they assessing her in the usual way that ladies doted on pretty children or as a tasty morsel to snack on later in the evening?

I got the names of all the ladies within minutes. There was Mrs. Eshton and two of her daughters. Of her daughters, who sat enchanted with my little charge, the eldest, Amy, was rather little and somewhat childlike herself in face and manner. The second, Louisa, was taller and more elegant in figure, very pretty, too. Mrs. Colonel Dent was less showy, but more ladylike. I'd centred on Lady Lynn, with her high forehead and dark eyes, as the one with most vampyric potential.

But the three most distinguished—partly, perhaps, because the tallest figures of the band—were the Dowager Lady Ingram and her daughters, Blanche and Mary. They were all three of the loftiest stature of women. The dowager gave an expression of almost insupportable haughtiness in her bearing and countenance. She had a fierce and a hard eye. It reminded me of Mrs. Reed's. If Blanche was no vampyre, I still couldn't be sure of her mother.

Blanche and Mary were of equal stature, both straight and tall as poplars. Mary was too slim for her height, but Blanche was moulded like a goddess. I regarded her, of course, with special interest. First, I wished to see whether her appearance accorded with Mrs. Fairfax's description. Second, whether it were such as I should fancy her likely to suit Mr. Rochester's taste. And third, if I could find some defect as to render her an unnatural being that must be removed from society and perhaps the very earth.

As far as her person went, she answered point for point Mrs. Fairfax's description. But her face had the same high features and haughty look of her mother's. I supposed men might overlook the haughtiness, or think it attractive on some level.

And her manner? Her laugh was satirical to match the habitual expression of her arched and haughty lip. She played: her execution was brilliant. She sang: her voice was fine. She spoke French apart to her mama, and she spoke it well, with fluency and with a good accent.

Had she placed herself under an enchantment to accomplish so much and to do it all well? Was she perhaps an ugly goblin under a glamour to make her appear as a beautiful woman? All things were possible, and I would be considering her every move.

Mary, Miss Ingram's sister, had a milder and more open countenance than Blanche, softer features, too, and a skin some shades fairer. But Mary was deficient in life. Her face lacked expression, her eye luster. She had nothing to say and, having once taken her seat, remained fixed like a statue in its niche. Very zombielike, if I was being honest, and it was entirely possible that she had died young and her vain sister had dug her up to act the foil. The sisters were both attired in spotless, unaccented white.

At last coffee was brought in, and the gentlemen were summoned. For some time, I had been in my little window nook observing unmolested Adele was content. No one needed or cared to notice me. The collective appearance of the gentlemen, like that of the ladies, was imposing. The gentlemen were all in black. Most of them were tall, equal in height to Mr. Rochester or taller. Some of them were young.

Henry and Frederick Lynn were dashing sparks indeed. Colonel Dent seemed a fine soldierly man. Sir George was a big country-looking sort. Mr. Eshton, the magistrate of the district, was gentleman-like with white hair but dark eyebrows and whiskers, which made him look a little theatrical. Lord Ingram, like his sisters, was tall, and also handsome, but he shared Mary's apathetic and listless look. He seemed to have more length of limb than vivacity of blood or vigour of brain. If Blanche had harvested one sibling, what was to stop her from cursing the second? It would serve her well when spending her brother's inheritance. She could control him, and his money.

And where was Mr. Rochester?

He came in last, a little after all the others. I looked away on purpose, though I saw him enter from the corner of my eye. I feigned attention to my knitting needles, to the meshes of the purse I was forming. But there he was. My mind flew back to our last meeting when he didn't want to let me go. What had occurred since to change his and my relative position? How distant, how far estranged, we were! I did not wonder when, without looking at me, he took a seat at the other side of the room and began conversing with some of the ladies.

I was safe to watch him without being observed. My gaze was drawn to his rough face, the olive complexion, square brow, deep eyes, firm mouth. Was he beautiful according to rule? Not in the way of the Ingrams perhaps, or not like the handsome younger Henry and Frederick Lynn. But he was beautiful to me. He quite mastered me. I had not intended to love him. The reader knows how hard I had tried to stop. Now, at the first renewed view of him, I couldn't deny my feelings. He made me love him without looking at me.

I compared him with his guests. What was the gallant grace of the Lynns, the languid elegance of Lord Ingram, even the military distinction of Colonel Dent, contrasted with Mr. Rochester's look of native pith and genuine power? He talked, at the moment, to Louisa and Amy Eshton. I wondered to see them receive with calm that look that seemed to me so penetrating. I expected their eyes to fall, their colour to rise under it; yet I was glad when it seemed they were in no sense moved.

Coffee was handed around. Conversation carried on. Blanche Ingram stood alone at the table, bending gracefully over an album. Mr. Rochester quit the Eshtons and went to stand on the hearth, solitary, giving her the perfect chance to confront him.

"Mr. Rochester, I thought you were not fond of children?" she asked, heading right over to his side.

"Nor am I."

"Then, what induced you to take charge of such a little doll as that?" She gestured to Adele as if she were an object, just a floppy puppet. "Where did you pick her up?"

"I did not pick her up. She was left on my hands."

"You should have sent her to school."

"I could not afford it. Schools are so dear."

"Why, I suppose you have a governess for her. I saw a person with her just now—is she gone? Oh, no! There she is still, behind the window curtain. You pay her, of course. I should think it quite as expensive, more so, for you have them both to keep in addition."

Oh, yes, I was quite the luxury item. I hated to be reminded that I was in his employ and not an equal, as Miss Ingram. But so be it.

"I have not considered the subject." He remained staring straight in front of him. I imagined he was sorry he'd set himself apart for conversation and was fancying he might step out for a cigar about now. If I had the kind of power over him that I'd suspected of Grace Poole, it was exactly the kind of thought I would put in his head.

"No, you men never do consider economy and common sense," Blanche, sensing she'd struck a point in her favour, carried on. "You should hear Mama on the chapter of governesses. Mary and I have had, I should think, a dozen at least in our day, half of them detestable and the rest ridiculous—were they not, Mama?"

"Did you speak, my own?"

The young lady thus claimed as the dowager's special property reiterated her question with an explanation, and Lady Ingram said, "My dearest, don't mention governesses. The word makes me nervous. I thank heaven I have now done with them!"

I was not disappointed to find myself amongst the very class who had driven Lady Ingram to distraction. I felt the pride of sisterhood with those who had gone before me. If only they had proven even more effective in their quest to do Lady Ingram in.

Mrs. Dent here bent over to the pious lady and whispered something in her ear. I supposed it was a reminder that one of the dreaded race was present.

"Very well. I hope it may do her good!" Lady Ingram went on. Then, in a lower tone, but still loud enough for me to hear: "I noticed her. I am a judge of physiognomy, and in hers I see all the faults of her class."

"What are they, madam?" inquired Mr. Rochester aloud.

"I will tell you in your private ear," replied she, wagging her turban three times with portentous significance.

"But my curiosity will be past its appetite. It craves food now." Mr. Rochester wore that vexing half smile, though he would still not meet my gaze.

"Ask Blanche. She is nearer you than I."

By now, I assumed it was so scandalous as to admit that her husband had preferred the company of governesses to that of his wife, and I would not be at all surprised. Intolerable woman!

"Oh, don't refer him to me, Mama! I have just one word to say of the whole tribe. They are a nuisance. Not that I ever suffered much from them. I took care to turn the tables. What tricks Theodore and I used to play on our Miss Wilsons, and Mrs. Greys, and Madame Jouberts! And then there was Miss Ross, the most disagreeable of them all. She caught on to all of our tricks. Tedo, remember how she broke all the mirrors in the house? But when we went outdoors, she would never chase after us. La, but we spent so much time out of doors when she was with us just to avoid her!"

"Yaas," Blanche's brother drawled. "And then, I told you, I saw her run straight into the tree branch one night, the night I refused to come in even after dark and she insisted on chasing me down. She tripped, landed on the branch, and poof! She turned to dust."

I listened with interest. They'd had a vampyre nanny! Was it possible that she'd turned one of them? Lady Ingram, perhaps? Or Tedo? I had narrowed my search.

"Oh, no, darlings," Lady Ingram put in. "She ran off with the music master. I was sure of it. Yet Theodore still insists on the story of hitting her head. Ho, now, you were such an inventive boy."

Tedo began to argue. I quite believed him, but would not tell him so. Besides, if they found governesses were so intolerable, it was a wonder the Ingrams kept hiring them.

"It sounds like the charges, not the governesses, may have been part of the problem," Mr. Rochester said in his inimitable way.

"Mark my words, Mr. Rochester. You're better off sending your charge to school. But enough of the topic," said Miss Ingram. "Signor Eduardo, are you in voice tonight?"

"Donna Bianca, if you command it, I will be."

"Then, signor, I lay on you my sovereign behest to furbish up your lungs and other vocal organs, as they will be wanted on my royal service."

Miss Ingram, who had now seated herself with proud grace at the piano, spread out her snowy robes in queenly amplitude. "Mr. Rochester, now sing! And I will play."

"I am all obedience," he said.

"Here then is a corsair song. Know that I dote on corsairs, and for that reason, sing it *con spirito*."

"Commands from Miss Ingram's lips would put spirit into a mug of milk and water."

Or bile into an empty stomach. I wished he would just get on with it. I meant to slip away as soon as he started singing. If there were vampyres amongst the guests, they hadn't made themselves known to the others yet, and it was likely they wouldn't this evening. I was not needed.

But he started, and the tones arrested me. Mrs. Fairfax had said Mr. Rochester possessed a fine voice. He did: a mellow, powerful bass, into which he threw his feelings, his force, finding a way through the ear to the heart, and there waking sensation strangely. I waited until the last deep and full vibration had expired, then quitted my sheltered corner and made my exit by the side door, which was fortunately near. I would send Sophie for Adele in a short time.

I'd made it to the hall, a narrow passage that led to the back staircase, when a voice behind me gave me pause.

I turned and stood face-to-face with Mr. Rochester.

"How do you do?" he asked.

"I am very well, sir."

"Why did you not come and speak to me in the room?"

"I did not wish to disturb you, as you seemed engaged, sir."

"What have you been doing during my absence?"

"Teaching Adele, as usual."

"And getting a good deal paler than you were—as I saw at first sight. What is the matter?"

"Nothing at all, sir."

"Did you take any cold that night you half drowned me?"

"Not the least."

"Return to the drawing room. You are deserting too early."

"I am tired, sir."

He looked at me for a minute. "And a little depressed. What about? Tell me."

"Nothing, sir. I am not depressed."

"But I affirm that you are. So much depressed that a few more words would bring tears to your eyes—indeed, they are there now, shining and swimming. If I had time and were not in mortal dread of a servant passing, I would know what all this means. Well, tonight, I excuse you. Tomorrow, and every night as long as my visitors stay, I expect you to appear in the drawing room. Now go, and send Sophie for Adele."

"Yes, sir." I could not meet his gaze. "Good night."

"Good night, my—" He stopped, bit his lip, and abruptly left me.

CHAPTER 21

I ALLOWED MYSELF TO JOIN in the festivities, just as Mr. Rochester requested. Merry days were these at Thornfield Hall, and busy days, too. Life was everywhere, movement all day long.

And plenty of excitement for night, too. On the second night of the visit, Lady Lynn claimed she woke to find someone in her room, leaning over her with hot breath that reeked of port. I thought immediately of Grace Poole, but I couldn't rule out a vampyre. I remembered holidays with the Reeds and how they would murder and dine on guests in their beds. I would have to be on my guard. Mr. Rochester simply suggested someone stumbled into the wrong room and warned his guests to lock their doors. I flashed him a look, but he appeared not to notice.

Tonight, they spoke of playing charades. The servants were called in, the dining-room tables wheeled away, the lights otherwise disposed, the chairs placed in a semicircle opposite the arch. Old storage chests were raided to yield items that might aid in the making of costumes. Mr. Rochester summoned the ladies around him and selected certain of their number to be amongst his party.

"Miss Ingram is mine, of course," he said, then he named the two Misses Eshton, and Mrs. Dent. He looked at me. I was near him as I had been fastening the clasp of Mrs. Dent's bracelet.

"Will you play?" he asked. I shook my head. He did not insist, which I rather feared he would do. He allowed me to return quietly to my usual seat.

He and his aides now withdrew behind the curtain. The other party, which was headed by Colonel Dent, sat down on the crescent of chairs. Ere long a bell tinkled, and the curtain drew up. Sir

George Lynn was seen enveloped in a white sheet on a table. Mr. Rochester dug in a patch of ground that appeared to be a graveyard and returned with some odd parts. I wondered if he meant to act the role of bokor? The curtains closed.

I guessed it as the novel *Frankenstein, or the Modern Prometheus*, which had caused such a stir amongst the girls at Lowood until Miss Scatcherd caught it going around and threw it in the fire. I'd always found it too eerily reminiscent of what we'd endured under Mr. Bokorhurst's rule at Lowood. Colonel Dent's crew gathered around in deliberation, but could not come to agreement without a second scene.

A considerable interval elapsed before the curtain again rose. Greenery from the conservatory was scattered around to resemble a woodland scene. Miss Ingram as Elizabeth, in her lovely costume, skipped through the makeshift trees until Sir George, made up to look gruesome, jumped out and murdered her. Sir George ran as Mr. Rochester emerged to bend, and grieve, over his ladylove.

"*Frankenstein!*" Colonel Dent finally guessed.

"Sir George, you make a fitting monster," Lord Ingram drawled.

A sufficient interval having elapsed for the performers to resume their ordinary costume, they reentered the dining room. Mr. Rochester led in Miss Ingram.

"Now, Dent," continued Mr. Rochester to the party, "it is your turn."

As the other party withdrew, he and his band took the vacated seats. Miss Ingram placed herself at her leader's right hand. The other diviners filled the chairs on either side of him and her. I tried to watch the actors to determine who amongst them could be a vampyre, but it was no use. The spectators absorbed my full attention. I watched Mr. Rochester turn to Miss Ingram, and Miss Ingram to him. I noticed how she inclined her head towards him, until her dark curls almost touched his shoulder and waved against his cheek. I heard their whisperings.

I have told you, reader, that I had learned to love Mr. Rochester.

I could not stop loving him now merely because I found that he had ceased to notice me in favour of a great lady who scorned to touch me with the hem of her robes as she passed. I could not stop even though I felt sure he would soon marry this very lady.

Nothing in these circumstances would cool or banish love, though much would create despair. I was not jealous, or rarely. Miss Ingram was a mark beneath jealousy, was too inferior to excite the feeling, despite her seeming superiority in class. She was showy, but not genuine. She had a fine person, many brilliant attainments, but her mind was poor, her heart barren. She was not good, not original. I most objected to the way she treated little Adele, pushing her away if she approached her, sometimes ordering her from the room, and always treating her with coldness and acrimony.

Other eyes besides mine watched these manifestations of character, watched them closely, keenly, shrewdly. Yes, the future bridegroom, Mr. Rochester himself. I couldn't imagine he approved her entirely, yet he showed her marked preference. Together, they had become the life and soul of the party. If he was absent from the room an hour, a perceptible dullness seemed to steal over the spirits of his guests; and his reentry was sure to give a fresh impulse to the vivacity of conversation.

The want of his animating influence appeared to be peculiarly felt one day when he had been summoned to Millcote on business and was not likely to return until late. The afternoon was wet. I'd stopped worrying that he would run into trouble on the road once I'd become more certain that he would know how to handle himself in a crisis. He'd been handling something here at home for years, apparently.

As for the rest of his party, I had no concern. Let the vampyres get them all. They had proposed to take a walk to see a Gypsy camp, lately pitched on a common beyond Hay, but the outing was deferred on account of the weather. Some of the gentlemen were gone to the stables. The younger ones, together with the younger ladies, were playing billiards in the billiard room. The Dowagers Ingram and Lynn sought solace in a quiet game at cards. Blanche Ingram refused all efforts of the others to engage her. She fetched a novel from the library and flung herself in haughty listlessness on a sofa. The room and the house were silent save for the occasional burst of merriment of the billiard players echoing from above.

It verged on dusk and the clock had already given warning of the hour to dress for dinner when little Adele, who knelt by me in the drawing-room window seat, suddenly exclaimed that she thought she heard Mr. Rochester's return.

I turned, and Miss Ingram darted forward from her sofa. But it was not Mr. Rochester returning on Mesrour with Pilot at his side. It was a carriage bearing a visitor. Miss Ingram berated Adele as "a tiresome monkey!" as the stranger rang the bell. He was soon led in to sit with the party and await Mr. Rochester's return. He bowed to Lady Ingram, as deeming her the eldest lady present.

"It appears I come at an inopportune time, madam," said he, "when my friend Mr. Rochester is from home, but I arrive from a very long journey. May I wait on him?"

His manner was polite. His accent struck me as somewhat unusual, not precisely foreign, but still not altogether English. His age might be about Mr. Rochester's. His complexion was singularly sallow. Otherwise he was a fine-looking man, at first sight especially. On closer examination, I detected something in his face that displeased, or rather that failed to please. His features were regular, but too relaxed. His eyes were large and well cut, but the life looking out of them was a tame, vacant life, at least so I thought.

I had more chance to study him after dinner, as the party returned to the drawing room and I kept my usual seat. I observed and learned more of him from listening to his talk with some of the gentlemen. Called Mr. Mason, he was but just arrived in England from some hot country, which explained why his face was so sallow, and why he sat so near the hearth and wore a coat in the house. Presently the words Jamaica, Kingston, Spanish Town, indicated the West Indies as his residence, and I gathered that he had met Mr. Rochester there. Curious, indeed. He spoke of his friend's dislike of the burning heats, the hurricanes, and the rainy seasons of that region. I knew Mr. Rochester had been a traveller, but I did not know he had spent time in the West Indies. I thought of Helen Burns's maid, the one who had told her of zombie curses and voodoo bokors. I wondered about Mr. Mason. What did he know of zombies?

I was pondering this when an incident, somewhat unexpected, broke the thread of my musings. Mr. Mason needed more coal on the fire. The footman who brought the coal, in going out, stopped near Mr. Eshton's chair and said something to him in a low voice, of which I heard only the words "old woman" and "quite troublesome."

"Tell her she shall be put in the stocks if she does not take herself off," replied the magistrate.

"No—stop!" interrupted Colonel Dent. "Don't send her away, Eshton. We'd better consult the ladies." Speaking aloud, he continued, "Ladies, you talked of going to Hay Common to visit the Gypsy camp. Sam here says that one of the old Mother Bunches is in the servants' hall at this moment and insists upon being brought in before 'the quality' to tell them their fortunes. Would you like to see her?"

I sat up straighter, suspicious now. That this strange Gypsy woman should come on the same night as a strange West Indies visitor? I'd learned to question coincidences and strangers. I remained on alert.

"What is she like?" inquired the Misses Eshton in a breath.

"A shockingly ugly old creature, miss."

"Why, she's a real sorceress!" cried Frederick Lynn. "Let us have her in, of course."

A sorceress? Aha, she could be one of Grace Poole's people.

Things had been quiet with regard to Grace Poole for some time, but I remained wary of her, too.

"I have a curiosity to hear my fortune told. Sam, order the beldam forward," spoke Blanche haughtily as she turned around on the piano stool, where until now she had sat silent, apparently examining sundry sheets of music.

Excitement instantly seized the whole party, a running fire of raillery and jests.

When Sam returned, he said, "She won't come now. She says it's not her mission to appear before the 'vulgar herd.' I must show her into a room by herself, and then those who wish to consult her must go to her one by one."

"Show her into the library, of course," Blanche said. "It is not my mission to listen to her before the vulgar herd either. I mean to have her all to myself."

"She's ready now," said the footman as he reappeared. "She wishes to know who will be her first visitor."

"I go first." Miss Ingram rose solemnly.

I thought I should perhaps stop her, in case evil awaited. But I had no desire to save Blanche Ingram from an evil fate, and I simply watched her go. The minutes passed slowly. Fifteen were counted before the library door again opened. Miss Ingram returned to us through the arch.

Would she laugh? Would she take it as a joke? All eyes met her with a glance of eager curiosity, and she met all eyes with one of rebuff and coldness. She looked neither flurried nor merry. She walked stiffly to her seat and took it in silence.

"Well, Blanche?" said Lord Ingram.

"What did she say, Sister?" asked Mary.

"Now, now, good people," returned Miss Ingram. "Don't press upon me. I have seen a Gypsy vagabond. She has practised in hackneyed fashion the science of palmistry and told me what such people usually tell. My whim is gratified, and now I think Mr.

Eshton will do well to put the hag in the stocks tomorrow morning, as he threatened."

Miss Ingram took a book, leaned back in her chair, and so declined further conversation. I watched her for nearly a half hour. During all that time, she never turned a page, and her face grew darker, more dissatisfied, and more sourly expressive of disappointment by the minute. She had obviously not heard anything to her advantage.

Meantime, Mary Ingram and Amy and Louisa Eshton declared they dared not go alone, yet they all wished to go. A negotiation was opened through Sam, and after much pacing to and fro, until, I think, Sam's calves must have ached with the exercise, permission was at last, with great difficulty, extorted from the rigorous sibyl for the three to wait upon her in a body.

Their visit was not so still as Miss Ingram's had been. We heard hysterical giggling and little shrieks from the library. After about twenty minutes they came running across the hall, as if they were half scared out of their wits.

"I am sure she is something not right!" they cried, one and all. "She told us such things! She knows all about us!" They sank breathless into the various seats the gentlemen hastened to bring them.

The others begged more information and the girls related how the woman knew such intimate particulars as their fondest wishes and what they dreamed at night.

In the midst of the tumult, and while my eyes and ears were fully engaged in the scene before me, I heard a hem close at my elbow. I turned and saw Sam.

"If you please, miss, the Gypsy declares that there is another young single lady in the room who has not been to her yet, and she swears she will not go until she has seen all. I thought it must be you. What shall I tell her?"

"Oh, I will go by all means." I was glad of the opportunity to gratify my much excited curiosity. I slipped out of the room and closed the door quietly behind me.

CHAPTER 22

THE LIBRARY LOOKED TRANQUIL enough, illuminated only by the light of the fire. The witch, if witch she was, was seated in an easy chair at the chimney corner. She had on a red cloak and a broad-brimmed Gypsy hat, tied down with a striped handkerchief under her chin. An extinguished candle stood on the table.

"Well, and you want your fortune told?" she said in a harsh voice.

"I don't care about it. You may please yourself. But I ought to warn you, I have no faith."

"It's like your impudence to say so. I heard it in your step as you crossed the threshold."

"Did you? You've a quick ear." I watched her carefully, thinking of the daggers I had strapped to my ankle in case of danger.

"I have, and a quick eye and a quick brain."

"You need them all in your trade."

"I do. Especially when I've customers like you to deal with. Why don't you tremble?"

"I'm not cold."

"You are cold. Cold because you are alone." She put a short black pipe to her lips and began smoking with vigour.

"You might say all that to almost anyone who you knew lived as a solitary dependent in a great house."

"I might say it to almost anyone, but would it be true of almost anyone? If you knew it, you are peculiarly situated, very near happiness. Yes, within reach of it. The materials are all prepared. There only wants a movement to combine them. Now, show me your palm."

"And I must cross it with silver, I suppose?"

"To be sure." She cackled again.

I gave her a shilling. She pocketed it and told me to hold out my hand. I did. She approached her face to the palm.

"It is too fine. I can make nothing of such a hand as that, almost without lines. I wonder what thoughts are busy in your heart during all the hours you sit in the window seat with the fine people flitting before you like shapes in a magic lantern. You see I know your habits—"

"You have learned them from the servants."

"Ah! You think yourself sharp. Well, perhaps I have. To speak truth, I have an acquaintance with one of them, Mrs. Poole—"

I started to my feet when I heard the name. Something wicked was in all this after all. My hand grasped at the stake I kept in my pocket.

"Don't be alarmed," continued the strange being. "She's a safe hand is Mrs. Poole. Close and quiet, anyone may repose confidence in her. But, as I was saying, sitting in that window seat, is there not one face you study? One figure whose movements you follow with at least curiosity?"

"I like to observe all the faces and all the figures."

"But do you never single one from the rest—or it may be, two?"

"I do frequently. When the gestures or looks of a pair seem telling a tale, it amuses me to watch them."

"What tale do you like best to hear?"

"Oh, I have not much choice! They generally run on the same theme, courtship and marriage." I relaxed my hold on the stake, feeling more secure.

"And do you like that monotonous theme?"

"I don't care about it. It is nothing to me."

"Nothing to you? When a lady, young and full of life and health, charming with beauty and endowed with the gifts of rank and fortune, sits and smiles in the eyes of a gentleman you—"

"I what?"

"You know—and perhaps think well of."

"I don't know the gentlemen here. I have scarcely interchanged a syllable with one of them."

"Will you say that of the master of the house?"

"He is not at home."

"A most ingenious quibble!"

"No, but I can scarcely see what Mr. Rochester has to do with the theme you had introduced."

"Can't you? You have seen love, have you not? And, looking forward, you have seen him married and beheld his bride happy?"

"Not exactly. Your witch's skill is rather at fault sometimes."

"What the devil have you seen, then?"

"Never mind. I came here to inquire, not to confess. Is it known that Mr. Rochester is to be married?"

"Yes, and to the beautiful Miss Ingram."

"Shortly?"

"Appearances would warrant that conclusion. But I gave her some intelligence that seemed to quite upset her. It seems she prefers to marry for fortune, and I assured her that Mr. Rochester was on the brink of ruin."

Ha. Fortune-teller indeed. It could be that his fortunes had been reduced, though I saw nothing of it. But on the brink of ruin? No wonder Blanche was most distressed.

"But, I did not come to hear Mr. Rochester's fortune. I came to hear my own, and you have told me nothing of it."

"Your fortune is yet doubtful. Chance has meted you a measure of happiness. She has laid it carefully on one side for you. It depends on you to stretch out your hand and take it up. The problem is that I can't tell whether you will do so, stubborn one. Kneel on the rug."

I leaned as if I would kneel, but instead retrieved my daggers and lunged at the old fraud, daggers extended, one in each hand. "What of the master not being at home? Who are you? Who sent you? Do you intend to rob me as you have perhaps robbed others tonight? Or are you about to perpetrate a foul scheme, with perhaps Grace Poole? Confess, or die!"

"Confess?" She stood to full height, taller than I imagined. Not intimidated, I slid a dagger under her throat. Much to my surprise, the old hag reacted with lightning speed, gripping my wrist and twisting my arm behind my back.

"What act is this?" The hag's voice deepened to a gravelly huskiness. "Daggers, Jane?"

She knew my name. No doubt I was right about her being in league with Grace Poole. I steadied my breathing, as Miss Temple had instructed, imagined my enemy's position behind me, and—

Slammed my head back into what should have been her head, but surely was only her chest. Still, the move was effective enough to startle my aggressor into dropping my wrist. I spun, reared up on my toes, and delivered a solid kick to the old witch's jaw. "Ha, take that!"

She slammed back into her chair, and I filled with that surge of power that accompanied such victories. "Now tell me your name, and your purpose!"

"No such thing." She bounced back with surprising skill, slamming into me, and pinioning me against the wall with supernatural strength. I gasped in surprise. Zombie or vampyre? I'd lost my daggers, but I still had a stake in my pocket if only I could twist my arm out of her viselike hold and—

"Enough, Jane," my aggressor said quietly, the voice registering in my mind. I knew that voice. I looked. I knew those eyes. "We could clearly engage in combat all night, but I had only thought to entertain you for a quarter hour. The guests will be getting anxious for you."

"The guests don't take any notice of me, Mr. Rochester. As you know. But what are you doing dressed up? Reading fortunes? Sir, what a strange idea."

He stepped back, freeing me while he removed his red cloak. "As strange as a governess armed with Egyptian daggers that she clearly knows how to use?" He picked them up and returned them to me after making a close study of the handles. "Exquisite workmanship."

"And stakes, sir. I have one in my pocket at all times. There are vampyres about."

"What do you mean, vampyres?"

"You explain first. What were you doing in costume?"

"Simply trying to amuse my guests."

"But with me, sir? It felt as if you were trying to draw me out."

"And so I have, Madam Assassin, speaking of acting a part. Do you forgive me, Jane?"

"I don't know yet. If, on reflection, I find I have fallen into no great absurdity, I shall try to forgive you."

"Oh, you have been very correct. And quite impressive."

I reflected, and thought, on the whole, I had. It was a comfort, but indeed I had been on my guard almost from the beginning of the interview. Something of masquerade I suspected, but my mind had been running on Grace Poole.

"I am no assassin, sir. There were zombies at Lowood. Before that, I lived with vampyres. I have learned a few things to—protect myself." And others, but I didn't want to embarrass him by mentioning the few vampyres I'd killed to protect him at our first meeting. "I seem to get a certain feeling when vampyres are present, and I have had that feeling since you arrived with your guests. I am sure one of them is not quite right. I think one of them meant to attack Lady Lynn in her bed the other night."

"One of them, you say. A sense for vampyres? What an unusual skill. But that one of my guests could be so unnatural? I had no idea."

"They often manage to go about in the population unnoticed."

"You were raised with them?"

"There is much about me you don't know, sir."

"There is much I would like to know, but my guests must be

growing impatient. Perhaps some other time. I suspect you have been watching out for the vampyre amongst them? Tell me what the people in the drawing room are doing."

"Discussing the Gypsy, I daresay. And, oh, are you aware, Mr. Rochester, that a stranger has arrived here since you left this morning?"

"A stranger? Who can it be? I expected no one. Is he gone?"

"No. He said he had known you long, and that he could take the liberty of installing himself here until you returned."

"The devil he did! Did he give his name?"

"His name is Mason, sir, from the West Indies." I hoped the name would draw Mr. Rochester out and allow him to tell me about his time in the West Indies. Did he know anything of voodoo? Did it have anything to do with Grace Poole?

"Mason!"

"Are you ill, sir?"

He shook his head, clearly distressed. He sat down, and made me sit beside him. "Jane, I wish I were on a quiet island with only you, and trouble, and danger, and hideous recollections removed from me."

"Can I help you, sir?"

"Yes. Fetch me a glass of wine from the dining room. They will be at supper there. Make note and tell me if Mason is with them, and what he is doing."

I went. I found all the party in the dining room at supper, as Mr. Rochester had said. They were not seated at the table. The supper was arranged on the sideboard. Each had taken what he chose, and they stood about here and there in groups, their plates and glasses in their hands. Every one seemed in high glee. Mr. Mason stood near the fire, talking to Colonel and Mrs. Dent, and appeared as merry as any of them. I filled a wineglass and saw Miss Ingram watch me with such a look, as if she'd caught me taking a liberty. I nodded in her direction and returned to the library.

Mr. Rochester seemed more collected. He took the glass from my hand.

"Here is to your health, ministrant spirit!" He swallowed the contents and returned it to me. "What are they doing, Jane?"

I gave my report. He nodded. "Go back now into the room. Take Mason aside quietly and tell him that Mr. Rochester has returned and wishes to see him. Show him in here and then leave us."

"Yes, sir."

I did his behest. The company all stared at me as I passed straight amongst them. I sought Mr. Mason, delivered the message, and preceded him from the room. I ushered him into the library, then I went upstairs.

At a late hour, after I had been in bed some time, I heard the visitors repair to their chambers. I distinguished Mr. Rochester's voice and heard him say, "This way, Mason, to your room."

He spoke cheerfully and it set my mind at ease. I was able to stop worrying, turn over, and go to sleep.

The moon was full, bright, and shining in my window, waking me up in the middle of the night. I had forgotten to draw my curtain, which I usually did, and also to let down my window blind. I got up to do so and stopped in my tracks at a sound.

A strange noise split the air: a savage, sharp, shrilly sound that ran from end to end of Thornfield Hall.

My pulse stopped. My heart stood still. The cry died and was not renewed. Indeed, whatever being uttered that fearful shriek could not soon repeat it, I daresay. It would have damaged its throat.

I knew it at once to be out of the third story, for it came from overhead, right over my room. I heard a struggle going on, a deadly one from the sound of it. A half-smothered voice called out for help, three times in rapid succession. Then, more scraping and banging. Finally, a cry for Mr. Rochester, which set me at some ease. A voice calling for Rochester meant that he was not in the middle of the fray.

Chamber doors opened. Someone ran, or rushed, along the gallery. Another step stamped on the flooring above and something fell. Then there was silence, more eerie than the noise.

I rushed into some clothes and armed myself with a few stakes in various pockets, full ready to take any action needed on this night. I stepped out to find the doors of curious tenants opening, closing, exclamations of bewilderment, and terrified murmurs. The gallery filled. Gentlemen and ladies alike had quitted their beds.

"Oh! What is it?"—"Who is hurt?"—"What has happened?"—"Fetch a light!"—"Is it fire?"—"Are there robbers?"—"Where shall we run?" was demanded confusedly on all hands. But for the moonlight they would have been in complete darkness.

"Now calm, all," I said. "I'm sure it's nothing. Back to bed." No one could be sure it was I who had spoken, for they did not often hear my voice, but there was some agreement. A few did start back.

"Where the devil is Rochester?" cried Colonel Dent. "I cannot find him in his bed."

"Here! here!" was shouted in return. "Be composed, all of you. I'm coming."

The door at the end of the gallery opened, and Mr. Rochester advanced with a candle. He had just descended from the upper story. Miss Ingram ran to him directly and seized his arm, nearly toppling the candle.

"What awful event has taken place?" said she. "Let us know the worst at once!"

Mr. Rochester's black eyes darted sparks more heated than the candle's flame. Calming himself by an apparent effort, he added, "A servant has had a nightmare. That is all. She's an excitable, nervous person. She construed her dream into an apparition, or something of that sort, no doubt, and has taken a fit with fright. Now, then, I must see you all back into your rooms, for until the house is settled, she cannot be looked after. Gentlemen, have the goodness to set the ladies the example. Miss Ingram, I am sure you will not fail in evincing superiority to idle terrors."

I did not return to my room to sit idly waiting for Mr. Rochester to come to me. I stayed while others went and finally approached him. "Am I wanted?"

"Have you a sponge in your room?" he asked in a whisper. "And volatile salts?"

"Yes to both."

"Fetch them, please, and follow me."

My slippers were thin. I could walk the matted floor as softly as a cat. I followed as he glided up the gallery and up the stairs and stopped in the dark, low corridor of the fateful third story. He paused outside a great black door with keys in his hand and turned to me.

"You don't turn sick at the sight of blood?"

"Not at all." What did he think? I'd just attacked him in his own library and confessed to be looking for a vampyre amongst his houseguests.

"Just give me your hand," he said. "It will not do to risk a fainting fit. Warm and steady now."

I didn't argue that I had no need for his support. I welcomed the chance for contact and I put my fingers into his. He turned the key and opened the door.

I saw a room I remembered to have seen before, the day Mrs. Fairfax showed me over the house. It was hung with tapestry, but the tapestry was now looped up in one part, revealing a door, which had then been concealed. The door was open. A light shone out of the room. I heard thence a snarling sound.

"Wait a minute," said Mr. Rochester, putting down his candle, and he went forward to the inner apartment. A shout of laughter greeted his entrance, noisy at first, and terminating in Grace Poole's own goblin *ha! ha!* She then was there. He made some sort of arrangement without speaking, though I heard a low voice address him. He came out and closed the door behind him.

"Here, Jane." He motioned me to the back of the room. I walked around to the other side of a large bed, which with its drawn curtains concealed a considerable portion of the chamber. An easy chair was near the bed. A man sat in it, dressed with the exception of his coat. He was still, his head back, his eyes closed. Mr. Rochester held the candle over him. I recognised the stranger, Mason. I saw, too, that his linen on one side, and one arm, were almost soaked in blood.

"Hold the candle," said Mr. Rochester, and I took it. He fetched a basin of water from the washstand. "Hold that," he said. I obeyed. He took the sponge, dipped it in, and moistened the corpselike face. Mr. Mason was not a zombie. I knew from the amount of blood and no sign of the green ooze. Mr. Rochester asked for my smelling bottle and applied it to the nostrils. Mr. Mason shortly opened his eyes and groaned. Mr. Rochester opened the shirt of the wounded man, whose arm and shoulder were bandaged. He sponged away blood, trickling fast down.

"Is there immediate danger?" murmured Mr. Mason.

"No—a mere scratch. Don't be so overcome, man. Bear up! I'll fetch a surgeon for you now and you'll be able to be removed by morning, I hope.

"Jane," Mr. Rochester said. "I must leave you in this room with this gentleman, for an hour, or perhaps two hours. You will sponge the blood as I do when it returns. If he feels faint, you will put the glass of water on that stand to his lips, and your salts to his nose. You will not speak to him on any pretext, and, Richard, it will be at the peril of your life if you speak to her. Open your lips, agitate yourself, and I'll not answer for the consequences."

Again the poor man groaned. He looked as if he dared not move. Fear, of death or of something else, appeared almost to paralyse him. Mr. Rochester put the bloody sponge into my hand, which I used as he had done.

"Remember, no conversation," he said, and then left.

I felt strange as the key grated in the lock and the sound of his retreating step ceased to be heard. Grace Poole was on the other side of the inner door, and what did she there? What had she done to Mr. Mason? I would have ignored Mr. Rochester's orders and queried Mr. Mason if I felt he was in any condition to speak, but I feared he had met his end or was about to. The "mere scratch" looked quite deep and caused a great loss of blood. I remembered what it was like to be shut up in a dark room bleeding, and I was glad to be there for Mr. Mason, glad to have a candle at my side.

Here then I was in the third story, fastened into one of its mystic cells, Grace Poole so close I could get up and go question her. I could see what vile form she'd transformed to, or what kind of spells she might hurl my way. I could decide if beheading or a stake to the heart would be a surer way to do her in. I could end Mr. Rochester's torments of the woman once and for all, but it wasn't my right to choose. If he kept her at Thornfield, he kept her for a reason. As long as that reason was not revealed to me, I could not take it upon myself to act.

Mr. Mason's wound needed constant attention, and he maintained eye contact, as if willing me to know that he still lived. He had survived some kind of terror at Grace Poole's hands. But what? What had he done? What had she done? How were they acquainted? They must have known each other, or why would he be on the third floor? Perhaps she was his wife? I wondered.

The candle expired just as I perceived streaks of grey light edging the window curtains. Dawn, and Mr. Rochester, approached. I could hear Pilot barking in the yard. In a few minutes more, the key turned in the lock and Mr. Rochester entered with Mr. Carter, the surgeon.

Mr. Rochester stripped off his jacket and rolled up his sleeves. "Now, Carter, be on the alert. I give you but a half hour for dressing the wound, fastening the bandages, getting the patient downstairs and all."

"But is he fit to move, sir?" Carter looked doubtful.

"No doubt of it. It is nothing serious. He is nervous. His spirits must be kept up. Come, set to work."

CHAPTER 23

IF I HAD HOPED to be dismissed, I was mistaken. I didn't mind staying so much when Mr. Rochester was there, needing me. He drew back the thick curtain, drew up the blind, and let in all the daylight he could. I was surprised and cheered to see what rosy streaks were beginning to brighten the east. Then he approached Mason, whom the surgeon was already handling.

"Now, my good fellow, how are you?"

"She's done for me, I fear" was the faint reply. I took that as confirmation of Grace Poole's guilt in the matter.

"Not a whit! Courage! You've lost a little blood is all. Carter, assure him there's no danger."

"I can't do that conscientiously," said Carter, who had now undone the bandages. "Only I wish I could have got here sooner. He would not have bled so much—but how is this? The flesh on the shoulder is torn as well as cut. This wound was not done with a knife. There have been teeth here!"

"She bit me," Mr. Mason murmured. "She worried me like a tigress when Rochester got the knife from her."

Bit? I found new interest in the mutterings of our patient. It made me wish I'd had the nerve to thwart Mr. Rochester and grill Mason earlier. But I was here now, and no one made any effort to shuffle me out of the room.

"You should not have yielded," Mr. Rochester said on a sigh. "You should have grappled with her at once."

"But under such circumstances, what could one do? Oh, it was frightful!" Mr. Mason added, shuddering. "And I did not expect it. She looked so quiet at first."

"I warned you. I said, 'Be on your guard when you go near her.' Besides, you might have waited until tomorrow, as I'd asked. If you'd had me with you, it would have turned out quite differently. It was mere folly to attempt the interview tonight, and alone."

"I thought I could have done some good."

"You thought! You thought!" Mr. Rochester paced, running his hand through his hair. "You have suffered and are likely to suffer enough for not taking my advice. I'll say no more. Carter—hurry! The sun will soon rise, and I must have him off."

"Directly, sir. The shoulder is just bandaged. I must look to this other wound in the arm. She has had her teeth here, too, I think."

"She sucked the blood. She said she'd drain my heart," said Mason.

"Come, be silent, Richard, and never mind her gibberish. Don't repeat it."

"I wish I could forget it."

"You will when you are out of the country. When you get back to Spanish Town, you may think of her as dead and buried—or rather, you need not think of her at all."

"Impossible to forget this night!"

"It is not impossible. Have some energy, man. You thought you were as dead as a herring two hours since, and you are all alive and talking now. Carter has done with you or nearly so. I'll make you decent in a trice. Jane"—Mr. Rochester turned to me for the first time since his reentrance—"take this key. Go down into my bedroom and walk straight forward into my dressing room. Open the top drawer of the wardrobe and take out a clean shirt and neckerchief. Bring them here, and be nimble."

Nimble I was, finding the articles named and returning with them.

"Now," he said, "go to the other side of the bed while I order his toilet, but don't leave the room. You may be wanted again."

I retired as directed.

"Was anybody stirring below when you went down, Jane?" inquired Mr. Rochester presently.

"No, sir. All was very still."

"There, Richard. You shall make your escape before any are the wiser for it. And it will be better, both for your sake, and for that of the poor creature in yonder."

Poor creature, he called her? After the damage she'd wrought? The danger she obviously presented?

Mr. Rochester went on, "I have striven long to avoid exposure, and I should not like it to come at last. Here, Carter, help him on with his waistcoat. Where did you leave your furred cloak? You can't travel a mile without that, I know, in this damned cold climate. In your room? Jane, run down to Mr. Mason's room, the one next to mine, and fetch a cloak you will see there."

Again I ran and again returned, bearing an immense mantle lined and edged with fur.

"Now, I've another errand for you," Mr. Rochester said. "This one's very important. Back to my chamber. In my toilet table, middle drawer, you will find a velvet casket. Open it. It's filled with little glass phials. Bring me one, er, make it two."

I flew thither and back, bringing the desired vessels.

"Excellent. Now, Doctor, I shall take the liberty of administering a dose myself, on my own responsibility. I got this cordial at Rome, of an Italian charlatan—a fellow you would have kicked, Carter. It is not a thing to be used indiscriminately, but it is good upon occasion. As now, for instance. Jane, a little water."

He held out the tiny glass, and I half filled it from the water bottle on the washstand.

"That will do. Now wet the lip of the phial."

I did so. He measured twelve drops of a crimson liquid and presented it to Mason.

"Drink, Richard. It will give you the heart you lack, for an hour or so."

"But will it hurt me? Is it inflammatory?"

"Trust me, man. You don't want to risk any ill effects, if you know what I mean. Drink!"

Ill effects? Whatever could he mean? What sort of elixir was this?

Mr. Mason obeyed because it was evidently useless to resist. He was dressed now. He still looked pale, but he was no longer gory and sullied. Mr. Rochester let him sit three minutes after he had swallowed the liquid, then took his arm.

"Now I am sure you can get on your feet. Try."

The patient rose.

"Carter, take him under the other shoulder. Be of good cheer, Richard. That's it!"

"I do feel better," remarked Mr. Mason.

"I am sure you do. Now, Jane, trip on before us away to the back stairs. Unbolt the side-passage door, and tell the driver of the post chaise you will see in the yard—or just outside, for I told him not to drive his rattling wheels over the pavement—to be ready, we are coming. And, Jane, if anyone is about, come to the foot of the stairs and hem."

By this time, it was half past five, and the sun was on the point of rising. Still, the kitchen was dark and silent. The servants would not be up for another little while. I followed Mr. Rochester's requests to the letter, though I had to go out into the yard to get the driver's attention. I did not mind. It was setting up to be a beautiful morning and I welcomed the fresh air and the twittering of the birds in the orchard trees.

The gentlemen now appeared. Mason, supported by Mr. Rochester and the surgeon, seemed to walk with tolerable ease. They assisted him into the chaise. Carter followed.

"Take care of him," said Mr. Rochester to the latter. "Follow the instructions I gave and keep him at your house until he is quite well. I shall ride over in a day or two to see how he gets on. Richard, how is it with you?"

"The fresh air revives me. But one thing?"

"Well, what is it?"

"Let her be taken care of. Let her be treated as tenderly as may be. Let her—" Mr. Mason stopped and burst into tears.

Such care for one who had nearly devoured him hours earlier?

"I do my best, as I have done, and will continue to do" was the answer. Mr. Rochester shut the chaise door, and the vehicle drove away.

"Yet would to God there was an end of all this!" he added as he closed and barred the heavy yard-gates. "Come where there is some freshness, for a few moments. That house is a mere dungeon. Don't you feel it so?"

"It seems to me a splendid mansion, sir." With not-so-splendid secrets. I didn't want to push. I hoped he would come out with what I longed to know.

He strayed down a walk edged with apple trees, pear trees, and cherry trees on one side, and a border on the other full of all sorts of old-fashioned flowers, primroses, pansies, and various fragrant herbs. They were fresh now as a succession of April showers and gleams, followed by a lovely spring morning, could make them. The sun was just entering the dappled east.

"Jane, will you have a flower?" He gathered a half-blown rose, the first on the bush, and offered it to me.

"Thank you, sir."

"Do you like this sunrise? That sky with its high and light clouds, which are sure to melt away as the day waxes warm?"

"I do, very much."

"You have passed a strange night."

"I've passed stranger. Or perhaps, equally strange."

"I suppose you have." His brow arched, but he did not press. "I would not have left you there in danger, you know. The door was locked. You were safe. I should have been a careless shepherd if I had left a lamb so near a wolf's den, unguarded."

"What will you do about Grace Poole, sir? Will she remain here?"

"Don't trouble your head about her. Put the thing out of your thoughts."

"Yet it seems to me your life is hardly secure while she stays. And what of those around you?"

"Mr. Mason took a ridiculous risk. It should never have happened. He knew what he was up against."

"Am I to ever know what he was up against, sir? I have no doubt of your faith in my confidence by now. I assure you, there is naught you could tell me that I would run from, fear, or disbelieve."

"And you have faith in me, I know. Please, don't lose your faith, Jane, and don't ask me to reveal secrets that might hurt you. It is enough that I bear such a burden."

"And Mr. Mason." And how many of the other servants? "You trust him not to spread the news of his attack?"

"Mason would never defy me, not willingly. Unintentionally, perhaps, he could in a moment let slip one careless word to deprive me, if not of life, yet forever of happiness."

"Then he must be cautious. Order it so! Let him know what you fear, and show him how to avert the danger."

"Would that it were so easily done." He picked up my hand, then seemed to rethink his actions and released it as quickly. "I cannot say, 'Beware of harming me, Richard,' for it is imperative that I should keep him ignorant that harm to me is possible. Now you look puzzled."

"I want to say the thing that will help you most. Not knowing the particulars of your situation, I know not how to guide you, or what course to recommend."

"You do guide me, Jane. Your mere presence guides me. You make me want to be a better man, to find my way to happiness. You have allowed me to think it possible I could be happy. I act, and I think to myself, 'What would Jane say to that?' and make sure I behave accordingly."

"You might have rethought your Gypsy ruse. I would not have recommended duping your guests."

"My guests? You have such concern for them, do you? I believe you mean you would not have recommended my playing the role with you."

I nodded. "I dislike deceptions, sir."

He took my hand and led me to a rustic seat in the arbour, an arch in the wall lined with ivy.

"Sit. The bench is long enough for two. You don't hesitate to take a place at my side, do you? Is that wrong, Jane?"

I had no answer. I sat beside him.

"Now, I'll put a case to you, which you must endeavour to suppose your own. Will you stay to hear? Are you comfortable?"

"It's a lovely spot. Had I no responsibilities to tend, I might find myself sitting here for most of the day. Perhaps with my paints and an easel." I breathed deep of the dewy air and felt reinvigorated after such a long, terrible night.

Sharing a sunrise, sitting so close to Mr. Rochester—my employer—did feel startlingly intimate and, perhaps, unwise. But the night was long and cold, so filled with death and threats that I embraced the little bit of contentment at the start of the new day without reservation.

"Very well. Jane, suppose you were no longer a girl well reared and disciplined, but a wild boy indulged from childhood upwards. You find yourself in a remote land, and there commit an error with such consequences that haunt you through the rest of your life. In time, the result of your choice becomes utterly insupportable. You take measures to obtain relief: unusual measures, but neither unlawful nor culpable. Still you are miserable, without hope as without sun or air."

He could not have touched on a better comparison to draw my

sympathy, for I had lived without hope or sun, though through no active choice on my part.

"You wander seeking rest in exile. You find no pleasure to blight the bitterness or bring the return of true happiness until you find a stranger filled with the good and bright qualities, which you have sought for fifteen years and never before encountered. Such society revives you. You feel better days come back—higher wishes, purer feelings. You desire to recommence your life, and to spend what remains to you of days in a way more worthy of an immortal being. To attain this end, are you justified in overleaping an obstacle of custom—a mere conventional impediment which neither your conscience sanctifies nor your judgment approves?"

"Sir, you must know, first, that not all immortal beings are worthy. There is great risk in supposing it. And next, if your conscience neither sanctifies nor approves, I don't think you need to hear my answer, for you know it well enough. And thirdly, your happiness never depends on a fellow creature. This stranger you speak of has some influence, perhaps, but ultimately bears no fault or credit for the changes you take to attain your own steps to happiness."

"Ah." He rose now and paced before the branches of the nearby tree. "I see your opinion of the matter. It makes sense. You would follow your conscience and judgment, even if it led you to misery when happiness was right within your grasp?"

"How could one be truly happy in purposely choosing what his conscience knows is not in the right? It would be troubling to you, sir. The happiness would be fleeting."

He sighed. "My little abbess."

"Sir?" By the change in his face, the softness fading, I knew my answer had not been the one he wanted to hear.

"Have you noticed my tender penchant for Miss Ingram?" His tone, too, changed from dreamy and melodic to harsh and sarcastic.

"I have. And you should know"—though I dreaded to inform him—"that she is not your vampyre. I've seen her in the sunlight."

"So it is true that vampyres can't abide the sun?"

"They burn to a crisp."

"You've seen it?"

"Not entirely. Though I have seen one scorched on the arm, just there." I pointed to a patch above my wrist. "I imagine it would be quite painful for them to go that way, sir."

"Indeed. So that rules out the Lynn boys, Sir George, Colonel Dent, and Eshton. I've seen them all ride in the sun."

As he paced and considered, my gaze was drawn to something behind him, under the lilac hedges. "Lord Ingram, sir!"

"Dash it, I'm not sure about Ingram. But it's possible. I've only ever seen him ride in a carriage, like one of the ladies."

"No, sir, I mean—Lord Ingram." I pointed to the charred body that even now gave off steam behind him as the sun rose and burned the rest of his exposed flesh. The face, shaded under the bush, was yet untouched. It was most definitely Lord Ingram. "There. I believe we've found our vampyre. And he should no longer be cause for concern."

"Jane." Mr. Rochester stopped before me so as to shield my view of the corpse. "Perhaps you should go in while I examine the body?"

"No, sir. We'll need to get him out of the sun, to alert the others. I can help."

"Bless me! There's Dent and Lynn in the stables. It's too late to worry about the state of the body now. And why raise concern? Go in by the shrubbery, through that wicket. I'll head them off and handle this."

As I went one way, he went another, and I heard him in the yard, saying with a cheer that no one else might recognise as false, "Mason got the start of you all this morning. He was gone before sunrise. I rose at four to see him off. He shared a carriage with Lord Ingram. It seems Ingram had business in London."

Later in the day, Mr. Rochester found me in the schoolroom with Adele. I dismissed her and waited until Sophie had taken her away.

"The body was gone," he explained. "By the time I got back to have a look, there was nothing left but ash and Ingram's clothes. I brought those in and burned them."

"I should have expected as much." I nodded. "It happens when one stakes them, too. Poof! They turn to dust. It's fascinating, really. Even a little pretty in the moonlight."

"You're stranger than I imagined, my little abbess." He gazed at me with something like admiration, or perhaps I was only imagining it, trying to recapture what we'd shared in the garden before his mood grew dark.

"But what of Lady Ingram and his sisters? Did they believe he ran off to London, so suddenly?"

"Oh, yes, yes." He waved off the question as if it were a minor irritation. "Tedo, as Blanche affectionately calls him, has been running off on a whim since he was young. It's not unlike him to just leave in the night without a word and show up again days or weeks later. They'll start to wonder eventually, when he does not return, but by then they will be long gone and look for explanations elsewhere."

"To disappear would be easier than having to explain his hunting habits. I wonder if he developed a fascination for vampyres after his experience with the governess? No doubt their Miss Ross was one of them, but not the one who turned him. Vampyres stop aging when they're bitten."

"How sad," Mr. Rochester said. "To stay young while all grow old around you?"

"That's exactly how I feel." Curious, that! "I wouldn't want to be one of them for anything. Tell me, do you think the rest of the Ingrams had any idea?"

"I doubt it. Lady Ingram wouldn't have abided it. She probably would have disowned him at once."

"Not so easy to do if she's reliant on him for her keeping." I had a sudden realisation that the death of Lord Ingram might mean the women stood in line to inherit his fortune, instead of merely being dependent on him. Perhaps Blanche would be free to marry elsewhere and leave Mr. Rochester alone!

"I do wonder how he ended up out of doors by dawn." Mr. Rochester paced in front of my chair.

"Perhaps he came upon us just as we were coming out to see to the carriage and get Mr. Mason away. It would have made for an awkward explanation to run into anyone then. He might have hid in the bushes waiting for us to go back in, and then he either nodded off or the sun started coming up before he expected it. Yes, that makes sense. At least he was not indoors eating his friends. He must have had some semblance of a conscience."

"A vampyre with a conscience? Is it possible?"

"I've known it to happen," I said, thinking of my uncle Reed. "They are the most unhappy of creatures. I'm certain he's better off."

"Perhaps he is. You think I should marry the sister then?"

It took me a second to answer. "Yes, if that is your inclination."

"Very well. Shake hands. What cold fingers! They were warmer last night when I touched them at the door of the mysterious chamber. Jane, will you keep watch with me again?"

"Whenever I can be useful, sir. But perhaps in better circumstances."

"For instance, the night before I am married? I am sure I shall not be able to sleep. Will you promise to sit up with me to bear me company?"

My stomach turned but I would not reveal it. "Yes, sir."

CHAPTER 24

AT VARIOUS TIMES IN my life, I've had presentiments. I have known others who have had them, too. When I was a little girl, only six years old, I one night heard Bessie say to Martha Abbot that she had been dreaming about a little child, and that to dream of children was a sure sign of trouble. The next day, Bessie was sent for home to the deathbed of her little sister.

Of late, I had often recalled this saying and this incident, for I had been dreaming of an infant. Sometimes, I hushed it in my arms. Others, I dandled it on my knee. It wailed one night and laughed the next, but day after day for a week, it appeared in my dreams. I grew nervous as bedtime approached and the hour of the vision drew near. I felt sure the recurrence of such an image occasioned bad news or ill tidings. I remained on my guard, considering the danger of Grace Poole still in the house, but I eventually fell asleep and there the dream came again. This time, I was trying to soothe the infant, rocking it in a cradle in the Reeds' red room, when Mrs. Reed came in and told me that if I couldn't stop it from crying, she would suck out all its blood, and every drop of my happiness with it. I ran with the child, out of Gateshead, through the woods, into a graveyard. Headstones leaned precariously. Some were toppled over, the ground soft from recent rain. And then I saw a hand snaking up through the dirt at my feet, a zombie hand missing the tip of the ring finger and dripping with pea green goo. I tried to run, but it gripped my ankle, the goo sticky against my bare skin. The baby cried louder and clutched at my breast. When I looked down, I saw that it had fangs, like an infant vampyre. Alarmed, I woke in a sweat, clutching my pillow to my chest. I struggled to catch my breath, and I was glad to see that it was day and I could dress and prepare for my tasks instead of trying to find sleep again.

That afternoon, I was summoned from the schoolroom by a message that someone wanted me in Mrs. Fairfax's room. On repairing thither, I found a man having the appearance of a gentleman's servant waiting for me. He was dressed in deep mourning, and the hat he held in his hand was surrounded with a crepe band.

"I daresay you hardly remember me, miss," he said, rising as I entered. "But my name is Leaven. I lived coachman with Mrs. Reed when you were at Gateshead, eight or nine years since, and I live there still."

"Robert! How do you do? And how is Bessie? You are married to Bessie?"

"Yes, miss. My wife is well, thank you. She brought me another little one about two months since—we have three now—and both mother and child are thriving."

"How sweet. And are the family well at the house, Robert?" Mourning clothes could mean only one thing, but mourning one of the Reeds seemed impossible. I ruled it out.

"I am sorry I can't give you better news of them, miss. They are very badly at present—in great trouble."

"You don't say? How can that be?"

"Mr. John died last week, at his chambers in London."

"John Reed? Dead?"

"Yes."

"You mean, gone dead? Not just—"

"Gone." He looked down respectfully.

"But, how? And how does his mother bear it?"

"Why, you see, Miss Slayre, it is not a common mishap. His life has been very wild. These last three years he gave himself up to strange ways, and his death was shocking."

"I heard from Bessie he was not doing well."

"He could not do worse. He ruined his mother's estate and got in amongst the worst of his kind. He got into debt and into jail, killed his jailors and escaped, no less, in a rather spectacular way."

Which was to say, dear reader, that he ate them and left the blood-drained bodies on the prison floor. I understood it distinctly.

"His mother helped him out twice, but as soon as he was free, he returned to his old companions and habits. His head was not strong. He came down to Gateshead about three weeks ago and wanted Missus to give up all to him. Missus refused. Her means have long been much reduced by his extravagance. So he went back again, and the next news was that he was dead. How he died, God knows! They say he killed himself."

Or, he'd run into some slayers who did the deed quite well for him. A stake through the heart, an end to his troubles. He might have sought them out on purpose, or he might have run into them in a misadventure. Or, perhaps, he'd run into a tree on his own devices and let a branch hit home, but I couldn't imagine John Reed would have the courage to attempt such a trick.

I was silent. The news was frightful. Yet, I was glad for it. What could one say?

"Missus had been out of health herself for some time. She had got very stout from hunting, but was not strong with it. Now she's unable to hunt at all, and she will not eat even what her daughters bring to her. The loss of money and fear of poverty were quite breaking her down. The information about Mr. John's death and the manner of it came too suddenly. It brought on a stroke."

"A stroke? Heavens!" Immortal and yet not immune to brain ailments such as stroke? Bad luck, that.

"Yes," Robert said. "She was three days without speaking, but last Tuesday she seemed improved. She appeared as if she wanted to say something and kept mumbling. It was only yesterday morning, however, that Bessie made out the words, 'Bring Jane—fetch Jane Slayre. I want to speak to her.' Bessie is not sure whether she is in her right mind or means anything by it, but she told Miss Reed and Miss Georgiana and advised them to send for you. The young ladies put it off at first, but their mother grew so restless and said, 'Jane, Jane,' so many times that at last they consented. I left Gateshead yesterday. If you can get ready, miss, I should like to take you back with me early tomorrow morning."

His words gave me quite a start. I didn't fancy ever returning to Gateshead, under any circumstances, and it didn't thrill me to contemplate making the journey now with Mrs. Reed unwell. I had no idea one of her kind could even suffer a stroke! It was quite a notion. Yet my heart went out in sympathy to the poor woman. To live forever in such a state? To lose her precious child in such a way and to know that she had to go on, though she had no means to recover her finances? "Yes, Robert, I shall be ready. It seems to me that I ought to go."

"I think so, too, miss. Bessie said she was sure you would not refuse, but I suppose you will have to ask leave before you can get off?"

"Yes, and I will do it now." I directed him to the servants' hall and recommended him to the care of John's wife, and the attentions of John himself. That settled, I went in search of Mr. Rochester.

He was not in any of the lower rooms, not in the yard, the stables, or on the grounds. I asked Mrs. Fairfax if she had seen him. Yes, she believed he was playing billiards. I hastened to the billiard room. The click of balls and the hum of voices resounded. Mr. Rochester, Miss Ingram, the two Misses Eshton, and their admirers were all busied in the game. It required some courage to disturb so interesting a party. However, I could not defer my errand, so I approached the master where he stood at Miss Ingram's side.

She turned as I drew near and looked at me haughtily. Her eyes seemed to demand, "What can the creeping creature want now?" and when I said, in a low voice, "Mr. Rochester," she made a movement as if tempted to order me away.

"Does that person want you?" she inquired of Mr. Rochester.

Mr. Rochester turned to see who the "person" was. He made a curious grimace—one of his strange and equivocal demonstrations—threw down his cue, and followed me from the room.

"Well, Jane?" he said as he rested his back against the school-room door, which he had shut.

"If you please, sir, I want leave of absence for a week or two."

"What to do? Where to go?"

"To see a sick lady who has sent for me."

"What sick lady? Where does she live?"

"At Gateshead, sir, in——shire."

"That is a hundred miles off! Who may she be that sends for people to see her at that distance?"

"Her name is Reed, sir—Mrs. Reed."

"Reed of Gateshead? There was a Reed of Gateshead, a magistrate."

"It is his widow, sir."

"And what have you to do with her? How do you know her?"

"Mr. Reed was my uncle—my mother's brother."

"The deuce he was! You never told me that before. You always said you had no relations."

"None that would own me, sir. Mr. Reed is dead, and his wife cast me off."

"Why?"

"Because I was poor, and burdensome, and she disliked me."

"But Reed left children? You must have cousins? Sir George Lynn was talking of a Reed of Gateshead yesterday who, he said, was one of the veriest rascals on town."

"More than a rascal, I'm given to understand, sir."

"Indeed." Mr. Rochester stroked his beard as if considering the situation. "They're the vampyres, then?"

I nodded. "John Reed is dead, sir. He ruined himself and half-ruined his family and is supposed to have committed suicide. The news so shocked his mother that it brought on an apoplectic attack."

"And what good can you do her? Nonsense, Jane! I would never think of running a hundred miles to see an old lady vampyre. Besides, you say she cast you off. I'd rather not send you back to such a woman."

He was standing too near. He was too male, too protective, too potent. I had the sudden urge to press myself to him, to cry out for him to love me and hold me and keep me from such dreadful fiends. But I could not. I was not that weak, that vulnerable, or that foolish. I could face the Reeds, and I could leave him. I remained calm.

"Sir, she needs me. I feel I must go."

He slipped his fingers under my chin and tipped my face up to meet his gaze. "You must? Now, Jane?"

"Now that her circumstances are so very reduced, so different from what they were, I cannot neglect her wishes."

"How long will you stay?"

"As short a time as possible, sir."

"Promise me only to stay a week—"

"I will not make a promise that I might be obliged to break."

"At all events you *will* come back. You will not be induced under any pretext to take up a permanent residence with her?"

"Oh, no! I shall certainly return if all be well."

"And who goes with you? You don't travel a hundred miles alone."

"No, sir, she has sent her coachman."

"A person to be trusted?"

"Yes, sir, he has lived ten years in the family. I know his wife quite well. They're perfectly human, the pair of them and their children."

"And they haven't been eaten?"

"The Reeds do not indulge in common blood."

"Oh, I see." Mr. Rochester meditated. "When do you wish to go?"

"Early tomorrow morning, sir."

"Well, you must have some money. You can't travel without money, and I daresay you have not much. I have given you no salary yet. How much have you in the world, Jane?" he asked, smiling.

I drew out my purse, a meager thing it was. "Five shillings, sir."

He took the purse, poured the hoard into his palm, and chuckled over it as if its scantiness amused him. Soon he produced his pocketbook.

"Here," said he, offering me a note. It was fifty pounds, and he owed me but fifteen. I told him I had no change.

"I don't want change. Take your wages."

I declined accepting more than was my due. He scowled at first, then, as if recollecting something, brightened again.

"Right, right! Better not give you all now. You would, perhaps, stay away three months if you had fifty pounds. There are ten. Is it not plenty?"

"Yes, sir, but now you owe me five."

"Come back for it, then. I am your banker for forty pounds."

"Mr. Rochester, I may as well mention another matter of business to you while I have the opportunity."

"Matter of business? I am curious to hear it."

"You have as good as informed me, sir, that you are going shortly to be married?"

"Yes, what then?"

"In that case, sir, Adele ought to go to school. I am sure you will perceive the necessity of it."

"To get her out of the way of my bride, who might otherwise walk over her rather too emphatically? There's sense in the suggestion, not a doubt of it. Adele, as you say, must go to school. And you, of course, must march straight to—the devil?"

I went there now, as it was. Heading back to the Reeds' house might as well have been jumping headfirst into the pits of hell. "I hope not, sir, but I must seek another situation somewhere."

"In course!" he exclaimed with a twang of voice and a distortion of features equally fantastic and ludicrous. He looked at me some minutes. "Good God, Jane, you deal me a blow to say you're leaving me for weeks, and then you come back with sending Adele to school so that you can leave me permanently? And old Madam

Reed, or the misses, her daughters, will be solicited by you to seek a place, I suppose?"

Deal him a blow? In leaving Adele without a governess, though she had a perfectly capable nurse? It wasn't as if I were abandoning my charge, merely her education for a short time. "No, sir. I am not on such terms with my relatives as would justify me in asking favours of them—but I shall advertise."

"You shall walk up the pyramids of Egypt!" he growled. "At your peril you advertise! I wish I had only offered you a sovereign instead of ten pounds. Give me back nine pounds, Jane. I've a use for it."

"And so have I, sir," I returned, putting my hands and my purse behind me. "I could not spare the money on any account."

"Just let me look at the cash."

"No, sir. You are not to be trusted," I said with a laugh.

"Jane," he said seriously.

"Sir?"

"Promise me some things."

"I'll promise you anything, sir, that I think I am likely to perform." My heart raced. I was likely to perform any request he would make of me.

He looked at me a moment, his eyes shifting as if he searched for answers in mine. Then he stepped back to the door. "To carry your stakes and your daggers. Not to advertise, and to trust this quest of a situation to me. I'll find you one in time."

"I shall be glad to do so, sir, if you, in your turn, will promise that Adele and I shall both be safely out of the house before your bride enters it."

"Very well! I'll pledge my word on it. You go tomorrow, then?"

"Yes, sir. Early."

"Shall you come down to the drawing room after dinner?"

"No, sir, I must prepare for the journey."

"Then you and I must bid good-bye for a little while?"

"I suppose so, sir."

"And how do people perform that ceremony of parting, Jane? Teach me. I'm not quite up to it."

"They say 'farewell,' or any other form they prefer."

"Then say it."

"Farewell, Mr. Rochester, for the present." I tried to make it sound like such an easy thing to say. In truth, my voice caught in my throat and I barely forced the sounds out.

"What must I say?"

"The same, if you like, sir."

"Farewell, Miss Slayre, for the present. Is that all?"

"Yes."

"It seems stingy, to my notions, and dry, and unfriendly. I should like something else, a little addition to the rite. If one shook hands, for instance? But, no—that would not content me either. So you'll do no more than say farewell, Jane?"

"It is enough. As much goodwill may be conveyed in one hearty word as in many." Such as, I love you! Please don't marry such a haughty shrew as Blanche Ingram!

"Very likely, but it is blank and cool—'farewell.' "

The dinner bell rang, and suddenly away he bolted, without another word. Indeed, perhaps farewell suited him more than he imagined. I saw him no more during the day and was off before he had risen in the morning.

CHAPTER 25

IT WAS FIVE IN the afternoon when I reached the lodge at Gateshead on the first of May. I stepped in to see Bessie before heading up to the hall. It wasn't quite dark yet, so the Reeds were likely abed.

The lodge had never looked better. It was bright, cheerful, and clean. The ornamental windows were hung with little white curtains, and the grate shone with the fire burning comfortably. Bessie sat on the hearth, nursing her last born, and Robert and his sister played quietly in a corner.

"Bless you! I knew you would come!" exclaimed Mrs. Leaven as I entered.

"Yes, Bessie. Don't get up." I approached and kissed her. "How is Mrs. Reed?"

"Badly, but more sensible and collected than she was. She spoke of you last night and wishing you would come, but they won't be up for hours yet. Will you rest yourself here a bit, miss, and then I will go up with you?"

Robert entered, and Bessie laid her sleeping child in the cradle and went to welcome him. She made us tea and wanted to know if I was happy at Thornfield Hall, and what sort of a person the mistress was. When I told her there was only a master, she asked whether he was a nice gentleman, and if I liked him. I told her that he treated me kindly, and I was content. Then I described to her the gay company that had lately been staying at the house. These details Bessie relished as they never entertained properly at Gateshead without later dining on the guests, and even that not for years now.

In such conversation, the hours passed. Bessie restored to me my pelisse and bonnet, and I accompanied her to Gateshead Hall, as nine years earlier I had accompanied her from the hall to my departing coach. I still felt as a wanderer on the face of the earth, but I experienced firmer trust in my own powers. The gaping wound of my wrongs, too, was now quite healed, and the flame of resentment extinguished.

"You shall go into the drawing room first," said Bessie as she preceded me through the hall. "The young ladies will be there."

In another moment I was within that apartment. Every article of furniture looked just as it did on the morning I was first introduced to Mr. Bokorhurst. I was not surprised to find the house unchanged, but it was a bit of a shock to meet the Reed sisters still as I remembered them, though quite different as well.

Eliza, Miss Reed, had been much taller than I when I was a child, but now we stood closer to the same height, as I had almost caught up to her size. But she was thin and sallow, and her face pinched and severe. As it ever was, I supposed, but I hadn't been used to vampyre features in some time. Something ascetic was in Eliza's look, which was augmented by the extreme plainness of a straight-skirted, black, stuff dress, a starched linen collar, and her hair combed away from the temples. She looked so much the part of a nun that I almost expected to find her holding a string of rosary beads.

The other was as certainly Georgiana, but not the slim and fairy-like girl of thirteen. Her face still had the puffy, precious quality of a child's, but it was overrouged and somewhat garish, like a child playing at being an adult. She was a full-blown, plump damsel, still pretty underneath the powder and rouge, with blue eyes that sparkled darkly and blond ringlets framing her face. She could pass for an older girl, but still a girl. One might guess she was her sister's age, fifteen, which explained how she had managed to come out in London and entice a lad to request her hand in marriage. Until the poor thing got himself and his family eaten, of course. Such a tragedy. For all her mother's dwindling fortunes, Georgiana kept herself clothed in the latest styles. I wondered if it wasn't only John Reed responsible for the family's imminent downfall.

In each of the sisters there was one trait of the mother—and only one. The thin and pallid elder daughter had her parent's onyx eyes. The blooming and luxuriant younger girl had Mrs. Reed's contour of jaw and chin—perhaps a little softened, but still imparting an indescribable hardness to the countenance otherwise so voluptuous. Both ladies, as I advanced, rose to welcome me, and both addressed me by the name of "Miss Slayre."

Eliza's greeting was delivered in a short, abrupt voice, without a smile, and with a quick return to her task of staring at the fire. Georgiana chattered on, starting with a friendly "How d'ye do?" and adding several commonplaces about my journey, the weather, and so on, uttered in rather a drawling tone that reminded me of Lord Ingram's style of speaking, and accompanied by sundry side glances that measured me from head to foot, now traversing the folds of my drab merino pelisse, and now lingering on the plain trimming of my cottage bonnet.

A sneer, however, whether covert or open, had now no longer that power over me it once possessed. As I sat between my cousins, I was surprised to find how easy I felt under the total neglect of the one and the semisarcastic attentions of the other. Eliza did not mortify, nor Georgiana ruffle, me. I had much more to occupy my thoughts. In the last few months, I'd experienced feelings more potent than any that could be raised in this house, pains and pleasures so much more acute and exquisite than any it was in their power to inflict. Had John Reed been alive and present, I doubted even he would raise me to alarm.

"How is Mrs. Reed?" I asked soon, looking calmly at Georgiana, who thought fit to bridle at the direct address, as if it were an unexpected liberty.

"Mrs. Reed? Ah! Mama, you mean. She is extremely poorly. I doubt if you can see her tonight."

"If you would just step upstairs and tell her I am come, I should be much obliged to you."

Georgiana almost started, and she opened her blue eyes wild and wide.

"I know she had a particular wish to see me," I added, "and I would not defer attending to her desire longer than is absolutely necessary."

"Mama dislikes being disturbed in an evening," remarked Eliza.

I soon rose, quietly took off my bonnet and gloves, uninvited, and said I would just step out to Bessie—who was, I dared say, in the kitchen—and ask her to ascertain whether Mrs. Reed was disposed to receive me tonight. I went and, having found Bessie and dispatched her on my errand, took further measures.

As a child, I might more easily have been put off. I might even have left after such a reception. But I had grown. I was no child, unlike the Reed sisters, who remained trapped in such a state. I had not come a hundred miles, had not left Mr. Rochester, just to be told I would not be seen. I imagined that Eliza and Georgiana actually had little control over household affairs, even with their mother in such a sorry condition. I took the liberty of addressing the housekeeper, asking her to show me a room, and telling her I would be a visitor here for a week or two. While my trunk was conveyed to my chamber, I met Bessie on the landing.

"Missus is awake," she said. "She's a little muddled today. Some days are better than others. But I have told her you are here. Come and let us see if she will know you."

I did not need to be guided to the well-known room, to which I had so often been summoned for chastisement or reprimand in former days. I hastened before Bessie, softly opened the door, and saw to it that a light burned low in the room, for it was dark. The great four-poster bed with amber hangings was as of old. There the toilet table, the armchair, and the footstool, at which I had a hundred times been sentenced to kneel, to ask pardon for offences by me uncommitted. I approached the casket, opened the curtains, and leaned over the high-piled pillows.

Well did I remember Mrs. Reed's face, and I eagerly sought the familiar image. It is a happy thing that time quells the longings of vengeance and hushes the promptings of rage and aversion. I had left this woman in bitterness and hate, and I came back to her now with no other emotion than a sort of ruth for sufferings she'd caused others, and a strong yearning to forget and forgive all injuries. I did not expect, nor did I desire, to be reconciled and clasp hands in amity.

The well-known face was there, stern, relentless as ever. There was that peculiar dark eye that nothing could melt, and the somewhat raised, imperious, despotic eyebrow. I stooped down and clasped her hand, which lay outside the sheet on the edge of the elaborate satin-lined coffin she slept in, open during the night, closed during the day to keep out any errant rays of sunshine.

She looked at me. "Is this Jane Slayre?"

"Yes, Aunt Reed. How are you, Aunt?"

I had once vowed that I would never call her aunt again. I thought it no sin to forget and break that vow now. Mrs. Reed took her hand away, and turning her face rather from me, she remarked that the night was warm.

I brought a chair to the coffin head. I sat down and leaned over the pillow. "You sent for me, and I am here; and it is my intention to stay until I see how you get on."

"Oh, of course! You have seen my daughters? My lovely girls!"

"Yes."

"Well, you may tell them I wish you to stay until I can talk some things over with you I have on my mind. Tonight it is too late, and I have a difficulty in recalling them. But there was something I wished to say—let me see . . ."

The wandering look and changed utterance told what wreck had taken place in her once vigorous frame. Turning restlessly, she drew the bedclothes around her. My elbow, resting on a corner of the quilt outside the coffin's edge, fixed it down. She was at once irritated.

"Sit up! Don't annoy me with holding the clothes fast. Are you Jane Slayre?"

"I am Jane Slayre."

"I have had more trouble with that child than anyone would believe. Such a burden to be left on my hands—and so much annoyance as she caused me, daily and hourly, with her incomprehensible disposition, and her sudden starts of temper, and her continual, unnatural watching of one's movements! I was glad to get her away from the house. What did they do with her at Lowood? The fever broke out there, and many of the pupils died. She, however, did not die, but I said she did—I wish she had died!"

"A strange wish, Mrs. Reed. She was out of your way by then. Why should it bother you whether she lived or died? Why do you hate her so?"

"I had a dislike to her mother always. She was my husband's only sister, and a great favourite with him. He opposed the family's disowning her when she made her low marriage. He wept like a simpleton on news of her death. He would have the baby, though I entreated him rather to put it out to nurse and pay for its maintenance. And when he went to gather the infant? Oh! He was attacked! A dreadful thing."

"The attack?"

"Yes, but he came back to me. Not the same, but he came back. And to think, I was so happy when I heard that we could live forever!"

"Forever is a very long time, Aunt. Perhaps too long."

"You learn such things the hard way. He changed me to what he was so we could live together always, and we planned to change the children when they came of age as well. And then, a new tragedy. My husband could not go on. He hated what he'd become."

"But you didn't hate it, Mrs. Reed? You preferred it."

"At first, and for so many years. It was a mistake to change the children, but John begged so. Oh, my poor boy! How he wanted to be like me. He warned me that if I failed to change him in time, he might die before he could have the chance. I didn't want him to die. I wanted him to live forever, my golden boy!"

"He was too indulged, Mrs. Reed. He wanted a firmer hand."

"Hmph." She smiled without mirth. "You might not judge. You didn't live for months on end with that Slayre baby, forever crying! I hated it the first time I set my eyes on it—a sickly, whining, pining thing! Mr. Reed pitied it, and he used to coo over it as if it had been his own. More, indeed, than he ever noticed his own at that age.

He would try to make my children friendly to the little beggar. The darlings could not bear it, and he was angry with them when they showed their dislike. In his last days, he had it brought continually to his bedside. But an hour before he died, he bound me by vow to keep the creature."

"I'm sure you did the best you could," I allowed her by way of forgiveness. It didn't hurt me any to comfort her now.

"John does not at all resemble his father, and I am glad of it. John is like me and like my brothers—he is quite a Gibson. Oh, I wish he would cease tormenting me with letters for money. I have no more money to give him. We are getting poor. I must send away half the servants and shut up part of the house or let it off. I can never submit to do that—yet how are we to get on? Two-thirds of my income goes in paying the interest of mortgages. John gambles dreadfully and always loses—poor boy! He drinks the blood of common rabble! John is sunk and degraded—his look is frightful—I feel ashamed for him when I see him." She burst into noisy tears.

Bessie persuaded her to take a sedative draught. Soon after, Mrs. Reed grew more composed and sank into a doze. I then left her.

More than ten days elapsed before I had any further conversation with her. She continued either delirious or lethargic. She took but little nourishment from what Eliza would provide.

I was surprised to learn that Eliza abhorred hunting or killing of any sort. She recognised its necessity to keep her alive, but allowed herself only meager portions. She trapped small forest animals in cages, as Jimmy the footman had showed her, then she killed them as humanely as possible and drained the blood out into cups. Georgiana, of course, hunted alone, and she had perhaps acquired her mother's skill at it. She was well fed, by the look of her, and she preferred not to share.

Eliza would sit half the night sewing, reading, or writing and scarcely utter a word either to me or to her sister. Georgiana would chatter nonsense to her canary by the hour and take no notice of me. But I had brought my drawing materials, and they served me for both occupation and amusement.

One night, for I had taken to following their schedule while I visited, I fell to sketching a face. What sort of a face it was to be, I did not care or know. I took a soft black pencil, gave it a broad point, and worked away. Soon I had traced on the paper a broad and prominent forehead and a square jaw. I smiled at it when I finished, and I felt a little less lonely even having him on paper to observe.

"Is that a portrait of someone you know?" asked Eliza, who had approached me unnoticed.

I responded that it was merely a study and hurried it beneath the other sheets. Georgiana also advanced to look. They both seemed surprised at my skill. I offered to sketch their portraits, and each, in turn, sat for a pencil outline. This put Georgiana at once into good humour. She proposed a walk on the grounds. I agreed, as walking at night was no longer such a challenge to me.

Before we had been out two hours, we were deep in a confidential conversation. She had favoured me with a description of the brilliant winter she had spent in London two seasons ago—of the admiration she had there excited—the attention she had received. I even got hints of the titled conquest she had made, before she took off after a deer and I went back to the house alone.

In the night, these hints were enlarged on. She liked to speak of her romantic conquests, which were more numerous than I'd imagined considering she had such a child's face. Strangely, she never once brought up her mother's illness, or her brother's death, or the gloomy state of the family prospects. Her mind seemed wholly taken up with reminiscences of past gaiety, and aspirations after dissipations to come. She passed about five minutes each day in her mother's sickroom, and no more.

Eliza still spoke little. Three times a night she studied a little book, which I found, on inspection, was a Common Prayer Book. She had found others of her kind, those who lived as she did, with an abhorrence of killing and a preference to feed their cravings as humanely as possible. I marvelled that she had found two such others in her own neighbourhood. Mostly, she seemed to want no company and little conversation. I believed she was happy in her way.

She told me one evening, when more disposed to be communicative than usual, that John's conduct, and the threatened ruin of the family, had profoundly afflicted her. Her own fortune she had taken care to secure, and she planned to use it to devote to a vampyre church in Italy, a place where those of her kind could go to seek forgiveness and learn new ways to live and deal with their affliction while still being answerable to God. I wished her well with her endeavour.

On a wet and windy night, Georgiana had fallen asleep on the sofa over the perusal of a novel. Eliza was gone to attend a saint's-day service with her church group, for in matters of religion she was a rigid formalist. I went upstairs to see how the woman fared who lay there almost unheeded. The very servants paid her but an intermittent attention. The hired nurse, being little looked after and entirely too human, would slip out of the room whenever she could. Abbot, I'd learned, had fallen down the stairs when carrying laundry, hit her head, knocked it loose, and was no more, a stunning loss for Aunt Reed. Bessie was faithful, the dear, but she had her own family to mind and could only occasionally come to the hall.

I found the sickroom unwatched, as I had expected. The patient lay still and seemingly lethargic. The fire was dying in the grate. I renewed the fuel, rearranged the bedclothes, gazed awhile on her who could not now gaze on me, and then I moved to the window.

"Who is that?" I knew Mrs. Reed had not spoken for nights. Was she reviving? I went up to her.

"It is I, Aunt Reed."

"Who—I? You are quite a stranger to me—where is Bessie?"

"She is at the lodge, Aunt."

"Aunt. Who calls me aunt? Why, you are like Jane Slayre!"

"I am." I explained how Bessie had sent for me.

"Is the nurse here? Or is there no one in the room but you?"

I assured her we were alone.

"Well, I have twice done you a wrong which I regret now. One was in breaking the promise which I gave my husband to bring you up as my own child."

"It is forgiven, Aunt. I have been quite happy with the life I have made."

"The other—" She stopped. She made an effort to alter her position, but failed. Her face changed. "Go to my dressing case, open it, and take out a letter you will see there."

I obeyed her directions and read the letter.

It was short and contained an inquiry into my health and whereabouts. The writer, my father's brother, desired to take over as my guardian with the purpose of not only overseeing my care and education, but to train me in the ways of the family, the Slayre ways passed from generation to generation. As he was unmarried and had no heirs, he was eager to adopt me and bequeath his fortune to me upon his death. It was signed, John Slayre, Madeira, and dated three years back.

"Why did I never hear of this?" I asked.

"Because I disliked you too fixedly and thoroughly denied ever to lend a hand in lifting you to prosperity. I told him you were dead. I could not abide your family vocation at the time. Slayers? The world did not need more of such cruelty in the name of justice. Justice? Bah! And I could not bear to think of you becoming one of them. I remembered the time, Jane, that you showed me the stake you had carved, all on your own, with no formal training or instruction. It is as your uncle always said: slaying is in your blood. It would be your destiny one way or another. And now I see the mercy in what you do, in what your uncle has done. I understand now that there is grace in it. There is beauty. There is goodness. I pray you, please, show me mercy."

"Mercy, Aunt? But I have forgiven you."

"Ah, no, dear. No, no. I am asking—nay, begging—you to do for me what your uncle did for my husband, your uncle Reed."

"What?"

"A stake! A stake through the heart. I cannot bear more than I have borne, Jane. I cannot live with so much death, so much blood and loss, on my conscience. My children have grown away from me. My John is—" She began to bawl. "Oh, my dear John. I am remorseful, Jane. I repent and I am ready to die. I wish to go to heaven, or to see if I can try. Do you believe I can get there, Jane? That God will make a place for me?"

I remembered my uncle's ghostly words. He had told me that only in death, following true repentance, could a vampyre be reunited with its soul to find the way to heaven. I could end my aunt's earthly torture. I had come armed with stakes and would not have been caught around Gateshead without several. I had one up my sleeve and two in my pocket even now.

But to do as she asked? She was my family, after all, as much as I had denied her in the past. "I don't know, Aunt Reed. Are you sure you are repentant?"

"I am." She shook her head and cried. "You'll never know the pain I suffer for my actions. How I blame myself for taking innocent lives, and for allowing my John to run astray, for cheating you of your uncle Slayre."

She seemed so earnest, so desperate. I felt it my duty to oblige.

"I suppose we should say a little prayer?" I offered.

"Pray for me once I am gone. The nurse could be back any minute. My daughters might come in and try to stop you. I don't want you to be stopped, Jane. I have written letters, in that same drawer where you got that one, to each of my daughters to explain. Now, I am ready. Send me on my journey, Jane, as only you can do."

She closed her eyes and stretched out, quite like a corpse, just awaiting my blow. I slid the stake out of my sleeve and studied her for some seconds. It was a mercy, she said. The same mercy my uncle Reed had begged of my father's brother, John, to spare him, to take his body and return his soul.

"God help me," I whispered as I held the stake in two hands, raised it over my head, and drove it home straight through Aunt Reed.

Though I had slain enough vampyres to know what to expect, I somehow thought she would cry, whimper, or at least jump from the shock. To change her mind at the last second and blame me for taking her life. To sit up, eyes gaping, and say, "What have you done, you evil child!" But she said nothing. She was simply gone, from body to dust. Aside from the top of her night rail sticking out, I couldn't even tell where she had been under the blankets. How would I explain it?

The letters, I remembered. I would bring the letters to Eliza and Georgiana and simply hope that they would understand. Be at God's peace, I bid my aunt before I left the room.

I almost wished Abbot had been around after all these years. Nothing like a little zombie beheading to take the edge off staking one's aunt.

CHAPTER 26

A MONTH ELAPSED BEFORE I quitted Gateshead. How I missed Thornfield, my home! Absence had not helped remove Mr. Rochester from my heart, but had only driven him deeper into it. I thought of him constantly. Had he married Miss Ingram? No, it had only been a month. But I was sure the wedding was imminent. My days with Mr. Rochester were numbered as it was, and I was missing out on them the longer I stayed.

We closed Aunt Reed's dust up in her coffin and buried her in the family plot next to Mr. Reed, John, and their numerous victims, with a small service and few tears. Bessie Leaven was the only one to cry, and I believe it was more for memories of times past than for Mrs. Reed. Mrs. Reed's perfectly human brother Mr. Gibson had come from London to settle the estate's affairs, and he took Georgiana back to London with him. I wasn't sure he knew what he was getting into, but it was no longer my concern.

Eliza requested me to stay another week to help look after the house, see to callers, and answer notes of condolence while she prepared for her journey to Italy.

"Good-bye, Cousin Jane Slayre," she said when we parted. "I wish you well. You have some sense."

How other people felt when they were returning home from an absence, long or short, I did not know. My journey seemed tedious, fifty miles one day, a night spent at an inn, and fifty miles the next day. I was glad, at least, to see the sun again. I mused that seeing Mr. Rochester would eclipse even my joy at feeling the warmth of daytime sunshine on my face.

I was going back to Thornfield, but how long was I to stay there? Just before I left to return, I had a letter from Mrs. Fairfax. She reported that the party at the hall was dispersed. Mr. Rochester had left for London three weeks ago, but he was then expected to return soon. Mrs. Fairfax surmised that he was gone to make arrangements for his wedding, as he had talked of purchasing a new carriage. She expected the event would take place soon.

The question followed, where was I to go? I dreamt of staking Aunt Reed. How much easier it was than I had imagined, how I had given her the peace she craved. Perhaps I should try to find my family. I had a name at last, John Slayre, Madeira. I didn't like the idea of travelling to Madeira on my own, but I would enjoy learning more of my parents and of my supposedly inherited skills at slaying. Was it possible I was denying my natural talents? Could I not provide a valuable service in restoring souls to those who had lost their way? Or in stopping fiends from turning more to their kind?

I wasn't sure I had it in me. All I wanted, in my dreams, was to live at Mr. Rochester's side, as man and wife. But I did not live in my dreams, and the real world was pointing me in a new direction, if only I knew what it was.

I had not notified Mrs. Fairfax of the exact day of my return for I did not wish a carriage to meet me at Millcote. I proposed to walk the distance quietly by myself. Upon arrival at Millcote, I left my box in the hostler's care to be delivered to Thornfield Hall later. I slipped away from the George Inn about six o'clock of a June evening and took the old road to Thornfield, a road that lay chiefly through fields and was now little frequented.

It was not a bright or splendid summer evening, though fair and soft. The haymakers were at work all along the road.

"Mrs. Fairfax will smile you a calm welcome, to be sure," I said to myself as I walked along. "And little Adele will clap her hands and jump to see you. But you know very well you are thinking of another than they, and that he is not thinking of you."

But sense would not stop me from dreaming and urging me on my way. "Hasten! Be with him while you may. But a few more days or weeks, at most, and you are parted from him forever!"

I began to run.

When I reached the fields near Thornfield, the labourers were just quitting their work and returning home with their rakes on their shoulders. I had but a field or two to traverse, then I would cross the road and reach the gates. I passed a tall briar, shooting leafy and flowery branches across the path. I saw the narrow stile with stone steps. And there—was I dreaming?—I saw Mr. Rochester sitting, a book and a pencil in his hand. He was writing.

For a moment I was beyond my own mastery. I did not think I should tremble in this way when I saw him or lose my voice or the power of motion. I thought to turn around, take the other way to the house, to avoid making a fool of myself. It would not do to cry and lose my faculties upon greeting him.

Too late. He saw me. He looked up, started as if seeing a ghost, and then began to wave.

"Hallo!" he cried. He put up his book and his pencil. "There you are! Come on!"

I kept going, somehow, though I don't know in what fashion. I lost awareness of my movements, my actions.

"And this is Jane Slayre?" he said as I neared. "Are you coming from Millcote, and on foot? Yes, just one of your tricks not to send for a carriage and come clattering over street and road like a common mortal, to steal into the vicinage of your home along with twilight, just as if you were a dream or a fairy. What the deuce have you done with yourself this last month?"

"I have been with my aunt, sir, who is dead."

"A true Janian reply! Good angels, be my guard! She comes from the other world—from the abode of people who are dead, she tells me so when she meets me alone here in the gloaming! If I dared, I'd touch you, to see if you are substance or shadow, you elf. Truant! Absent from me a month, and forgetting me, I'll be sworn!"

My heart raced and my breath came faster. He had spoken of Thornfield as my home—would that it were my home!

He did not leave the stile, and I hardly liked to ask to go by. I inquired if he had not been to London.

"Yes. I suppose you found that out by second sight."

"Mrs. Fairfax told me in a letter."

"And did she inform you what I went to do?"

"Oh, yes, sir! Everybody knew your errand."

"You must see the carriage, Jane, and tell me if you don't think it will suit Mrs. Rochester exactly, and whether she won't look like a queen leaning back against those purple cushions. I wish I were a trifle better adapted to match with her externally. Tell me now, my fairy, can't you give me a charm, or a philter, or something of that sort, to make me a handsome man?"

"It would be past the power of magic, sir," I said, delighted at teasing him again, then added, "A loving eye is all the charm needed. To such you are handsome enough, or rather your sternness has a power beyond beauty."

Mr. Rochester smiled at me, outshining the warmth of the summer sun when it reached its highest point in the sky.

"Pass, Jane," said he, making room for me to cross the stile. "Go up home, and stay your weary, little, wandering feet at a friend's threshold."

All I had now to do was to obey him in silence. No need for me to speak and risk my emotions further. But a strange impulse took hold and forced me to turn around once I'd safely passed him.

"Thank you, Mr. Rochester, for your great kindness. I am strangely glad to get back again to you, and wherever you are is my home—my only home."

I turned again and walked on so fast that even he could hardly have overtaken me had he tried. Little Adele was half-wild with delight when she saw me. Mrs. Fairfax received me with her usual plain friendliness. Leah smiled, and even Sophie bid me "*Bonsoir*" with glee.

A fortnight of dubious calm succeeded my return to Thornfield Hall. Nothing was said of the master's marriage, and I saw no preparation going on for such an event. Almost every day I asked Mrs. Fairfax if she had yet heard anything decided. Her answer was always in the negative. Once, she said she had actually put the question to Mr. Rochester as to when he was going to bring his bride home, but he had answered her only by a joke and one of his queer looks, and she could not tell what to make of him.

One midsummer eve, Adele, weary with gathering wild strawberries in Hay Lane half the day, had gone to bed with the sun. I watched her drop to sleep, and when I left her, I sought the garden.

It was now the sweetest hour of the twenty-four. The sky was a deep blue, nearly purple, with blazes of jewel red where the sun dipped down to set. I walked awhile on the pavement, but a subtle, well-known scent—that of a cigar—stole from some window. I saw the library casement open a handbreadth. I knew I might be watched thence, so I went apart into the orchard.

No nook in the grounds was more sheltered and more Edenic. It was full of trees and abloom with flowers. A winding walk, bordered with laurels and terminating at a giant horse-chestnut tree circled at the base by a seat, led down to the fence. Here one could wander unseen, but in threading the flower and fruit parterres at the upper part of the enclosure, enticed there by the light the rising moon cast on this more open quarter, my step was once more stayed by a warning fragrance.

I knew it well—it was Mr. Rochester's cigar. I looked around and listened. I saw trees laden with ripening fruit. I heard a nightingale warbling in a wood half a mile off. No moving form was visible, no coming step audible, but that perfume increased. I made for the wicket leading to the shrubbery, and I saw Mr. Rochester entering. I stepped aside into the ivy recess, where I'd sat with him the morning after the attack on Mr. Mason. He would not stay long, I reasoned. He would soon return whence he came, and if I sat still, he would never see me.

But eventide was as pleasant to him as to me, and this antique garden as attractive. He strolled on through the fruit trees. A great moth went humming by me. It stopped on a plant at Mr. Rochester's foot. He bent to examine it.

"Now, he has his back towards me," I said to myself. "Perhaps, if I walked softly, I could slip away unnoticed."

I hadn't even stood before his voice stopped me. "Jane, come and look at this fellow. He reminds me rather of a West Indian insect. There! He has flown."

The moth roamed away. I was sheepishly retreating also, but Mr. Rochester followed me.

"Turn back?" he said when we reached the wicket. "On so lovely a night, it is a shame to sit in the house. Thornfield is a pleasant place in summer, is it not?"

"Yes, sir."

He walked to one side of the horse chestnut. I, to the other.

"You must have become in some degree attached to the house." He peeked through a branch.

"I am attached to it, indeed."

"And though I don't comprehend how it is, I perceive you have acquired a degree of regard for that foolish little child Adele, too. And even for simple dame Fairfax?"

"Yes, sir. In different ways, I have an affection for both."

"You would be sorry to part with them?"

"Yes."

"Pity!" He sighed and paused. "It is always the way of events in this life. No sooner have you got settled in a pleasant place than a voice calls out to you to rise and move on."

"Must I move on, sir? Must I leave Thornfield?"

"I believe you must, Jane." A few wisps of hair had strayed loose from my bun. He reached out and smoothed them back. "I am sorry, Jane, but I believe indeed you must."

This was a blow, but I did not let it prostrate me.

"Well, sir"—I straightened up—"I shall be ready when the order to march comes."

"I must give it tonight."

"Then, you *are* going to be married, sir?"

"I have every hope that it will happen soon. Adele must go to school, and you, Miss Slayre, must get a new situation."

"Of course, sir. I will advertise immediately."

"No need to advertise. I have already, through the esteemed Lady Ingram, heard of a place that she thinks will suit. It is to undertake the education of the five daughters of Mrs. Derby O'Gall of Bitternutt Lodge, Connaught, Ireland. You would like Ireland, I think. They're such warmhearted people there, they say."

"It is a long way off, sir."

"From what, Jane?"

"From England and from Thornfield; and—"

"Well?"

"From you, sir." The tears I had struggled against since he first said I must go began to fall. I narrowly avoided sobbing. The thought of Mrs. O'Gall and Bitternutt Lodge struck cold to my heart. "It is a long way."

"It is, to be sure. Probably why the old lady recommended it. She might have noticed the way I sometimes look at you when you're sitting in your nook watching over our party. Or the way I look mournful when you're not there. Have you noticed, Jane?"

"The way you look when I'm not there? How could I, sir?"

"No." He laughed and drew closer. "The way I sometimes look at you. As if you're the only woman in the room. I daresay it would be vexing to the woman who fancies herself the object of my affections, and her mother, who is eager to secure the match, or at least my fortune, for her daughter. We have been good friends, Jane. Have we not?"

"Yes, sir."

"And when friends are on the eve of separation, they like to spend the little time that remains to them close to each other. Here is the chestnut tree. Come, we will sit on the bench at its roots in peace tonight, though we might never more be destined to sit together." He seated us, making sure we sat close.

Too close. I could feel him breathing. I fancied I could feel the beating of his heart in time with my own. But then, I was a fanciful girl at times.

"It is a long way to Ireland, Jane, but I can't do better in finding you a position. Can you imagine a way it could be helped?"

Well, by him not marrying Blanche Ingram, to be sure, but I couldn't find my voice to speak.

"I think we are much alike in some regards, Jane. I sometimes have a queer feeling with regard to you—especially when you are near me, as now. It is as if I had a string somewhere under my left ribs, tightly and inextricably knotted to a similar string situated in the corresponding quarter of your little frame." He made a gesture as if to indicate the string running from his ribs to mine. My breath caught. "And if that boisterous channel, and two hundred miles or so of land come broad between us, I am afraid that cord of communion will snap. And then I've a nervous notion I should take to bleeding inwardly. As for you, you'd forget me."

"I could never forget you. I—" I almost confessed how desperately I loved him, but I stopped the words in time.

"Jane, do you hear that nightingale singing in the wood? Listen." It was just like him to sense my distress and create a distraction to give me time to compose myself.

But I could not regain my composure! In listening, I sobbed convulsively. No longer could I repress my feelings. I blubbered something about how I wished I had never been born, never come to Thornfield.

"Because you are sorry to leave it?"

I was overcome. It all came out in a flood. "I grieve to leave Thornfield! I love Thornfield. I love it because I have lived in it a full and delightful life. I have not been trampled on. I have not been petrified. I have not been buried with inferior minds and excluded from every glimpse of communion with what is bright and energetic and high. I have known you, Mr. Rochester, and it strikes me with terror and anguish to feel I absolutely must be torn from you forever. I see the necessity of departure, and it is like looking on the necessity of death."

I struggled to catch my breath, to calm down. I had said it. There was no going back.

"Where do you see the necessity?" he asked suddenly.

"Where? You, sir, have placed it before me. You're taking a bride."

"What bride? I have no bride!"

"But you will have."

"Yes. I will!" He set his teeth.

"Then I must go. You have said it yourself." At last I was able to speak evenly, without emotion. I had mastered myself.

He placed a hand under my chin and tipped my face up to his. "The only time you go will be with me, at my side, if I can yet convince you."

"I don't understand."

"I have teased you too much, Jane. Don't be angry. I needed to know that your feelings were the same as mine, and I could not think how to accomplish it." He shifted in his seat, taking both my hands in his. "Marry me, Jane. I want *you* to be my bride. I offer you my hand, my heart, and a share of all my possessions."

I gasped. It was not real. I was convinced that I was in bed, asleep, and dreaming. I put my hand to his face, the side of his cheek, the roughness of his day's growth of beard on that stubborn, square chin. I did not sleep. I was in the garden, on a bench, at his side. It was real. All of it, real. "Sir?"

"I ask you to pass through life at my side. To be my second self, and my best earthly companion."

"Oh, sir." It was too wonderful! Too wonderful, and too amazing, too shocking, all at once. I could not answer properly. I could only marvel. "Sir."

I began to cry.

Mr. Rochester sat quiet, looking at me gently and seriously. He put his arm around me and pulled me closer again, cradling me into his shoulder.

"But what of Miss Ingram?"

"What love have I for Miss Ingram? None; and that you know. What love has she for me? None; as I have taken pains to prove. I started a rumor that my fortune was not a third of what was supposed, and after that I presented myself to see the result. It was coldness both from her and her mother. I would not—I could not—marry Miss Ingram. You—you strange, you almost unearthly thing! I love you as my own flesh. I love you." He kissed my brow. "I entreat you to accept me as a husband. Jane, I must have you for my own—entirely my own. Will you be mine? Say yes, quickly."

His face was much agitated and much flushed, and strong workings were in the features, and strange gleams in the eyes. I was silent, examining him. Then I realised that what I was feeling was not entirely overwhelming affection, though love and surprise were certainly part of it. I had that queer feeling again. I looked around the garden. It had grown quite dark. I could not see anything amiss, but I sensed it near.

"Oh, Jane, you torture me!" he exclaimed. "With that searching and yet faithful and generous look, you torture me!"

"How can I do that? If you are true, and your offer real, my only feelings to you must be gratitude and devotion—they cannot torture." I tried to focus on my one true love and not the shadows that fell around us.

"Gratitude? Jane accept me quickly. Say, 'Edward'—give me my name—'Edward, I will marry you.' "

"Are you in earnest? Do you truly love me? Do you sincerely wish me to be your wife?" By now, I knew he did, but I must stall and hope that our garden villain showed himself.

"I do. If an oath is necessary to satisfy you, I swear it."

"Then, sir, I will marry you."

"Edward—my little wife!"

"Dear Edward!" I thought I heard something, behind the tree, off towards the hedgerow.

"Come to me—come to me entirely now." He embraced me. "God pardon me! And man meddle not with me. I have her and will hold her."

"There is no man to meddle, sir." Only, perhaps, a vampyre in the underbrush, who had still not made himself known. "Edward. I have no kindred to interfere."

"No, that is the best of it."

If I had loved him less, I should have thought his accent and look of exultation savage, but sitting by him, roused from the nightmare of parting, called to the paradise of union, I thought only of the bliss given me to drink in so abundant a flow. The bliss, and the vampyre, drawing nearer by the minute. I had waited long for this bliss, and so help me, no skulking night-creature would interfere!

Again and again he said, "Are you happy, Jane?"

And again and again I answered, "Yes."

But what had befallen the night as we embraced? The moon was not yet set, and we were all in shadow. I could scarcely see my master's face, near as I was. The chestnut tree writhed, while wind roared in the laurel walk and came sweeping over us.

"We must go in. The weather changes. I could have sat with you until morning, Jane."

"And so could I with you," I said, then jumped as a livid spark leapt out of a cloud at which I was looking, and there was a crack, a crash, and a close rattling peal, and I caught sight of it at last in the bright burst, the vampyre, as he slowly crept up on us and barely managed to hide on the other side of the chestnut's trunk. I had a split second to act while Mr. Rochester was still overcome with the lightning and his emotions, and while the thing lurked, ready to pounce. I pretended to bury my eyes against Mr. Rochester's shoulder while I reached up my sleeve, retrieved a stake, took aim, and hurled it with all my might through the air.

All at once, the rain rushed down, framing the vampyre in silhouette, there one second, gone the next. Fortunately I had sharpened that stake just this morning and my aim was as true as my love for Mr. Rochester, for I would not have had a second chance. As the rain fell, he hurried me up the walk, through the grounds, and into the house. We were quite wet before we could pass the threshold. He took off my shawl and shook the water out of my loosened hair, running his hands through it as if it were wet gold. The lamp was lit.

"Hasten to take off your wet things," he said. "And before you go, good night—good night, my darling!"

He leaned his head down and caught my lips in a kiss, gentle at first then growing more urgent, drawing me close against him though we were both wet through and through. His body was warm against mine. I wished the kiss would never end, but he eventually released me.

When I looked up, on leaving his arms, there stood Mrs. Fairfax, her face registering shock. I only smiled at her and ran upstairs. Explanation would have to do for another time.

Still, when I reached my chamber, I felt a pang at the idea she should even temporarily misconstrue what she had seen. But joy soon effaced every other feeling. The wind blew loud and thunder crashed near and fierce. Lightning gleamed. But I experienced no fear and little awe. Mr. Rochester came thrice to my door during it, to ask if I was safe and tranquil, and that was comfort, that was strength for anything.

Before I left my bed in the morning, little Adele came running in to tell me that the great horse-chestnut tree at the bottom of the orchard had been struck by lightning in the night, and half of it split away.

CHAPTER 27

As I ROSE AND dressed, I thought over what had happened and still wondered if it was a dream. I could not be certain of the reality until I had seen Mr. Rochester again and heard him renew his words of love and promise.

While arranging my hair, I looked at my face in the glass and felt it was no longer plain. I took a clean and light summer dress from my drawer and put it on. It seemed no attire had ever so well become me, because none had I ever worn in so blissful a mood.

I felt pretty, lighthearted, without a care in the world! I never imagined I could feel so. I was not surprised, when I ran down into the hall, to see that a brilliant June morning had succeeded to the tempest of the night. The rooks cawed, and birds sang, but nothing was so merry or so musical as my own rejoicing heart.

"Miss Slayre, will you come to breakfast?" Mrs. Fairfax greeted me with a grave air. I could feel her disapproval as she looked at me, but I couldn't say anything until Mr. Rochester had announced it. I ate what I could, then I hastened upstairs to meet Adele leaving the schoolroom.

"Where are you going? It is time for lessons."

"Mr. Rochester has sent me away to the nursery."

"Where is he?"

"In there." She pointed to the apartment she had left. I went in, and there he stood.

"Come and bid me good morning," he said.

I gladly advanced and received now not merely a cold word, nor even a shake of the hand, but an embrace and a kiss. A deep, loving kiss, like the one we'd exchanged last night. It seemed natural. It seemed genial to be so well loved, so caressed by him.

"Jane, you look blooming, and smiling, and pretty. Is this my pale little elf? This little, sunny-faced girl with the dimpled cheek, rosy lips, smooth hazel hair, and radiant green eyes?"

"It is Jane Slayre, sir."

"Soon to be Jane Rochester. In four weeks, Jane, not a day more. Do you hear?"

I did, and I could not quite comprehend it. "Jane Rochester. It seems so strange."

"Yes, Mrs. Rochester. Young Mrs. Rochester—Edward Rochester's girl-bride."

"Human beings never enjoy complete happiness in this world, do they? Could it be? It all seems a fairy-tale dream."

"Which I can and will realise. I shall begin today. This morning I wrote to my banker in London to send me certain jewels he has in his keeping, heirlooms for the ladies of Thornfield. In a day or two I hope to pour them into your lap."

"Oh, sir! Never rain jewels! Jewels for Jane Slayre sounds unnatural and strange. I would rather not have them."

"I will myself put the diamond chain round your neck. I will clasp the bracelets on these fine wrists and load these fairylike fingers with rings. I will attire my Jane in satin and lace, and she shall have roses in her hair. And I will cover the head I love best with a priceless veil. This very day I shall take you in the carriage to Millcote, and you must choose some dresses for yourself. The wedding is to take place quietly, in the church down below yonder, and then I shall waft you away at once to town. After a brief stay there, I shall bear my treasure to regions nearer the sun, to French vineyards and Italian plains."

"We will travel, sir?"

He nodded. "Paris, Rome, and Naples. Florence, Venice, and Vienna. I want to show you the world as I have known it, and to live it all again through your eyes, my angel."

I blushed at his endearment. "I am no angel. I am only Jane. And I ask you, sir, please, don't send for the jewels, and don't crown me with roses. I'm not one for such extravagances."

He laughed. "Very well. I will win you over to it, a little at a time. I can't help wanting to shower you with gifts. Make a request of me. What do you want? It is yours. Some fine new daggers, perhaps?"

"No, sir, it is far simpler. Communicate your intentions to Mrs. Fairfax. She saw me with you last night in the hall, and she was shocked. Give her some explanation before I see her again. It pains me to be misjudged by so good a woman."

"Very well. Go to your room and put on your bonnet. I mean you to accompany me to Millcote this morning, for dresses you will need and have, and while you prepare for the drive, I will enlighten the old lady's understanding. Did she think, Jane, you had given the world for love and considered it well lost?"

"I believe she thought I had forgotten my station, and yours, sir."

"Station! Your station is in my heart, and on the necks of those who would insult you, now or hereafter. Go."

I was soon dressed, and when I heard Mr. Rochester quit Mrs. Fairfax's parlour, I hurried down to it. She sat, staring straight ahead, looking a bit shocked.

Seeing me, she roused herself. "I feel so astonished. I hardly know what to say to you, Miss Slayre. Can you tell me whether it is actually true that Mr. Rochester has asked you to marry him? And have you accepted him?"

"Yes."

She looked at me bewildered. "Equality of position and fortune is advisable in such cases, and there are twenty years of difference in your ages."

I was nettled. "Mr. Rochester looks as young, and is as young, as some men at five-and-twenty."

"Is it really for love he is going to marry you?"

I was hurt by her coldness. Tears rose to my eyes.

"I am sorry to grieve you," pursued the widow. "Mr. Rochester, I daresay, is fond of you. I have always noticed that you were a sort of pet of his. Last night I cannot tell you what I suffered when I sought all over the house and could find you nowhere, or the master either, and then saw you come in with him."

"Well, never mind that now. It is enough that all was right."

Happily, Adele ran in.

"Let me go, let me go to Millcote, too!" she cried. "Mr. Rochester won't allow it, though there is so much room in the new carriage. Beg him to let me go, mademoiselle."

"That I will, Adele." I hastened away with her, glad to quit Mrs. Fairfax lest she offer more advice or admonishment. The carriage was ready. They were bringing it around to the front, and my master was pacing the pavement, Pilot following him backwards and forwards.

"Adele may accompany us, may she not, sir?"

"I told her no. I'll have only you."

"Do let her go, Mr. Rochester, if you please. It would be better."

He sighed. "Then off for your bonnet, Adele, and back like a flash of lightning!"

She obeyed him with what speed she might.

"After all, a single morning's interruption will not matter much," he said, "when I mean shortly to claim you—your thoughts, conversation, and company—for life."

❦

The hour spent at Millcote was somewhat harassing me. Mr. Rochester obliged me to go to a certain silk warehouse. There I was ordered to choose a half dozen dresses. I hated the business. I begged leave to defer it. No, he was insistent. It should be gone through with now. If I could not choose, he vowed he would select himself, and he did. He fixed on a rich silk of the most brilliant amethyst dye, and a superb pink satin. Before he chose the rest in crimson or spun of pure gold, I persuaded him to add some sober black satins and a pearl-grey silk.

According to the warehouse manager, unfortunately, one black satin was not the same as the next. There were shades of black—onyx, ebony, midnight—and satins of varying sheens. He could have his assistant, quite the expert eye in blacks, show me a few while he showed the gentleman some fine manly patterns for waistcoats and ascots. I tried to refuse, but Mr. Rochester insisted that he keep Adele with him while I had a look and chose the very ones that I preferred. I sensed the shop manager simply wanted more of Mr. Rochester's money, but there was no point in arguing. I allowed the dreary assistant to show me to the store of black satins.

After seeing skeins after skeins of black satins, I still couldn't tell a bit of difference between them.

"Perhaps if there was more light?" I said, feeling anxiously torn between them. "Could we go near a window?"

"Heavens, no," she said. Her black hair, possibly ebony but perhaps closer to midnight, was pulled back so tight that her eyes seemed constricted. "Natural light is the worst thing for viewing fabrics. I'll fetch a lamp."

A lamp? It occurred to me that the entire warehouse was kept rather dark for showing fabrics, but the back room was so dark I could barely tell between black and grey, let alone distinguish between shades of the same colour. That's when I knew that my anxiety was not simply brought on by nerves from shopping. My queer feeling was at work, a warning. The assistant was a vampyre!

She returned with the lamp and began to show me what she stated to be the differences between one and the next.

"I think I begin to see," I said, holding up one that looked every bit the same as the next. "This one is rather like your eyes. Quite an unnatural hue."

"Dark eyes run in my family." She might have blushed if she had the ability.

"How did you come to be working in a silk warehouse? It seems too dreary an occupation for a young woman. But perhaps there's plenty to eat."

"I don't know what you mean."

"Don't you? Travellers must come from all over to sell you their wares. I wonder, how many of them make it safely back home to their families?"

She glared, rather like Georgiana Reed used to glare at Eliza, her round face becoming sharp and shrewish. With a shrug, she lowered one skein and pretended to reach for another, but instead she gripped me by the throat and bared her fangs. "What do you know of it? Do you want a bite, then?"

"No indeed." Her grip was solid, and I knew I could not break out of it by pulling away.

Instead, I dropped straight to the ground in a move that Miss Temple once showed me and I hadn't tried in years, one leg forward, one leg back. She called it the splits. The sudden move disoriented my opponent and allowed me to reach into my skirt for my stakes and spring back to my feet in fighting form. I faced her, stakes extended.

"Oh, you like to play," she purred, casually strolling towards me. "Mother always warned me not to play with my food."

Before I could adequately prepare for combat, she flew through the air with acrobatic speed and delivered a solid kick to my solar plexus. It knocked me back a few feet, right to the floor. I couldn't catch my breath! I couldn't move. And she kept coming at me. I had to think fast. I remained down and let her come. At the last second, as she leapt for me, I rolled to the side and sprang to my feet. Bolts of fabric lined the walls to cushion her impact. She bounced back and snarled in my direction.

I could tell she was prepared to make another run at me. In the back of the room, on the other side, there was a door. My one hope was that the door led to the outdoors, and sunlight. I ran for it. As predicted, she ran after me, close on my heels. Vampyres, unlike zombies, were fast. My lungs burned with the effort of making it to the door before she made it to me.

My hand on the knob, I turned. So focused on devouring me, perhaps, she didn't notice I was at the door, she flew at me in a fury. At the last second, I turned the knob, opened the door, and sunlight flooded in, causing her to recoil, hands over her face.

"No!" she screamed. "No, stop! It burns. It burns!"

While she was still protecting her face from the sun, I stepped forward and stabbed the stake right through her heart. Poof! Dust. I didn't bother extricating my stake from her frock, which pooled on the floor. I had plenty more at home.

The warehouse manager peeked his head in the door at the other side of the room, followed closely by Mr. Rochester and Adele. "Was that a scream?"

"Yes." I indicated the open door. "The oddest thing. Your assistant decided that I was hopeless to choose one black satin from another. It drove her to such distraction that she ran screaming right out that door. Any black satin will do. I leave it in your capable hands." He would no doubt simply choose the most expensive. Turning to Mr. Rochester, I said, "Shall we go, sir?"

I moved past the men to take little Adele by the hand and lead the way back to the front of the shop.

Glad was I to get him out of the silk warehouse, and then out of a jeweler's shop. As we reentered the carriage and I sat back feverish and fagged, I remembered what, in the hurry of events, dark and bright, I had wholly forgotten—the letter of my uncle John Slayre to Mrs. Reed, his intention to adopt me and make me his legatee.

It would indeed be a relief, I thought, to have a small independency, some income of my own. I would feel more of an equal to my husband and less like his dependent. Yes, that would be ideal! I decided to write to Madeira at once, as soon as I got home, to tell my uncle John that I was alive and to be married, and to whom. Feeling better at the thought, I ventured once more to meet my future husband's eye.

He smiled. I settled little Adele, who also had some new things and was quite content now to sleep on the way home, on the seat to my other side and looked with a serious air at Mr. Rochester.

"I will have you know," I said, "that I do not want to be crushed by obligations. Do you remember what you said of Celine Varens? Of the diamonds, the cashmeres, you gave her? I will welcome a few presents, like the dresses today, which will be needed for our travels, and I thank you. But I will not be your English Celine Varens. I shall continue to act as Adele's governess; by that I shall earn my board and lodging, and thirty pounds a year besides. In future, I'll furnish my own wardrobe out of that money, and you shall give me nothing but—"

"Well, but what?"

"Your regard. And if I give you mine in return, that debt will be quit."

"Well, for cool native impudence and pure innate pride, you haven't your equal." We were now approaching Thornfield. "Will it please you to dine with me today?"

"No, thank you, sir."

"And what for 'no, thank you?' if one may inquire."

"I never have dined with you, sir, and I see no reason why I should now until we are married."

"Do you suppose I eat like an ogre or a vampyre, that you dread being the companion of my repast?"

"I simply want to go on as usual for another month."

"You will give up your governessing slavery at once."

"Indeed, begging your pardon, sir, I shall not. I shall just go on with it as usual. I shall keep out of your way all day, as I have been accustomed to do. You may send for me in the evening, when you feel disposed to see me, and I'll come then, but at no other time."

"Very well, little tyrant. It is your time now, but it will be mine once we're wed."

He said this as he helped me to alight from the carriage, and while he afterwards lifted out Adele. I entered the house and made good my retreat upstairs.

The month of courtship fled by, its very last hours being numbered. I had nothing more to do. My trunks were packed, locked, corded, arranged in a row along the wall of my little chamber. Tomorrow, at this time, they would be far on their road to London, and so should one Jane Rochester, a person whom as yet I knew not.

My wedding clothes hung in the closet, the pearl-coloured robe and the vapoury veil. I shut the closet to conceal the strange, wraith-like apparel it contained. I paced, then decided to go out for a walk, though it was nine o'clock. Not only did the hurry of preparation make me restless, or the anticipation of the great change—the new life that was to commence tomorrow. Both these circumstances had their share, doubtless, in producing that excited mood that hurried me forth at this late hour into the darkening grounds—but a third cause influenced my mind more than they.

The previous night, something had happened that I could not

comprehend, perhaps did not want to accept. Mr. Rochester that night was absent from home, and he remained absent for the next few hours. Business had called him to a small estate of two or three farms he possessed thirty miles off, business it was requisite he should settle in person, before his meditated departure from England. I waited now his return, eager to seek of him the solution of the enigma that perplexed me. Stay until he comes, reader; and when I disclose my secret to him, you shall share the confidence.

CHAPTER 28

I SOUGHT THE ORCHARD, DRIVEN to its shelter by the wind, which had all day blown strong and full from the south. Descending the laurel walk, I faced the wreck of the chestnut tree. The cloven halves were not broken from each other, for the firm base and strong roots kept them together below.

"You did right to hold fast to each other," I said, as if the monster splinters were living things and could hear me.

As I looked up at them, the moon appeared momentarily in that part of the sky that filled their fissure. Her disk was bloodred and half overcast. She seemed to throw on me one bewildered, dreary glance, then buried herself again instantly in the deep drift of cloud.

"I wish he would come!" I exclaimed, seized with hypochondriac foreboding. Not my usual queer feeling. I was certain no vampyres roamed. But I had expected his arrival before tea. Now it was dark. What could keep him?

I set out for the gate, thinking to meet him there. I walked fast, but not far ere I heard the tramp of hooves. A horseman came on, full gallop. A dog ran by his side.

"There!" he exclaimed as he stretched out his hand and bent from the saddle. "You can't do without me. Step on my boot toe. Give me both hands, mount!"

I obeyed. Joy made me agile. I sprang up before him. A hearty kissing I got for a welcome, and some boastful triumph, which I swallowed as well as I could.

"I thought you would never come. I could not bear to wait in the house for you, especially with this rain and wind."

"Yes, you are dripping like a mermaid. Pull my cloak around you." He nestled me closer. "But I think you are feverish, Jane. Both your cheek and hand are burning hot. I ask again, is there anything the matter?"

"I'll tell you all about it once we get warm before the library fire."

He helped me down once we reached the stable. John took his horse. He followed me into the hall, told me to make haste and put something dry on, then to return to him in the library, where I met up with him not long afterwards. He sat with a small supper waiting for us both.

"Take a seat and bear me company, Jane. Please God, it is the last meal but one you will eat at Thornfield Hall for a long time."

I sat down near him, but told him I could not eat. "I cannot see my prospects clearly tonight, and I hardly know what thoughts I have in my head. Everything in life seems unreal."

"Except me. I am substantial enough. Touch me."

"You, Edward, are the most phantomlike of all. You are a mere dream."

"Is that a dream?" he said, laughing, placing his hand close to my eyes.

"Yes, though I touch it, it is a dream." I put it down from before my face. "Have you finished supper?"

"Yes, Jane."

I rang the bell and ordered away the tray. When we were again alone, I stirred the fire, then took a low seat at his knee.

"It is near midnight," I said.

"Yes, but remember, Jane, you promised to wake with me the night before my wedding."

"I did, and I will keep my promise, for an hour or two at least. I have no wish to go to bed." Absolutely no wish, if only he knew.

"Are all your arrangements complete?"

"All, sir."

"And on my part likewise. I have settled everything. We shall leave Thornfield tomorrow, within half hour after our return from church. But, you hinted a while ago at something which had happened in my absence. Let me hear it. You have overheard the servants talk?"

"No." It struck twelve. I waited for the chimes to stop, then continued, "All day yesterday, I was very busy, and very happy in my ceaseless bustle. I think it a glorious thing to have the hope of living with you, because I love you. Edward, don't caress me now—let me talk undisturbed. Yesterday, I trusted well in Providence and believed that events were working together for your good and mine. It was a fine day, if you recollect. I walked a little while after tea, thinking of you. Sophie called me upstairs to look at my wedding dress, which they had just brought. And under it in the box I found your present, the veil, which, in your princely extravagance, you sent for from London. I smiled as I unfolded it and devised how I would tease you about your aristocratic tastes. I had prepared myself a simple square of unembroidered blond to use as a veil, but yours, Edward. It was extraordinary."

"Was? But what did you find in the veil besides its embroidery? Did you find poison, or a dagger, that you look so mournful now?"

I shook my head. "Besides the delicacy and richness of the fabric, I found nothing save Edward Rochester's pride, and that did not scare me because I am used to the sight of that particular demon. But, sir, as it grew dark, the wind rose. I wished you were at home. For some time after I went to bed, I could not sleep—a sense of anxious excitement distressed me."

"Your vampyre feeling? Tell me you were safe, that none came?"

"Not vampyres. Once I finally fell asleep, I continued in dreams the idea of a dark and gusty night. I had another dream that Thornfield Hall was but a ruin, a charred and abandoned place. On waking, a gleam dazzled my eyes. I thought, 'Oh, it is daylight!' But I was mistaken. It was only candlelight. Sophie, I supposed, had come in. There was a light on the dressing table, and the door of the closet, where, before going to bed, I had hung my wedding dress and veil, stood open. I heard a rustling there. I asked, 'Sophie, what are you doing?' No one answered. A form emerged from the closet. It took the light, held it aloft, and surveyed the wedding garments that were hanging. I had risen up in bed. I bent forward. First surprise, then bewilderment, came over me, and then my blood crept cold through my veins. Mr. Rochester, this was not Sophie, it was not Leah, it was not Mrs. Fairfax. It was not—no, I was sure of it, and am still—it was not even that strange woman, Grace Poole."

"It must have been one of them," interrupted my Edward.

"I solemnly assure you to the contrary. The shape standing before me had never crossed my eyes within the precincts of Thornfield Hall. The height, the contour, the form, were new to me."

"Describe it, Jane."

"It seemed a woman, tall and large, with thick and dark hair hanging long down her back."

"Did you see her face?"

"Not at first. But presently she took my veil from its place. She held it up, gazed at it long, and then she threw it over her own head, and turned to the mirror. At that moment I saw the reflection of the visage and features quite distinctly in the glass."

"And how were they?"

"Fearful and ghastly to me—oh, I never saw a face like it! It was a reflection, so I knew at once it was not a vampyre. Witch, ghoul, or fiend, I could not tell. She was no zombie! Zombies are listless unless in a frenzy for flesh, then still quite slow. This one was fierce! It was a discoloured face—it was a savage face. I wish I could forget the roll of the red eyes and the fearful blackened inflation of the lineaments!"

"Ghosts are usually pale, Jane."

"This was purple. The lips were swelled and bloody, with teeth protruding, such long, sharp teeth. The nose! It was more like a snout. She might have been lightly furred. It was dark. I could not tell."

"Ah! What did it do?"

"It removed my veil from its monstrous head, rent it in two parts with its hands, quite like paws, and flung the destroyed veil on the floor and trampled on it."

"Afterwards?"

"It drew aside the window curtain and looked out. Perhaps it saw dawn approaching, for, taking the candle, it retreated to the door. Just at my bedside, the figure stopped. The fiery eyes glared upon me. She thrust up her candle close to my face and extinguished it under my eyes."

"And she left you then? Dear God, Jane, she didn't try to hurt you?"

"Then she left me," I said, leaving off the rest of the narrative for the time.

"Thank God" he exclaimed, "that if anything malignant did come near you last night, it was only the veil that was harmed! Oh, to think what might have happened!"

He pulled me up onto his lap and hugged me to him, and I accepted the comfort for now, leaning into his strong arms, breathing in his soothing scent of spice and cigars. He was home, and I was glad.

To think what might have happened, indeed!

While she was on me, dear reader, I gripped my daggers under the sheet, and I thought about how best to strike. I knew it would give me a fight,and I debated how prepared I was to take on such a foe. I was alone, no Mr. Rochester down the hall to come running to my assistance. I had seen what she had done to Mr. Mason. I was prepared to defend myself should the need arise, but I was not prepared to attack without provocation, not knowing quite what I was up against. Great was my relief when it simply blew out the candle and started back for the third-story door.

I gave it a minute to get well enough ahead of me, then I grabbed my shawl, daggers, and stakes and followed carefully. The gallery was dark. I peeked out my door, my heart racing, and heard the third-story door creak open and footfalls on the stairs. Even then, I was not satisfied. I waited a minute, went back into my room, and lit a candle, which I then carried with me to the door and up the stairs. At the top of the stairs, I heard voices.

The tapestry was askew, but I could see that the door behind it was shut and, I suspected, locked again. I could not make out a conversation directly, but one voice seemed to cluck and admonish while the other made that deep, low laugh. Curious, that! I could only conclude that Grace Poole had been the blameless victim of my suspicions. She was most definitely not the creature I'd seen in my room. Most likely she was its keeper, an occasionally lax keeper at that. That she had it all locked up again did not make me any lighter of heart.

The question remained, what was it? And why did Edward keep it in his home? I hoped he would volunteer some answers to my questions. On the eve of my wedding, I was willing to accept what he would offer without wanting to press him for more. It was enough to know that I was safe, that whatever it was might have murderous intentions on Mr. Rochester and anyone who came near to challenge it in its lair, but it seemed to be mostly under lock, and in control, and not out to generally injure or attack the other members of the household. Still, when I was married, I would demand my answers, and it would have to go.

"Afterwards, did you sleep?" he asked at length, once he had held me long enough to perhaps regain command of his senses.

"Sleep was out of the question. I rose, bathed my head and face in water, and determined that to none but you would I impart this vision. Now, sir, tell me who and what that woman was?"

"The creature of an overstimulated brain, that is certain."

"Depend on it, my nerves were not in fault. The thing was real. The transaction actually took place, and I have proof. My beautiful wedding veil, the precious gift from you, is destroyed. I found it on my floor, irreparable."

He considered my words carefully.

Again he drew me into his embrace. He strained me so close to him, I could scarcely breathe. At last he released me.

"Now, Janet, you suspect there is more to the employment of Grace Poole than you've been told. You are right, indeed. You are too clever to doubt the evidence when it is standing right in front of you ripping your veil. I see you would ask why I keep such a creature in my house. When we have been married a year and a day, I will tell you; but not now. Are you satisfied, Jane? Do you accept my solution of the mystery?"

I knew him. I trusted him. I had faith that he would keep his word, and that he held the information back, for now, for reasons of his own. I was not entirely satisfied, but I was accepting.

"I do," I answered him with a contented smile.

"Does not Sophie sleep with Adele in the nursery?" he asked as I got up to light a candle.

"Yes."

"And there is room enough in Adele's little bed for you. You must share it with her tonight, Jane." He got up, too, and stood behind me. He cupped my shoulders and spoke low, his warm breath brushing my ear. "I am not surprised that the incident you have related should make you nervous, and I would rather you did not sleep alone. Promise me to go to the nursery."

"I shall be very glad to do so." I turned to face him, again with a reassuring smile.

"And fasten the door securely on the inside. Wake Sophie when you go upstairs to request her to rouse you in good time tomorrow. You must be dressed and have finished breakfast before eight. And now, no more sombre thoughts. Chase dull care away, Jane. Don't you hear to what soft whispers the wind has fallen? And there is no more beating of rain against the window. Look here." He strolled to the window and lifted up the curtain. "It is a lovely night!"

I joined him to look out. It was. Half heaven was pure and stainless. The clouds, now trooping before the wind, which had shifted to the west, were filing off eastward in long, silvered columns. The moon shone peacefully.

"Well," said Mr. Rochester, gazing inquiringly into my eyes, "how is my Janet now?"

"The night is serene, Edward, and so am I."

"And you will not dream of separation and sorrow tonight, but of happy love and blissful union."

This prediction was but half-fulfilled. I did not indeed dream of sorrow, but as little did I dream of joy. I never slept at all. With little Adele in my arms, I watched the slumber of childhood—so tranquil, so passionless, so innocent—and waited for the coming day. All my life was awake and astir in my frame. As soon as the sun rose, I rose, too.

It was my wedding day.

CHAPTER 29

BEFORE SOPHIE CAME AT seven to help dress me, I'd had my bath and arranged my hair and felt I was nearly ready to dress and go. Sophie had other ideas. My hair, in my usual bun, was not right. She asked, in indignant French, if I thought it was just like any other day. Then, how she fussed over me! She took down my hair and brushed it again. I thought she would be brushing for hours. Then she twisted it into an elegant, soft chignon with stray curls framing my face. She smoothed my brow and plucked at stray hairs and pinched my cheeks to a soft glow. She was just adjusting my veil, the plain square of blond after all, to my hair with a brooch when Mr. Rochester, apparently impatient for my appearance, sent word up the stairs to hurry me along. Eager to join him, I almost flew out from Sophie's hands as she still worked. She steadied me.

"Stop!" she cried in French. "Look at yourself in the mirror. You have not taken one peep."

I hardly recognised the image staring back. I looked like a fantasy of myself, like the little fairy or angel that Mr. Rochester was always accusing me of being. I thanked her and hurried down to meet my groom.

He received me at the foot of the stairs.

"Lingerer!" he said before even looking up. "My brain is on fire with impatience, and you tarry so long!" He surveyed me keenly, then pronounced, "My dearest, you have taken my breath clean away. You are as fair as a lily, nay, fairer. The pride of my life, and desire of my eyes."

I laughed at him. I could not imagine Mr. Rochester losing his breath over anything, much less my appearance, but I thanked him for the compliments and returned them in the only way he would expect.

"You look tolerably handsome yourself." I smiled.

In truth, to my eyes, he looked like a prince stepped out of a novel. He was clean-shaven, and his hair, though recently trimmed, still had a touch of wildness about it, the way I liked it. He wore a dark suit, but he might as well have been clad in medieval armor, for he was my shining protector. My heart surged with pride.

He told me he would give me but ten minutes to eat some breakfast. He rang the bell. One of his lately hired servants, a footman, answered it.

"Is the luggage brought down?"

"They are bringing it down, sir."

"And the carriage?"

"The horses are harnessing."

"We shall not want it to go to church, but it must be ready the moment we return, all the boxes and luggage arranged and strapped on, and the coachman in his seat."

"Yes, sir."

"Jane, are you ready?"

I rose. There were no groomsmen, no bridesmaids, no relatives, to wait for or marshal, none but Mr. Rochester and I. Mrs. Fairfax stood in the hall as we passed. I would have spoken to her, but I was hurried along by a stride I could hardly follow.

At the churchyard wicket, he stopped. He discovered I was quite out of breath.

"Am I cruel in my love?" he said. "Delay an instant. Lean on me, Jane."

Now I can recall the picture of the grey old house of God rising calm before me, of a rook wheeling round the steeple, of a ruddy morning sky beyond. I have not forgotten, either, two figures of strangers straying amongst the low hillocks and reading the mementos graven on the few mossy headstones. I noticed them because, as they saw us, they passed round to the back of the church, and I suspected they were going to enter by the side door to witness the ceremony. I did not mind. I would gladly share my happiness with all.

We entered the quiet and humble temple. The priest waited in his white surplice at the altar, the clerk beside him. All was still. Two shadows only moved in a remote corner. As I thought, the strangers had slipped in before us, and they now stood by the vault of the Rochesters, their backs towards us, viewing through the rails the old, time-stained marble tomb, where a kneeling angel guarded the remains of Damer de Rochester, slain at Marston Moor in the time of the civil wars, and of Elizabeth, his wife.

We took our places at the communion rail. The service began. The explanation of the intent of matrimony was gone through, then the clergyman came a step farther forward and, bending slightly towards Mr. Rochester, went on:

"I require and charge you both, as ye will answer at the dreadful day of judgment, when the secrets of all hearts shall be disclosed, that if either of you know any impediment why ye may not lawfully be joined together in matrimony, ye do now confess it; for be ye well assured that so many as are coupled together otherwise than God's word doth allow, are not joined together by God, neither is their matrimony lawful."

He paused, as the custom is. When is the pause after that sentence ever broken by reply? Not, perhaps, once in a hundred years. The clergyman, who had not lifted his eyes from his book and had held his breath but for a moment, proceeded, his hand already stretched towards Mr. Rochester.

"Wilt thou have this woman for thy wedded wife?"

The sound of someone drawing closer culminated in a voice. "The marriage cannot go on. I declare the existence of an impediment."

The clergyman looked up at the speaker and stood mute. The clerk did the same.

Mr. Rochester moved slightly, as if an earthquake had rolled under his feet. "Proceed," he said, his voice deep and low, rolling through the church as if God's very own. He took a firmer footing and did not turn his head or his eyes.

"I cannot proceed without some investigation into what has been asserted, and evidence of its truth or falsehood," Mr. Wood said quietly.

"The ceremony is over," subjoined the voice behind us. "I am in a condition to prove my allegation. An insuperable impediment to this marriage exists."

Mr. Rochester heard, but heeded not; he stood stubborn and rigid, making no movement but to take my hand. What a hot and strong grasp he had! And how like quarried marble was his pale, firm, massive front at this moment! How his eyes shone, still watchful, and yet wild beneath!

Mr. Wood seemed at a loss. "What is the nature of the impediment? Perhaps it may be got over—explained away?"

"Hardly. I have called it insuperable, and I speak advisedly." The speaker came forward and leaned on the rail. "It simply consists in the existence of a previous marriage. Mr. Rochester has a wife now living."

My nerves vibrated to those low-spoken words as they had never vibrated to thunder. My blood felt their subtle violence as it had never felt frost or fire, but I was collected, and in no danger of swooning. I looked at Mr. Rochester. I made him look at me. His whole face was colourless rock. His gaze was both spark and flint. He seemed as if he would defy all things. Without speaking, without smiling, without seeming to recognise in me a human being, he only twined my waist with his arm and riveted me to his side.

I knew, now, that the accusations would have to be answered, and that the answer would not please me. I thought of the thing in the attic, and I knew. I knew that Mr. Rochester's long-desired happiness was now as impossible as my own.

He would not give up as easily. "Who are you?"

"My name is Briggs, a solicitor from London."

"And you would thrust on me a wife?"

"I would remind you of your lady's existence, sir, which the law recognises, if you do not."

"Favour me with an account of her—with her name, her parentage, her place of abode."

"Certainly." Mr. Briggs calmly took a paper from his pocket and read out in a sort of official, nasal voice, " 'I affirm and can prove that Edward Fairfax Rochester, of Thornfield Hall, and of Ferndean Manor, England, was married to my sister, Bertha Antoinetta Mason, daughter of Jonas Mason, merchant, and of Antoinetta, his wife, a Creole, of Spanish Town, Jamaica. The record of the marriage will be found in the register of the church—a copy of it is now in my possession. Signed, Richard Mason.' "

"That—if a genuine document—may prove I have been married, but it does not prove that the woman mentioned therein as my wife is still living."

"She was living three months ago," returned the lawyer.

"How do you know?"

"I have a witness to the fact, whose testimony even you, sir, will scarcely controvert."

"Produce him—or go to hell."

"I will produce him. Mr. Mason, have the goodness to step forward."

Mr. Rochester, on hearing the name, set his teeth. He experienced, too, a sort of strong convulsive quiver.

The second stranger, who had hitherto lingered in the background, now drew near. Mr. Rochester turned and glared at him. For a moment, I feared he would strike the man, who was indeed the pale, withering Mr. Mason.

"What have you to say?" Mr. Rochester dared Mr. Mason with his eyes.

An inaudible reply escaped Mason's white lips.

"The devil is in it if you cannot answer distinctly. I again demand, what have you to say?"

"Sir—sir," interrupted the clergyman, "do not forget you are in a sacred place." Then, addressing Mason, he inquired gently, "Are you aware, sir, whether or not this gentleman's wife is still living?"

"Courage," urged the lawyer. "Speak out."

"She is now living at Thornfield Hall," said Mason in more articulate tones. "I saw her there last April. I am her brother."

Her brother, indeed! That explained Mason's bold midnight visit. He supposed himself a comforting force, perhaps, to his sister, who flew off and attacked him anyway. What was she? Was I at last to know? What was that thing in the attic that had somehow become my love's wife, for she was no longer human if indeed she had ever been.

"At Thornfield Hall!" The clergyman could not contain his disbelief. "Impossible! I am an old resident in this neighbourhood, sir, and I never heard of a Mrs. Rochester at Thornfield Hall."

I saw a grim smile contort Mr. Rochester's lips. "No, by God! I took care that none should hear of it—or of her under that name. Enough! There will be no wedding today. I have been married, and the woman to whom I was married lives. You say you never heard of a Mrs. Rochester at the house up yonder, Wood? But I daresay you have many a time inclined your ear to gossip about the mysterious creature kept there under watch and ward. Some have whispered perhaps that she is my bastard half sister, some, my cast-off mistress. I now inform you that she is my wife of fifteen years, Bertha Mason by name, sister of this resolute personage, who is now, with his quivering limbs and white cheeks, showing you what a stout heart men may bear. Cheer up, Dick! Never fear me! I'd almost as soon strike a woman as you."

"I had to say something." Mr. Mason looked at me as if he would make apologies, but Mr. Rochester stepped in front of me as if to shield me from all.

"Briggs, Wood, Mason, I invite you all to come up to the house and visit Mrs. Poole's patient, and *my wife*!"

The words pained me, but not for my own sake. I ached for him. I knew at last what he'd been trying to hide, to escape, for all these years, the past mistake he could not put behind him to find his way to happiness.

"You shall see what sort of a being I was cheated into espousing and judge whether or not I had a right to break the compact and seek sympathy with something at least human. This girl"—he looked at me, at last, and my heart broke with the sorrow in his gaze—"she knew no more than you, Wood, of the disgusting secret. She thought all was fair and legal and never dreamt she was going to be entrapped into a feigned union with a defrauded wretch, already bound to a bad, mad, and embruted partner! Come all of you—follow!"

Still holding me fast, he left the church, the three gentlemen trailing behind. At the front door of the hall, we found the carriage.

"Take it back to the coach house, John," said Mr. Rochester coolly. "It will not be wanted today."

At our entrance, Mrs. Fairfax, Adele, Sophie, and Leah advanced to meet and greet us.

"To the right-about—every soul! Away with your congratulations! Who wants them? Not I! They are fifteen years too late!"

He passed on and ascended the stairs, still holding my hand, and still beckoning the gentlemen to follow him, which they did. The low, black door, opened by Mr. Rochester's master key, admitted us to the tapestried room, with its great bed and its pictorial cabinet.

"You know this place, Mason," said our guide. "She bit and stabbed you here."

He lifted the hangings from the wall, uncovering the second door. This, too, he opened. In a room without a window, there burned a fire guarded by a high and strong fender, and a lamp suspended from the ceiling by a chain. Grace Poole bent over the fire, apparently cooking something in a saucepan. In the deep shade, at the farther end of the room, a figure ran backwards and forwards.

What it was, whether beast or human being, one could not, at first sight, tell. It groveled, seemingly, on all fours. It snatched and growled like some strange wild animal, but it was covered with clothing, and a quantity of dark, grizzled hair, wild as a mane, hid its head and face.

"Good morrow, Mrs. Poole!" said Mr. Rochester. "How are you? How is your charge today?"

"We're tolerable, sir, I thank you," replied Grace. "Rather snappish, but not 'rageous."

A fierce cry seemed to give the lie to her favourable report. The clothed wolf rose up and stood tall on its hind feet.

"Ah! Sir, she sees you!" Grace warned. "You'd better not stay."

"Only a few moments, Grace, You must allow me a few moments."

"Take care then, sir! For God's sake, take care!"

The creature bellowed. She parted her shaggy locks and looked out. I recognised well that purple face, those bloated features, though she was not quite in the beastly state at which I had seen her, and probably not in full form even then. I remembered such a creature from fairy stories Bessie had told me in my youth, a creature with a curse of transforming from human to wolf under the glow of a full moon. A werewolf.

Mrs. Poole advanced.

"Keep out of the way," said Mr. Rochester, thrusting her aside. "She has no knife now, I suppose, and I'm on my guard."

"One never knows what she has, sir. She is so cunning."

"We had better leave her," whispered Mason.

"Go to the devil!" was his brother-in-law's recommendation.

"'Ware!" cried Grace.

The three gentlemen retreated simultaneously. Mr. Rochester flung me behind him, and a good thing, for I hadn't thought to arm myself with stakes on my wedding day, if stakes could even affect such a beast. The creature sprang and grappled his throat viciously. She tried to bite his cheek, but he dodged her teeth. She was a big woman, in stature almost equaling her husband, and corpulent besides. She showed virile force in the contest—more than once she almost throttled him, athletic as he was. He could have settled her with a well-planted blow, but he would not strike. He would only wrestle.

At last, he mastered her arms. Grace Poole gave him a cord, and he pinioned them behind her. With more rope, which was at hand, he bound her to a chair. The operation was performed amidst the fiercest yells and the most convulsive plunges. Mr. Rochester then turned to the spectators. He looked at them with a smile both acrid and desolate.

"That is my wife. Such is the sole conjugal embrace I am ever to know. Such are the endearments. And this is what I wished to have." He laid his hand on my shoulder. "This woman, who stands so grave and quiet at the mouth of hell, looking collectedly at the gambols of a demon. Wood and Briggs, look at the difference! Compare these clear eyes with the red balls yonder—this face with that mask—this form with that bulk, and then judge me, priest of the gospel and man of the law, and remember with what judgment ye judge ye shall be judged! Off with you now. I must shut up my prize."

We all withdrew. Mr. Rochester stayed a moment behind us, to give some further order to Grace Poole. The solicitor addressed me as he descended the stair.

"You, madam, are cleared from all blame. Your uncle will be glad to hear it—if, indeed, he should be still living—when Mr. Mason returns to Madeira."

"My uncle! What of him? Do you know him?"

"Mr. Mason does. Mr. Slayre has been the correspondent of his house for some years in the region. When your uncle received your letter intimating the contemplated union between yourself and Mr. Rochester, Mr. Mason, who was staying at Madeira to recruit his health, on his way back to Jamaica, happened to be with him. Mr. Slayre mentioned the intelligence, for he knew that my client here was acquainted with a gentleman of the name of Rochester. Mr. Mason, astonished and distressed as you may suppose, revealed the real state of matters. Your uncle, I am sorry to say, is now on a sick-bed, from which, considering the nature of his disease, decline, and the stage it has reached, it is unlikely he will ever rise. He would have come if he could have to extricate you from the snare into which you had fallen, but he implored Mr. Mason to lose no time in taking steps to prevent the false marriage. He referred him to me for assistance. Were I not morally certain that your uncle would be dead ere you reach Madeira, I would advise you to accompany Mr. Mason back. As it is, though, I think you had better remain in England until you can hear further from me, or from your uncle himself. Have we anything else to stay for?" the solicitor inquired of Mr. Mason.

"No, no—let us be gone" was the anxious reply. Without waiting to take leave of Mr. Rochester, they made their exit at the hall door. The clergyman stayed to exchange a few sentences, either of admonition or reproof, with his haughty parishioner. This duty done, he, too, departed.

I heard him go as I stood at the half-open door of my own room, to which I had withdrawn. The house cleared, I shut myself in, fastened the bolt that none might intrude, and took off the wedding dress to replace it by the stuff gown I had worn yesterday.

I stretched out on my bed, suddenly weak and tired. I thought over all that had happened. Where was the Jane Slayre of yesterday? Where was her life? Where were her prospects? I looked on my cherished wishes, yesterday so blooming and glowing. Today, they lay stark, chill, livid corpses that could never revive.

One idea only still throbbed lifelike within me—a remembrance of my uncle Reed entreating me to my Slayre mission. Had I sought others like me, had I trained, would I not have been prepared to slay the vile werebeast as she'd stood over me the other night? If I had, I would be married now. I would have saved Mr. Rochester from his burden and freed the thing that roamed the attic. Was she remorseful? Did she want to be free to go to God? Did it matter?

I would not even have found Mr. Rochester had I been off seeking others of my kind. I would not have come to Thornfield Hall to love him, or to know of that creature, his wife. My life would be very different, but perhaps I would be doing what I was meant to do.

It was clear to me, when Mr. Rochester would not strike it, that he viewed that thing he married with compassion. I couldn't imagine the particulars that had brought about their union, but I know he regretted it now. Still, he would not kill her. It would have been so easy to find the way to get it done, to have rid himself of such an encumbrance as a werewolf wife, but that was not his way.

He pitied her. He kept her. He hired a servant to keep her safe from harm, and to keep her from hurting others in turn. He was passionate, caring. I could see that if I'd killed the thing, he would probably not have approved, and where would we be then? The same place we were now, torn asunder.

I felt the tears begin to come, and once they started, there was no stopping them.

CHAPTER 30

SOMETIME IN THE AFTERNOON I raised my head and looked around. The western sun gilded the sign of its decline on the wall. My head swam as I stood. I was weak with grief and, probably, hunger, for I had taken no breakfast. I decided to get some nourishment, and I opened the door and practically fell into Mr. Rochester, who stood on the other side.

"You come out at last. Well, I have been waiting for you long, and listening."

"All day? You have been here waiting?"

He nodded. A chair was placed nearby, so I assumed he hadn't spent the whole time standing, but there he was outside my door. "I started to worry that you were dead. I haven't heard a movement, not an oath, or a whisper, or even a tear, all afternoon. Five more minutes and I planned to break the door down."

"No need. I had to come out sometime."

"So you shun me? You shut yourself up and grieve alone. I expected a scene of some kind. Well, Jane? Not a word of reproach? Nothing bitter—nothing poignant? You regard me with a weary, passive look."

"What is to be said that can help the situation now?" Kill your wife, sir, or let me have at her. I will find a way! I sensed it was not the right thing to say.

"Jane, I never meant to wound you thus. Will you ever forgive me?"

Such deep remorse was in his eye, such true pity in his tone, such manly energy in his manner. Besides, such unchanged love was in his whole look and manner. The only thing to forgive, as far as I could tell, was that he should have trusted in me sooner with the news. I should not have had to hear it as I did. That he was married to that thing upstairs? He may have been married once, but I could not consider him married now. But that a formal union could not exist between us, that the vows we'd been about to speak would have been false? He should have told me. Still, looking at him, knowing what he suffered and how he'd been seeking my happiness as well as his, I could not blame him.

Reader, I forgave him at the moment and on the spot.

"You know I am a scoundrel, Jane?" ere long he inquired wistfully—wondering, I suppose, at my continued silence and tameness, the result rather of weakness than of will.

"Yes, sir."

"Then tell me so roundly and sharply—don't spare me."

"Sir." I placed my hand tenderly on his chest. His heart beat fierce under my fingers. "I would love to berate you as you deserve, but I cannot. I am tired and weak with hunger. I need water."

I wasn't waxing melodramatic. It was true. My knees buckled under me as I spoke and he had to catch me up in his arms. He carried me downstairs and set me down. I felt the reviving warmth of a fire. Summer as it was, I had become icy cold in my chamber. He put wine to my lips. I tasted it and revived. I ate something he offered me and was soon myself. I was in the library, in his favoured chair. He took the one opposite and pulled it close.

I could not stay in the house with that thing, now that I knew what she was, now that everyone knew she was his wife. What was to be done? Had he never attempted to marry me, had I never written my uncle, things might have stayed as they were.

"How are you now, Jane?"

"Much better. I shall be well soon."

"You must have a strange opinion of me. To think I tried to marry you all the while keeping a wife in the attic upstairs. She's so much more than what she looks."

"I know, Edward. A werewolf. I don't think this house a suitable environment for a child. I believe Adele needs to go to school." It wasn't the main issue that needed to be settled between us, but I figured I would bring it up as it came to mind.

"Oh, Adele will go to school. I have settled that already; nor do I mean to torment you with the hideous associations and recollections of Thornfield Hall. Jane, you shall not stay here, nor will I. I was wrong ever to bring new people to Thornfield Hall, knowing as I did how it was haunted. I charged them to conceal from you, before I ever saw you, all knowledge of the curse of the place, merely because I didn't think Adele yet ready for school and never would have a governess to stay if she knew with what inmate she was housed. My plans would not permit me to remove the fiend elsewhere. Though I possess an old house, Ferndean Manor, even more retired and hidden than this, where I could have lodged her safely enough, it seemed an unhealthy situation. Probably those damp walls would soon have eased me of her charge, but to each villain his own vice. Mine is not a tendency to indirect assassination, even of what I most hate."

This point, I sensed, would be the separation of us. He had no tendency towards even indirect assassination, while I saw the mercy in killing the afflicted. Did Bertha Mason wish to live as a fiend? Did she not deserve to be set free of such unnatural earthly bonds? Yet, I understood his desire for mercy. Shutting her away to die of illness and neglect would never do. One wanted a sure hand to end her suffering immediately, phut! No drawing it out.

"I should shut up Thornfield Hall. I'll nail up the front door and board the lower windows. I'll give Mrs. Poole two hundred a year to live here with my wife. Grace will do much for money, and she shall have her son, the keeper at Grimsby Retreat, to bear her company and be at hand to give her aid in the paroxysms, when my wife senses a full moon and is prompted by her familiar to burn people in their beds at night, to stab them, to bite their flesh from their bones, and so on—"

"Edward," I interrupted, "you speak of her with hate—with vindictive antipathy. She cannot help what she is."

"Jane, my little darling, you misjudge me. It is not because she is a werewolf, or even mad, that I hate her. If you were mad or afflicted with such a curse, do you think I should hate you?"

"I do indeed."

"Then you are mistaken. Every atom of your flesh is as dear to me as my own. In pain and sickness, it would still be dear. Your mind is my treasure, and if it were broken, it would be my treasure still. If you raved and grew fur and fangs, my arms should confine you, and not a strait waistcoat. Your grasp, even in fury, would have a charm for me. If you flew at me as wildly as that woman did this morning, I should receive you in an embrace, at least as fond as it would be restrictive. I should not shrink from you with disgust as I did from her. In your quiet moments, you should have no watcher and no nurse but me. I could hang over you with untiring tenderness, though you gave me no smile in return, and never weary of gazing into your eyes, though they had no longer a ray of recognition for me. I love you, Jane. I love you as I have never loved before, and I will always love you."

"Then, you never loved her? And why did you marry her? How did she come to be this way? Please, help me understand."

He leaned back in his chair, tented his fingers, and exhaled. "Jane, did you ever hear or know that I was not the eldest son of my house, that I had once a brother older than I?"

"So Mrs. Fairfax told me once."

"And did you ever hear that my father was an avaricious, grasping man?"

"I have understood something to that effect."

"Well, Jane, being so, it was his resolution to keep the property together. He could not bear the idea of dividing his estate and leaving me a fair portion. All, he resolved, should go to my brother, Rowland. Yet as little could he endure that a son of his should be a poor man. His solution was that I must be provided for by a wealthy marriage, and he sought me a partner. Mr. Mason, a West Indies planter and merchant, was his old acquaintance. He was certain his possessions were real and vast. He made inquiries. Mr. Mason, he found, had a son and daughter; and he learned from him that he could and would give the latter a fortune of thirty thousand pounds. That sufficed."

"And you were agreeable?"

"This hardly mattered to my father. When I left college, I was sent out to Jamaica. My father said nothing about her money. He told me Miss Mason was the boast of Spanish Town for her beauty, and this was no lie. At the time, she was a fine woman: tall, dark, and majestic. They showed her to me in parties, splendidly dressed. I seldom saw her alone and had very little private conversation with her. She flattered me and lavishly displayed for my pleasure her charms and accomplishments. Being ignorant, raw, and inexperienced, I thought I loved her. A marriage was achieved almost before I knew where I was. Oh, I have no respect for myself when I think of that act! I never loved, I never esteemed, I did not even know her."

"But you were young. And you were deceived?"

He nodded. "I understood that my bride's mother was dead. Once the honeymoon was over, I learned the truth. She was shut up in a lunatic asylum, stark raving mad. The elder brother, whom you have seen, will probably be in the same state one day. My father and my brother, Rowland, knew all this, to the fullest extent, but they thought only of the thirty thousand pounds and joined in the plot against me."

"I'm so sorry. Your own father and brother!"

"These were vile discoveries, but except for the treachery of concealment, I should have made them no subject of reproach to my wife, even when I found her nature wholly alien to mine, her tastes obnoxious to me, her cast of mind common, low, narrow, and singularly incapable of being led to anything higher. When I perceived that I should never have a quiet or settled household because no servant would bear the continued outbreaks of her violent and unreasonable temper, or the vexations of her absurd, contradictory, exacting orders—even then I restrained myself. I tried to devour my repentance and disgust in secret. I repressed the deep antipathy I felt."

"This repression must have been very difficult for one so naturally outspoken as yourself."

"Jane, I lived with that woman upstairs four years, and before that time she had tried me indeed. Her character ripened and developed with frightful rapidity. Her vices sprang up fast and rank. They were so strong, only cruelty could check them, and I would not use cruelty. Bertha Mason, the true daughter of an infamous mother, dragged me through all the hideous and degrading agonies which must attend a man bound to a wife at once intemperate and unchaste. And worse. One of her lovers had been afflicted with what they called in the West Indies *lob hombre*. In short, he was a werewolf, and when he bit her in their lovemaking, he infected her with the condition as well. In the next full moon, she revealed her transformation. She tore apart the housekeeper in her bed and devoured a footman and a maid before I managed to restrain her."

"But, she's never bitten you?"

"How she's tried! But, no, she's never broken skin. I have made sure to keep up my physical strength and to give myself every advantage of her."

"Not so, Mr. Mason," I realised. "She did bite him."

"Ah, yes, thus the Italian potion. If administered soon enough, it might prevent any effects, or he might end up a mad werewolf himself yet. But, back to my tale. My wife was genetically predisposed to madness, and in the course of our first four years together, a werewolf as well. My brother in the interval was dead, and at the end of the four years my father died, too. I was rich enough, yet I could not rid myself of it by any legal proceedings, for the doctors now realised that my wife was showing signs of full-blown madness, too. Jane, shall I defer the rest to another day? You look unwell."

"No, finish it now. What did you do when you found she was mad?"

"I approached the verge of despair. A remnant of self-respect was all that intervened between the gulf and me. In the eyes of the world, I was associated with her. I remembered I had once been her husband—that recollection was then, and is now, inexpressibly odious to me; moreover, I knew that while she lived, I could never be the husband of another and better wife. Though five years my senior, she was likely to live as long as I, being as robust in frame as she was infirm in mind. Thus, at the age of twenty-three, I was hopeless."

"So young."

"And yet older than you are now. One night I had been awakened by her yells. Since the medical men had pronounced her mad, she had, of course, been shut up. I wouldn't trust her to an institution due to her unique condition. It was indeed a night of a full moon, and a fiery West Indian night besides, one of the sorts that frequently precede the hurricanes of those climates. Being unable to sleep, I got up and opened the window. The air was like sulfur steams—I could find no refreshment anywhere. Mosquitoes buzzed in. The sea rumbled dull like an earthquake, black clouds casting up over it. The moon was setting in the waves, broad and red, like a hot cannonball. I was physically influenced by the atmosphere and scene, and my ears were filled with the howls of my creature-wife as she made her transformation. She momentarily mingled my name with such a tone of demon hate, with such language and wolfish shrieks."

"And the laugh?"

"Ah, yes, she was yet perfecting her vocal stylings. At last, I'd had enough, or so I'd thought. 'This life,' said I at last, 'is hell. Let me break away and go home to God!' But a wind fresh from Europe blew over the ocean and rushed through the open casement. The air grew pure. I then framed and fixed a resolution. I would go and live in Europe again. I would have to take the creature with me to England, as I could not trust her with anyone else. I would confine her with due attendance and precautions at Thornfield, then travel and form what new ties I liked. She was not my wife, I reasoned. Not really. She was barely human. No one would know of her relation to me. My father and brother had not made my marriage known to their acquaintance. Far from desiring to publish the connection, they were as anxious to conceal it as myself."

"They acted badly," I said.

"But they were dead and without a chance to meet the charmer my wife had become. I should have thought of it sooner. To England, then, I conveyed her. A fearful voyage I had with such a monster in the vessel. Glad was I when I at last got her to Thornfield and saw her safely lodged in that third-story room, of whose secret inner cabinet she has now for ten years made a wild beast's den. I had some trouble in finding an attendant for her, as it was necessary to select one on whose fidelity dependence could be placed, for her ravings would inevitably betray my secret. Besides, she had lucid intervals of days—sometimes weeks—which she filled up with abuse of me. At last I hired Grace Poole from the Grimsby Retreat. She and the surgeon, Carter, are the only two I have ever admitted to my confidence."

"I owe Grace Poole my thanks and many apologies. I've thought so ill of her."

"It is my fault, for I helped in creating the impression. She doesn't need approval when there's money to be made. Mrs. Fairfax may indeed have suspected something, but she could have gained no precise knowledge as to facts. Grace has, on the whole, proved a good keeper, though, owing partly to a fault of her own, her vigilance has been more than once lulled and baffled. The lunatic is both cunning and malignant. She has never failed to take advantage of her guardian's temporary lapses, once to secrete the knife with which she stabbed her brother, and twice to possess herself of the key of her cell and issue forth in the nighttime. On the first of these occasions, she perpetrated the attempt to burn me in my bed."

"And the cows, Edward. She attacked the cows." I still was not sure if she was responsible for killing the charwoman, but no need to mention her. Edward had not been at home.

"The cows?"

"Later that night, there were two found mutilated. One in the pasture and one dragged straight through the yard."

"Ah, yes. Before she set my bed afire, she went for a rampage in the surroundings. Thank God for the cows, easy targets, or she might have gone after a person. I'm sure they filled her up suitably. It was the first time she made it out of the house during a full moon. She probably wouldn't have even returned had it not been for attacking the cows fueling her excitement to murderous intent. She has always had it in for me, Jane. I believe she meant to devour me rather than just burn me in bed, but perhaps she knocked over the candle and frightened herself to seek the safety of the third-story sanctuary. Hard to say how it all came about."

"The main thing is that you were safe, sir."

"That we were all safe, Jane, my angel. On her second escape, she paid that ghastly visit to you. I thank Providence, who watched over you, that she spent her fury on your wedding apparel. On what might have happened, I cannot endure to reflect."

"It wasn't quite a full moon. I think she was yet more lunatic than wolf. But back to your story—once you got her settled here at Thornfield Hall, what did you do?"

"What did I do? I transformed myself into a will-o'-the-wisp. Where did I go? I pursued wanderings that could take me far and wide. My fixed desire was to seek and find a good and intelligent woman whom I could love: a contrast to the fury I left at Thornfield."

"But you could not marry, sir."

"I had determined and was convinced that I could and ought. It was not my original intention to deceive, as I have deceived you. I meant to tell my tale plainly and make my proposals openly. For ten long years I roved about, living first in one capital, then another. Provided with plenty of money and the passport of an old name, I could choose my own society. No circles were closed against me. I sought my ideal of a woman in all countries of my travel, and I could not find her. You are not to suppose that I desired perfection, either of mind or person. I longed only for what suited me, for the antipodes of the Creole, and I longed vainly. Yet I could not live alone, so I tried the companionship of mistresses."

"Celine Varens." I nodded.

"She was the first. You already know what she was, and how my liaison with her terminated. She had two successors: an Italian, Giacinta, and a German, Clara; both considered singularly handsome. What was their beauty to me in a few weeks? Giacinta was unprincipled and violent. I tired of her in three months. Clara was honest and quiet, but heavy, mindless, and not one whit to my taste. I was glad to give her a sufficient sum to set her up in a good line of business and so get decently rid of her. But, Jane, I see by your face you are not forming a very favourable opinion of me just now. You think me an unfeeling, loose-principled rake, don't you?"

"I don't like you so well as I have done sometimes. Did it not seem to you in the least wrong to live in that way, first with one mistress and then another? You talk of it as a mere matter of course."

"It was with me, and I did not like it. Hiring a mistress is the next worse thing to buying a slave: both are often by nature, and always by position, inferior, and to live familiarly with inferiors is degrading. I now hate the recollection of the time I passed with Celine, Giacinta, and Clara."

I felt the truth of these words, and I drew from them the certain inference that if I were so far to forget myself and all the teaching that had ever been instilled into me to become the successor of these poor girls, he would one day regard me with the same feeling that now in his mind desecrated their memory. I did not give utterance to this conviction. It was enough to feel it. I impressed it on my heart, that it might remain there to serve me as aid in the time of trial.

"You are looking grave. You disapprove of me still, I see. But let me come to the point. Last January, rid of all mistresses, in a bitter frame of mind—the result of a useless, roving life—recalled by business, I came back to England. On a frosty winter afternoon, I rode in sight of Thornfield Hall. Abhorred spot! I expected no peace, no pleasure there. On Hay Lane I saw a quiet, little figure standing in the road. I passed it as negligently as I did the pollard willow opposite to it. I had no presentiment of what it would be to me, no inward warning that the arbitress of my life waited there in humble guise. I did not know, even when, on the occasion of Mesrour's accident, it came up and gravely offered me help. I was surly, but the thing would not go. It stood by me with strange perseverance and looked and spoke with a sort of authority. I must be aided, and by that hand; and aided I was.

"When once I had pressed the frail shoulder, something new—a fresh sap and sense—stole into my frame. It was well I had learnt that this elf must return to me, that it belonged to my house down below, or I could not have felt it pass away from under my hand and seen it vanish behind the dim hedge without singular regret. I heard you come home that night, Jane, though probably you were not aware that I thought of you. The next day I observed you while you played with Adele in the gallery. Adele claimed your attention for a while, yet I fancied your thoughts were elsewhere. Still, you were very patient with her. You talked to her and amused her a long time.

"Impatiently I waited for evening, when I might summon you to my presence. An unusual character I suspected was yours. I desired to search it deeper and know it better."

"Don't talk any more of those days," I interrupted, dashing away some tears from my eyes. His language was torture to me. I knew what I must do—and do soon—and all these reminiscences and these revelations of his feelings only made my work more difficult.

"No, Jane. What necessity is there to dwell on the past, when the present is so much surer—the future so much brighter? You see now how the case stands—do you not? After a youth and manhood passed half in unutterable misery and half in dreary solitude, I have for the first time found what I truly love. I have found you. You are my better self, my good angel. It was because I felt and knew this that I resolved to marry you. To tell me that I had already a wife is empty mockery. You know now that I have but a hideous demon. I was wrong to attempt to deceive you, but I wanted to have you safe before hazarding confidences. This was cowardly. I should have appealed to your nobleness and magnanimity, shown to you not my resolution, but my resistless bent to love faithfully and well, where I am faithfully and well loved in return. Then"—he dropped to his knees at my feet—"I should have asked you to accept my pledge of fidelity and to give me yours. Jane, give it me now."

My gaze searched his. How could I? How could I not? He wrapped his arms around my knees, dropped his head on my lap, and looked up again.

"Why are you silent, Jane?"

A hand of fiery iron grasped my vitals. Terrible moment, full of struggle! Not a human being that ever lived could wish to be loved better than I was loved. I knew how I felt about his wife, his very much alive creature of a wife. In name only, perhaps, but here she was, now known to all. Here, she lived. She shared his name. It left me one option, and he had told me how he'd felt about his mistresses.

"Jane, you understand what I want of you? Just this promise—'I will be yours, Mr. Rochester.' "

"Mr. Rochester, I will not be yours."

Another long silence.

"Jane!" he cried with a gentleness that broke me down with grief. "Jane, do you mean to go one way in the world, and to let me go another?"

"I do."

"Jane." He rose and stood over me, pulling me to my feet so that I stood right up against him, so close to him I could feel him breathing. "Do you mean it now?"

"I do."

"And now?" He dropped soft kisses on my forehead, my cheek, the tip of my nose. He wrapped his arm around my waist and pulled me even closer. He kissed me as I'd never been kissed, and it aroused something wild in me that demanded exploration. I tasted him, the tobacco and the wine, until I was trembling and breathless and—insane! It was insane, to allow him to come so close, to nearly convince me.

"I do." With two hands on his shoulders, I pushed him away hard.

"Oh, Jane, this is bitter! This—this is wicked. It would not be wicked to love me."

"It would to obey you."

A wild look raised his brows and crossed his features. "One instant, Jane. Give one glance to my horrible life when you are gone. What have I without you? I have but the maniac upstairs. As well might you refer me to some corpse in yonder churchyard."

That could be done, I thought, but did not say. I had a past, too. It served me well to remember it now. I'd stood up to vampyres and zombies and ended miserable lives with mercy and kindness. I was Jane Slayre, and I was strong.

"You have neither relatives nor acquaintances whom you need

fear to offend by living with me." He stepped closer, as if to try his seduction again. I stepped back.

Still indomitable was the reply. I cared for myself. I knew what it could cost me to stay as his inferior, to live a life that would never be all that we wanted for ourselves, with his wife in the shadows between us.

I retired to the door.

"You are leaving me?"

"Yes."

"Withdraw, then. I consent. But remember, you leave me here in anguish. Go up to your own room. Think over all I have said, and, Jane, cast a glance on my sufferings—think of me."

He turned away.

I had already gained the door; but, reader, I walked back. I turned his face to me. I kissed his cheek. I smoothed his hair with my hand.

"God bless you, my dear Edward! God keep you from harm and wrong, direct you, solace you, and reward you well for your past kindness to me."

"Your love would have been my best reward. Without it, my heart is broken."

Up the blood rushed to his face, forth flashed the fire from his eyes. He held his arms out, but I evaded the embrace and at once quitted the room.

"Farewell!" was the cry of my heart as I left him. Despair added, "Farewell forever!"

That night I thought I would never sleep, but the events of the day must have taxed me more than I'd imagined, for I fell to a heavy slumber as soon as I lay down in bed. I was transported in thought to the scenes of childhood. I dreamt I lay in the red room at Gateshead, that the night was dark, and my mind impressed with strange musings. The light that had long ago struck me into syncope, recalled in this vision, seemed glidingly to mount the wall, and tremblingly to pause in the centre of the obscured ceiling. I lifted up my head to look. The roof resolved to clouds, high and dim. The gleam was such as the moon imparts to vapours she is about to sever. I watched her come—watched with the strangest anticipation. She broke forth as never moon yet burst from cloud. A hand first penetrated the clouds and waved them away. Then, not a moon, but a white human form shone in the azure, inclining a glorious brow earthward. It gazed and gazed on me. It spoke to my spirit. Immeasurably distant was the tone, yet so near it whispered in my heart:

"My daughter, follow your instincts. Seek the Slayres."

"Mother, I will."

So I answered after I had waked from the trancelike dream. It was yet night, but July nights are short. Soon after midnight, dawn comes. If I didn't go now, I would never go.

I rose. I dressed. I gathered some linen, a locket, a ring, six stakes, my daggers. In seeking these articles, I encountered the beads of a pearl necklace Mr. Rochester had gifted me a few days ago. I left that. It was not mine. It belonged to the visionary bride who had melted in air, like a vampyre after a staking. I pocketed my purse, containing twenty shillings, all I had. I tied on my straw bonnet, pinned my shawl, gathered my parcel and my slippers, which I would not yet put on, and stole from my room.

"Farewell, kind Mrs. Fairfax!" I whispered as I glided past her door.

"Farewell, my darling Adele!" I said as I glanced towards the nursery.

No thought could be admitted of entering to embrace her. I had to deceive a fine ear. For all I knew, it might now be listening.

I would have got past Mr. Rochester's chamber without a pause, but as my heart momentarily stopping its beat at that threshold, my foot was forced to stop also. No sleep was there. He walked restlessly from wall to wall, and again and again he sighed while I listened. A heaven—a temporary heaven—was in this room for me, if I chose.

That kind master, who could not now sleep, was waiting with impatience for day. He would send for me in the morning. I would be gone. He would have me sought for, all efforts in vain. He would feel himself forsaken, his love rejected. He would suffer. He might grow desperate. His conduct was all under his control, not mine. Still, my hand moved towards the lock. I caught it back and glided on.

Drearily I wound my way downstairs. I knew what I had to do, and I did it mechanically. I got some water. I got some bread. All this I did without one sound. I opened the door, passed through, and shut it softly. Dim dawn glimmered in the yard. The great gates were closed and locked, but a wicket in one of them was only latched. Through that I departed. It, too, I shut. I was out of Thornfield.

A mile off, beyond the fields, was a road that stretched in the contrary direction to Millcote, a road I had never travelled, but often noticed, and wondered where it led. There I went. No reflection was to be allowed now. Not one glance was to be cast back, or forward. I simply walked, one step at a time, away from all I knew and loved. I followed my instincts, as instructed by my ghostly dream or visitor of last night.

My conscience warned me not to turn, that I could not give in. Even as I prepared to marry him, I was too aware of my inferiority of position. Would he not begin to resent me? Mr. Rochester was social by nature. How would he get on cut off from all his friends? Bad enough that he would marry his governess, but to simply take her as a mistress? I did not care what other people might say as much as I thought of me. Could I live as less than I should be? A mistress, instead of a wife. A dependent, instead of an equal. A merciful keeper, instead of a mercy killer.

Instinct told me I was not yet the woman I should be. I had much to accomplish, much to learn. I would follow my instinct to my destiny.

I walked on, through cramps and fatigue, until I reached the road. When I got there, I needed to sit and rest under a tree. I heard wheels and saw a coach coming. I stood up and lifted my hand. It stopped. I asked the driver where it was going, and he named a place a long way off, somewhere I was sure Mr. Rochester had never mentioned and probably had no connections. I negotiated a price. He asked for thirty shillings. I had twenty. He said he would try to make do. He further gave me leave to get in, as the vehicle was empty. I entered, was shut in, and it rolled on its way.

Gentle reader, may you never feel what I then felt! May your eyes never shed such stormy, scalding, heart-wrung tears as poured from mine. May you never have to be the instrument of evil to what you wholly love.

CHAPTER 31

TWO DAYS LATER, THE coachman set me down at a place called Whitcross. He could take me no farther for the sum I had given, and I was not possessed of another shilling in the world. I was alone, the coach long gone, before I realised that I'd left my parcel behind on the seat. It was too late to retrieve it. I was absolutely destitute.

My instincts had led me here. Perhaps my instincts were a little off and not to be trusted.

Whitcross, I quickly discovered, was not a town, nor even a hamlet. It was a stone pillar, whitewashed with four arms pointing in four directions, set up at the meeting of four roads. According to my trusty guidepost, the nearest town to which these pointed was ten miles off, the farthest, a distance of twenty miles. From the well-known names of these towns, I learned in what county I had lighted, a north-midland shire, dusk with moorland, ridged with mountain. Great moors were behind and on each hand of me, and waves of mountains far beyond that deep valley at my feet. I guessed the population to be thin, and I saw no signs of passersby to help direct me or to offer a weary traveller assistance. Or a bit of bread and cheese. Hunger gnawed at me. Even Lowood's porridge would seem appetizing now, so long had it been since I'd eaten. But it seemed it would be longer.

Not a tie held me to human society. Not a charm or hope called me where my fellow creatures were. None that saw me would have a kind thought or a good wish for me, surely, as I was dusty from the road and worn in appearance. I had no relative but the universal mother, Nature. I sought her breast and asked repose.

I struck straight into the heath. I wandered until I found a moss-blackened granite crag at a hidden angle, and I sat down under it. High banks of moor were about me. The crag protected my head. The sky was over that.

Some time passed before I felt tranquil even here. I imagined wild cattle or deer roaming nearby, and that brought to mind the creatures that might hunt such beasts. I had a stake up my sleeve in case of vampyres. If a werewolf came at a charge, I had no idea what to do. Soon, the weather became more a concern than even the wildest creature. The wind whistled, growing sharp. Could rain be far behind?

The next time a ghostly spirit opted to pop in for a visitation, I would tell it to please go prey on a less worthy subject. I could be at home in bed in Thornfield. In Mr. Rochester's bed, warm at his side as his pretend wife. What was I to do now? Where to go? Mr. Rochester was no doubt at home, worried and equally unable to sleep but much better fed.

Regrets would do me no good. I touched the heath. It was dry, yet warm with the heat of the summer day. I looked at the sky. It was pure, no rain in sight. A kindly star twinkled just above the chasm ridge. Nature seemed to me benign and good. Suddenly, I noticed ripe bilberries in a patch off to one side. I gathered a handful and ate them, my hunger somewhat appeased. I said my evening prayers, then made my couch in the heath. I folded my shawl double and spread it over me for a coverlet. A low, mossy swell was my pillow. Thus lodged, I was not too cold.

The next day I felt refreshed and renewed. Everywhere sunshine. Life was yet in my possession, with all its requirements, and pains, and responsibilities. I got up, looked around me, and set out.

Whitcross regained, I followed a road that led from the sun, now fervent and high. I walked a long time, and when I thought I had nearly done enough and might conscientiously yield to the fatigue that almost overpowered me and, sitting down on a stone I saw near, submit to the apathy that clogged heart and limb—I heard a church bell.

I turned in the direction of the sound, and there, amongst the romantic hills, whose changes and aspect I had ceased to note an hour ago, I saw a hamlet and a spire. The valley at my right hand was full of pastures and cornfields, and wood, with a glittering stream running through the varied shades of green. Recalled by the rumbling of wheels to the road before me, I saw a heavily laden wagon labouring up the hill, and not far beyond were two cows and their drover. Human life and human labour were near.

By the early afternoon, I entered the village. At the bottom of its one street, there was a little shop with some cakes of bread in the window. Without bread, I wasn't sure how I would proceed. Had I nothing about me I could offer in exchange for a roll? I considered. I had a small silk handkerchief tied around my throat. I had my gloves. I could hardly tell how men and women in extremities of destitution proceeded. I did not know whether either of these articles would be accepted.

I entered the shop. A woman was there. Seeing a respectably dressed person, a lady as she supposed, she came forward with civility. How could she serve me? I was seized with shame. My tongue would not utter the request I had prepared. I only begged permission to sit down a moment, as I was tired. Disappointed in the expectation of a customer, she coolly acceded to my request. She pointed to a seat. I sank into it. Soon I asked, "Is there any dress-maker or plain-work woman in the village?"

"Yes, two or three." Quite as many as there was employment for.

"Do you know of any place in the neighbourhood where a servant is wanted?"

"Nay. I couldn't say."

"What is the chief trade in this place? What do most of the people do?"

"Some are farm labourers. A good deal work at Mr. Oliver's needle factory, and at the foundry."

"Does Mr. Oliver employ women?"

"Nay." She smiled as if it were an idiot's question. "It is men's work."

"And what do the women do?"

"I knawn't. Some do one thing, and some another. Poor folk get on as they can. We don't like strangers much in this town, miss. We've had trouble."

"What sort of trouble?"

She wouldn't offer more. She seemed to be tired of my questions. Indeed, what claim had I to importune her? A few neighbours came in. My chair was evidently wanted. I took leave.

I passed up the street, looking as I went at all the houses to the right hand and to the left. I left them and came back again, and again I wandered away, always repelled by the consciousness of having no claim to ask—no right to expect interest in my isolated lot. In crossing a field, I saw the church spire before me. I hastened towards it.

Near the churchyard, and in the middle of a garden, stood a well-built though small house, which I had no doubt was the parsonage. I remembered that strangers who arrive at a place where they have no friends, and who want employment, sometimes apply to the clergyman for introduction and aid. Renewing then my courage, and gathering my feeble remains of strength, I pushed on. I reached the house and knocked at the kitchen door. An old woman opened. I asked was this the parsonage, and if so, was the clergyman in?

"He was called away by the sudden death of his father. He's at Marsh End now, some three miles off, and he will very likely stay there a fortnight longer."

She was housekeeper, I discovered, and of her, reader, I could not bear to ask the relief for want of which I was sinking. I could not yet beg. I went away.

A little before dark I passed a farmhouse, at the open door of which the farmer was sitting, eating his supper of bread and cheese.

"Will you give me a piece of bread?" I asked. "For I am very hungry."

He cast on me a glance of surprise. Without answering, he cut a thick slice from his loaf and gave it to me. I imagine he did not think I was a beggar, but only an eccentric sort of lady who had taken a fancy to his brown loaf. As soon as I was out of sight of his house, I sat down and ate it.

I could not hope to get a lodging under a roof and sought it in the wood. But my night was wretched, my rest broken. The ground was damp, the air cold. Besides, a group of intruders passed near me, and I had to huddle into the bushes to avoid their notice. There were three of them, two men and a woman, and I couldn't help overhearing them.

"I've got to eat something," one of the men said. "I haven't had a taste since Tuesday, and my stomach's like to cave in on itself."

"Rest easy, love. There's a farmhouse at the edge of town, looked to be some livestock milling about i'the yard."

"Farm? I don't want another pig, Hyacinth."

"Listen, Jack, will you? Where there's farms, there's people, eh? A whole row of houses down the line. We should ha' no trouble picking 'em off one at a time. Georgy's there setting 'em all up for us."

Vampyres! My stomach tensed. My instinct warned. I was grateful for the damp chill and wind for helping to hide my scent. I made every effort to control my movements, not even daring to breathe.

My supposed lack of noble blood wouldn't turn the appetites of this lot, I was certain.

"Looks like an austere sort of place," the other male said. "I like it better when they're prone to vice. They're so sweet when their blood's all tainted with whiskey and mead."

"Not as sweet as your mother was on Tuesday," the first male, Jack, added with a wicked laugh.

"I rather thought ye fancied his wee brother Charlie best, love," the woman jested in a sharp-edged drawl.

"No matter," the other male said with a wave of his hand that came dangerously close to my hiding place. "It serves 'em all right for turning me out without a cent, don't it? They ain't scoffing at ol' Desmond now, huh?"

They all laughed, a pack of hyenas, as they rambled towards the town.

Despite my weakness from hunger and weariness from cold, I felt recharged. I still had a stake up my sleeve. I couldn't possibly handle all three of them, plus the referenced Georgy on the inside, but I could possibly warn the family. At best, I could take out the female, who seemed to be the brains of the group. At worst, I would end up as dinner, but it seemed I was headed towards a bad end as it was. I might as well go out with a fight. My uncles Reed and Slayre would be proud.

I could no longer see the trio up ahead, but I could still hear their voices and an occasional ribald comment in entirety when the wind died. Aware that their senses were sharper than my own, I moved with caution, not too fast or too clumsily. After some minutes of silence, I feared I'd lost them, or that they planned an ambush as Mrs. Reed used to do with her children to corner sheep. I stopped and leaned against a tree, taking a moment to catch my breath and listen carefully. I thought I detected sounds of merriment from afar. When I came around the trees to start down the slope, I saw a light in the window of the farmhouse where the farmer had given me bread earlier in the day. And there, just entering, was the vampyre trio. They'd made quick progress, probably eager to get inside and find their meal.

I didn't have the energy to run, and what little I did have might be better saved for self-defense. Before long, I was standing at the entrance. I went around to look in the window, which proved too high for me to see in, so I went to the back hoping to find a better window. There was no window, but there was an open door. I could see the trio seated at a round table with a woman and two other men, one of them the farmer who had shared his bread. The woman was petite, but round with curves. I could not get a look at her face. They seemed to be having a friendly conversation, but from the way one of the men from the woods kept leaning over, as if to drink in the aroma wafting from the man next to him, I assumed the humans were in imminent danger.

My heart raced, more with excitement than with fear. I realised I was gripping my stake tightly in one hand. As I pondered my next course of action—making a noise to distract them, perhaps, and telling the humans to run when they came out—the second vampyre female turned around, the one called Georgy. I got a better look at her face and nearly fainted. Georgiana!

She was heavily rouged and, from the look of her, perhaps intoxicated. Hadn't she gone to London with her uncle Gibson? I could only surmise that they must have had a falling out once he realised her lifestyle greatly differed from his own. At any rate, she had sunk low to be running with such a crowd, perhaps as low as her brother had before his death. I shuddered to think what Eliza would make of her sister now.

Dread rolled through my stomach. Georgiana was out murdering innocents, or worse, turning them to monsters like herself. She had to be stopped. She was my cousin but—I had to stop her. I had killed Aunt Reed, perhaps, but it was different to think of staking Georgiana. I knew Aunt Reed had repentance in her heart. I could take comfort in that I was reuniting her with her mortal soul. In the case of Georgiana, I was certain she was beyond remorseful thoughts. If I drove a stake through her heart, I would be sending her to hell, eternal damnation—a choice, in all fairness, she had already made for herself.

Then she would no longer prey on the unsuspecting nor create more vampyres to murder more souls in turn. I saw the need for it. I sensed what I had to do. My pulse thrummed with that familiar feeling of power. I had to stop them from eating the farmer and the other man, who looked to be his brother. I wondered how Georgiana had persuaded strangers to let her in when I'd had so much trouble earlier in the day. Perhaps if I simply called out to her and—

I was suddenly wrenched away from the door.

"What are you doing here?" a low voice said in my ear. "I've been tracking this group"—he gestured to the door with a nod—"and you're not one of them. Or, are you?"

In the gleam of lamplight that streamed from the door, I saw the face of the man who held me. He was the sort of man I used to fear before I fell in love with Mr. Rochester, a classically handsome youth. He was probably between twenty-eight and thirty, tall, slender, with a face that riveted the eye, pure in outline, with a straight nose and an Athenian mouth and chin. I contemplated using my stake, but he didn't quite have the look of a vampyre. He studied me intently, as if trying to make up his mind about me as well.

"There are vampyres inside," I warned him, too worried and perhaps light-headed from hunger to be concerned with his opinion of my mental health. "Those people are at risk."

"How would you know unless you're a risk as well?" He narrowed his eyes. "You're not one of them," he said decisively as if he had just come to that conclusion somehow.

"No. I overheard a plot and followed from the woods. I—"

"It's a dangerous night to be out. Run on home now! Run home to safety, young lady. Read your psalms once you arrive."

"Psalms!" I twisted free of him. "I have read enough psalms to last a lifetime. Rest assured, I can look after myself."

"Then look!" he shouted, and once again got his hands on me, this time to pull me close only to shove me in the other direction, right into hedges.

When I landed and looked up, I knew why. He was tangling in a new embrace, this one of a vampyre male with extended canines. I looked from left to right. His friends—and Georgiana—could not be far behind. My stake! I'd dropped it when he tossed me.

I scrambled in the dirt, under the hedges, searching for my weapon. By the time I found it and looked up, the stranger had a dusty pile at his feet and was putting a stake into a second.

"How—how did you?" I stared down at the pool of clothes and up, as the other one evaporated to a fine powder. "How did you do that?"

He turned to show me his hand, covered in some sort of gauntlet. As I started towards him for a better look, suddenly Georgiana leapt on him in a fury, all teeth and claws.

"How could you?" she practically hissed. "How could you kill them? I worked so hard to train them!"

Train them? Georgiana was their leader?

She was on him with a vengeance, getting the upper hand with the element of surprise. He'd been knocked to the ground, his hands pinned under him, and she'd bared her fangs as she leaned over him, reminding me all too much of John Reed bending over me while Georgiana—petted, spoiled Georgiana—cheered him on in the background.

"Enough!" Before I realised what I was about, I had her by the shoulders. "Georgiana, enough!"

She looked up and shock registered. "Why if it isn't Cousin Jane! What on earth—you're the last person I expected to run into in a quaint old village as this." She rose.

"Indeed, Georgiana," I said. "Snacking on common blood? Now what would your dear mother say?"

She tipped her head back and laughed, a cackle really, more like something I might expect from a witch, not from a vampyre. "Oh, Jane, you always were a singular delight. You know this fellow?"

She gestured to the stranger.

"Yes," I lied. "We're together."

She snorted. "Not bad, Jane. Not bad." She wiped her mouth with the back of her hand and licked at the corner of her lips. "Tasty, too."

He got to his feet. I gestured for him to stay back. Surprisingly, he did. But only, I realised, because he was reloading the device that was at the centre of his gauntlet.

"Georgiana," I said, a distraction. "You didn't enjoy London?"

"I adored London!" She laughed. "Oh, dear me, such fun. Uncle Gibson was a delight. Absolutely. Down to the last drop."

I stifled a gasp. Her own uncle? She had murdered her uncle?

"Don't look so shocked, Jane. He was horrid. He wanted to marry me off to an apothecary, for God's sake."

"I can't imagine," I muttered, keeping track of the stranger's movements with my eyes. He stood back, as if allowing me to finish my conversation before doing what I knew he meant to do. "So you narrowly escaped?"

"The apothecary? Yes. And do you know? He tasted like quinine!" She grimaced. "But his shop was near a tavern, where I met this lot. We're taking a little country tour. We heard this place was a good one to lie low, find some good blood. Join us, Jane! Have you ever considered becoming a vampyre?"

"Yes," I lied again. Convincingly, I hoped. "You always suspected how much I wanted to be like you."

"I did!" She practically sparkled with the news. "I knew it, Jane! And you're a good sort, honestly. You did off Mother, but no loss really, hm? She'd become such a bother, really. She would die to hear me say, but—oh, well, she's already dead, isn't she?" She broke off in a laugh, then resumed, "I could do it. It won't hurt. I drink your blood. You drink some of mine. It's that simple. We could do your friend, too." She smiled in a way I thought to be lecherous. "And him, and you, and me, and Hyacinth—what happened to Hyacinth?" She broke off and looked around. "Hy! Hy, darling!"

While she was distracted with looking for Hyacinth, I stepped closer to her. I indicated, with a nod, that the stranger should hold back. He seemed ready to strike. I knew, suddenly, that I couldn't allow it. I could not allow this strange, handsome youth to brutally stake my cousin, thus sending her to hell, because—

Because, I wanted to give Georgiana Reed her due. I felt the power surging through my veins, and I knew. I knew.

It had to be me.

The wood of the stake was smooth against my palm. I was a Slayre. It was in my blood.

I was a Slayre.

"Georgiana," I called her to attention as I stepped close enough to embrace her.

"Yes," she said, blinking her eyes in that familiar way of hers, the batting of the lashes that would win her mother over and convince Abbot to do anything she liked—not that it was a stretch with Abbot being a zombie under her mother's control.

"I always used to wonder how such a pretty little girl could be so hideous at the same time."

"What?" She blinked again, this time in shock. "Jane?"

"Hideous," I affirmed, shaking my head. "And I'm sorry, Georgy, but it's time—"

I raised the stake and drove it home, in one solid motion that broke the skin and, possibly, bone and pierced her heart. I was surprised I still had the strength. "It's time for you to go."

She blinked once, twice, then her eyelids shriveled, with the rest of her skin, and her eyes turned to dust, and she was no more. A pile of dust in an unflattering frock jumbled in a heap at my feet.

I felt a surge of elation, and then I was overwhelmed. I fell to my knees. I could not get back on my feet. I saw Hyacinth, Georgiana's vampyre friend, the one from the woods, emerge from around the corner, dabbing at her lips as if she'd recently finished a five-course meal.

"Georgy? Jack? Where did everyone go? I started without you. Just a quick bite, a taste. I couldn't resist, but there's plenty—"

Just as quickly, I saw a stake in her chest and watched her shrivel and fall, poof!

I looked back at the stranger. He removed his gauntlet, tucked it under his arm, approached, and extended his hand. "I told you to get to safety. You're obstinate."

"I just need to rest a moment. I've been wandering, sleeping out of doors, and I've had naught but a crust of bread and handful of berries to eat in three days. I suddenly feel on the verge of collapse."

"Can you hold on, just a moment? I need to check on Mr. Marshall inside, to make sure everyone is well."

I nodded. I could not move to go anywhere.

He came back within minutes. "Mr. Marshall is well. His brother just got a bite in the neck and passed out from fear, but he'll recover. It's a good thing his wife took the kids to visit her mother last week. Are you conscious?"

I muttered a yes. He offered me his hand. I took it and he pulled me to my feet, but I was yet unsteady. I fell into him. He supported me with one arm. "I can but die and I believe in God. Let me try to wait His will in silence."

"All men must die," he said, "but not all are condemned to meet a lingering and premature doom, such as yours would be if you perished here of want."

Upon hearing those words, I collapsed in the good stranger's arms.

❧

When I opened my eyes, I was still in the support of strong arms, standing on a covered porch, at a door.

"Is it you, Mr. St. John?" a woman said. She looked to be an elder maidservant.

"Yes. Open quickly."

"Well, how wet and cold you must be, such a wild night as it is!

Come in—your sisters are quite uneasy about you. What have you there?"

"A woman in need of assistance. She collapsed from want."

"Mr. St. John, there've been bad folk about i'the village of late. Is it safe to trust beggars and vagrants and the like?"

"Hush, Hannah! I have a word to say to the woman. I think this is a peculiar case. I must at least examine into it." He set me on my feet. I wobbled, but managed to stay upright. "Young woman, try to pass before me into the house."

With difficulty, I obeyed him. Presently I stood within a clean, bright kitchen—on the hearth—trembling, sickening, conscious of my aspect in the last degree ghastly, wild, and weather-beaten. Two young ladies, Mr. St. John, and the old servant were all gazing at me.

"St. John, who is it?" I heard one ask.

"I found her on the road."

"She does look white," said Hannah.

"As white as clay or death," another responded. "She will fall. Let her sit."

Indeed my head swam as it had not swum in years, not since my youth when I was bitten and beaten and dragged off to the red room dripping blood.

"Perhaps a little water would restore her. Hannah, fetch some. But she is worn to nothing. How very thin, and pale!"

"A mere specter!"

"Is she ill, or only famished?"

"Famished, I think. Hannah, is that milk? Give it me, and a piece of bread."

One of the women, the taller one with long curls, broke some bread, dipped it in milk, and put it to my lips. "Try to eat."

"Yes—try," repeated the other gently. Her hand removed my sodden bonnet and lifted my head. I tasted what they offered me, feebly at first, eagerly soon.

"Not too much at first—restrain her, Diana," Mr. St. John said.

"She has had enough." He withdrew the cup of milk and the plate of bread.

I felt I could speak. "My name is Jane Spencer." Anxious as ever to avoid discovery, I had before resolved to assume an alias.

"And where do you live? Where are your friends?"

"I have no home or friends."

"Can we send for anyone you know?"

I shook my head.

"What account can you give of yourself?"

Somehow, now that I had once crossed the threshold of this house and was brought face-to-face with its owners, I felt no longer outcast by the wide world. I began once more to know myself, but I wasn't sure how much to offer. "Sir, I can give you no details to-night."

"But what, then," said he, "do you expect me to do for you?"

"I will trust you. If I were a dog, I know that you would not turn me from your hearth tonight. As it is, I really have no fear. Do with me and for me as you like, but excuse me from much discourse. My breath is short—I feel a spasm when I speak."

A pleasant stupor was stealing over me as I sat by the genial fire. One of the young ladies was giving directions to Hannah. Ere long, with the servant's aid, I contrived to mount a staircase. My dripping clothes were removed. Soon a warm, dry bed received me. I thanked God, experienced amidst unutterable exhaustion a glow of grateful joy, and slept.

CHAPTER 32

THE NEXT THREE DAYS and nights were not clear in my mind. I slept. When I wasn't sleeping, it was if I lived a waking dream, still half-asleep but yet somewhat aware. I knew I was in a small room and in a narrow bed. I knew the difference between night and day, as always since my childhood with night having played so key a role in my youth, but I was not aware of the time. I observed when anyone entered or left the apartment. I could tell who they were and understand what was said when the speaker stood near to me. But, I could not answer. To open my lips or move my limbs seemed equally impossible.

Hannah, the servant, was my most frequent visitor. Diana and Mary, as I learned their names from their conversations, appeared in the chamber once or twice a day. They would whisper at my bedside.

"It is very well we took her in."

"Yes. She would certainly have died there in the road had St. John not found her and brought her to us. I wonder what she has gone through."

"Strange hardships, I imagine, poor, pallid wanderer."

"She is not an uneducated person, I should think, by her manner of speaking. Her accent was quite pure, and the clothes she took off, though splashed and wet, were little worn and fine."

"She has a peculiar face, like a pixie's. I rather like it."

Never once in their dialogues did they reveal any hint of dissatisfaction for taking me in, which comforted me.

Mr. St. John came but once. He looked at me and said my lethargy was a reaction to excessive and protracted fatigue. He pronounced it needless to send for a doctor. Nature, he was sure, would manage best left to herself. He said every nerve had been overstrained in some way, and the whole system must sleep torpid awhile, and then, he imagined, my recovery would be rapid enough. These opinions he delivered in a few words, in a quiet, low voice, and added, after a pause, in the tone of a man little accustomed to expansive comment, "Rather an unusual face."

"Oh, yes," responded Diana (I thought it must be Diana). "To speak truth, St. John, my heart rather warms to the poor little soul."

"She has come from somewhere, from family, from home. We may, perhaps, succeed in restoring her to them, if she is not obstinate." He stood considering me some minutes, then added, "She looks sensible."

On the third day, I was better. On the fourth, I could speak, move, rise in bed, and turn. Hannah had brought me some gruel and dry toast, about, as I supposed, the dinner hour. I had eaten with relish. When she left me, I felt comparatively strong and revived. I wished to rise, but what could I put on?

The answer waited on a chair by the bedside: my own things, clean and dry. My black silk frock hung against the wall, in fine shape. My shoes and stockings were purified and rendered presentable. The means of washing were in the room, and a comb and brush to smooth my hair. After a weary process, resting every five minutes, I succeeded in dressing myself. My clothes hung loose on me, for I was much wasted. I covered deficiencies with a shawl, and once more clean and respectable, I crept down a stone staircase with the aid of the banister, to a narrow, low passage and found my way to the kitchen.

It was full of the fragrance of new bread and the warmth of a generous fire. Hannah was baking.

When she saw me come in tidy and well dressed, she even smiled. "What, you have got up! You are better, then. You may sit down in my chair on the hearthstone, if you will."

She pointed to the rocking chair. I took it. She bustled about, examining me every now and then from the corner of her eye.

"Did you ever go a-begging afore you came here?" she asked bluntly, turning to me as she took some loaves from the oven.

"You are mistaken in supposing me a beggar. I am no beggar any more than you or your young ladies."

After a pause she said, "I dunnut understand that: you've like no house, nor no brass, I guess?"

"The want of house or brass, by which I suppose you mean money, does not make a beggar in your sense of the word."

"Are you book-learned?"

I crossed my arms over my chest. "Yes, very."

"But you've never been to a boarding school?"

"I was at a boarding school eight years."

She opened her eyes wide. "Whatever cannot ye keep yourself for, then?"

"I have kept myself and, I trust, shall keep myself again." She brought out a basket of fruit. "What are you going to do with these gooseberries?"

"Mak' 'em into pies."

"Give them to me and I'll pick them."

"Nay."

"But I must do something. Let me have them."

She consented, and she even brought me a clean towel to spread over my dress "lest," as she said, "you should mucky it."

She remarked, "Ye've not been used to sarvant's wark, I see by your hands. Happen ye've been a dressmaker?"

"Never mind what I have been. Where am I now? This house has a name?"

"Some calls it Marsh End, and some calls it Moor House."

"And the gentleman who lives here is called Mr. St. John?"

"Nay, he doesn't live here. He is only staying awhile. When he is at home, he is in his own parish at Morton."

"That village a few miles off?"

"Aye."

"And what is he?"

"Never mind what he is," Hannah said, flashing a saucy smile.

I remembered the answer of the old housekeeper at the parsonage, when I had asked to see the clergyman. "This, then, was his father's residence?"

"Aye. Old Mr. Rivers lived here, and his father, and grandfather, and great-grandfather afore him."

"The name, then, of that gentleman is Mr. St. John Rivers?"

"Aye. St. John is like his christened name."

"And his sisters are called Diana and Mary Rivers?"

"Yes."

"Their father is dead?"

"Dead three weeks sin' of a stroke."

"They have no mother?"

"The mistress has been dead for years."

"Have you lived with the family long?"

"I've lived here thirty years. I nursed them all three."

"That proves you must have been an honest and faithful servant. I will say so much for you, though you have had the incivility to call me a beggar."

She again regarded me with a surprised stare. "I believe I was quite mista'en in my thoughts of you, but there is so many cheats goes about, you must forgive me."

"That will do—I forgive you now. Shake hands."

She put her floury and horny hand into mine and smiled. Hannah was evidently fond of talking. While I picked the fruit, and she made the paste for the pies, she gave me sundry details about her deceased master and mistress, and "the childer," as she called the young people.

Old Mr. Rivers, she said, was a plain man enough, but a gentleman, and of as ancient a family as could be found. Marsh End had belonged to the Riverses ever since it was a house and was, she affirmed, "aboon two hundred year old—for all it looked but a small, humble place, naught to compare wi' Mr. Oliver's grand hall down i' Morton Vale."

The Riverses were gentry in the old days, she informed me. The old master preferred to get on as common folk, with interests in farming and shooting. The mistress was a great reader; Hannah supposed the "bairns," as she called them, had taken after their mother. Nothing like them was in these parts, nor had ever been. They had liked learning, all three, almost from the time they could speak. Mr. St. John, when he grew up, would go to college and be a parson. The girls, as soon as they left school, would seek places as governesses. Their father lost a great deal of the family money to a trusted friend who turned out to be no friend at all, and so they all had to provide for themselves and work hard to make enough money to provide for St. John's experiments and his mission.

"His mission? And experiments?" Here I stopped Hannah's rambling narrative to ask some questions.

"Oh, aye. Mr. St. John has always been fond o'fiddling with old junk to mak' 'em into new things. His 'speriments offtimes just make more junk t' fill the shed, but some of 'em done work for the mission. It's a school he runs, training the childer to grow up and fight the vampyres like his uncle taught him when he was a lad."

"His uncle? His uncle was a slayer?"

She slanted her eyes and looked at me as if I'd struck a nerve, then told me if I wanted to know more about it, I would have to ask Mr. St. John directly. Having finished my task of gooseberry picking, I asked where the two ladies and their brother were now.

"Gone over to Morton for a walk. But they would be back in half an hour to tea."

They returned within twenty minutes. They entered by the kitchen door. Mr. St. John, when he saw me, merely bowed and passed. The two ladies stopped.

"You should have waited for my leave to descend," Diana said. "You still look very pale—and so thin! Poor girl!"

Diana's whole face seemed to me full of charm. Mary's countenance was equally intelligent, her features equally pretty. Her expression was more reserved, and her manners, though gentle, more distant than her sister's. Diana looked and spoke with authority.

"And what business have you here?" she continued. "It is not your place. Mary and I sit in the kitchen sometimes because at home we like to be free, even to license—but you are a visitor and must go into the parlour."

"I am very well here."

"Not at all, with Hannah bustling about and covering you with flour."

Still holding my hand, Diana made me rise and led me into the inner room.

"Sit there," she said, placing me on the sofa, "while we take our things off and get the tea ready. It is another privilege we exercise in our little moorland home—to prepare our own meals when we are so inclined, or when Hannah is baking, brewing, washing, or ironing."

Diana closed the door, leaving me alone with Mr. St. John, who sat opposite, a book in his hand. I examined first the parlour, then its occupant.

The parlour was rather a small room, plainly furnished, yet comfortable. The old-fashioned chairs were bright, and the walnut table was like a looking glass. A few strange, antique portraits of the men and women of other days decorated the walls. A cupboard with glass doors contained some books and an ancient set of china. No superfluous ornament was in the room—not one modern piece of furniture, save a brace of workboxes that stood on a side table and a lady's desk in rosewood. Everything, including the carpet and curtains, looked at once well worn and well saved.

Mr. St. John, sitting as still as one of the dusty pictures on the walls, was easy enough to examine. Earlier, I made note of his physique and his classic, handsome features. In the better light of day, I could see that his eyes were large and blue, with brown lashes. His high forehead, colourless as ivory, was partially streaked over by careless locks of fair hair.

This is a gentle delineation, is it not, reader? Yet he whom it describes scarcely impressed one with the idea of a gentle, a yielding, or even a placid nature. He did not speak to me one word, nor even direct to me one glance, until his sisters returned.

Diana, as she passed in and out preparing tea, brought me a little cake. "Eat that now. You must be hungry. Hannah says you have had nothing but some gruel since breakfast."

I did not refuse it, for my appetite was awakened and keen.

Mr. Rivers now closed his book, approached the table, and, as he took a seat, fixed his blue pictorial-looking eyes full on me. "You are very hungry."

"I am, sir."

"It is well for you that a low fever has forced you to abstain for the last three days. There would have been danger in yielding to the cravings of your appetite at first. Now you may eat, though still not immoderately. When you have indicated to us the residence of your friends, we can write to them, and you may be restored to home."

"That, I must plainly tell you, is out of my power to do, being absolutely without home and friends."

The three looked at me more with curiosity than distrust. I sensed no suspicion in their glances.

"Do you mean to say," he asked, "that you are completely isolated from every connection?"

"I do. Not a tie links me to any living thing. Not a claim do I possess to admittance under any roof in England."

"I believe you had a cousin?" he asked after a minute. "Perhaps more than one?"

"I have no more like her. She was the last of my relations. I am, as I have said, quite alone in the world."

"A most singular position at your age!"

Here I saw his glance directed to my hands, which were folded on the table before me. "You have never been married? You are a spinster?"

Diana laughed. "Why, she can't be above seventeen or eighteen years old, St. John."

"I am near nineteen, but I am not married. No."

I felt a burning glow mount to my face. They all saw the embarrassment and the emotion.

"Where did you last reside?" he now asked.

"The name of the place where, and of the person with whom I lived, is my secret," I replied concisely. I had no idea to what lengths Mr. Rochester might go to discover my whereabouts. The less they knew, the easier it was for me to remain concealed.

"Yet if I know nothing about you or your history, I cannot help you," he said. "And you need help, do you not?"

I had now swallowed my tea. Refreshed as I was, I had strength returned enough to tell the portion of my tale I wished to share.

"Mr. Rivers," I said, turning to him, and looking at him, as he looked at me, openly and without diffidence. "You and your sisters have done me a great service. You have rescued me, by your noble hospitality, from death. This benefit conferred gives you an unlimited claim on my gratitude, and a claim, to a certain extent, on my confidence. I am an orphan, the daughter of a clergyman. My parents died before I could know them. I was brought up a dependent in a rather unusual household and educated in a charitable institution. I passed six years as a pupil, and two as a teacher at Lowood orphan asylum. You will have heard of it, Mr. Rivers?"

"I have seen the school."

"I left Lowood nearly a year since to become a private governess. I obtained a good situation. This place I was obliged to leave four days before I came here. The reason of my departure I cannot and ought not to explain. No blame was attached to me."

St. John nodded, obviously satisfied so far and eager to hear more. "Go on."

"I observed but two points in planning my departure: speed, and secrecy. To secure these, I left everything behind me but a small parcel, which I forgot to take out of the coach that brought me to Whitcross. The ride took every shilling I owned. I arrived in your neighbourhood as a wanderer, quite destitute. I slept two nights in fields out of doors and lived on very little food, whatever I could find. I scoured the nearby forest looking for a place to die in peace when I was interrupted by a conversation between strangers plotting wicked deeds. I followed them at some length. I knew their sort, and not to get too close. They met their coconspirator in the farmhouse. I dared not go in. But I looked in to debate my next move, how I should go about warning the residents to safety, when a girl turned and I recognised her as my cousin."

"You had no idea she would be there?"

"I thought she was in London, and I believe you overheard some of our conversation to that effect."

"Before you staked her."

Diana and Mary gasped.

"Yes," I said quietly. The memory came rushing back, and with it the same surge of power I'd felt at the scene.

"I retrieved your stake. Fine work. How did you know?"

"How did I know what, sir?"

"That it takes a wooden stake to the heart to kill a vampyre?"

"I had a vision," I said quite simply. "I lived with a family of vampyres—the unusual household of my reference—when I was a child and I learned to protect myself."

"How was it they never consumed you?"

"The family had noble blood, and they believed that I did not. For some reason, my aunt was convinced that common blood would taint the family with illness."

He made a noise, but it was not quite a laugh. "Unusual indeed. Your cousin seemed to have changed her mind on that point."

"And her brother before her. They are both gone now. Perhaps they should have obeyed their mama."

"And your aunt?"

"She died repentant, sir, as my uncle did years earlier. Both sought the mercy of death from slayers."

He narrowed his eyes. "Your name is Spencer, you say?"

"It is the name by which I think it expedient to be called at present, but it is not my real name, and when I hear it, it sounds strange to me."

"Your real name you will not give?"

"No. I fear discovery above all things; and whatever disclosure would lead to it, I avoid. Once fully recovered, I am stronger than you imagine. I have a quick mind and capable physique. I understand you have a mission, Mr. St. John. I would like to train with you to help you in it. I would also like to work. I need to find a position. Please let me stay until I have found suitable employment."

"Indeed you shall stay here," said Diana, putting her hand on my head.

"You shall," repeated Mary.

"My sisters, you see, have a pleasure in keeping you," said Mr. St. John. "You're not strong enough to consider training, and at any rate you're a woman. As for employment, my sphere is narrow. I am but the incumbent of a poor country parish. My aid must be of the humblest sort."

"I will be a dressmaker. I will be a plain-work woman. I will be a servant, a nurse-girl, if I can be no better. I am not afraid of hard work or physical labour. And I wouldn't be the first woman to become a slayer. Women have done so before me. I know of at least one."

I thought of my mother, who had, I believed, reached out to me, as my uncle did before her, to guide me on my way.

"Right," said Mr. St. John quite coolly. "If such is your spirit, I promise to aid you, in my own time and way. In short, regain your strength and we will discuss it at a later time. No more on the subject for now."

He now resumed the book with which he had been occupied before tea. I soon withdrew, for I had talked as much as my strength would permit.

CHAPTER 33

THE MORE I KNEW of the inmates of Moor House, the better I liked them. In a few days I had so far recovered my health that I could sit up all day and walk out sometimes. I could join Diana and Mary in all their occupations, converse with them as much as they wished, and aid them when and where they would allow me.

They discovered I could draw. Their pencils and colour boxes were immediately at my service. My skill, greater in this one point than theirs, surprised and charmed them. Thus occupied, and mutually entertained, days passed like hours, and weeks like days. As to Mr. St. John, the intimacy that had so naturally and rapidly arisen between his sisters and me did not extend to him. One reason for this distance was that he was comparatively seldom at home. A large proportion of his time appeared devoted to visiting the sick and poor amongst the scattered population of his parish, and also I suspected to his training mission.

He would often return home with heightened colour and slicked with perspiration that could only have come from intense physical activity. Oftentimes, he slept later during the day and went out just as it was growing dark. I suspected he was hunting at night—vampyre hunting. With my strength returning, I was waiting to find a way to reintroduce the subject of his mission with him.

Meantime a month was gone. Diana and Mary were soon to leave Moor House and return to the far different life and scene that awaited them, as governesses in a large, fashionable south-of-England city, where each held a situation in families by whose wealthy and haughty members they were regarded only as humble dependents. Mr. St. John had said nothing to me yet about the employment he had promised to obtain for me, yet it became urgent that I should have a vocation of some kind. One morning, being left alone with him a few minutes in the parlour, I ventured to approach the desk consecrated as a kind of study. I was going to speak, but I first observed that he was sketching a sort of weapon, a type of crossbow.

"You would do better to make the bow more curved here." I pointed. "And raise this part here, and bring this nub back a bit, to increase the tension." I had no idea about weapons, but it seemed a natural argument based on artistic principles and natural law.

He looked up, his mouth twisting to a sneer. "I designed it. I believe I know what I am doing."

"Very well." I shrugged and continued looking. "It is brilliant, in concept. That roller there, on the bottom? I assume it allows for rapid fire of preloaded stakes?"

"Did you have a question to ask of me?" he said, continuing with his sketch and ignoring my comments. Not entirely ignoring, for I noticed he had made some adjustments in keeping with the very changes I'd pointed out.

"Yes. I wish to know whether you have heard of any service I can offer myself to undertake?"

"I devised something for you three weeks ago, but as you seemed both useful and happy here—as my sisters had evidently become attached to you, and your society gave them unusual pleasure—I deemed it inexpedient to break in on your mutual comfort until their approaching departure from Marsh End should render yours necessary."

"And you thought they would protest the idea of my being in danger? Or worse, you feared they might get a notion that they could be slayers, too?"

He glared at me.

"They will go in three days now," I added.

"Yes, and when they go, I shall return to the parsonage at Morton. Hannah will accompany me, and this old house will be shut up."

"What is the employment you had in view, Mr. Rivers? I hope this delay will not have increased the difficulty of securing it."

"Oh, no, since it is an employment which depends only on me to give, and you to accept. Let me frankly tell you, I have nothing eligible or profitable to suggest. I am poor, for I find that, when I have paid my father's debts, all the patrimony remaining to me will be this crumbling grange, the row of scathed firs behind, and the patch of soil, with the yew trees and holly bushes in front. I am obscure. Rivers is an old name, but a good one. And since I am myself poor and obscure, I can offer you but a service of poverty and obscurity."

"Well?" I said as he again paused. "Proceed."

"I believe you will accept the post I offer you. Despite the many dangers and arduous training, long hours, and very little recompense except for the satisfaction of creating a safer world. I shall not stay long at Morton now that my father is dead, and that I am my own master. I shall leave the place probably in the course of a twelvemonth for India."

"India?" I asked, surprised.

"The vampyre populations grow wild, unchecked. I plan to combine missionary work with slaying, to leave our world a better place. But while I do stay, I will exert myself to the utmost for its improvement. Morton used to be a thriving community, with two or three times the current population. But, about twenty years ago, vampyres ravaged the area, killing many and scaring away the others. My uncles, my mother's brothers, made it their mission to drive all the vampyres from the surroundings, as their fathers before them had done the same in other regions, as I will do in India. Recently, vampyres have begun to return to this region, drawn here perhaps for the immense woods that surround us and create shade, for their kind cannot tolerate direct sunlight."

I smiled. "Growing up in what felt like eternal darkness, I know it all too well."

"Indeed. I sense you have a unique perspective, and talents I can use. Morton, when I came back to it two years ago, was a defenseless community, and getting poorer and more defenseless as people were reluctant to return. I established a training school for boys. I mean now to open a second one for girls. In learning to protect themselves, they will keep vampyres from attaching to the area and draining it continually. Over time, Morton will thrive again."

"A noble cause." I approved.

"My mother and my aunt were killed in helping my uncles', as you say, noble cause. They bravely chose to fight. Miss Oliver, the only daughter of the sole rich man in my parish—Mr. Oliver, the proprietor of a needle factory and iron foundry in the valley—also lost her mother to an attack, and she feels strongly attached to our project. She is too delicate to train, but she has given us the funding for the school. I have hired a building for the purpose, with a cottage of two rooms attached to it for the mistress's house. Her salary will be thirty pounds a year. Her house is already furnished, very simply, but sufficiently, by the kindness of a lady. Miss Oliver also means to provide an assistant for the school's mistress, an orphan from the workhouse that she will agree to clothe and fund. Will you be the school's mistress?"

"I thank you for the proposal, Mr. Rivers, and I accept it with all my heart."

"But you comprehend me? It is a village school. Your scholars will be only poor girls—cottagers' children—at the best, farmers' daughters. They are used to rough work, which serves us well, but they may not be up to the level of education you expect."

"Perhaps there will be time to help them with some reading, writing, and ciphering between training sessions."

"You know what you undertake, then?"

"I do."

He now smiled, and not a bitter or a sad smile, but one well pleased and deeply gratified. "We will go to my house to begin your training tomorrow and open the school, if you like, next week."

"Very well. So be it."

Diana and Mary Rivers became more sad and silent as the day approached for leaving their brother and their home.

"He will sacrifice all to his long-framed resolves," Diana said. "St. John looks quiet, Jane, but he hides a fever in his vitals."

St. John, at that moment, passed the window reading a letter. He entered and said, "Our uncle John is dead."

Both the sisters seemed struck, not shocked or appalled.

"Dead?" Diana repeated.

"Yes. Read." He threw the letter into her lap. She glanced over it and handed it to Mary. Mary perused it in silence and returned it to her brother. All three looked at each other, and all three smiled—a dreary, pensive smile.

"At any rate, it makes us no worse off than we were before," remarked Mary.

"Only it forces rather strongly on the mind the picture of what might have been," said Mr. Rivers, "and contrasts it somewhat too vividly with what is."

He folded the letter, locked it in his desk, and again went out.

For some minutes no one spoke.

Diana then turned to me. "Jane, you will wonder at us and our mysteries and think us hard-hearted beings not to be more moved at the death of so near a relation as an uncle; but we have not seen him since we were children. He was my mother's brother. My father and he quarreled long ago, after my mother's death."

Aha, I thought. No doubt their father blamed their uncle, for St. John had revealed how his mother died, fighting alongside his uncle.

"My father disapproved of my uncle's vocation, and he did not like to see my mother encouraging St. John to learn the ways of her family from my uncle. Once Mother died, why—" Here, Diana composed herself before she could continue. "They parted in anger and were never reconciled. My uncle continued pursuing his mission in other areas, where he also went on to make some successful business dealings and build a fortune. To add insult, my father lost money in his own speculations at around the same time."

"Yes, that must have seemed so unfair."

"Our uncle never married and had no near kindred but ourselves and one other person, not more closely related than we. My father always cherished the idea that my uncle would atone for my mother's death by leaving his possessions to us. That letter informs us that he has bequeathed every penny to the other relation, with the exception of thirty guineas, to be divided between St. John, Diana, and Mary Rivers, for the purchase of three mourning rings. He had a right, of course, to do as he pleased. It was not his fault our mother chose to fight and was struck down, along with our aunt and uncle, the parents of our other relation. I'm sure he fancied that we have each other, and that is a fortune unto itself. Our aunt and uncle had no other children. Still, a momentary damp is cast on the spirits by the receipt of such news. Mary and I would have esteemed ourselves rich with a thousand pounds each, and to St. John such a sum would have been valuable for the good it would have enabled him to do."

This explanation given, the subject was dropped, and no further reference made to it by either Mr. Rivers or his sisters. The next day I left Marsh End for Morton. The day after, Diana and Mary quitted it for their work. In a week, Mr. Rivers and Hannah repaired to the parsonage, and so the old grange was abandoned.

CHAPTER 34

My home, as mistress of St. John's training school, was a cottage. I had a little room with whitewashed walls and a sanded floor, containing four painted chairs and a table, a clock, a cupboard, with two or three plates and dishes, and a set of tea-things. Above was a chamber of the same dimensions as the kitchen, with a deal bedstead and chest of drawers that was small, yet too large to be filled with my scanty wardrobe. Through the kindness of my gentle and generous friends, I had a modest stock of such things as are necessary.

The first evening of my first day teaching twenty girls the moves that St. John had only recently shown me, I ached from head to toe. I expected the work to be physically challenging, but the repetition of the movements revealed muscles and joints I did not know my body possessed. With the fee of an orange, I dismissed the orphan who served as my assistant so I could groan over my pains in private.

Most of my students were unmannered, rough, and intractable, but all that might serve them well against such violent opponents. Others were docile, with a wish to learn and a disposition that pleased me.

To torture myself in the quiet hours, I thought of the life I might be living as Mr. Rochester's mistress. Just now, I might be settling to sleep in a bed of silk, in a southern clime, amongst the luxuries of a pleasure villa, delirious with his love half my time.

Yes, I had spent time in handsome St. John's arms—but to learn fighting holds and releases, not to be loved. I held Mr. Rochester in my heart, and it would ever be so.

I felt I had made the right choice, and yet, alone in my cottage, I wept. I hid my eyes and leant my head against the stone frame of my door, but soon a slight noise near the wicket, which shut in my tiny garden from the meadow beyond it, made me look up. A dog—old Carlo, Mr. Rivers's pointer, as I saw in a moment—was pushing the gate with his nose, and St. John himself leant upon it with folded arms. I asked him to come in.

"No, I cannot stay. I have only brought you a little parcel. It contains pencils and paper. I want you to look at some sketches and see how you might improve on them. You seem to have a knack with engineering. The ideas you had for my rapid-fire crossbow worked out perfectly."

"Thank you." I approached to take the parcel, and the roll of sketches. He examined my face, I thought, with austerity, as I came near. The traces of tears were doubtless visible upon it.

"Have you found your first day's work harder than you expected?" he asked.

"Oh, no! On the contrary, I think in time I shall get on with my scholars very well."

"More frequent exercise should increase your endurance. I counsel you to resist firmly every temptation that would incline you to look back on what you had. Pursue your present career steadily, for some months at least."

"Good evening, Mr. Rivers," a sweet voice hailed, turning our attention. "And good evening, old Carlo. Your dog is quicker to recognise his friends than you are, sir. He pricked his ears and wagged his tail when I was at the bottom of the field, and you had your back towards me."

Mr. Rivers had started at the first of those musical accents, as if a thunderbolt had split a cloud over his head. A youthful, graceful woman, clad all in white, approached. After bending to caress Carlo, she lifted her head, and there bloomed a face of perfect beauty. No charm was wanting. The girl had regular and delicate features: dark eyes, sweetly formed lips, even and gleaming teeth, and the ornament of rich, plenteous tresses. Nature had surely formed her in a partial mood.

What did St. John Rivers think of this earthly angel? He had already withdrawn his eye from her and was looking at a humble tuft of daisies by the wicket.

"A lovely evening, but late for you to be out alone," he said as he crushed the snowy heads of the closed flowers with his foot.

"Oh, I only came home this afternoon. Papa told me you had opened your school, and that the new mistress had come. I put on my bonnet after tea and ran up the valley to see her."

"This is she, Miss Jane Spencer," said St. John, gesturing to me in an offhand manner. He nodded, addressing me now. "Your benefactress, Miss Rosamond Oliver."

"Do you think you shall like Morton?" she asked me with a direct and naive simplicity of tone and manner.

"I hope I shall. I have many inducements to do so."

"Do you like your house?"

"Very much."

"And have I made a good choice of an assistant for you in young Dinah Winn?"

"You have indeed. She is teachable and handy."

"I shall come up and help you sometimes," Miss Oliver added. "You will have to teach me, too, at first, as Mr. Rivers has not encouraged me at all. He thinks it unbecoming for a lady to fight. Well, if my mother knew at least how to defend herself, things may have been so very different." She sighed sweetly. "I admire you, Miss Slayre. I'm not much for fighting, I know, but I do mean to learn a few tricks. I was at a ball and dancing until two o'clock this morning! If I can dance with such stamina, I daresay perhaps I can fight."

"I agree, Miss Oliver." I ignored her comment revealing St. John's opinion of a lady fighting. I was aware that he did not wish his sisters to take on the cause. Perhaps it escaped his notice that I was a lady, or he set me to a different standard somehow. I recalled that his mother and his aunt died fighting. He must wish to protect the women he loved, and I did not fall under that category. Miss Oliver, on the other hand, must have been in his heart.

It seemed to me that Mr. St. John's upper lip curled a moment. He lifted his gaze, too, from the daisies, and turned it on her. An unsmiling, searching gaze it was.

As he stood, mute and grave, she again fell to caressing Carlo. "Poor Carlo loves me. He is not stern and distant to his friends. Oh, I forgot! I am so giddy and thoughtless! Do excuse me. Diana and Mary have left you, and Moor House is shut up, and you must be lonely. I am sure I pity you. Do come and see Papa."

"Not tonight, Miss Rosamond. And you should head on home before it gets dark."

"Well, if you are so obstinate, I will leave you. But expect me to repeat the invitation soon. Good evening!"

She held out her hand. He just touched it.

"Good evening!" he repeated in a voice low and hollow as an echo.

She turned twice to gaze after him as she walked away. He never turned at all.

"It's a pleasant evening. You needn't have stayed on my account. Miss Oliver seemed very eager to get you to herself," I said, calling his attention back from the crushed daisies.

"We have business. I need an assistant in my workshop, someone to help me reason through my designs and see them to fruition. Your keen insights might prove most valuable to me. It is too late to bring you there tonight. I shall leave you to your rest. But if you could be so kind as to look over the sketches and make some additional notes, I would be grateful. In a few days, once the girls have picked up some of the basic stances, we might grant them leave to take a day off and spend that time with my inventions."

"That sounds agreeable. I will have a look. While we're there, might I have a look at your library? You've mentioned some volumes I should like to peruse."

"Of course," he agreed readily. "I am glad you have interest in further study."

I was pleased to be of use. He and his sisters had been so good to me and I liked to feel I had something to give back to him. Also, his inventing fascinated me. Lastly, I wondered if I might find some books in his library of paranormal references, which might aid in my research on werewolves.

I continued training the village girls as actively and faithfully as I could. It was truly hard work at first, and besides training with the girls half the day, I trained with St. John on my own, just the two of us. He taught me new holds and evasive moves and worked with me to improve my strength and endurance. I mourned daily the loss of my daggers. They were left in my parcel on the coach. No vampyres had been reported to have newly moved into the area, and while I was glad of it, I was eager for the chance to put my new skills to the test.

Fortunately, Mr. St. John's shop had much work to keep me occupied. He had shown me the gauntlet he'd used on that first night when I'd encountered him. It fit securely over the hand and contained a trigger that could be activated with one finger, sending a stake from a loaded wrist chamber to fire out with deadly force. The fault of the design, besides its being nearly too heavy to lift with one hand—a drawback I overcame as I gained strength—was that it could only hold one stake at a time.

Reloading was not always possible if one suddenly became surrounded by vampyres. St. John, with my help, improved on his design for a rapid-fire crossbow, one that held several stakes in a track to fire them in succession without delay. Together, we also developed what he called a mechanical, automatic, crank-operated six-stake shooter; I shortened this name to the more efficient stake-o-matic. With six barrels each holding a stake and a crank-driven launching device, the stake-o-matic could, like the crossbow, shoot stakes with great force in rapid succession. The crossbow had the advantage of being lighter and easier to aim, but the stake-o-matic held more stakes at a time, could be reloaded more efficiently, and fired effectively from a greater distance.

While St. John busied himself with adding our design modifications as we devised them, I searched through his many volumes on paranormal and supernatural beings to learn all I could about werewolves, what might be their weaknesses, and how one might be brought down.

When not teaching, studying, or tinkering, I made some effort to become acquainted with my students and their families. I believe I became a favourite in the neighbourhood. Whenever I went out, I heard on all sides cordial salutations and was welcomed with friendly smiles. To live amidst general regard with working people was like always sitting in the sunshine, feeling peaceful warmth spread through me.

At this period of my life, my heart far oftener swelled with thankfulness than sank with dejection. I used to rush into strange dreams at night, amidst unusual scenes, charged with adventure, with agitating risk and romantic chance, where I still again and again met Mr. Rochester, always at some exciting crisis. The sense of being in his arms, hearing his voice, meeting his eye, touching his hand and cheek, loving him, being loved by him—the hope of passing a lifetime at his side—would be renewed, with all its first force and fire.

Then I would wake. Then I would recall where I was, and how situated. Then I would cry fresh tears and convulse with despair. I would get out of bed and renew my research into werewolves and how to stop them.

Miss Oliver made good on her promise of frequent visits to the school. She came during her morning ride, cantering up to the door on her pony. The children adored her and seemed to work harder in her presence. It helped me to judge my students' progress as they enthusiastically volunteered to correct Miss Oliver's small mistakes in stance or form.

Miss Oliver, I suspected, had ulterior motives for her frequent visits. She generally came at the hour when Mr. Rivers was due to stop by to give one of his lessons. For his part, a sort of instinct seemed to warn him of her entrance. His cheek would glow, and his marble features, though they refused to relax, changed indescribably.

Miss Oliver also honoured me with frequent visits to my cottage. I had learned her whole character, which was without mystery or disguise.

She said I was like Mr. Rivers, only, certainly, she allowed, "not one-tenth so handsome, though you are a nice, neat little soul enough, but he is an angel." I was, however, good, clever, composed, and firm, like him.

One evening while she was rummaging the cupboard and the table drawer of my little kitchen, she discovered my drawing materials and some sketches. She was first transfixed with surprise, then electrified with delight.

"Did you do these pictures?" she asked. What a love—what a miracle I was! I drew better than her drawing master. Would I sketch a portrait of her, to show to Papa?

"With pleasure," I replied, and I felt a thrill of delight at the idea of copying from so perfect and radiant a model. I took a sheet of fine cardboard and drew a careful outline. As it was getting late then, I told her she must come and sit another day.

She made such a report of me to her father that Mr. Oliver himself accompanied her next evening—a tall, massive-featured, middle-aged, and grey-headed man. The sketch of Rosamond's portrait pleased him highly. He said I must make a finished picture of it. He insisted, too, on my coming the next day to spend the evening at Vale Hall.

I went and found it a large, handsome residence, showing abundant evidences of wealth in the proprietor.

While I waited for Rosamond and her father to return from an outing, a servant brought me a glass of water. Her finger came off in my hand as she gave it to me. I looked up in surprise to hand it back, ignoring the light sheen of green goo in the socket.

"Were you, by chance, educated at Lowood?" I asked as I handed back her finger. Her cheeks were indeed gaunt, her colouring grey.

"Aye," she responded listlessly, reattaching her finger as she spoke. "For two years. Then I was sent away to work."

"Have you always worked here since then?"

"Nay. I was a maid for Lady Granby, but she turned me out for clumsiness. Miss Rosamond took me in."

"How kind of her."

The maid shrugged. So, the Olivers couldn't be very much attached to her. Might they not even notice if she suddenly went missing? I spied a balcony off the parlour where I waited and I had an idea. "Could you do me one favour? I wonder what the view is from the balcony through those doors. Could you open it up so I could walk out and have a look?"

Without another word, she dutifully followed my orders, as I knew she would. When she headed for the doors, I looked quickly around the room for something to make short work of her. A pity Mr. Oliver did not seem to be a collector of swords. I did find a brass letter opener and an umbrella in a corner holder, and they would have to do. When she leaned to shift the latch on the door. I clocked her with the umbrella. She made a dazed groan. To my surprise, she reached up and grabbed the umbrella before I could hit her again. I'd made the crucial mistake of underestimating her reaction time. She groaned, more forcefully now, and flipped me over her head through the one now-open door. I landed with a thud on the balcony, the umbrella still in my hand. She came at me—slowly. I had time to spring to my feet, letter opener in one hand, umbrella extended in the other.

"I mean to set you free," I explained. "You deserve to be free of this servitude."

She stopped and looked at me. "Servi-wha?"

"Service. Domestic service. Drudgery." Oh, never mind. While she puzzled over this, I charged forth and whacked her again with the umbrella. I'd thought I might have to cut her somehow with the letter opener, but fortunately she was one of Mr. Bokorhurst's earlier works, like Martha Abbot. Her head blew clean off with the second solid whack. Now to dispose of the head, and body, before green goo oozed all over the rug.

I stepped back out and looked over the balcony's edge. As I'd hoped, the balcony overlooked a wooded area. Unless someone belowstairs saw the body land, it could easily go unnoticed for months, or longer. I dragged the corpse to the rail and heaved it over with all my might. It landed with a hollow thunk on a leaning poplar. When I went back in for the head, I could hear that someone was rapidly approaching. Oh dear, no time to spare! I retrieved the head and hurled it through the doors, right over the edge to land I knew not where, quickly closed the doors, and just narrowly avoided slipping on a patch of ooze on the way back to the sofa, where I had originally been seated in wait.

When Rosamond came in, I had been just about to sit, but I made as if I were standing to greet her. She professed to be "so pleased" to see me and was full of glee all the time I stayed. Her father was affable, and when he conversed with me after tea, he expressed in strong terms his approbation of what I had done in Morton school and said he only feared, from what he saw and heard, I was too good for the place and would soon quit it for one more suitable. By more suitable, I was sure he meant teaching more suitable subjects than how to pierce a heart with a stake or how to escape a choke hold.

"Indeed," cried Rosamond, "she is clever enough to be a governess in a high family, Papa."

I smiled at the compliment. At the same time, I noticed a large hawk flying off through the trees with the maid's head in its talons!

"Oh dear!" I said aloud, then wished I could take it back in case Rosamond and her father, who fortunately sat in chairs opposite with backs facing the windows, turned to see what I meant. "Dear, I have spilled my tea."

That got their attention. I pretended to sop it up, but Mr. Oliver had already started on a new topic. The hawk flew out of sight.

Mr. Oliver spoke of Mr. Rivers—of the Rivers family—with great respect. He obviously fancied a match between his daughter and St. John, and he took pains to point out how desirable the alliance with such a respectable old name would be. He accounted it a pity that so fine and talented a young man should have formed the intent of going out as a missionary.

I changed the subject by bringing up something nearer to my heart. It did not escape my notice that Mr. Oliver owned the foundry, as well as the needle factory, and I needed his assistance. I showed him some of my sketches of an adaptation of the stake-o-matic that could fire silver bullets rather than launching wooden stakes. Silver, I'd recently read, had the power to subdue a werewolf long enough to ensure its destruction, slowing their regenerative powers long enough to allow for the fatal crushing of heart and brain. By the end of the meeting, I had secured a promise that Mr. Oliver would make some silver bullets for me in exchange for my portrait of Rosamond, as well as perhaps influencing Mr. St. John towards making a match with Miss Oliver, if appropriate opportunity should arise. My influence was not needed, I assured them, but I left feeling satisfied with my accomplishment.

❦

It was the fifth of November, and a holiday. My little servant, after helping me to clean my house, was gone, well satisfied with the fee of a penny for her aid. All about me was spotless and bright—scoured floor, polished grate, and well-rubbed chairs. I had also made myself neat and had now the afternoon before me to spend as I would.

The translation of a few pages of German occupied an hour. Next, I sketched from memory a picture of Bertha Mason, and some alterations of face and figure through what she must look like when she was in transition, and finally in full wolf mode. I shuddered and put the drawing away. I fell to the more soothing occupation of completing Rosamond Oliver's miniature. The head was already finished, with but the background to tint and the drapery to shade off.

I was executing these nice details when, after one rapid tap, my door opened, admitting St. John Rivers.

"I am come to see how you are spending your holiday," he said. "Not, I hope, in thought? I have brought you new modifications to the stake-o-matic. The smaller barrels could accommodate the silver bullets, as you asked, and as silver is heavier than wood, I have increased the firepower to add force as well. I think we'll be able to make a smaller weapon, lighter for you. However, I still don't understand this obsession with werewolves. There have been no sightings in these parts. They remain legend."

"Werewolves are quite real. I've seen one, up close. But that is all I will say on it."

"Yes, well, my uncle would agree with you. It is the reason he left England, after all. He was offered a great sum to protect a winemaker's family from werewolves rampant in the area, and also to try to find a cure for family members already affected. Oh." St. John paused. "In fact, I've had news from uncle's estate. He left a book of his notes that might interest you."

"Of course! You can show me tomorrow, and perhaps we can work on the modifications to the stake-o-matic then as well."

"See what you think." He handed me his sketches and notes.

While I looked through his modifications, which all seemed workable and well planned, St. John stooped to examine my drawing. He sprang up with a start. He said nothing. He shunned my eye. I knew his thoughts well and could read his heart plainly. I had been entrusted to make a case for Rosamond, and now was my chance.

"Take a chair, Mr. Rivers. Is this portrait like?"

He almost started at my sudden and strange abruptness. He looked at me astonished. "A well-executed picture. Very graceful and correct drawing."

"I will promise to paint you a careful and faithful duplicate of this very picture, provided you admit that the gift would be acceptable to you. Would it comfort or would it wound you to have a similar painting?"

He now furtively raised his eyes. He glanced at me, irresolute, disturbed. He again surveyed the picture. "That I should like to have it is certain. Whether it would be judicious or wise is another question."

It seemed to me that, should he become the possessor of Mr. Oliver's large fortune, he might do as much good with it here in England, rather than to follow his plan to chase new vampyre uprisings in all areas of the globe.

"As far as I can see," I said, "it would be wiser and more judicious if you were to take to yourself the original at once."

By this time he had sat down. He had laid the picture on the table before him and, with his brow supported on both hands, hung fondly over it.

"She likes you, I am sure." I stood behind his chair. "And her father respects you. You ought to marry her."

"Does she like me?"

How could he not know? "Certainly. Better than she likes anyone else. She talks of you continually. There is no subject she enjoys so much or touches upon so often."

"I like her, too. I love her. It is strange that while I love Rosamond Oliver so wildly, I experience at the same time a consciousness that she would not make me a good wife, that she is not the partner suited to me, that I should discover this within a year after marriage, and that to twelve months' rapture would succeed a lifetime of regret. This I know."

"Strange indeed."

"While something in me is acutely sensible to her charms, something else is as deeply impressed with her defects. They are such that she could sympathize in nothing I aspired to—cooperate in nothing I undertook. Rosamond a fighter, a slayer, a female apostle? Rosamond a missionary's wife? No!"

"But you need not be a missionary. You might relinquish that scheme. There are plenty of vampyres in England to pursue. Until we have eradicated them here, there is no need, perhaps, to seek them abroad. And as for preaching, you are an excellent clergyman. Morton embraces you. You need go no further."

"Relinquish! My vocation? My great work? My hopes of being numbered in the band who have merged all ambitions in the glorious one of bettering their race—of carrying knowledge into the realms of ignorance—of substituting the hope of heaven for the fear of hell? It is what I have to look forward to, and to live for."

"And Miss Oliver? She has come to training. She has tried her best. Granted, she is no natural when it comes to fighting, and I can't imagine she will ever manage more than to defend herself, not to slay vampyres." I thought suddenly of her appalling lack of skills, though she did try. "Honestly, I doubt she could even manage to defend herself in any event. Still, she has made the effort. Why not let her decide what kind of life she would prefer to lead?"

"Miss Oliver enjoys balls and fetes and luxuries. She is ever surrounded by suitors and flatterers. In less than a month, my image will be effaced from her heart. She will forget me and marry someone who will make her far happier than I should do."

"You speak coolly enough; but you suffer in the conflict. You are wasting away."

"No. If I get a little thin, it is with anxiety about my prospects, yet unsettled—my departure, continually procrastinated. Only this morning, I received intelligence that the successor, whose arrival I have been so long expecting, cannot be ready to replace me for three months to come yet. And perhaps the three months may extend to six."

"You tremble and become flushed whenever Miss Oliver enters the schoolroom."

"You are original. And not timid. There is something brave in your spirit, as well as penetrating in your eye. I almost dread to inform you that you partially misinterpret my emotions. Know me to be what I am—a cold, hard man."

I smiled incredulously. Having said this, he took his hat, which lay on the table beside my palette. Once more he looked at the portrait.

"She is lovely," he murmured.

"And may I not paint one like it for you?"

"Cui bono? No." He drew over the picture the sheet of thin paper on which I was accustomed to rest my hand in painting, to prevent the cardboard from being sullied. What he suddenly saw on this blank paper was impossible for me to tell. Something had caught his eye. He took it up with a snatch. He looked at the edge, then shot a glance at me that seemed to take and make note of every point in my shape, face, and dress. His lips parted, as if to speak, but he checked the coming sentence, whatever it was.

"What is the matter?" I asked.

"Nothing in the world." As he replaced the paper, I saw him dexterously tear a narrow slip from the margin. It disappeared in his glove. With one hasty nod and "Good afternoon," he vanished.

I, in my turn, scrutinised the paper, but saw nothing on it save a few dingy stains of paint where I had tried the tint in my brush. I pondered the mystery a minute or two, but dismissed and soon forgot it.

CHAPTER 35

WHEN MR. ST. JOHN left, it was beginning to snow. The whirling storm continued all night. The next day a keen wind brought fresh and blinding falls. By twilight the valley was drifted up and almost impassable. I sat down at the fire with St. John's sketches and my research notes.

I heard a noise. The wind, I thought. No, it was St. John Rivers himself, who, lifting the latch, came in out of the frozen hurricane—the howling darkness—and stood before me. The cloak that covered his tall figure was all white as a glacier.

"Any ill news?" I demanded. "Has anything happened? Are there vampyres about?"

"No. How very easily alarmed you are!" He removed his cloak and hung it against the door. He stamped the snow from his boots. "I shall sully the purity of your floor, but you must excuse me for once." He approached the fire to warm his hands. "I have had hard work to get here, I assure you. One drift took me up to the waist. Happily, the snow is quite soft yet."

"But why have you come?"

"Rather an inhospitable question to put to a visitor, but since you ask it, I answer simply, to have a little talk with you. I got tired of my tinkering. The model of your Rivers Gun is complete, by the way. I call it a Rivers Gun because stake-o-matic makes no sense when you will shoot silver bullets instead of stakes. I couldn't drag such a machine through the snow, but I did bring you my uncle's notes. Besides, since yesterday I have experienced the excitement of a person to whom a tale has been half-told, and who is impatient to hear the sequel."

"You confuse me," I said as he sat down. "I wish Diana or Mary would come and live with you. It is too bad that you should be quite alone. You are recklessly rash about your own health."

"Not at all. I care for myself when necessary. I am well now. What do you see amiss in me?"

I saw nothing amiss. In fact, he'd never looked so handsome, so chiseled. His face glowed in the fire and seemed to glow from the inside, too. He seemed careless, almost happy. It was a new side to St. John Rivers, one I never thought I would see. It must have been the snow. Perhaps he had experienced a bit of frostbite—to his brain.

"How long were you out in the snow?" I asked.

"Not long."

"Have you heard from Diana and Mary lately?" Perhaps communication with his sisters explained his mood.

"Not since the letter I showed you a week ago."

"There has been no change made about your own arrangements? Do you plan to leave England sooner than you expected?"

"I fear not, indeed. Such chance is too good to befall me."

"It's a shame we had to cancel training today. We may lose more days to snow if the weather keeps up. But, Christmas comes. Mr. Oliver means to give the whole school a treat at Christmas," I said, drawing the subject nearer to St. John's beloved in hope of drawing him out.

"I know. His daughter's suggestion, I think."

"It is like her. She is so good-natured."

"Yes."

Again came the blank of a pause. The clock struck eight strokes.

He uncrossed his legs, sat straight, and turned to me. "Leave your sketches a moment, and come a little nearer the fire."

Wondering, and of my wonder finding no end, I complied.

"I spoke of my impatience to hear the sequel of a tale," he said. "On reflection, I find the matter will be better managed by my assuming the narrator's part."

"Very well," I agreed, anything so he would get to the point.

"Twenty years ago, a poor curate—never mind his name at this moment—fell in love with a rich man's daughter. She fell in love with him and married him, against the advice of all her friends, who consequently disowned her immediately after the wedding. Before two years passed, the rash pair were both killed while trying to eradicate vampyres from the region and laid quietly side by side under one slab. I have seen their grave. It formed part of the pavement of a huge churchyard surrounding the grim, soot-black, old cathedral of an overgrown manufacturing town not far from Morton. They left a daughter. Charity carried the friendless thing to her rich maternal relations. She was reared by an aunt-in-law, called—I come to names now—Mrs. Reed of Gateshead. You start—did you hear a noise?"

"Not at all. Go on." He'd left out the part about Mr. Reed being attacked on his way to bring the baby home and turning the whole family to vampyres, save for the orphan charge, but it was not common knowledge, and as I knew, at last, what St. John was finally getting at, I kept silent.

"Mrs. Reed kept the orphan ten years. Whether the girl was happy or not with her, I cannot say, never having been told. But at the end of that time she transferred her charge to a place you know—being no other than Lowood school. It seems her career there was very honourable. From a pupil, she became a teacher, like yourself. Really it strikes me there are parallel points in her history and yours. She left the school to be a governess. There, again, your fates were analogous. She undertook the education of the ward of a certain Mr. Rochester."

"Mr. Rivers!" I interrupted. The mere pronouncing of the name sent a wave of longing through me. Now he knew. Sweet torture!

"I can guess your feelings," he said. I doubted it. "But restrain them for a while. I have nearly finished. Of Mr. Rochester's character I know nothing, but the one fact that he professed to offer honourable marriage to this young girl, and that at the very altar she discovered he had a wife yet alive, though a lunatic. What his subsequent conduct and proposals were is a matter of pure conjecture. But when an event transpired which rendered inquiry after the governess necessary, it was discovered she was gone. No one could tell when, where, or how. She had left Thornfield Hall in the night. Every research after her course had been vain."

My breathing came shallow. A hollow, anxious feeling gripped me to the core.

"The country had been scoured far and wide," he went on. "No vestige of information could be gathered respecting her. That she should be found is become a matter of serious urgency. Advertisements have been put in all the papers. I myself have received a letter from one Mr. Briggs, a solicitor, communicating the details I have just imparted. Is it not an odd tale?"

I snapped like a whip. What could I do? "Dear God, St. John, what has happened? What of Mr. Rochester? Is he well? Has something happened to him? How and where is he?"

St. John merely shrugged. "I am ignorant of all concerning Mr. Rochester. The letter never mentions him but to narrate the fraudulent and illegal attempt I have adverted to. You should rather ask the name of the governess, the nature of the event which requires her appearance."

"Did no one go to Thornfield Hall, then? Did no one see Mr. Rochester?" I felt somewhat relieved. I had so feared that he was building up to dreadful news of Mr. Rochester.

"I suppose not."

"But they wrote to him?"

"Of course."

"And what did he say? Who has his letters?"

"Mr. Briggs intimates that the answer to his application was not from Mr. Rochester, but from a lady. It is signed 'Alice Fairfax.' "

I felt cold and dismayed. My worry remained. What had my departure done to him? He had, in all probability, left England and rushed in reckless desperation to some former haunt on the Continent. Oh, my poor master—once almost my husband—whom I had often called "my dear Edward"!

"He must have been a bad man," observed Mr. Rivers.

"You don't know him—don't pronounce an opinion upon him," I said with warmth.

"Very well," St. John answered quietly. "And I have my tale to finish. Since you won't ask the governess's name, I must tell it of my own accord. Stay! I have it here—it is always more satisfactory to see important points written down, fairly committed to black and white."

He displayed the corner he had ripped off my work before leaving me the other day. Aha, it had my signature. I had forgotten to write Jane Spencer, and I left him the clue he needed to solve his mystery. Jane Slayre.

"Briggs wrote to me of a Jane Slayre," he said. "The advertisements demanded a Jane Slayre. I knew a Jane Spencer. I confess I had my suspicions, but it was only yesterday afternoon they were at once resolved into certainty. You own the name and renounce the alias?"

"Yes, but where is Mr. Briggs? He perhaps knows more of Mr. Rochester than you do."

"Briggs is in London. I should doubt his knowing anything at all about Mr. Rochester. This has nothing to do with Rochester. It is not Mr. Rochester who seeks you, Jane Slayre. At least, not in that concerns me. You forget essential points in pursuing trifles. You do not inquire why Mr. Briggs sought after you—what *he* wanted with you."

"Well, what did he want?"

"Merely to tell you that your uncle, Mr. Slayre of Madeira, is dead. That he has left you all his property, and that you are now rich—merely that, nothing more."

"I—rich?"

"Yes, you, rich. Quite an heiress."

Silence succeeded.

"You must prove your identity of course," resumed St. John presently. "A step which will offer no difficulties. You can then enter on immediate possession. Your fortune is vested in the English funds. Briggs has the will and the necessary documents."

It is a fine thing, reader, to be lifted in a moment from indigence to wealth—a very fine thing, but not a matter one can comprehend, or consequently enjoy, all at once.

Besides, the words *legacy* and *bequest* go side by side with the words *death* and *funeral*. I had heard that my uncle was dead. Ever since being made aware of his existence, I had cherished the hope of one day seeing him. Now, I never should.

"You unbend your forehead at last," said St. John. "I thought Medusa had looked at you and you were turning into stone. Perhaps now you will ask how much you're worth."

"How much?"

"Oh, a trifle! Nothing of course to speak of—twenty thousand pounds, I think they say—but what is that?"

"Twenty thousand pounds?"

Here was a new stunner. I had been calculating on four or five thousand. This news actually took my breath for a moment. Mr. St. John, whom I had never heard laugh before, laughed now.

"Well," said he, "if you had committed a murder, and I had told you your crime was discovered, you could scarcely look more aghast."

"It is a large sum. Don't you think there is a mistake?"

"No mistake at all."

I again felt rather like an individual of but average gastronomical powers sitting down to feast alone at a table spread with provisions for a hundred. Mr. Rivers rose now and put on his cloak.

"If it were not such a very wild night, I would send Hannah down to keep you company. But Hannah, poor woman, she could not make it in this weather. I must leave you to your thoughts. Good night."

"Stop one minute!" I cried. "You leave off the best part of the story."

"How is that?"

"It puzzles me to know why Mr. Briggs wrote to you about me, or how he knew you, or could fancy that you, living in such an out-of-the-way place, had the power to aid in my discovery."

"Oh! I am a clergyman. And the clergy are often appealed to about odd matters." Again the latch rattled.

"Clergymen are honest, and you are being less than forthright. Satisfy me with the rest of the tale, St. John."

"Another time."

"No. Now." And as he turned from the door, I placed myself between it and him. He looked rather embarrassed. "You certainly shall not go until you have told me all."

"I would rather not just now. I would rather Diana or Mary informed you. I apprised you that I was a hard man, difficult to persuade."

"And I am a hard woman, impossible to put off."

"And then, I am cold. No fervour infects me."

"Whereas I am hot, and fire dissolves ice. The blaze there has thawed all the snow from your cloak. By the same token, it has streamed onto my floor and made it like a trampled street. As you hope ever to be forgiven, Mr. Rivers, for spoiling my sanded kitchen, tell me what I wish to know."

He threw up his hands. "I yield. If not to your earnestness, to your perseverance. Your name is Jane Slayre?"

"Of course. That was all settled before."

"You are not, perhaps, aware that I am your namesake? That I was christened St. John Slayre Rivers?"

"No, indeed! I remember now seeing the letter *S* comprised in your initials written in books you have at different times lent me, but I never asked for what name it stood."

"My mother's name was Slayre. She had two brothers, one a clergyman, who married Miss Jane Reed, of Gateshead. The other,

John Slayre, Esq., merchant, late of Funchal, Madeira. Mr. Briggs, being Mr. Slayre's solicitor, wrote to us last August to inform us of our uncle's death, and to say that he had left his property to his brother the clergyman's orphan daughter, overlooking us, in consequence of a quarrel, never forgiven, between him and my father. He wrote again a few weeks since, to intimate that the heiress was lost, and asking if we knew anything of her. A name casually written on a slip of paper has enabled me to find her out. You know the rest."

Again St. John was going, but I set my back against the door. "Do let me speak. Let me have one moment to draw breath and reflect." I paused.

He stood before me, hat in hand, looking composed enough. I suspected as much, but to hear it confirmed, how happy it made me.

"Your mother was my father's sister?"

"Yes."

"My aunt consequently?"

He bowed.

"My uncle John was your uncle John? You, Diana, and Mary are his sister's children, as I am his brother's child?"

"Undeniably."

"You three, then, are my cousins."

"We are cousins, yes. Slayres are Slayers. It is the family way. I had a vague suspicion when you excelled at training. Indeed, when you killed your Reed cousin. Was the whole family afflicted? You grew up with vampyres?"

"Mr. Reed was surrounded and attacked when he carried me, as a baby, back to his house. He managed to hide me. I believe I was the reason he agreed to become one of them, to be able to bring me home to safety. And then his wife demanded immortality, and the children, well, they were always so spoiled and indulged. As I've mentioned, it was my aunt's belief that common blood was tainted and would destroy them. Things didn't end well for the Reeds, all but Eliza, who has taken the vows and lives as a nun with a sect of vampyres who keep a remorseful, peaceful existence."

"That is odd. But would that they would all find God and peace."

"It seems a rather rare occurrence amongst vampyres." I now clapped my hands in sudden joy. My pulse bounded. My veins thrilled. "But we are cousins, St. John! This is greater fortune to me than the wealth, though that is welcome indeed. It may be of no moment to you. You have sisters and don't care for a cousin. But I had nobody, and now three relations—or two, if you don't choose to be counted—are born into my world full grown. I am glad!"

I walked fast through the room. Those who had saved my life could now benefit. I could reunite them. Were we not four? Twenty thousand pounds shared equally would be five thousand each, justice enough. Now the wealth did not weigh on me. It was a legacy of life, hope, and enjoyment.

"Write to Diana and Mary tomorrow," I said. "Tell them to come home directly. Diana said they would both consider themselves rich with a thousand pounds, so with five thousand they will do very well."

"Tell me where I can get you a glass of water," said St. John. "You must really make an effort to calm yourself."

"Nonsense! Mary and Diana work to keep themselves and to send money to you for your training schools. Now they don't have to do it. They can come home and live together happily with their studies at Moor House. What effect will the bequest have on you? Will it keep you in England, induce you to marry Miss Oliver, and settle down like an ordinary mortal?"

"Perhaps, if you explained yourself a little more fully, I should comprehend better."

"What is there to explain? You cannot fail to see that twenty thousand pounds, the sum in question, divided equally between the nephew and three nieces of our uncle, will give five thousand to each? What I want is that you should write to your sisters and tell them of the fortune that has accrued to them."

"This is acting on first impulses. You must take days to consider such a matter, ere your word can be regarded as valid."

"Oh! If all you doubt is my sincerity, I am easy. You see the justice of the case?"

"It is not a matter of justice. The entire fortune is your right. Our uncle chose to leave it to you."

"And I choose to share it. That is my right."

"You think so now," rejoined St. John, "because you do not know what it is to possess, nor consequently to enjoy, wealth."

"And you cannot at all imagine the craving I have for fraternal and sisterly love. I must and will have them now. You are not reluctant to admit me and own me, are you?"

"Jane, I will be your brother—my sisters will be your sisters—without stipulating for this sacrifice of your just rights."

"This is my wish, to share my fortune equally amongst us. We will all be rich, or quite comfortable. I will not change my mind should I think it over another hundred years. Please, accept my wishes. Say again you will be my brother. When you uttered the words, I was happy. Repeat them, if you can, repeat them sincerely."

"I feel I can easily and naturally make room in my heart for you as my third and youngest sister."

"Thank you. That contents me for tonight. Now you had better go, for if you stay longer, you will perhaps irritate me afresh by some mistrustful scruple."

"And the training school, Miss Slayre? It must now be shut up, I suppose?"

"No. I will retain my post of mistress until you get a substitute. I still intend to keep up my training with you, St. John."

He smiled approbation. We shook hands, and he took leave.

As I drifted off to sleep that night, my heart felt lighter. I could meet Mr. Rochester as an equal now, no longer as a dependent. Unfortunately, there was still the matter of what to do about his wife.

CHAPTER 36

It was near Christmas by the time all was settled. I left Morton training school in care of my young assistant, Miss Dinah Winn, who, though only sixteen, seemed a most capable mistress. Should trouble arise, most of the youth and indeed some of the adults in Morton could capably launch a defense against vampyre aggressors. There hadn't been any trouble for months, but it paid to be prepared.

"Do you consider you have got your reward for a season of exertion?" asked Mr. Rivers after my last day with the girls at school. "Does not the consciousness of having done some real good in your day and generation give pleasure?"

"Doubtless."

"And you have only toiled a few months! Would not a life devoted to the task of keeping the world safe from evil be well spent?"

"Yes, but I am out of it and disposed for full holiday."

He looked grave. "What now? What do you plan to do?"

"To be active, as active as I can. And first I must beg you to set Hannah at liberty and get somebody else to wait on you."

"Do you want her?"

"Yes, to go with me to Moor House. Diana and Mary will be at home in a week, and I want to have everything in order against their arrival."

"I understand. Hannah shall go with you."

"Tell her to be ready by tomorrow then, and here is the schoolroom key. I will give you the key of my cottage in the morning."

He took it. "You give it up very gleefully. I don't quite understand your lightheartedness because I cannot tell what employment you propose to yourself as a substitute for the one you are relinquishing. What aim, what purpose, what ambition in life, have you now?"

"My aim will be to clean down Moor House from chamber to cellar. Afterwards I shall go near to ruin you in coals and peat to keep up good fires in every room. My purpose, in short, is to have all things in an absolutely perfect state of readiness for Diana and Mary before next Thursday. My ambition, at present, is to give them a beau ideal of a welcome when they come."

St. John smiled slightly. Still he was dissatisfied. "It is all very well for the present, but, seriously, I trust that when the first flush of vivacity has passed, you will look a little higher than domestic endearments and household joys."

"I am trained and ready to take on what may come. You know I intend to keep perfecting our designs."

"And studying your werewolves?"

"Indeed. Our uncle's notes have proven most helpful. It's possible to save some of the infected. There's an Italian potion, a remedy. I believe I have even seen it in use." I thought of the vials Mr. Rochester kept in his drawer, the one he slipped to Richard Mason after Bertha bit him. "The key seems to be to administer it early after exposure, and again during a full moon as the transformation process begins. It's complicated. I'm still analyzing our uncle's experiments with it."

I could see St. John's lack of interest in the subject. He still couldn't fathom werewolves becoming a problem near the same scope as the one presented by vampyres. Nor had he ever been in a position to dismember zombies, either.

"Jane, I excuse you for the present. Unless danger presents itself, two months' grace I allow you for the full enjoyment of your new position, and for pleasing yourself with this late-found charm of relationship. But, I hope you will begin to look beyond Moor House and Morton, and sisterly society, and the selfish calm and sensual comfort of civilised affluence. I hope your energies will then once more trouble you with their strength."

I smiled. He was so serious, far too serious for his own good. "Be sure to come greet Mary and Diana when they arrive, brother."

I rose on my toes to kiss him on the cheek with sisterly affection, but he seemed taken aback by the gesture. His cheeks turned red and he looked away.

Happy at Moor House I was, and hard I worked. So did Hannah. She was charmed to see how jovial I could be amidst the bustle of a house turned topsy-turvy. I had purchased new furniture and made alterations to some rooms, while keeping others mostly the same so that Diana and Mary would still recognise Moor House as their home.

The eventful Thursday at length came. They were expected about dark, and ere dusk fires were lit upstairs and below. The kitchen was in perfect trim. Hannah and I were dressed, and all was in readiness.

To my surprise, St. John arrived first. He found me in the kitchen, watching the progress of cakes for tea.

"Are you at last satisfied with housemaid's work?" he said, leaning over the hearth and practically whispering in my ear.

I looked up to see a strange look in his eye.

"Come," I said, leaving my cakes and taking his hand. "I will show you the whole house from top to bottom, and we will see what you think of my labours."

He just looked in at the doors I opened. When he had wandered upstairs and downstairs, he said I must have gone through a great deal of fatigue and trouble to make such considerable changes in so short a time. Not a syllable did he utter to indicate any pleasure in the improved aspect of his abode.

This silence damped me. I thought perhaps the alterations had disturbed some old associations he valued. I inquired whether this was the case, no doubt in a somewhat crestfallen tone.

"Not at all," he said. "On the contrary, you have scrupulously respected every association. I fear you must have bestowed more thought on the matter than it was worth."

He took down a book and withdrew to his preferred window recess to read.

Now, I did not like this, reader. St. John was a good man, but I began to feel he had spoken truth of himself when he said he was hard and cold. The humanities and amenities of life had no attraction for him, its peaceful enjoyments no charm. He would never rest, nor approve of others resting round him. I comprehended all at once that Miss Oliver had made a decent escape. He would hardly make a good husband. He was right to choose a missionary career.

"They are coming!" cried Hannah, throwing open the parlour door. At the same moment old Carlo barked joyfully. The vehicle had stopped at the wicket. The driver opened the door. First one well-known form, then another, stepped out. They laughed, kissed me, then Hannah, patted Carlo, who was half-wild with delight, asked eagerly if all was well, and, being assured in the affirmative, hastened into the house.

Sweet was that evening. My cousins, full of exhilaration, were so eloquent in narrative and comment that their fluency covered St. John's taciturnity. I was afraid the whole of the ensuing week tried his patience.

It was Christmas week. We took to no settled employment, but spent it in a sort of merry domestic dissipation. The air of the moors, the freedom of home, the dawn of prosperity, acted on Diana's and Mary's spirits like some life-giving elixir. They were gay from morning until noon, and from noon until night. St. John did not rebuke our vivacity, but he escaped from it. He was seldom in the house. His parish was large, the population scattered, and he found daily business in visiting the sick and poor in its different districts.

One morning at breakfast, Diana, after looking a little pensive for some minutes, asked him if his plans were yet unchanged.

"Unchanged and unchangeable." He informed us that his departure was now definitively fixed for the ensuing year, for England was growing quiet with fewer vampyre attacks while news was spreading of an increase in activity in India, which needed his special skills more than we did here at home.

"And Rosamond Oliver?" suggested Mary, the words seeming to escape her lips involuntarily, for no sooner had she uttered them than she made a gesture as if wishing to recall them.

"Rosamond Oliver," said he, closing the book he habitually kept open, "is about to be married to Mr. Granby, grandson and heir to Sir Frederic Granby. I had the intelligence from her father yesterday."

We all three looked at him. He was serene as glass.

"The match must have been got up hastily," said Diana. "They cannot have known each other long."

"But two months. They met in October at a county ball. But where there are no obstacles to a union, as in the present case, where the connection is in every point desirable, delays are unnecessary. They will be married as soon as Sutton Place, which Sir Frederic gives up to them, can be refitted for their reception."

The first time I found St. John alone after this communication, I felt tempted to inquire if the event distressed him. But he seemed well enough, so I left it alone. Besides, I was out of practise in talking to him. He had not kept his promise of treating me like his sisters. He felt more distant to me than he had even when I was not known to be his relation, when we worked together in his shop, or training the children, or when he would teach me new ways to avoid a trap, or to grip a vampyre from behind to hold him steady while I planted the stake in his chest. When I remembered how far I had once been admitted to his confidence, I could hardly comprehend his present frigidity.

As the holiday passed and Diana, Mary, and I settled into a quieter character and we resumed our usual habits and regular studies, St. John stayed more at home. He sat with us in the same room, sometimes for hours together while we all pursued our own courses of study.

I often noticed him looking at me. I wondered what it meant. I wondered, too, at the satisfaction he never failed to exhibit on my weekly visit to the Morton school to train with my former students. And still more was I puzzled when, if the day was unfavourable, if there was snow or rain or high wind, and his sisters urged me not to go, he would invariably make light of their solicitude and encourage me to accomplish the task without regard to the elements.

"Jane is not such a weakling as you would make her," he would say, beaming proudly at me in a way that looked almost ridiculous for a man of St. John's habitual calm. "She can bear a mountain blast, or a shower, or a few flakes of snow, as well as any of us."

One evening, on returning home later than planned, I nearly ran into a small group of strangers in the woods. At once, my instinct warned me what they were. I had thought they hadn't seen me, and I was without weapons save for a few stakes in my sleeve. I chose to avoid confronting them in favour of coming home to get St. John and the protection of some of our inventions first. But one followed me. He must have picked up my scent and, perhaps eager to keep a tasty morsel to himself, did not inform his friends of my presence. I felt his step gaining on me as I skirted through trees and stayed off the regular path to escape his notice. I did not want to lead him to Moor House. I hid behind a tree trunk and believed he had passed, but then he gripped me from the side.

"Late for a lady to be out," he drawled. "Perhaps I could accompany you home?"

"What a sweet offer," I replied, furtively dropping a stake from each sleeve into my waiting palms. "But thank you, I can find my way."

I sized him up. He was barely twenty, just a little taller than myself and not stout, or so it seemed. He wore a coat several sizes too big, something he'd possibly stripped off a previous victim.

"Mm, no. I don't think you can. Did your mother never warn you not to speak to strangers?" His dark hair fell with rakish abandon into his sharp black eyes.

"My mother is dead," I answered, keeping up the conversation as I judged whether I had a better chance to lunge at him full on, or if I should try to put the tree between us and stake him from the side.

"Poor little orphan," he said with a lecherous smile. "Is there no one to take care of you? I could offer you a family, love. A whole new world."

"What do you mean?" I returned his smile, as if considering. Perhaps it would help if I could get close without his putting up a fight. If he thought I was complacent prey, willing to offer up my neck, I could stake him when he went in for the bite.

He paused as I drew near. "You smell so sweet. I haven't eaten in weeks."

"Surely, you don't mean to eat me, sir?"

"Aha." He wrapped his arm around my waist and drew me closer. "That was my original plan. But perhaps you might enjoy a little game? I bite you, you bite me. It could be quite amusing."

"What about your friends? How many, four? Five? If you mean to adopt me, I think you should know that I prefer to belong to a big family."

He was distractedly sniffing at my neck. I was about to make my move and stake him, but he had more to add. "We're all family, love. There are twenty-two more of them at home. They come tomorrow. The few of us are just here to take the lay of the land, so to speak."

"I know the land and could be helpful should you need assistance getting settled."

"Delightful. You might be very useful to keep around. Now give us a taste, hm?"

He bared his fangs and moved in towards my neck. I raised my arm, about to stake him through the back, praying I had properly calculated the location of his heart, when he, somehow, seemed to guess my purpose.

Spinning around, he caught my wrist and slammed me into the trunk of a tree.

"Ah, ah! Now I'll have to kill you after all. Pity." He slapped me full across the face and I went tumbling off to the side.

He pounced, but I rolled out of the way in time. I ran at him, stake extended. He dodged left, right, got hold of my arm, knocked me to the ground, and wrenched the stake from my hand.

"How did you know? Who warned you we were coming?" he demanded.

"No one. I always carry stakes. Everyone in these parts believes in being prepared."

"In Morton? It never before was such." He clucked and rolled atop me, clearly believing me disarmed. "I'll have to be on my guard. In the meantime, a snack!"

His voice trailed off as he bared his fangs again. Memories of John Reed came flooding back, urging me to fight, but yet I froze. Would I not be better off to let him bite me? I could continue my slaying as one of them. True, I would sacrifice my soul, but think of the access I would have to their inner circles, the power I would gain! Was it not worth losing myself to help the greater good? I felt his teeth pierce my neck, my blood begin to drain. I grew weaker, but somehow blissfully dazed. I felt my attacker moving against me, taking pleasure in the warmth of my body and my blood. It would be over soon. I would drink from him and be strong again. But for now, I gave in to the exquisite sensation of, for once, being weak. Of choosing the wrong path instead of the right. If only I had chosen Mr. Rochester . . .

Mr. Rochester! I could never be known to him again if I let myself go. I would be shamed. Defeated. With the remaining trace of strength I had, I raised my hand over my attacker. I did not hesitate to guess at my target. With as much force as I could muster, I simply rammed the stake, in my left hand, straight into his chest. He disintegrated, but perhaps because I was light-headed from blood loss, it seemed to take longer than usual. I watched his head rise from my neck, his face registering shock. His eyes rolled back. And then his skin seemed to dissolve, his eyes shrivel. From flesh, to bone, and finally—he disintegrated atop me. I shuddered, brushed him off—the overlarge coat rolling off with him—brushed brown leaves and muck from my dress with my hands. I steadied myself, getting to my feet with the aid of a branch, and then I leaned against the trunk of a tree to catch my breath and get my bearings.

A few great gasps of clean, fresh air seemed to restore me to my senses. How close I had come to losing myself, and all hope, forever! The feeling of triumph over not only the vampyre but over my own dark thoughts pulsed fierce in my veins, helping to recharge my sapped strength. Recovered at last, I ran home to warn St. John.

After I delivered my report, relating the attack, but not all that had transpired, St. John remained calm, as if nearly catatonic. Having heard what I'd been through—only that I had been attacked and bitten, not that I'd considered the worst—and my fear of the potential danger to the village, all he could say was "Jane, your dress. It's torn."

I looked down. Indeed, a slit in my skirts ran straight up to midthigh, baring my leg. I covered it and blushed, but St. John stared as if transfixed.

"Come," he said at last. "Let's get the weapons and warn the villagers."

After a quick change of frock, I led St. John to the edge of the woods where I'd seen the strangers gathering. The vampyres were there, now four of them, and St. John slew each one from a distance, taking them by surprise before they even realised what had happened. The stake-o-matic was a stunning success. I, armed with the lighter, recently improved version of the rapid-fire crossbow, never even needed to take a shot.

By the next afternoon, we'd alerted, gathered, trained, and armed most of Morton. It helped that the children knew basic techniques and could demonstrate for the adults. Before the vampyres arrived, the men and boys, led by St. John, waited in the moors and woods with stake-o-matics loaded and ready. My assignment was to keep watch over the women and younger children in the schoolroom so that none could be killed or terrorized in their homes. The girls who knew how to fight were prepared to do so, under the guidance of their new teacher, Dinah Winn, with my assistance.

As night fell and we waited for reports from the men, one of the girls, a former student, expressed her fear that vampyres might make it into town and she would have to employ the techniques she'd learned in school.

"I know what to do," she said. "I've practised. I just never imagined I would actually have to act in my own defence."

"If the time comes, you'll be able to trust your instincts," I assured her. "But the men are well armed and quite capable. I doubt any vampyres could infiltrate the village with Mr. St. John Rivers on guard. If it would help you to feel more secure, we could step out of doors and have some target practise with the crossbows?"

She declined, either confident in St. John's abilities or too afraid to venture into the open square. I thought of going out on my own. I enjoyed target practise, though it wasn't as satisfying as the actual charge of power that hummed in my veins after killing a vampyre.

"I wish Mother were here," the baker's daughter said after a moment.

"She isn't here?" I looked around. I'd thought Dinah had taken a count of heads, but perhaps she'd missed one or two in the tumult of assembling all in one place. "Where is she?"

"There were loaves in the oven and more ready to bake. We can ill afford to waste good flour. She instructed me to run on ahead and say that she was here, but she's not and I'm worried." The girl began to sob. I put her in the care of an older girl, then put Dinah Winn in charge of guarding the bunch. Armed with a loaded crossbow and pack of stakes, I set off in search of the baker, the widow Watson.

The moon lit my path and I found no reason to be alarmed along the way. When I reached Watsons' shop, which they lived above, the door was ajar. It was dark inside, but a light was in a window abovestairs. I proceeded carefully to the door, leading the way with my crossbow, and peeked inside, squinting through the darkness. There was the empty table I'd sat at my first day in Morton, when I'd tried to get information on employment as I'd struggled to find a way to trade my gloves for bread. The pastry cases sat empty, but the aroma of fresh-baked bread lingered. As I started towards the ovens in back, the sound of something crashing drew my attention overhead.

A stream of light led me to the stairs, and graceful on my feet though I wore boots St. John had provided me, I went up without making a sound. There, at the top of the stairs, I heard them.

"That's it," a deep voice crooned. "Let me drink my fill and then you have a taste of me."

"No, Richard." A woman cried softly. "Think of Lily. Someone's got to take care of Lily."

The widowed baker referred to her daughter. I followed the voices, rounded a corner, and saw what had crashed, a vase that might have been hurled or thrown, broken and scattered along the floor leading to a stout vampyre pressing a slender woman up against the wall, fangs bared as if poised to take a bite.

"Back away from her," I said in the harshest tone I could muster. "Release her and back away."

I couldn't get a shot at him without potentially harming her. The vampyre laughed in response, shaking his head before turning around, prepared to pounce on me until his black eyes widened at the sight of my well-aimed crossbow. A large man, he could not close his coat around his sizable belly, making him an easy target for me, except—

The woman screamed at the sight of me. Could she not see that I was trying to save her? "You don't understand," she said in shaky voice as she was still crying. "He's my husband."

I paused, the fatal pause St. John had always warned me about in training. The vampyre's reaction wasn't to be expected. He didn't lunge at me or try to wrest away my weapon. He reached behind him and pulled the baker to the fore, using her as a sort of shield from my attack.

"I'll drain her," he said, menace in his tone. "I'll drain her and come get you."

"Lily was worried about you," I informed Mrs. Watson. "She sent me to bring you back."

Mrs. Watson cried harder, but the vampyre held her fast in front of him, his pudgy arms wrapped around her waist, his canines extended and hovering over her throat. I suspected I'd come just in time. He would have killed her or made her a vampyre as well.

"Don't you care about young Lily, Mr. Watson?" I addressed the vampyre by name. "She'll grow up without a mother. Or worse, raised by vampyres. It's no life for a child."

They could trust me on that.

"Bothersome chit," Mr. Watson conceded. "Always making a fuss and getting in the way. Even now."

He loosed his hold slightly, or so it seemed as the dimples in his hands relaxed. I kept my gaze narrowed, my aim focused.

I sniffed the air. "Is that burning bread?"

The air still smelled fragrant, but the threat of burned bread made Mrs. Watson start for the door, and I took full advantage of her brief separation from her husband to fire off a stake. Phut! It hit him in the chest, left of centre. It took a few seconds longer than usual, or so it seemed, for that big pile of flesh to disintegrate to a pile of cloth and dust. Watching it, I felt the usual sense of relief and power, a surge of triumph over evil singing in my veins.

Mrs. Watson was safe, and I could restore her to her daughter. I thought of my own mother and smiled. Had she led me here on purpose, to look after these people? To make sure no daughter had to be separated from her mother by vampyres again? I could not be sure, but it felt right that I was here now, preserving life amongst good working people. I turned to check on the baker just as she started to shriek.

I put down the weapon. "Mrs. Watson, I'm sorry. I had to do it."

Quickly, she regained control of her emotions, only sobbing lightly when she spoke again. "You don't understand. I'm relieved, I am. He—" She choked on a sob. "He was always so angry and bullying. He left the baking to me and went to work in the needle factory, and then he was attacked. He was never the same afterwards. He went away. I said he was dead. I didn't think I would see him again, and then I was putting loaves in the oven and turned, and there he was."

She covered her mouth with her hands and went over to examine her husband's remains.

"He's truly gone," I assured her. "But you might want to check on that bread."

We brought fresh loaves back to the crowd gathered at the school. Lily and her mother had a happy reunion.

Fortunately, St. John soon returned to put us all at ease with his report. I watched from the window and I knew him by his walk—a strong, measured stride. St. John believed that we were no longer in imminent danger of attack. He and his men had kept watch as the vampyres headed into town, travelling in smaller groups and meeting up at the edge of the woods. The men allowed them to gather, then surrounded them, moving in until it was certain the stake-o-matics were within range. Once the first vampyres began to drop, the others began to run. But it was too late. Our men had them in sight, targeted, until they were shot down, eighteen in all. Some of the men were staying on to patrol the woods around Morton, but most were headed home.

"But what of Miss Oliver?" one of the girls, the baker's daughter, asked. "She never came. What if there are vampyres at Vale Hall?"

I met St. John's gaze. We both were struck by the same sense of alarm.

"Vale Hall!" I said. "If any had investigated the area in advance, it might be the likeliest place they would go to establish a base. The vampyre who attacked me last night said there had been twenty-two, but we've only accounted for nineteen."

"Grab your crossbow," St. John said. "Let's go have a look."

When we arrived at Vale Hall, all seemed dark and quiet inside, to be expected considering the late hour. A creak and a bang spun us in our tracks as we approached the front door.

"Oh, thank God," Rosamond Oliver lowered her weapon, one of the rapid-fire crossbows she had picked up from the school. "I thought you were more vampyres. When the servants came home with the news, the house was in a panic. I managed to sneak out before they barred the doors. I shot three right over there."

St. John went over to inspect the remains. "Well done."

He sounded amazed. I was equally surprised.

"Indeed, Miss Oliver. You were really paying attention in class," I said.

"I deserve very little credit. This is truly an amazing weapon. Ingenious design, Mr. Rivers."

"Miss Slayre is partly to credit for the design. Your father's generous Christmas donations, and your support of the school, helped us make it possible to arm all the citizens," St. John said. "The credit for that belongs to your father and to you."

She beamed with pride. "I suppose it's safe to go to bed now?"

"The danger has passed," St. John affirmed. "Allow us to escort you inside."

Days later, once things had again settled down, Mary and Diana planned a trip into Morton, but I had to excuse myself as I had come down with a terrible cold.

I sat working on my German translation skills while St. John sat nearby puzzling over some scrolls. I happened to look his way and found myself under the influence of the ever-watchful blue eyes. So keen were they, yet so cold, I felt for the moment superstitious, as if I were sitting in the room with something uncanny.

"Jane, I want you to give up German and learn Hindustani."

"You are not in earnest?"

"In such earnest that I must have it so, and I will tell you why."

He was studying Hindustani, he explained, and it would help him to have a pupil with whom he might go over the elements and so fix them thoroughly in his mind. Would I do him this favour?

St. John was not a man to be lightly refused. I consented. When Diana and Mary returned, they laughed that he had been able to persuade me to such a step.

"I know it," he answered quietly. "Jane is a good deal more interested in adventure than any other woman I've ever known."

"I daresay Rosamond Oliver proved more adventurous than you ever suspected, and she possesses a fair amount of courage. Do you regret letting her go now?" I asked.

He shook his head, not taking a moment to gather his answer. "Her courage was born of temporary excitement," he stated decisively. "Impressive, but fleeting. If confronted with a crisis on a regular basis, she would throw up her hands and run. She would prefer to live in her pretty house with her Mr. Granby sitting docilely at her side. She's not the type of woman suited to me. In fact, the more time passes, the more I wonder quite what I ever saw in her."

That evening at bedtime, his sisters and I stood around him, bidding him good-night. He kissed each of them, as was his custom. As was equally his custom, he gave me his hand.

"St. John!" Diana exclaimed in a frolicsome humour. "You used to call Jane your third sister, but you don't treat her as such. You should kiss her, too."

She pushed me towards him. I thought Diana very provoking and felt uncomfortably confused. St. John bent his head. His Greek face was brought to a level with mine. His eyes questioned mine piercingly. Before I could protest, he kissed me.

It was not a lover's kiss, but not quite a brother's, either. When given, he viewed me to learn the result. It was not striking. I am sure I did not blush. Perhaps I went pale. I might have trembled.

He never omitted the ceremony afterwards, and the gravity and quiescence with which I underwent it seemed to invest it for him with a certain charm.

CHAPTER 37

PERHAPS YOU THINK I had forgotten Mr. Rochester, reader, amidst these changes of place and fortune? Not for a moment. The craving to know what had become of him followed me everywhere. When I was at Morton, I thought of him every evening as I sat alone in my cottage. Now at Moor House, I sought my bedroom each night to brood over him.

In my necessary correspondence with Mr. Briggs about the will, I had inquired if he knew anything of Mr. Rochester's present residence and state of health. But, as St. John had conjectured, Mr. Briggs was quite ignorant of all concerning him. I then wrote to Mrs. Fairfax, entreating information on the subject. I had calculated with certainty on this step answering my end. I felt sure it would elicit an early answer. I was astonished when a fortnight passed without reply, but when two months wore away, and day after day the post arrived and brought nothing, I fell prey to the keenest anxiety.

I wrote again. Perhaps my first letter had missed. Renewed hope followed this renewed effort, but not a line, not a word, reached me. When half a year was wasted in vain expectancy, my hope died out, and then I felt dark indeed.

A fine spring shone around me, which I could not enjoy. Summer approached. Diana tried to cheer me. She said I looked ill and wished to accompany me to the seaside. This St. John opposed. He said I did not want dissipation. I wanted employment. He increased our time training together and studying Hindustani as if the additional hours spent pouring over the intricate language would bring me cheer. I could not even find satisfaction in our training sessions, though it normally lifted my spirits considerably to shoot targets with the crossbow or to wrestle St. John to the ground.

I could not stop loving Mr. Rochester, and I couldn't imagine why I had ever left him. We were equals now. I could return to him with my own fortune, as my own woman, without any reason to feel inferior or worry that he might begin to regret my dependency. True, he had a wife. And now, all of our acquaintance knew he had a wife. I could be nothing but his mistress. It was hopeless, I knew, to think that he would ever let me kill Bertha Mason. He believed in mercy and would not stand for harming or killing her. He would not accept that in releasing her from her earthly bonds, I would be setting her free. Indeed, I wasn't sure of it myself.

Was she evil, like a vampyre? Soulless? Nothing in my reading indicated that she had chosen her current state and willingly given up her chance at heaven. By all accounts, she was a slave to her cursed nature, unable to resist the transformation under a full moon. Adding to her blameless state, she was a lunatic. It was a terrible combination of circumstances, but my argument that killing her would be saving others from harm would fail to impress the man that I loved. I loved him because of his reason and compassion, amongst other things, and to strike at Bertha Mason went against his very ideals.

What, then, did this leave us? Was it better that I become his mistress, and sacrifice my pride, or that we endure the torture of being apart for the rest of our lives? I was no longer certain I could bear the separation. But now that I had written and had no reply from Mrs. Fairfax, I wondered if I had been forgotten more easily than I imagined possible. Perhaps, with time, they all—including Mr. Rochester—had replaced me in their hearts and moved on.

St. John called me to his side to read. In my effort to do this, my voice failed me. Words were lost in tears. We two were the only occupants of the parlour. Diana was practising her music in the drawing room. Mary was gardening. This fine May day was clear, sunny, and breezy. My companion expressed no surprise at this emotion, nor did he question me as to its cause.

"We will wait a few minutes, Jane, until you are more composed."

I stifled my sobs. I wiped my eyes and muttered something about not being well that morning. I resumed my task and succeeded in completing it.

"Now, Jane, you shall take a walk with me." St. John put away our books.

The sun was high as we walked out to the road along the glen. As we advanced and left the track, we trod a soft turf, mossy fine and emerald green, dotted with tiny white flowers.

"Let us rest here," said St. John as we reached some rocks at the edge of a little waterfall, a picturesque spot.

I took a seat. St. John stood near me.

"Jane, I go in six weeks. I have taken my berth in an East Indiaman, which sails on the twentieth of June. There is much trouble there with vampyres. The population grows unchecked and at an alarming rate."

"God will protect you, for you have undertaken His work."

"Yes, there is my glory and joy. I am the servant of an infallible master. One day, we will rid this world of vampyres and evil creatures."

"One day, perhaps."

"Jane, come with me to India. You, too, are blessed with the Slayre skills. It is right that we have found each other to help each other with the tasks ahead."

"To India? India?" Impossible! So far away from Mr. Rochester? There would be no hope, absolutely no hope, of ever meeting him again.

"India, Jane. Think of it."

"There are still vampyres here. There is work to be done here at home. India is your choice. Not mine."

"Jane," he said calmly as if confident of his ability to persuade me. "I knew you were meant for me the moment you came in, breathless from fighting in the wood, with your skirts ripped, your hair undone. You were a vision."

A blush spread over my cheeks. I could not believe what I was hearing! That he had ever thought of me that way?

"St. John! You should not have noticed. And if you had, you should not be telling me so. Remember our circumstances, sir."

"Our circumstances? That we're cousins? If we're suited, I hardly see how that matters—and I believe we are suited, Jane. Very much. With you at my side, I feel stronger, more capable somehow. You—you inspire me."

"That is a compliment." I sighed. I was not accustomed to compliments. "I understand now why you wanted me to learn Hindustani."

"Humility, Jane, is the groundwork of Christian virtues. Who that ever was truly called believed himself worthy of the summons? Think like me, Jane—trust like me. We both were chosen."

"Thanks, in part, to your training, I am somewhat skilled at vampyre slaying, I grant you. But I am not called to a missionary life."

"Jane, you are docile, diligent, faithful, constant, and courageous, very gentle, and very heroic. Cease to mistrust yourself. I can trust you unreservedly. As a conductress of Indian schools for training, and a helper amongst Indian women, your assistance will be to me invaluable." He waited for an answer.

I could do what he asked of me, I reasoned. To join St. John in India meant doing worthy work, indeed. Was it the work I was born to do? Was it what my uncle Reed wanted of me when he told me of my history? Was it what my mother wanted of me when she appeared to me under the moon and told me to flee, to follow my instincts? What mattered was what *I* wanted.

I wanted to be loved. I wanted Mr. Rochester. I did not want to go to India. And yet, I had no Mr. Rochester. I had no love. What else did I have but my natural abilities and my family now? St. John was my family, and he needed me. Was it right to abandon him for a dream that had passed me by?

St. John would never love me. He would approve me. I would not disappoint him. Yes, I could work as hard as he could, and with as little grudging. But he did not love me, and I did not love him. We could never marry.

"I am ready to go to India if I may go free," I said. "I do not think we should marry."

He shook his head. "Adopted fraternity will not do in this case. Either our union must be consecrated and sealed by marriage, or it cannot exist. Practical obstacles oppose themselves to any other plan. Do you not see it, Jane? Consider a moment—your strong sense will guide you. You would not be safe to travel alone with a man who was not your husband."

"You don't love me."

"I desire you, Jane. We could manage well as a married couple. I would make it easy for you."

"It would never be easy, St. John. You know I love another."

"But for India," he said, his blue eyes entreating. "Do it for India."

"For India?" I laughed. "I will do that for no one but myself, sir, myself and the man that I love. He is not you."

"I tell you again, it could work between us. Think again. Don't be hasty in answering. Take more time. Think of all the good we could accomplish."

I did think of the good. It gave me pause.

As I walked by his side homeward, I read well in his iron silence all he felt towards me: the disapprobation of a cool, inflexible judgment that has detected in another feelings and views in which it has no power to sympathise.

That night, after everyone else was in bed, I was awake pacing. Had I made the right choice? I was certain I had. How could I follow St. John to India with no real love between us? How could I be with him without continually thinking of the man I loved, the man I could never have?

The one candle flickered, dying out. The room was full of moonlight. My heart beat fast. I heard its throb. Suddenly it stood still to an inexpressible feeling that thrilled it through and passed at once to my head and extremities. The feeling was not like an electric shock, but it was quite as sharp, as strange, as startling. It acted on my senses as if their utmost activity hitherto had been but torpor, from which they were now summoned and forced to wake.

I heard a voice.

"Jane! Jane! Jane!"

And nothing more.

It did not seem in the room, not in the house, not from the garden. It did not come from anywhere near, I knew. It was a voice I knew, and loved, and hadn't heard in quite some time, but he called to me now. From wherever he was, Edward Fairfax Rochester called to me.

And I would answer his call.

CHAPTER 38

I DID NOT SLEEP. I spent the rest of the night packing and staring out the window in silence by turns. I longed to hear his voice again. Inwardly I replied, "I'm coming!" But long-distance telepathy was a skill I had yet to develop. I would have to hope to see him in person at Thornfield.

At breakfast, I was spared having to see St. John as he had already left for his daily visits to parishioners. I sensed he was avoiding me as well, perhaps giving me time to think. I announced to Diana and Mary that I was going on a journey and should be absent at least four days.

"Alone, Jane?" they asked.

They knew me to battle vampyres to the death and to be in possession of a deadly range of weapons designed by their brother and myself, yet they would worry about my taking a carriage ride alone?

"Yes," I said simply. "I seek news of a friend about whom I have for some time been uneasy."

I had no doubt they had believed me to be without any friends save them, for it is indeed what I had often told them. I doubted St. John had ever informed them of a certain Mr. Rochester, and what he thought my past was with that man I could only guess.

"But, it's so sudden," Diana said. "You look pale. Perhaps you should wait a day?"

"I can wait no longer. I'm sorry. I must go at once."

I left Moor House and soon after I stood at the foot of the signpost of Whitcross, waiting the arrival of the coach that would take me to distant Thornfield. It was the same vehicle whence, a year ago, I had alighted one summer evening on this very spot—how desolate and hopeless and objectless! It stopped as I beckoned. I entered, not now obliged to part with my whole fortune as the price of its accommodation.

It was a journey of thirty-six hours. I had set out from Whitcross on a Tuesday afternoon, and early on the succeeding Thursday morning the coach stopped to water the horses at a wayside inn, in the midst of green hedges, vast fields, and low pastoral hills so different from Morton's moors and woods. Yes, I knew the character of this landscape. I was sure I was nearly home.

Home! Yet I still thought of Thornfield Hall as home. How could I not? Home would ever be where Mr. Rochester was. How foolish of me to feel that I could ever keep away from him.

"How far is Thornfield Hall from here?" I asked of the hostler.

"Just two miles, ma'am, across the fields."

"I will stop here." I got out of the coach and gave a box I had into the hostler's charge, to be kept until I called for it. I paid my fare, satisfied the coachman, and I was going. The brightening day gleamed on the sign of the inn, and I read in gilt letters THE ROCHESTER ARMS. My heart leapt. I was already on Mr. Rochester's very lands.

I cautioned myself. For all I knew, he was not at home. He could be in any one of his old haunts. He could be with friends. If he was at home at Thornfield Hall, so would be his wife. What then? She would always be between us.

I thought perhaps to enter the inn, to ask after the house, the residents. Why not see what I could find out before running all the way home? Alas, I could not wait to even do as much as that. My feet started on the path, and before I knew it, I was running, running, eager for the first view of the woods.

At last the woods rose. A loud cawing broke the morning stillness. The rookery was near. I hastened on, another field crossed, a lane threaded, and there were the courtyard walls, the back offices. The house itself and the rookery still hid behind trees.

"My first view of it shall be in front," I determined. "Where its bold battlements will strike the eye nobly at once, and where I can single out Mr. Rochester's very window. Perhaps he will be standing at it. He rises early. Perhaps he is now walking in the orchard, or on the pavement in front."

I had coasted along the lower wall of the orchard and turned its angle. A gate was just there, opening into the meadow, between two stone pillars. From behind one pillar I could view unseen the full front of the mansion. From there I could ascertain if any bedroom window-blinds were yet drawn up. Battlements, windows, front—all from this sheltered station were at my command.

I closed my eyes and inhaled deeply of the earthy scent I knew as Thornfield, pungent grass, fecund soil, and all the sweet flowers of the orchard. I could not smell the orchard's flowers now. Perhaps the winds carried their delicate perfumes in another direction. Slowly, I opened my eyes—and could not believe what I saw. Perhaps I had fallen asleep and was dreaming. I had had this dream before—the nightmare of Thornfield burned down. But it was day. I did not dream. My eyes could not be mistaken.

Reader, I could not contain my gasp. Indeed, I saw no need. Who would hear me in the desolate emptiness? The Thornfield Hall I'd expected—stately, majestic, waiting to welcome me home—was no more. What greeted me was a blackened ruin.

The lawn was patchy, with spots of fresh green shoots just poking up here and there in a sea of char. The walkway, crumbled. The facade stood, albeit not intact, the wall yet beginning to fall to decay. The windows all were broken, gone. The silence of death was now about this place, the solitude of a lonesome wild.

I knew why my letters had been unanswered. But what story belonged to this disaster? What loss, other than mortar and marble and woodwork, had followed upon it? Had life been wrecked as well as property? If so, whose? My heart ached and fluttered in a panic.

Nothing but pain was in wandering around the shattered walls and through the devastated interior. Judging from the ruins, it had not been a recent tragedy. Grass and weed grew here and there between the stones and fallen rafters. And where were the residents? Mr. Rochester?

I ran all the way back to the inn for news.

The host himself brought my breakfast into the parlour. I requested him to shut the door and sit down.

"You know Thornfield Hall, of course?" I managed to say at last.

"Yes, ma'am. I lived there once. I was the late Mr. Rochester's butler."

The late! I startled. I seem to have received, with full force, the blow I had been trying to evade.

I gasped. "Is he dead?"

"I mean the present gentleman's, Mr. Edward's father."

I breathed again. My blood resumed its flow. The present gentleman. He was alive!

"Is Mr. Rochester living at Thornfield Hall now?" I asked, knowing, of course, what the answer would be, but yet desirous of deferring the direct question as to where he really was.

"No, ma'am—oh, no! No one is living there. I suppose you are a stranger in these parts, or you would have heard what happened last autumn. Thornfield Hall is quite a ruin. It was burnt down just about harvesttime. A dreadful calamity! Such an immense quantity of valuable property destroyed. The fire broke out at dead of night, and before the engines arrived from Millcote, the building was one mass of flame. It was a terrible spectacle. I witnessed it myself."

"At dead of night!" I muttered. I knew, then, that it was her doing. Had she tried to burn him, again, in his bed? She was indeed a danger to herself, and to others. And yet, he would keep her alive, and keep her near!

"You are not perhaps aware," he continued, edging his chair a little nearer the table, and speaking low, "that there was a lady—a—a lunatic, kept in the house?"

"I have heard something of it."

"She was kept in very close confinement, ma'am. No one, for

many years, was certain of her existence. Rumors persisted, of course. Some said she was a ghost. Others that she was a demon. Who or what she was, it was difficult to conjecture. They said Mr. Edward had brought her from abroad, and some believed she had been his mistress. But a queer thing happened a year since—a very queer thing."

I feared now to hear my own story. I endeavoured to recall him to the main fact.

"And this lady?"

"This lady, ma'am, turned out to be Mr. Rochester's wife! The discovery was brought about in the strangest way. There was a young lady, a governess at the hall, that Mr. Rochester fell in—"

"But the fire," I suggested.

"I'm coming to that, ma'am—that Mr. Edward fell in love with this girl. The servants say they never saw anybody so much in love as he was. Mr. Rochester was about forty, and this governess not twenty. Yet, they would marry."

"But they could not," I said, to hurry him along. "Because he was married. Was it suspected that this lunatic, Mrs. Rochester, had any hand in it?"

"You've hit it, ma'am. It's quite certain that it was her, and nobody but her, that set it going. She had a woman to take care of her called Mrs. Poole, an able woman in her line, and very trustworthy, but for one fault. When Mrs. Poole was fast asleep after too much gin, the mad lady—who was as cunning as a witch they say and may have been one after all—would take the keys out of her pocket, let herself out of her chamber, and go roaming about the house, doing any wild mischief that came into her head. They say she had nearly burnt her husband in his bed once, but I don't know about that."

"But this time? She went after him again?"

"Oh, no, ma'am. On this night, she set fire first to the hangings of the room next her own, and then she got down to a lower story and made her way to the chamber that had been the governess's—

she was like as if she knew somehow how matters had gone on and had a spite at her—and she kindled the bed there."

I stifled my gasp at these words, not wishing to interrupt. Mr. Rochester had thought she would do me no harm, but he was wrong. I could have been killed had I stayed. Except that we would have been away, on our honeymoon, or what would have served as one. "And the governess?"

"The governess had run away two months before, and for all Mr. Rochester sought her as if she had been the most precious thing he had in the world, he never could hear a word of her. They say he grew savage—quite savage on his disappointment. He would be alone, too. He sent Mrs. Fairfax, the housekeeper, away to her friends at a distance. He did it handsomely, though. He settled an annuity on her for life."

"So when the fire broke out, she was safely not at home." I was relieved. Dear Mrs. Fairfax.

"Miss Adele, a ward he had, was put to school. He broke off acquaintance with all the gentry and shut himself up like a hermit at the hall. At night, he walked just like a ghost about the grounds and in the orchard as if he had lost his senses—which it is my opinion he had. He was wild, spirited, and full of life, and then dejected and empty."

"Then Mr. Rochester was at home when the fire broke out?"

"Yes, indeed, and he went up to the attics when all was burning above and below and got the servants out of their beds and helped them down himself, and went back to get his mad wife out of her cell, where she went back, apparently, after she started the place ablaze. And then they called out to him that she was on the roof, where she was standing, waving her arms, above the battlements, and shouting out until they could hear her a mile off. I saw her and heard her with my own eyes. I witnessed, and several more witnessed, Mr. Rochester ascend through the skylight onto the roof. We heard him call, 'Bertha!' We saw him approach her. And then, ma'am, she yelled and gave a spring, and the next minute she lay smashed on the pavement."

"Dead?"

"Dead! Ay, dead as the stones on which her brains and blood were scattered."

"Good God! You're sure her brains were scattered? And her heart?"

"Crushed, too, I'm sure. It was frightful!" He shuddered.

"And afterwards?"

"Well, ma'am, afterwards the house was burnt to the ground. There are only some bits of walls standing now."

"Were any other lives lost?"

"No. Perhaps it would have been better if there had. Poor Mr. Edward! Some say it was a just judgment on him for keeping his first marriage secret, and wanting to take another wife while he had one living. I pity him, for my part."

"You said he was alive? Why? How?" My blood was again running cold. "Where is he? Is he in England?"

"He is stone-blind," the host said at last. "Yes, he is stone-blind, is Mr. Edward."

I had dreaded worse. I had dreaded he was mad or had been bitten. Perhaps yet he was. I summoned strength to ask what had caused this calamity.

"It was all his own courage and, a body may say, his kindness, in a way, ma'am. He wouldn't leave the house until everyone else was out before him. As he came down the great staircase at last, after Mrs. Rochester had flung herself from the battlements, there was a great crash—all fell. He was taken out from under the ruins, alive, but sadly hurt. A beam had fallen in such a way as to protect him partly, but his sight was dazed. He is now helpless, indeed—blind."

"Where is he? Where does he now live?"

"At Ferndean, about thirty miles off. Quite a desolate spot."

"Who is with him?"

"Old John and his wife. He is quite broken-down, they say."

"Have you any sort of conveyance?"

"We have a chaise, ma'am. A very handsome chaise."

"Order it to be ready instantly, and if your postboy can drive me to Ferndean before dark this day, I'll pay both you and him twice the hire you usually demand."

CHAPTER 39

THE MANOR HOUSE OF Ferndean was of considerable antiquity, moderate size, and no architectural pretensions, deep buried in a wood. Mr. Rochester often spoke of it and sometimes went there. His father had purchased the estate for the sake of the game covers. Ferndean remained uninhabited and unfurnished, with the exception of some two or three rooms fitted up for the accommodation of the squire when he went there in the season to shoot.

I made it there before dark, as the sky turned cold and rain began to fall. I walked the last mile over rough terrain, having dismissed the chaise and the driver with double remuneration as I had promised. Even when within a short distance of the manor house, one could see nothing of it, the woods were so thick and dark. I passed through iron gates between granite pillars and crossed a grass-grown track to reach the dwelling.

I began to fear I had taken a wrong direction and lost my way. The darkness of natural as well as of sylvan dusk gathered over me. I looked around, but saw no other road, no opening, anywhere. I proceeded. At last my way opened, the trees thinned a little. Presently I beheld a railing, then the house. The house presented two pointed gables in its front. The windows were latticed and narrow. The front door was narrow, too, one step leading up to it. The whole looked, as the host of the Rochester Arms had said, "quite a desolate spot."

I heard a movement. The narrow front door opened and some shape was about to issue from the grange. A figure came out into the twilight and stood on the step. A man without a hat. He stretched forth his hand as if to feel whether it rained. It was my Edward Fairfax Rochester.

I forced myself to stay in place, to watch. His form was of the same strong and stalwart contour as ever. He stood tall, not stooped or hunched as the Rochester Arms host had led me to fear. His hair was still raven black, and his features regular and fine. Only his expression had changed. He looked desperate and brooding.

And, reader, do you think I feared him in his blind ferocity? I could not wait to run up and throw myself in his arms and kiss him, but wait I did. I would not accost him yet. Rain began to fall on him.

At this moment John approached him from some quarter. "Will you take my arm, sir? There is a heavy shower coming on. Had you not better go in?"

"Leave me alone."

John withdrew without having observed me. Mr. Rochester now tried to walk about but stopped, groped his way back to the house, and, reentering it, closed the door.

I now drew near and knocked. John's wife opened for me.

"Mary, how are you?"

"Is it really you, miss, come at this late hour to this lonely place?" She looked at me with wide eyes, as if looking at a ghost.

"It is Jane, Mary. Your eyes do not deceive you." I followed her into the kitchen, where John now sat by a good fire. He started to rise, but I bid him to keep his seat. I explained to them, in few words, that I had heard all that had happened since I left Thornfield, and that I had come to see Mr. Rochester.

I asked John to go down to the turnpike house, where I had dismissed the chaise, and bring my trunk, which I had left there. Then, while I removed my bonnet and shawl, I asked Mary if I could be accommodated at the house for the night. Arrangements to that effect, though difficult, would not be impossible. I informed her I should stay. Just at this moment the parlour bell rang.

"When you go in," I said, "tell your master that a person wishes to speak to him, but do not give my name."

"I don't think he will see you. He refuses everybody."

When she returned, I inquired what he had said.

"You are to send in your name and your business 'or go to hell.' Excuse me, but those were his words." She then filled a glass with water and placed it on a tray, together with candles.

"Is that what he rang for?"

"Yes. He always has candles brought in at dark, though he is blind."

"Give me the tray. I will carry it in."

I took it from her. The tray shook as I held it. The water spilt from the glass. My heart struck my ribs loud and fast. Mary opened the door for me, then shut it behind me.

The parlour looked gloomy. A fire burned low in the grate, and leaning over it, his head supported against the high, old-fashioned mantelpiece, appeared the blind tenant of the room. His old dog, Pilot, lay on one side, out of the way, and coiled up as if afraid of being inadvertently trodden upon. Pilot pricked up his ears when I came in. Then he jumped up with a yelp and a whine and bounded towards me. He almost knocked the tray from my hands. I set it on the table, then patted him and said softly, "Lie down!"

Mr. Rochester turned mechanically to see what the commotion was, but as he could not see a thing, he returned and sighed.

"Give me the water, Mary."

I approached him with the now only half-filled glass. Pilot followed me, still excited.

"What is the matter?"

"Down, Pilot!" I again said.

Mr. Rochester checked the water on its way to his lips and

seemed to listen. He drank, then put the glass down. "This is you, Mary, is it not?"

"Mary is in the kitchen."

He put out his hand with a quick gesture, but not seeing where I stood, he did not touch me.

"Who is this? Who is this?" he demanded, trying, as it seemed, to see with those sightless eyes. "Answer me—speak again!" he ordered imperiously and aloud.

"Will you have a little more water, sir? I spilt half of what was in the glass."

"Who is it? What is it? Who speaks?"

"Pilot knows me, and John and Mary know I am here. I came only this evening."

"Come here, come here at once! I must feel, or my heart will stop and my brain burst. Whatever—whoever you are—be perceptible to the touch or I cannot live!"

He groped. I arrested his wandering hand and imprisoned it in both of mine.

"Her very fingers!" he cried. "Her small, slight fingers! If so there must be more of her."

The muscular hand broke from my custody. He seized me around the waist, pulled me to him, and nestled his face in between my neck and shoulder. "Oh, the smell of you! My Jane! Is it Jane? She is her shape and size."

"And her voice. She is all here. Her heart, too. God bless you, sir! I am glad to be so near you again."

"Jane Slayre! Jane Slayre."

"My dear Edward, I have found you. I have come back to you."

"My living darling! How I have searched for you. It is a dream. Tell me it is not a dream? Such dreams as I have had at night when I have clasped her once more to my heart, as I do now. And kissed her, and felt that she loved me, and would not leave."

"Which I never will, sir, from this day."

" 'Never will,' says the vision? But I always wake alone abandoned, my life dark, lonely, hopeless. Kiss me, Jane. Kiss me and prove that you are real."

"There, sir—and there!' " I pressed my lips to his brilliant and now sightless eyes. I swept his hair from his brow and kissed that, too.

"Oh, Jane! It is you! You have come back to me then?"

"I am."

"And you do not lie dead in some ditch under some stream? And you are not a pining outcast amongst strangers? Oh, the terrible things I had feared!"

"Sir, I am alive, and I am an independent woman now. My uncle in Madeira is dead, and he left me five thousand pounds."

"What, Janet! You are a rich woman."

"If you won't let me live with you, I can build a house of my own close up to your door, and you may come and sit in my parlour when you want company of an evening."

"But as you are rich, Jane, you have now, no doubt, friends who will look after you and not suffer you to devote yourself to a blind—a man like me?"

"I told you I am independent, sir, as well as rich. I am my own mistress."

"And you will stay with me?"

"Certainly—unless you object. I will be your neighbour, your nurse, your housekeeper. If I find you lonely, I will be your companion—to read to you, to walk with you, to sit with you, to wait on you, to be eyes and hands to you. Cease to look so melancholy, my dear master. You shall not be left desolate so long as I live."

He sighed. "You think so, Jane? You see my sightless eyes, and you think it is well enough. What are lost eyes to you who can see for me? But you don't understand, Jane. You don't know the whole of it."

"And I don't care. I love you. I am here now. We will work through anything that arises."

He remained grave. "I don't want you for a servant, Jane. I have enough who can wait on me. I want you for my wife, but I have no right to ask."

"That didn't stop you when it was true. What holds you back now? Your wife is dead, or so I have come to understand. Did I hear wrong?"

I swore to God if she was in the attic now, I was going to dig out my gun with the silver bullet and march right upstairs and shoot her, right or wrong. Against his wishes or with his blessing.

"She is dead. I have no wife. But, Jane, please. You must not go. Not yet. I have barely touched you, heard you, felt the comfort of your presence. I cannot give up these joys. I have little left in myself—I must have you."

"You have me. I am here. I am here in any way you want me. I will never run from you again."

"You must know. Before you make promises. Things have changed."

"I see that. It makes no difference to me."

"It's more than you think. The night of the fire, I tried to save her. The house was wild with flames. I made sure everyone got out, and I went back for her. God help me, I couldn't let her die. I found her on the third story, in her usual haunt. It wasn't quite a full moon. She was not in her full state, but somewhat altered. She would not come. I thought perhaps I could get her to chase me, but she wouldn't move. She sat there as if waiting for the flames."

"Poor thing." I couldn't help it. She reminded me of my aunt Reed, for I was sure it was a sign that she wanted to die, and perhaps she'd died remorseful.

"The *poor thing* jumped on me, all teeth and claws. We had minutes to get out, if that, and she decided to take me down with her. I finally got her off, and she ran for the roof. I tried, once more, to bring her down, but she jumped to her death. It was only later, while escaping the flames, did I realise she had bitten me when we grappled. More than once. She broke the skin."

"Oh! Oh, sir."

He sighed heavily. "Indeed, Jane. I'd already dismissed all but the necessary servants. Adele was sent to school. I set Sophie up in a little house near her to look after her when school was out of session. Mrs. Fairfax has an income and a small house in the country. Grace Poole, well, after the fire, I let her go. John and Mary are my jailors now, when, once a month, the moon is full. They lock me in the attic, Jane. Can you bear it?"

I wrapped my arms around him. "I can bear anything, Edward! Anything. As long as I have you."

"But I am a monster now. I'm the dangerous one."

"You always were a bit of a danger, sir. Those moods of yours! And, well, it is only once a month. You're not a lunatic, as well, for that is not contagious. So you're a werewolf. It is good that I have come." I parted his thick and long, uncut locks. "For I see you are taking it on as a sort of fashion statement. We will need to keep this hair cut shorter, no? The worst of it is, one is in danger of loving you too well for all this, and making too much of you."

"I thought you would be revolted, Jane, when you saw my face and heard of it."

"Did you? Don't tell me so, lest I should say something disparaging to your judgment. Now, let me leave you an instant to make a better fire and have the hearth swept up. Can you tell when there is a good fire?"

"Yes. I see a glow—a ruddy haze."

"And you see the candles?"

"Very dimly—each is a luminous cloud."

"Can you see me?"

"No, my fairy, but I am only too thankful to hear and feel you."

"When do you take supper?"

"I never take supper."

"But you shall have some tonight. I am hungry. So are you, I daresay, only you forget."

Summoning Mary, I soon had the room in more cheerful order. I prepared him, likewise, a comfortable repast. My spirits were excited, and with pleasure and ease I talked to him during supper.

"Tell me," I said. "Those vials, like the ones you gave to Richard Mason, do you still have them or did they burn?"

"It is what delayed me further on my way out of the house. I went back for them. They contain a special potion from Italy meant to reduce or put off the effects of the disease that turns one to a wolflike state. Not a cure entirely, but as close as one can get. I took one right after the fire, or the next day, it was, by then. And I have taken another before each full moon. My transformations have been weak, but I fear they may, like Bertha's did, get stronger over time."

"I believe we can get even closer to a cure than that, perhaps cure you entirely. I've been researching. My uncle, in addition to being a vampyre slayer, studied werewolves and successfully cured a few. I have his notes."

Mr. Rochester sat up straighter. "But, Jane, this is wonderful news! How is it to be done?"

"Never mind that for now." It was dangerous and I didn't want to think of it. "But I think I know the way."

After supper, he began to ask me many questions, of where I had been, what I had been doing, how I had found him out, but I gave him only partial replies. It was too late to enter into particulars that night.

"You are altogether a human being, Jane? You are certain of that?"

"What, and do you think me a werewolf, too? Or a zombie? Or perhaps you prefer a vampyre? But I cannot be, you know, for I travelled to you all the day, and it has made me quite exhausted. Human I must be."

"Yet how, on this dark and doleful evening, could you so suddenly rise on my lone hearth? Like a fairy you appeared, as if out of the air. Not the first time you came to me such, I might add."

"I did not suddenly appear, as I already told you, but I have had grueling days of journeying and much walking, nay running, to and fro to try and find you."

"And there is enchantment in the very hour I am now spending with you. How can it be that Jane is with me, and says she loves me? Will she not depart as suddenly as she came? Tomorrow, I fear I shall find her no more."

It was useless to argue. I merely asked for a comb.

"A what?"

"A comb, sir. If I were a fairy, I would merely wrap my magic around you and fix your appearance at once. As it is, your hair is wild and I mean to tame it. Being perfectly human, I need a comb."

"Am I hideous, Jane?"

"Very, sir. You always were, you know."

"Humph! The wickedness has not been taken out of you, wherever you have sojourned."

"Yet I have been with good people, far better than you. I will need to write to them tomorrow and tell them I have had a change in plans. And perhaps I will invite them to our wedding, for I mean to accept you this time, and you won't be allowed to produce any excuses to stop me."

"Who the deuce have you been with?"

"If you twist in that way, you will make me pull the hair out of your head, and then I think you will cease to entertain doubts of my substantiality."

"Who have you been with, Jane?"

"You shall not get it out of me tonight, sir. You must wait until tomorrow. There, you have the security to know I will still be here in the morning, for I have promised you my tale. Your hair is combed. You look decent. Now I am very tired and going up to bed. Good night."

"Just one word, Jane. Were there only ladies in the house where you have been?"

I laughed and made my escape, still laughing as I ran upstairs.

❧

Early the next morning I heard him up and astir, wandering from one room to another.

As soon as Mary went down, I heard the questions. "Is Miss Slayre here? Which room did you put her into? Was it dry? Is she up? Go and ask if she wants anything, and when she will come down."

I came down as soon as I thought there was a prospect of breakfast. Entering the room softly, I had a view of him before he discovered my presence. It was mournful, indeed, to witness the subjugation of that vigorous spirit to a corporeal infirmity. The powerlessness of this strong man touched my heart to the quick; still, I accosted him with what vivacity I could.

"It is a bright, sunny morning, sir. The rain is over and gone, and there is a tender shining after it. You shall have a walk soon."

"Oh, you are indeed there, my skylark! Come to me. You are not gone, not vanished?"

"Skylark this morning? Last night I was a fairy. It feels a bit like a demotion, sir."

Most of the morning was spent in the open air. I led him out of the wet and wild wood into some cheerful fields. I described to him how brilliantly green they were, how the flowers and hedges looked refreshed, how sparkingly blue was the sky. I sought a seat for him in a hidden and lovely spot, a dry stump of a tree. I sat at his feet. Pilot lay beside us. All was quiet. He wrapped his arms around my shoulders and clasped me to him.

"Cruel, cruel deserter! Oh, Jane, what did I feel when I discovered you had fled from Thornfield and taken so little with you, that you had taken no money, nor anything which could serve as an equivalent. A pearl necklace I had given you lay untouched in its little casket. Your trunks were left corded and locked as they had been prepared for the bridal tour. What could my darling do, I asked, left destitute and penniless? And what did she do? Let me hear now."

Thus urged, I began the narrative of my experience for the last year. I told him all, leaving off parts of the suffering from sleeping outside and starving. I was proud to tell him about my fighting skills, and all I had accomplished, how I had learned to slay and, also, how to find the goodwill to let live. I informed of how I'd prepared to come back and kill Bertha, then thought the better of it because he wouldn't have approved.

I should not have left him thus, he said, without any means of making my way. I should have told him my intentions. I should have confided in him. He would have given me half his fortune, without demanding so much as a kiss in return, rather than I should have flung myself friendless on the wide world. I had endured, he was certain, more than I had confessed to him.

"Well, whatever my sufferings had been, they were very short." I told him that if I had informed him of my intentions, I doubted I could have ripped myself away.

"Better still you should never have left me." Here he pulled me up even closer, to sit on his lap.

I told him more about Moor House, the accession of fortune, and discovery of my relations.

"This St. John, then, is your cousin? You have spoken of him often. Do you like him?"

"He was a very good man, sir. I could not help liking him."

"A good man. Does that mean a respectable, well-conducted man of fifty? Or what does it mean?"

"St. John is only twenty-nine, sir."

"Tell me he was ugly, a person of low stature, phlegmatic, and plain. A person whose goodness consists rather in his guiltlessness of vice, than in his prowess in virtue."

"He is untiringly active. Great and exalted deeds are what he lives to perform."

"But his brain? That is probably rather soft? He means well, but you shrug your shoulders to hear him talk?"

"He talks little, sir. What he does say is ever to the point. His brain is first-rate, I should think not impressible, but vigorous."

"A thoroughly educated man?"

"St. John is an accomplished and profound scholar."

"His manners, I think, you said are not to your taste? Priggish and dull?"

"I never mentioned his manners, but they are polished, calm, and gentlemanlike."

"His appearance, again? I forget what description you gave of his appearance. A sort of raw curate, half-strangled with his white neckcloth, eh?"

"St. John dresses well. He is a handsome man, tall, fair, with blue eyes, and a Grecian profile."

"Damn him! But, did you like him, Jane?"

"Yes, Mr. Rochester, I liked him. But you asked me that before."

"Perhaps you would rather not sit any longer on my knee, Miss Slayre?" was the next, somewhat unexpected observation.

"Why not, Mr. Rochester?"

"The picture you have just drawn is suggestive of a rather too overwhelming contrast. Your words have delineated very prettily a graceful Apollo. And here you have me."

"I much prefer you. What use have I for a man prettier than me?"

He laughed. I loved the sound.

"You had a little cottage near the school, you say. Did he ever come there to see you?"

"Now and then."

"Of an evening?"

"Once or twice."

A pause. "How long did you reside with him and his sisters after the cousinship was discovered?"

"Five months. Yes, he spent much time at home. We all studied together a great deal."

"What did you study?"

"Hindustani."

"Rivers taught you Hindustani?"

"Yes, sir."

"And his sisters also?"

"No. Only me."

"Did you ask to learn?"

"No. He asked me to learn it. He intended me to go with him to India."

"Ah! Here I reach the root of the matter. He wanted you to marry him?"

"He asked me to marry him."

"That is a fiction—an impudent invention to vex me."

"I beg your pardon, it is the literal truth. He asked me more than once and was as stiff about urging his point as ever you could be."

"Miss Slayre, I repeat it, you can leave me. How often am I to say the same thing? Why do you remain perched on my knee when I have given you notice to quit?"

"Because I am comfortable there. Because I love you, and only you. Now stop your jealous inquiries. I did not wish to marry St. John, and he never loved me."

"What, Jane! Is this true? Is such really the state of matters between you and Rivers?"

"Absolutely, sir! Oh, you need not be jealous. All my heart is yours, sir. It belongs to you, and with you it would remain were fate to exile the rest of me from your presence forever."

He kissed me. As he turned aside his face a minute, I saw a tear slide from under the eyelid and trickle down the manly cheek.

"Jane, you will marry me?"

"Yes, sir."

"A poor blind man, whom you will have to lead about by the hand?"

"Yes, sir."

"A wolf that might attack and try to eat you in the night?"

"Yes, sir."

"Truly, Jane?"

"Most truly, sir."

"The case being so, we have nothing in the world to wait for. We must be married instantly."

He looked and spoke with eagerness. His old impetuosity was rising.

"We must become one flesh without any delay, Jane. There is but the license to get, and after the first full moon, we marry. I need you to see what I can be like once transformed before I bind you to me forever."

"I'll not consider myself bound, sir. I shall be connected to you in the freest, most wonderful way. And as I've told you, I believe we have a cure. I've read my uncle's notes. If you are willing to place yourself in my hands, I think we can drive the wolf straight out of you."

"There is no one I trust more. In your hands is where I long to be. Do you know, Jane, I have your little pearl necklace at this moment fastened around under my cravat? I have worn it since the day I lost my only treasure, as a memento of her."

I smiled, but he could not see. "We will go home through the wood. That will be the shadiest way."

He pursued his own thoughts without heeding me. "Jane! You think me, I daresay, an irreligious dog, but my heart swells with gratitude to the beneficent God of this earth just now. I did wrong. I would have sullied my innocent flower—breathed guilt on its purity. The Omnipotent snatched it from me. Of late, Jane, only of late, I began to see and acknowledge the hand of God in my doom. I began to seek repentance, the wish for reconcilement to my Maker. I began sometimes to pray. Some days since—four days to be exact, it was last Monday night—a singular mood came over me, one in which grief replaced frenzy. I had long had the impression that since

I could nowhere find you, you must be dead. Late that night, I supplicated God that, if it seemed good to Him, I might soon be taken from this life and admitted to that world to come, where there was still hope of rejoining Jane. I longed for you, Jane! I called out your name, three times. 'Jane! Jane! Jane!' "

"Did you speak these words aloud?"

"I did. I shouted."

"Monday night, somewhere near midnight?"

"Yes, but the time is of no consequence. What followed is the strange point. You will think me superstitious. As I exclaimed, 'Jane! Jane! Jane!' a voice—I cannot tell whence the voice came, but I know whose voice it was—replied, 'I am coming.' In spirit, I believe we must have met. You no doubt were, at that hour, in unconscious sleep, Jane. Perhaps your soul wandered from its cell to comfort mine, for the voice was yours. I thank God for your return."

Then he stretched his hand out to be led. I took that dear hand, held it a moment to my lips, then let it pass around my shoulder. We entered the wood and wended homeward.

CHAPTER 40

READER, I BURIED HIM.

Following the instructions in my uncle's journal precisely, on the rising of the full moon—the first full moon we were together again—I tethered Edward's hands and feet with silver chains and filled him full of potion.

Twelve vials remained of the potion Edward Rochester had saved from the fire, and I made him drink three for good measure. Uncle John mentioned a specific potion that could be got in Rome to chase the lycanthropy—as he called it—from an infected body, but he never specified the volume of potion required for a cure. If this was indeed the very potion, and I prayed it was, then I knew two wouldn't kill him, for Richard Mason had drunk two at Mr. Rochester's urging and he'd lived to walk away. Three seemed a more potent possibility. Four might have been too much. As it was, the fever broke over Edward and he began to writhe in a pretransformation dance as he drank. John had to help me hold him to force the third down his throat.

Edward became agitated and powerfully strong, despite the silver chains that were to help weaken him, and John and I had to hurry through the ritual to accomplish our goals in time. I feared we wouldn't make it. Halfway through the digging of the grave, I began to cry, but soldiered on.

Edward twisted in his bindings. We doubled them. His nose and mouth turned to something of a snout, and all my earlier efforts to cut and tame his hair had come to naught. Hair grew all over him, including a considerable length on his already abundantly tressed head. I shuddered to see him thus, but I tenderly addressed him and refused to look away. Still, I was wise to avoid drawing close enough to get bitten. I was glad, now, he couldn't see because the worst was about to come.

John and I had to lift Edward into a box that would serve as his temporary coffin and bury his body in the temporary grave. It was as my uncle advised. The potion would eventually work its magic, slowing the heart and the breathing, shutting down all but the most necessary body functions. In short, it would bring on a condition closely resembling death, necessary for the body to heal. To facilitate this process, my uncle Slayre advised digging a hole, like a grave, and covering the body with dirt.

Why was it advisable? It seemed a tad too hard for me to bear. But bear it I did. My uncle documented his experiments, and a number of the potion-treated werewolves who were not buried broke into a murderous rage, escaping their bindings and killing many of my uncle Slayre's assistants. The burial was a safeguard in case of the the worst, the potion having an inflaming effect on the drinker. Burying the werewolf made it harder for him to escape and attack in such an event. And in the best case—that the potion worked properly—the body functions were shut down to the extent that the drinker needed little oxygen to survive for the eight hours required.

In the best case, I would dig up my Edward in the morning, in the hour before sunrise, to find that he was alive and well—and cured. In the worst case, I would find a corpse. It was a tremendous risk.

Would it not have been better, reader, to let nature take its course once a month? To lock him up until it passed and hope he would never break free? It seemed to me it would. But Edward would not hear of it. If there was a cure, he wanted it. He had been through enough with Bertha to ever imagine himself in that wolf-like condition, to think that he could be in a murderous state with his precious Jane near. So, a cure was tried.

The potion consumed, the hole dug, the box ready, all that remained was to wrestle our enormous, beasty Rochester into his temporary coffin and bury him in his grave. It was accomplished more easily than John or I imagined, for Edward had begun to settle down. I hoped it meant the potion was beginning to take effect. Edward's gaze met my own as I closed the lid, and I felt certain in that second that he could see me. Curious, that! And not only that he could see me, that he recognised me with love in his eyes. Once I closed the lid, I kissed the top and rained tears all over it.

John urged Mary to lead me to a chair and bid me to drink some wine, to calm me, while he finished shoveling the dirt onto the coffin, filling the hole.

All that remained was the waiting. It was the longest night of my life.

CHAPTER 41

THREE DAYS AFTER THE full moon, reader, I married him.

We had a quiet wedding in a church with only the parson and the clerk as witnesses. Edward had become superstitious about having guests at a wedding, and I couldn't blame him, though I knew he no longer had anything to fear or to hide.

On the night of the full moon, after the eight hours had passed, I'd cried all over again when we'd opened the coffin and found Edward, not a wolf, but a man, smiling sweetly in his sleep. He awakened, groggy but alive, some minutes afterwards and declared that my face was the most beautiful sight that ever met his eyes. He had his vision back, as well as being free from the lycanthropy. Our happiness on that morning was exceeded only by the elation we knew at finally being pronounced man and wife.

When we got back from the wedding, I went into the kitchen of the manor house, where Mary was cooking the dinner and John cleaning the knives.

"Mary, I have been married to Mr. Rochester this morning," I said.

Mary and John were both calm, unexcitable people, but Mary dropped her ladle and looked up with a start, and one of John's knives clattered to the floor. Then, as if I'd announced we had just got back from a walk, as on any other day, she picked up her ladle, calm as anything.

"Have you, miss? Well, for sure!" she said. "I saw you step out with the master, but I didn't know you were gone to church to be wed." She went back to basting her chickens.

John, when I turned to him, was grinning from ear to ear. "I told

Mary how it would be. I knew what Mr. Edward would do, and I was certain he would not wait long. He's done right. I wish you joy, miss!" John left his knives and came over and gave me a hug, prompting Mary to do the same.

"Thank you both. Mr. Rochester told me to give you and Mary this." I put into John's hand a five-pound note. Without waiting to hear more, I left the kitchen.

I wrote to Moor House immediately, to say what I had done, fully explaining the situation. Diana and Mary approved the step unreservedly. Diana announced that she would just give me time to get over the honeymoon, and then she would come and see me.

"She had better not wait until then, Jane," Edward said when I read her letter to him. "If she does, she will be too late, for our honeymoon will shine our life long."

How St. John received the news, I don't know. He never answered the letter in which I communicated it. Six months after it, he wrote to me without mentioning Mr. Rochester's name or alluding to my marriage. His letter was then calm and, though serious, kind. He has maintained a regular, though not frequent, correspondence updating me now and then on his mission, how many vampyres he has destroyed, and telling me of his latest inventions. He always adds that he hopes I am happy and trusts I am not of those who live without God in the world and only mind earthly things.

My tale draws to its close. I have now been married ten years. I know what it is to live entirely for and with what I love best on earth. I hold myself supremely blessed—blessed beyond what language can express. I am my husband's life as fully as he is mine.

We have built a large manor house in the meadow near where Thornfield Hall used to stand. Adele comes to visit us with Sophie on holidays, though less frequently through the years as she has established her own society of friends and admirers in Paris, where Edward only hopes she does not decide to make her debut on the stage. We have two children of our own, a boy and a girl, and neither of them can deny the Slayre blood in their veins. My daughter's favourite story is the one I tell of dispatching the zombies at Lowood. My son shows remarkable skill at sharpening stakes and hitting targets with the rapid-fire crossbow that I have taught him to use, with supervision, and that I occasionally practise shooting along with him.

One never knows when such skills may come in handy. According to St. John Rivers, the vampyre populations have waned in India and he suspects there'll be another rise in England soon.

I will be ready.

READING GROUP GUIDE

JANE SLAYRE

Charlotte Brontë and Sherri Browning Erwin

INTRODUCTION

Raised by vampyre relatives, young Jane Slayre is forced to adhere to a nocturnal schedule, never enjoying a sunny afternoon or the sight of a singing bird. But things change for Jane when the ghost of her uncle visits her, imparts her parents' vampyre slayer history, and charges her with the responsibility or striking out on her own to find others of her kind and learn the slayer ways. She begins at Lowood, a charity school run by a severe, stingy headmaster, who Jane quickly discovers is reanimating dying students to be trained for domestic service. With the help of head teacher Miss Temple, Jane frees the souls of her friends and ends their zombified misery. Eventually, she decides to venture out once more, this time as a governess to the ward of wealthy Mr. Rochester, whose dark good looks hide an even darker secret. Deeply in love, she agrees to trust him against her better instincts, until a surprise revelation at the altar brings her dreams of marriage to an end. Determined not to become his mistress—for Rochester is already married to a mad werewolf, who he keeps locked in his attic—Jane secretly departs. Alone, penniless, and starving, she is rescued from the brink of death by local clergyman St. John, who shelters her with his sisters. Jane recovers and thrills to discover that St. John is a slayer, like her. Together they work to develop new weaponry and train the local children to kill vampyres, but when St. John proposes that Jane marry and accompany him on missionary work to hunt vampyres in India, she must decide once and for all where her future lies.

DISCUSSION

1. What seems to be more repugnant to the Reeds—that Jane is a dependent of common blood, or that she's human? Do you think Mrs. Reed is more irritated that her niece has a continuous flow of warm blood on tap and she doesn't, or that Jane won't share? What finally induces her to beg that Jane help release her soul?
2. Bessie suggests to Jane that much of the Reed children's nasty disposition can be attributed to their vampyre nature. Do you agree? Could there be another explanation? Do you think they would be such immortal brats if they'd been allowed to finish puberty before Mrs. Reed turned them into vampyres? Discuss the effects of being stuck in a child's body forever.
3. John Reed constantly threatens Jane, who believes his habit of taking small bites of her flesh indicates that he sees her as little more than food. But more astute critics have noted the complexity of John's personality: left without a male role model, this sad, misunderstood boy in a house full of women may simply be "pulling pigtails" to get Jane's affection. What effect does his expression of unrequited love have on Jane's adult interactions with men?
4. The Reeds are famous for hosting extravagant parties featuring buffets of noble-blooded guests. Why do you suppose people keep coming to Gateshead? Is it possible no one cares that so many rich folk have gone missing? How are vampyre-related disappearances explained throughout the novel?
5. Jane's charge to kill vampyres and release their souls is a Godly mission, yet she feels far less angelic than her friend, Helen Burns. If Helen is such a paragon of goodness and devotion, why doesn't Jane want to be more like her? Does Helen inspire

or annoy the crap out of you? Were you surprised that Jane didn't cut off her head sooner? What would you have done?

6. The zombies in this novel appear in two major roles: as poor charity-case students and as domestic servants, both groups for whom life is defined by obedience. To kill a zombie, one must take off its head. Do you think the author is making a statement here, or are the zombies just another excuse for the gore so common to nineteenth-century novels, which have been deemed vulgar by today's more genteel standards. If the former, what do you think the author might be saying?
7. Once she leaves Gateshead, where she's been exposed to vampyres, zombies, and stories of so much more, Jane develops a tendency to suspect nearly everyone of being unnatural. Is she simply obsessed with killing monsters as surrogates for the Reeds (especially John Reed), or does this reflect a more innate narrowness of thought crucial to her slayer destiny? Or perhaps, do you agree with critics that she's a Victorian feminist expressing her sexual frustration? Do you think it's a coincidence that she zeroes in most on people who make her uncomfortable, like Grace Poole or Lady Ingram? Is it possible that her instinct is correct—all people are really just monsters in disguise?
8. At Thornfield, Jane spends a good deal of time ignorant of and then denying her feelings for Mr. Rochester. He seems to drop a lot of hints that she simply doesn't catch. Do you think her inability to see what's right in front of her (aside from unnatural creatures) is a product of a childhood absent of love, or is it a necessary feature for a vampyre slayer, as natural to Jane's character as her killing instinct? Do you believe she can ever really love anyone? Why or why not?
9. On page 269, Mr. Rochester exclaims that in revealing the truth about his wife, others may judge "whether or not I had a right to break the compact." Do you think he's justified, or is he just another Englishman looking to unload his stroppy cow of

a wife? Is it significant that Bertha becomes increasingly difficult at the full moon? Do you think Rochester is compassionate to care for Bertha, albeit secretly, or is her confinement crueler than simply killing her, as Jane would have done?

10. In this novel, killing is a kindness more often than it's a sin. What makes it so in Jane's mind? Do you think she's right in her assessment that she should have killed Bertha Mason and released her from her cursed life? Imagine if Bertha was merely been mad and not a werewolf—would your opinion be different? Do you think Rochester would really have minded if Jane *had* killed his wife, or doth he protest too much?
11. Jane's discovery that St. John, Mary, and Diana are her cousins fills her with joy, but what does it say about the sisters that they choose to distract themselves with such unimportant activities as education when there are monsters to be rid of? Jane often remarks on her desire to be useful; do you think the other women in this novel (except, perhaps, Miss Temple) endeavor to be use*less*? Why or why not?
12. Ultimately, Jane's union with her cousin St. John seems a fulfillment of her Uncle's charge to go forth and find other slayers to learn from. St. John's offer to take her to India gives her the opportunity to destroy perhaps hundreds of vampyres in a place where they menace unchecked. Why then, does she shun her destiny as a slayer in favor of shacking up with Rochester? Do you think she's made the right decision, or will it come back to haunt her eventually?
13. Like so many young women dating older men, Jane suffers when her seemingly perfect romance with Rochester is ruined by his beastly ex's refusal to move out, disappear, or just die (and his refusal to simply kill her). Do you think she's really horrified to find him blind and infected with his wife's disease when they are reunited, or is there a bit of her that feels he's gotten his just desserts? How difficult do you think it really is

for her to bury him six feet deep after all he's put her through? Would his ordeal be enough to satisfy you, to allow your lover to emerge from the grave with a clean slate?

ENHANCE YOUR BOOKCLUB

1. Armed with Jane's description of vampyres, zombies, and werewolves, visit a crowded public place such as the mall or a party at night and see if you can spot the unnatural walking among us. (Note: it is unadvisable for untrained citizens to attempt the work of a slayer. Don't try to stake or behead anyone.)
2. An abridged version of the novel is available under the title *Jane Eyre*. It's been hailed by some as a truer representation of Victorian England than the original, but others believe its deletion of all vampyres, zombies, werewolves and the like has made it much duller. Read a few chapters and compare the two versions, sharing your opinion with your book club.
3. Coauthor Sherri Browning Erwin has established a website where you can go to learn more about her and find out about her other books on vampyres and romance. You'll also find links to her blog and social media pages, where you can share with her your encounters with the undead and unnatural. Visit her at www.sherribrowningerwin.com.